A RUSSIAN PROPHECY

A RUSSIAN PROPRIETOR

A
RUSSIAN PROPRIETOR

AND OTHER STORIES

BY

LEO N. TOLSTOY

Fredonia Books
Amsterdam, The Netherlands

A Russian Proprietor and Other Stories

by
Leo N. Tolstoy

ISBN: 1-58963-693-7

Reprinted from the 1902 edition

Fredonia Books
Amsterdam, The Netherlands
http://www.fredoniabooks.com

INTRODUCTION

SIX of the narratives included in the present volume
are representative of Count Tolstoï's literary activity in the years 1856, 1857, and 1859; the first, which
gives the volume its name, is of earlier date, having been
written in 1852, the same year as "Childhood, Boyhood,
and Youth." Literally translated, the title, *Utro Pomye-
shchika*, means "A Proprietor's Morning," and was probably intended as a part of a projected novel; but it is
complete in itself, representing the experiences of a con-
scientious young Russian in dealing with his serfs, endeavoring to lift them from their degradation, and finding
their ingrained obstinacy and conservatism too powerful
to overcome. One cannot help feeling that it is autobio-
graphical, or at least founded on similar experiences,
Count Tolstoï, it will be remembered, having suddenly
quitted the University of Kazan, in spite of the entreaties of his friends, and retired to his paternal estate
of Yasnaya Polyana near Tula. The aunt, whose letter
is cited in the first chapter, must have been Tolstoï's aunt
mentioned in the second chapter of "My Confession."

The "Recollections of a Billiard-marker" and "Two
Hussars" are both evidently reminiscent of Count Tolstoï's gambling days. Both must have been suggested
by some such terrible experience as that told of his
gambling debt in the Caucasus. The style of the first
is peculiarly rugged and staccato, with a quite wonderful skill in reproducing the slang of the billiard-saloon.
The other is a powerful delineation of the contrast between the dissipated, high-handed, bold hussar of the
early days, with his freaks of generosity, with his nobility
and gallantry, and his son, no less dissipated, but mean,
contemptible, and narrow.

"Lucerne" and "Albert" are likewise evidently transcripts from the author's own experiences. The Quixotic benefactor, the autobiographic Prince Nekhliudof, who in the one case patronizes the strolling Swiss singer and in the other tries to rescue the drunken violinist from himself, is Count Tolstoï.

"Family Happiness" is a romance complete in itself. It is the autobiography of a young, passionate, and susceptible woman, who, being thrown into the society of her guardian, marries him, and too late discovers that the love which she has to bestow is met by a philosophic liking so cold as thoroughly to disenchant her. She narrowly escapes shipwreck, not through any inherent badness, but by the force of inertia, which lets her drift with the stream toward the chasm of illicit passion. She wins a certain serenity, and happiness returns in her acceptance of the inevitable and in her devotion to duty. It is a wonderful study of a woman's soul, and is the most poetic of Count Tolstoï's works; it is shot through and through with the music of nightingales.

In interesting contrast to these characteristic stories is the little gem entitled *Kavkazsky Plyennik*, or "A Prisoner in the Caucasus." It is founded on a personal experience thus related by Count Tolstoï's brother-in-law, C. H. Behrs, in his "Recollections":—

"A certain Sodo, of the tribe of the Tchetchenians, and with whom the count was on friendly terms, had bought a young horse, and one day proposed to him to take a ride into the country surrounding the fortress, where the detachment of the Russian army in which he then served was posted. Two other officers of the artillery joined the party. Though all such excursions had been strictly forbidden by the military authorities in consequence of the serious dangers with which they were accompanied, not one of them, except Sodo, was furnished with any other weapon than the ordinary Circassian saber. Having tried his own horse, Sodo begged his friend to mount it, and himself leaped on the count's trotter, which, of course, was no good at a fast gallop. They were already about five versts from the fortress when suddenly they saw close before them a band of Tchetchenians, some twenty in number. The Tchetchenians began to pull their guns from their covers, and divided themselves into two parties. One-half of them set off in chase of the two officers, who were already making what speed they could back to the fortress, and soon overtook them. One of the officers was pulled from his horse and hacked to pieces; the other was taken prisoner. Sodo, followed by Lyof Nikolayevitch, pushed off in another direction toward a Cossack picket that was posted at about a verst distant. Their pursuers were close upon them, and there was nothing before them but death or captivity, with its usual accompaniment, to be put into a pit neck high and left there to starve, for the mountaineers were noted for their cruel treatment of the unlucky wretches who fell into their hands. It was possible for Lyof Nikolayevitch to escape on his friend's swift-footed steed, but he would not abandon him. Sodo, like a true mountaineer, had not failed to bring his gun with him, but unfortunately it was unloaded. He none the less aimed at his pursuers, and with a wild cry of defiance made as if he were on the point of firing. To judge from what followed, we may presume it was their intention to take them both prisoners, in order that they might better revenge themselves on Sodo. At any rate they none of them fired. It was this alone that saved their lives. They managed to get within sight of the picket, whence the sharp-eyed sentry had from a distance seen the danger they were in, and instantly gave the alarm. The Cossacks soon turned out, and before long compelled the Tchetchenians to cease their pursuit."

The style is perfectly simple and lucid; the pictures of life in the Tartar aul among the mountains are intensely vivid, painted with strong masterly touches; the heroism of the young officer in standing by his friend and fellow-captain is most affecting, and the reader will not soon forget the little black-eyed laughing maiden Dina, with the rubles jingling in her braided hair. She stands forth as one of the most fascinating of the author's creations, as the story itself is one that well deserves to be called classic.

CONTENTS

CONTENTS

A RUSSIAN PROPRIETOR

CHAPTER I

PRINCE NEKHLIUDOF was nineteen years of age when, at the end of his third term at the university, he came to spend his summer vacation on his estate, and was alone there all summer.

In the autumn he wrote, in his unformed boyish hand, a letter to his aunt, the Countess Bieloretsky, who, according to his notion, was his best friend, and the most talented woman in the world. The letter was in French, and was to the following effect: —

DEAR AUNT, — I have adopted a resolution on which must depend the fate of my whole existence. I have left the university in order to devote myself to a country life, because I feel that I was born for it. For God's sake, dear aunt, don't make sport of me. You say that I am young. Perhaps I am still almost a child ; but this does not prevent me from feeling sure of my vocation, from wishing to accomplish it successfully, and from loving it.

As I have already written you, I found our affairs in indescribable confusion. Wishing to bring order out of chaos, I made an investigation, and discovered that the principal trouble was due to the most wretched, miserable condition of the peasants, and that this trouble could be remedied only by work and patience.

If you could only see two of my peasants, David and Ivan, and the way they and their families live, I am convinced that one glance at these two unfortunates would do more to persuade you than all I can tell you in justification of my resolve. Is not my obligation sacred and clear, to labor for the welfare of these seven hundred human beings for whom I must be responsible to God? Would it not be a sin to leave them to the mercy of harsh elders and overseers, so as to carry out plans of enjoyment or ambition? And why should I seek in any other sphere the opportunity of being useful, and doing good, when such a noble, brilliant, and paramount duty lies right at hand?

I feel that I am capable of being a good manager [1] and in order to make myself such a one as I understand the word to mean, I do not need my diploma as "candidate" or the rank which you so expect of me. Dear aunt, do not make ambitious plans for me; accustom yourself to the thought that I am going on an absolutely peculiar path, but one that is good, and, I think, will bring me to happiness. I have thought and thought about my future duties, have written out some rules of conduct, and, if God only gives me health and strength, I shall succeed in my undertaking.

Do not show this letter to my brother Vasya; I am afraid of his ridicule. He generally dictates to me, and I am accustomed to give way to him. Whilst Vanya may not approve of my resolve, at least he will understand it.

The countess replied to her nephew in the following letter, also written in French: —

Your letter, dear Dmitri, showed nothing else to me than that you have a warm heart; and I have never had reason to doubt that. But, my dear, our good qualities do us more harm in life than our bad ones. I will not tell you that you are committing a folly, that your behavior annoys me; but I will do my best to make one argument have an effect on you. Let us reason together, my dear.

You say you feel that your vocation is for a country life; that you wish to make your serfs happy, and that you hope to be a good manager.

In the first place, I must tell you that we feel sure of our vocation only when we have once made a mistake in one; secondly, that it is easier to win happiness for ourselves than for others; and thirdly, that, in order to be a good master, it is necessary to be a cold and austere man, which you will never in this world succeed in being, even though you strive to make believe that you are.

You even consider your arguments irresistible, and go so far as to adopt them as rules for the conduct of life; but at my age, my dear, people don't care for arguments and rules, but only

[1] *Khozyaïn.*

for experience. Now, experience tells me that your plans are childish.

I am now in my fiftieth year, and I have known many fine men ; but I have never heard of a young man of good family and ability burying himself in the country under the pretext of doing good.

You have always wished to appear original, but your originality is nothing else than morbidly developed egotism. And, my dear, choose some better-trodden path. It will lead you to success ; and success, if it is not necessary for you as success, is at least indispensable in giving you the possibility of doing good which you desire. The poverty of a few serfs is an unavoidable evil, or, rather, an evil which cannot be remedied by forgetting all your obligations to society, to your relatives, and to yourself.

With your intellect, with your kind heart, and your love for virtue, no career would fail to bring you success ; but at all events choose one which would be worth your while, and bring you honor.

I believe that you are sincere, when you say that you are free from ambition ; but you are deceiving yourself. Ambition is a virtue at your age, and with your means ; it becomes a fault and an absurdity when a man is no longer in the condition to satisfy this passion.

And you will experience this if you do not change your intention. Good-by, dear Mitya. It seems to me that I have all the more love for you on account of your foolish but still noble and magnanimous plan. Do as you please, but I forewarn you that I shall not be able to sympathize with you.

The young man read this letter, considered it long and seriously, and finally, having decided that his genial aunt might be mistaken, sent in his petition for dismissal from the university, and took up his residence on his estate.

CHAPTER II

THE young proprietor had, as he wrote his aunt, devised a plan of action in the management of his estate ; and his whole life and activity were measured by hours, days, and months.

Sunday was reserved for the reception of petitioners, domestic servants, and peasants, for the visitation of the poor serfs belonging to the estate, and the distribution of assistance with the approval of the Commune, which met every Sunday evening, and was obliged to decide who should have help, and what amount should be given.

In such employments more than a year passed, and the young man was now no longer a novice either in the practical or theoretical knowledge of estate management.

It was a clear June Sunday when Nekhliudof, having finished his coffee and run through a chapter of "Maison Rustique," put his note-book and a packet of banknotes into the pocket of his light overcoat, and started out of doors. It was a great country house with colonnades and terraces where he lived, but he occupied only one small room on the ground floor. He made his way over the neglected, weed-grown paths of the old English garden, toward the village, which was distributed along both sides of the highway.

Nekhliudof was a tall, slender young man, with long, thick, wavy auburn hair, with a bright gleam in his dark eyes, and a clear complexion, and rosy lips where the first down of young manhood was now beginning to appear.

In all his motions and gait could be seen strength, energy, and the good-natured self-satisfaction of youth.

The serfs, in variegated groups, were returning from church : old men, maidens, children, mothers with babies in their arms, dressed in their Sunday best, were scattering to their homes; and as they met the barin they bowed low and made room for him to pass.

After Nekhliudof had walked some distance along the street, he stopped, and drew from his pocket his notebook, on the last page of which, inscribed in his own boyish hand, were several names of his serfs with memoranda. He read, "*Ivan Churisenok*[1] *asks for aid;*" and

[1] Diminutive of Churis ; the *e* on which falls the stress is pronounced like *yo*.

then, proceeding still farther along the street, entered the gate of the second *izba*, or cottage, on the right.

Churisenok's domicile consisted of a half-decayed structure, with musty "corners," as the rooms are called; the sides were rickety. It was so buried in the ground, that the banking, made of earth and dung, almost hid the two windows. The one on the front had a broken sash, and the shutters were half torn away; the other was small and low, and was stuffed with flax. A boarded entry with rotting sills and low door, another small building still older and still lower-studded than the entry, a gate, and a wattled closet were clustered about the principal izba.

All this had once been covered by one irregular roof; but now only over the eaves hung the thick straw, black and decaying. Above, in places, could be seen the framework and rafters.

In front of the yard were a well with rotten curb, the remains of a post, and the wheel, and a mud-puddle stirred up by the cattle, where some ducks were splashing.

Near the well stood two old willows, split and broken, with their whitish green foliage. They were witnesses to the fact that some one, sometime, had taken interest in beautifying this place. Under one of them sat a fair-haired girl of seven summers, watching another little girl of two, who was creeping at her feet. The watch-dog, gamboling about them, as soon as he saw the barin, flew headlong under the gate, and there set up a quavering yelp expressive of panic.

"Is Ivan at home?" asked Nekhliudof.

The little girl seemed stupefied at this question, and kept opening her eyes wider and wider, but made no reply. The baby opened her mouth and set up a yell.

A little old woman, in a torn checkered skirt, belted low with an old red girdle, peered out of the door, and also said nothing. Nekhliudof approached the entry, and repeated his inquiry.

"Yes, he's at home, benefactor," replied the little old

woman, in a harsh voice, bowing low, and growing more and more scared and agitated.

After Nekhliudof had asked after her health, and passed through the entry into the narrow yard, the old woman, resting her chin in her hand, went to the door, and, without taking her eyes off the barin, began gently to shake her head.

The yard was in a wretched condition, with heaps of old blackened manure that had not been carried away; on the manure were thrown in confusion a rotting block, pitchforks, and two harrows.

There were penthouses around the yard, under one side of which stood a *sokha*, or peasants' wooden plow, a cart without wheels, and a pile of empty good-for-nothing beehives thrown upon one another. The roof was in disrepair; and one side had fallen in so that the covering in front rested, not on the supports, but on the manure.

Churisenok, with the edge and head of an ax, was breaking off the wattles that strengthened the roof. Ivan Churis was a peasant, fifty years of age, of less than the ordinary stature. The features of his tanned oval face, framed in a dark auburn beard and hair where a trace of gray was beginning to appear, were handsome and expressive. His dark blue eyes gleamed with intelligence and lazy good-nature, from under half-shut lids. His small, regular mouth, sharply defined under his sandy, thin mustache when he smiled, betrayed a calm self-confidence, and a certain bantering indifference toward all around him.

By the roughness of his skin, by his deep wrinkles, by the veins that stood out prominently on his neck, face, and hands, by his unnatural stoop and the crooked position of his legs, it was evident that all his life had been spent in hard work, far beyond his strength.

His garb consisted of white hempen drawers, with blue patches on the knees, and a dirty shirt of the same material, which kept hitching up his back and arms. The shirt was belted low in the waist by a girdle, from which hung a brass key.

"Good-day,"[1] said the barin, as he stepped into the yard.

Churisenok glanced around, and kept on with his work; making energetic motions, he finished clearing away the wattles from under the shed, and then only, having struck the ax into the block, he came out into the middle of the yard.

"A pleasant holiday, your excellency!" said he, bowing low and smoothing his hair.

"Thanks, my friend. I came to see how your affairs[2] were progressing," said Nekhliudof, with boyish friendliness and timidity, glancing at the peasant's garb. "Just show me what you need in the way of supports that you asked me about at the last meeting."

"Supports, of course, sir, your excellency, sir.[3] I should like it fixed a little here, sir, if you will have the goodness to cast your eye on it; here this corner has given way, sir, and only by the mercy of God the cattle did n't happen to be there. It barely hangs at all," said Churis, gazing with an expressive look at his broken-down, ramshackly, and ruined sheds. "Now the girders and the supports and the rafters are nothing but rot; you won't see a sound timber. But where can we get lumber nowadays, I should like to know?"

"Well, what do you want with the five supports when the one shed has fallen in? The others will be soon falling in too, won't they? You need to have everything made new, rafters and girders and posts; but you don't want supports," said the barin, evidently priding himself on his comprehension of the case.

Churis made no reply.

"Of course you need lumber, but not supports. You ought to have told me so."

"Surely I do, but there's nowhere to get it. Not all of us can come to the manor-house. If we all should get into the habit of coming to the manor-house and asking your excellency for everything we wanted, what kind of serfs should we be? But if your kindness went

---

[1] *Bog pomoshch'*; literally, God our help.
[2] *Khozyaïstvo.* [3] *Batyushka vashe siyatelstvo.*

so far as to let me have some of the oak saplings that are lying idle over by the threshing-floor," said the peasant, making a low bow and scraping with his foot, "then, maybe, I might exchange some, and piece out others, so that the old would last some time longer."

"What is the good of the old? Why, you just told me that it was all old and rotten. This part has fallen in to-day; to-morrow that one will; the day after, a third. So, if anything is to be done, it must be all made new, so that the work may not be wasted. Now tell me what you think about it. Can your premises[1] last out this winter, or not?"

"Who can tell?"

"No, but what do you think? Will they fall in, or not?"

Churis meditated for a moment.

"Can't help falling in," said he, suddenly.

"Well, now you see you should have said that at the meeting, that you needed to rebuild your whole place,[1] instead of a few props. You see I should be glad to help you."

"Many thanks for your kindness," replied Churis, in an incredulous tone and not looking at the barin. "If you would give me four joists and some props, then, perhaps, I might fix things up myself; but if any one is hunting after good-for-nothing timbers, then he'd find them in the joists of the hut."

"Why, is your hut so wretched as all that?"

"My old woman and I are expecting it to fall in on us any day," replied Churis, indifferently. "A day or two ago a girder fell from the ceiling and struck my old woman."

"What! struck her?"

"Yes, struck her, your excellency; hit her on the back, so that she lay half dead all night."

"Well, did she get over it?"

"Pretty much, but she's been ailing ever since; but then she's always ailing."

"What, are you sick?" asked Nekhliudof of the old

[1] *Dvor.*

woman, who had been standing all the time at the door, and had begun to groan as soon as her husband mentioned her.

"It bothers me here more and more, especially on Sundays," she replied, pointing to her dirty, lean bosom.

"Again?" asked the young master, in a tone of vexation, shrugging his shoulders. "Why, if you are so sick, don't you come and get advice at the dispensary? That is what the dispensary was built for. Haven't you been told about it?"

"Certainly we have, benefactor, but I have not had any time to spare; have had to work in the field, and at home, and look after the children, and no one to help me; if I weren't all alone...."

CHAPTER III

NEKHLIUDOF went into the hut. The uneven smoke-begrimed walls of the dwelling were hung with various rags and clothes, and, in the living-room, were literally covered with reddish cockroaches clustering around the holy images and benches.

In the middle of this dark, fetid apartment, not fourteen feet square, was a huge crack in the ceiling; and, in spite of the fact that it was braced up in two places, the ceiling hung down so that it threatened to fall from moment to moment.

"Yes, the hut is very miserable," said the barin, looking into the face of Churisenok, who, it seems, had not cared to speak first about this state of things.

"It will crush us to death; it will crush the children," said the woman, in a tearful voice, attending to the stove which stood under the loft.

"Hold your tongue," cried Churis, sternly; and with a subtle, almost imperceptible smile playing under his quivering mustaches, he turned to the master. "And I haven't the wit to know what's to be done with it, your excellency, — with this hut and props and planks. There's nothing to be done with them."

"How can we live through the winter here? *Okh, okh!* — Oh, oh!" groaned the old woman.

"There's one thing — if we put in some more props and laid a new floor," said the husband, interrupting her with a calm, practical expression, "and threw over one set of rafters, then perhaps we might manage to get through the winter. It is possible to live; but you'd have to put some props all over the hut, like that; but if it gets shaken, then there won't be anything left of it. As long as it stands, it holds together," he concluded, evidently perfectly contented that he appreciated this contingency.

Nekhliudof was both vexed and grieved that Churis had got himself into such a condition, without having come to him long before; since he had more than once, during his sojourn on the estate, told the peasants, and insisted on it, that they should all apply directly to him for whatever they needed.

He now felt some indignation against the peasant; he angrily shrugged his shoulders, and frowned. But the sight of the poverty in the midst of which he found himself, and Churis's calm and self-satisfied appearance in contrast with this poverty, changed his vexation into a sort of feeling of melancholy and hopelessness.

"Well, Ivan, why on earth didn't you tell me about this before?" he asked, in a tone of reproach, as he took a seat on the filthy, unsteady bench.

"I didn't dare to, your excellency," replied Churis, with the same scarcely perceptible smile, shuffling with his black, bare feet over the uneven surface of the mud floor; but this he said so fearlessly and with such composure, that it was hard to believe that he had any timidity about going to his master.

"We are mere peasants; how could we be so presuming?" began the old woman, sobbing.

"Hush up," said Churis, again addressing her.

"It is impossible for you to live in this hut; it's all rotten," cried Nekhliudof, after a brief silence. "Now, this is how we shall manage it, my friend."[1] ....

---

[1] *Bratyets*, brother.

"I will obey," replied Churis.

"Have you seen the improved stone cottages that I have been building at the new farm, — the ones with the undressed walls?"

"Indeed, I have seen them," replied Churis, with a smile which showed his white teeth still unimpaired. "Everybody's agog at the way they're built. Fine cottages! The boys were laughing, and wondering if they wouldn't be turned into granaries; they would be so secure against rats. Fine cottages," he said, in conclusion, with an expression of absurd perplexity, shaking his head, "just like a jail!"

"Yes, they're splendid cottages, dry and warm, and no danger of fire," replied the barin, a frown crossing his youthful face, for he was evidently annoyed at the peasant's sarcasm.

"Without question, your excellency, fine cottages."

"Well, then, one of these cottages is just finished. It is twenty-four feet square, with an entry and a barn, and it's entirely ready. I will let you have it on credit if you say so, at cost price; you can pay for it at your own convenience," said the barin, with a self-satisfied smile, which he could not control, at the thought of his benevolence. "You can pull down this old one," he went on to say; "it will make you a granary. We will also move the pens. The water there is splendid. I will give you enough land for a vegetable-garden, and I'll let you have a strip of land on all three sides. You can live there in a decent way. Now, does not that please you?" asked Nekhliudof, perceiving that as soon as he spoke of settling somewhere else, Churis became perfectly motionless, and looked at the ground without even a shadow of a smile.

"It's as your excellency wills," he replied, not raising his eyes.

The old woman came forward as if something had stung her to the quick, and began to speak; but her husband anticipated her.

"It's as your excellency wills," he repeated resolutely, and at the same time humbly glancing at his master, and tossing back his hair. "But it would never do for us to live on a new farm."

"Why not?"

"Nay, your excellency, not if you move us over there; here we are wretched enough, but over there we could never in the world get along. What kind of peasants should we be there? Nay, nay, it is impossible for us to live there. But it is as you will."

"But why not, pray?"

"We should be totally ruined, your excellency."

"But why can't you live there?"

"What kind of a life would it be? Just think! it has never been lived in; we don't know anything about the water, no pasture anywhere. Here we have had hemp-fields ever since we can remember, all manured; but what is there there? Yes, what is there there? A wilderness! No hedges, no corn-kilns, no sheds, no nothing at all! Oh, yes, your excellency; we should be ruined if you took us there; we should be perfectly ruined. A new place, all unknown to us," he repeated, shaking his head thoughtfully but resolutely.

Nekhliudof tried to point out to the peasant that the change, on the contrary, would be very advantageous for him; that they would plant hedges, and build sheds; that the water there was excellent, and so on: but Churis's obstinate silence exasperated him, and he accordingly felt that he was speaking to no purpose.

Churis made no objection to what he said; but, when the master finished speaking, he remarked, with a crafty smile, that it would be best of all to remove to that farm some of the old domestic servants, and Alyosha the fool, so that they might watch over the grain there.

"That would be worth while," he remarked, and smiled once more. "This is foolish business, your excellency."

"What makes you think the place is not inhabitable?" insisted Nekhliudof, patiently. "This place here isn't habitable, and hasn't been, and yet you live here. But there, you will get settled there before you know it; you will certainly find it easy...."

"But, your excellency, kind sir,[1] how can it be compared?" replied Churis, eagerly, as if he feared that the master would not accept a conclusive argument. "Here is our place in the world; we are happy in it; we are accustomed to it, and the road and the pond .... where would the old woman do her washing? where would the cattle get watered? And all our peasant ways are here; here from time out of mind. And here's the threshing-floor, and the little garden, and the willows; and here my parents lived, and my grandfather; and my father gave his soul into God's keeping here, and I too would end my days here, your excellency. I ask nothing more than that. Be good, and let the hut be put in order; we shall be always grateful for your kindness: but no, not for anything, would we spend our last days anywhere else. Let us stay here and say our prayers," he continued, bowing low; "do not take us from our nest, batyushka!"

All the time that Churis was speaking, there was heard in the place under the loft, where his wife was standing, sobs growing more and more violent; and when the husband said "batyushka, — little father," she suddenly darted forward, and with tears in her eyes threw herself at the barin's feet.

"Don't destroy us, benefactor; you are our father, you are our mother! Where are you going to move us to? We are old folks; we have no one to help us. You are to us as God is," lamented the old woman.

Nekhliudof leaped up from the bench, and was going to lift the old woman; but she, with a sort of passionate despair, beat her forehead on the earth floor, and pushed aside the master's hand.

"What is the matter with you? Get up, I beg of you. If you don't wish to go, it is not necessary. I won't oblige you to," said he, waving his hand, and retreating to the door.

When Nekhliudof sat down on the bench again, and silence was restored in the room, interrupted only by the sobs of the old woman, who was once more busy

[1] *Batyushka vashe siyatelstvo.*

under the loft, and was wiping away her tears with the sleeves of her shirt, the young proprietor began to comprehend what was meant for the peasant and his wife by the dilapidated little hut, the crumbling well with the filthy pool, the decaying stalls and sheds, and the broken willows which could be seen before the crooked window; and the feeling that arose in him was burdensome, melancholy, and touched with shame.

"Why didn't you tell the Commune last Sunday, Ivan, that you needed a new hut? I don't know, now, how to help you. I told you all, at the first meeting, that I had come to live in the country, and devote my life to you, that I was ready to deprive myself of everything to make you happy and contented; and I vowed before God, now, that I would keep my word," said the young proprietor, not knowing that such a manner of opening the heart is incapable of arousing faith in any one, and especially in the Russian, who loves not words but deeds, and is reluctant to be stirred up by feelings, no matter how beautiful they may be.

But the simple-hearted young man was so pleased with this feeling that he experienced, that he could not help speaking.

Churis leaned his head to one side, and, slowly blinking, listened with constrained attention to his master, as to a man to whom he must needs listen, even though he says things not entirely good, and absolutely foreign to his way of thinking.

"But you see, I cannot do all that everybody asks of me. If I did not refuse some who asked me for wood, I myself should be left without any, and I could not give to those who really needed. When I made this rule, I did it for the regulation of the peasants' affairs; and I put it entirely in the hands of the Commune. This wood now is not mine, but yours, you peasants', and I cannot any longer dispose of it; but the Commune disposes of it, as you know. Come to the meeting to-night. I will tell the Commune about your request; if they are disposed to give you a new hut, well and good; but I haven't any more wood. I wish with all my soul to help you; but if you are n't willing to move, then it is no longer my affair, but the Commune's. Do you understand me?"

"Many thanks for your kindness," replied Churis, in some agitation. "If you will give me some lumber, then we can make repairs. What is the Commune? It's a well-known fact that ...."

"No, you come."

"I obey. I will come. Why should n't I come? Only this thing is sure: I won't ask the Commune."

CHAPTER IV

THE young proprietor evidently desired to ask some more questions of the peasants. He did not move from the bench; and he glanced irresolutely, now at Churis, now at the empty, unlighted stove.

"Well, have you had dinner yet?" he asked at last.

A mocking smile arose to Churis's lips, as if it were ridiculous to him for his master to ask such foolish questions; he made no reply.

"What do you mean, — dinner, benefactor?" said the old woman, sighing deeply. "We've eaten a little bread; that's our dinner. We could n't get any vegetables to-day so as to boil some soup,[1] but we had a little kvas, — enough for the children."

"To-day was a fast-day for us, your excellency," remarked Churis, sarcastically, taking up his wife's words. "Bread and onions; that's the way we peasants live. Howsomever, praise be to the Lord, I have a little grain yet, thanks to your kindness; it's lasted till now; but there's plenty of our peasants as ain't got any. Everywheres there's scarcity of onions. Only a day or two ago they sent to Mikhaïl, the gardener, to get a bunch for a farthing: could n't get any anywheres. Have n't been to God's church scarcely since Easter. Have n't had nothing to buy a taper for Mikola[2] with."

Nekhliudof, not by hearsay nor by trust in the words

---

[1] *Shchets* for *shchi*.   [2] St. Nicholas.

of others, but by the evidence of his own eyes, had long known the extreme depth of poverty into which his peasantry had sunken; but the entire reality was in such perfect contrast to his own bringing up, the turn of his mind, and the course of his life, that in spite of himself he kept forgetting the truth of it; and every time when, as now, it was brought vividly, tangibly, before him, his heart was torn with painful, almost unendurable melancholy, as if some absolute and unavoidable punishment were torturing him.

"Why are you so poor?" he exclaimed, involuntarily expressing his thought.

"How could such as we help being poor, sir,[1] your excellency?   Our land is so bad, you yourself may be pleased to know, — clay and sand-heaps; and surely we must have angered God, for this long time, ever since the cholera, the corn won't grow.   Our meadows and everything else have been growing worse and worse. And some of us have to work for the farm, and some detailed for the manor-lands.   And here I am with no one to help me, and I'm getting old.   I'd be glad enough to work, but I have not any strength.   And my old woman's ailing; and every year there's a new girl born, and I have to feed 'em all.   I get tired out all alone, and here's seven dependent on me.   I must be a sinner in the eyes of the Lord God, I often think to myself. And, if God would take us off, I feel it would be easier for me; just as it's better for them, than to lead such a dog's life here." ....

"Oh, okh!" groaned the old woman as a sort of confirmation of her husband's words.

"And this is all the help I have," continued Churis, pointing to the white-headed, unkempt little boy of seven, with a huge belly, who at this moment, timidly and quietly pushing the door open, came into the hut, and, resting his eyes in wonder and solemnity on the master, clung hold of Churis's shirt-band with both hands.

"This is all the assistance I have here," continued Churis, in a sonorous voice, laying his shaggy hand

[1] *Batyushka vashe siyatelstvo.*

on the little lad's white hair. "When will he be good for anything? But my work is n't much good. When I reach old age I shall be good for nothing; the rupture is getting the better of me. In wet weather it makes me fairly scream. I am getting to be an old man, and yet I have to take care of my land.[1] And here 's Yermilof, Demkin, Ziabref, all younger than I am, and they have been freed from their land long ago. Well, I have n't any one to help me with it; that 's my misfortune. There are so many to feed; that 's where my struggle lies, your excellency."

"I should be very glad to make it easier for you, truly. But how can I?" asked the young barin, in a tone of sympathy, looking at the serf.

"How make it easier? It 's a well-known fact, if you have the land you must do enforced labor[2] also; that 's the regulation. I expect something from this youngster. If only you 'd be good enough to let him off from going to school. But just a day or two ago, the officer[3] came and said that your excellency wanted him to go to school. Do let him off; he has no capacity for learning, your excellency. He 's too young yet; he won't understand anything."

"No, brother, you 're wrong there," said the barin. "Your boy is old enough to understand; it 's time for him to be learning. I am telling you what is for your interest. Just think of it! How he 'll grow up, and learn about farming; yes, and he 'll know his a-b-c's, and know how to read; and read in church. He 'll be a great help to you if God lets him live," said Nekhliudof, trying to make himself as plain as possible, and at the same time blushing and stammering.

---

[1] The lands belonging to the Russian commune, or *mir*, were periodically distributed by allotment, each full-grown peasant receiving as his share a *tiaglo*, representing what the average man and his wife were capable of cultivating. When the period was long — ten years, for instance — it sometimes happened that a serf, by reason of illness, laziness, or other misfortune, would find it hard to cultivate his share, pay the tax on it, and also do the work required of him on his barin's land. Such was Churis's complaint. — ED.

[2] *Barshchina :* work on the master's land.   [3] *Zemski.*

"Very true, your excellency. You don't want to do us an injury, but there's no one to take care of the house; for while I and the old woman are doing the enforced labor, the boy, though he's so young, is a great help, driving the cattle and watering the horses. Whatever he is, he's a true muzhik;" and Churisenok, with a smile, took the lad's nose between his fat fingers, and squeezed it dry.

"Nevertheless, you must send him to school, for now you are at home, and he has plenty of time, — do you hear? Don't you fail."

Churisenok sighed deeply, and made no reply.

CHAPTER V

"There's one other thing I wished to speak to you about," said Nekhliudof. "Why don't you haul out your manure?"

"What manure, sir, your excellency? There isn't any to haul out. What cattle have I got? One mare and colt; and last autumn I sold my heifer to the porter, — that's all the cattle I've got."

"I know you haven't much, but why did you sell your heifer?" asked the barin, in amazement.

"What have I got to feed her on?"

"Didn't you have some straw for feeding the cow? The others did."

"The others have their fields manured, but my land's all clay. I can't do anything with it."

"Why don't you dress it, then, so it won't be clay? Then the land would give you grain, and you'd have something to feed to your stock."

"But I haven't any stock, so how am I going to get dressing?"

"That's an odd *cercle vicieux*," said Nekhliudof to himself; and he actually was at his wits' ends to find an answer for the peasant.

"And I tell you this, your excellency, it's not the manure that makes the corn grow, but God," continued

Churis. "Now, one summer I had six ricks on one little undressed piece [1] of land, and only a tithe as much on that which was manured well. No one like God," he added, with a sigh. "Yes, and my stock are always dying off. Five years past I have n't had any luck with 'em. Last summer one heifer died; had to sell another, had n't anything to feed her on; and last year my best cow perished. They were driving her home from pasture; nothing the matter, but suddenly she staggered and staggered. And so now it's all empty here. Just my bad luck!"

"Well, brother, since you say that you have no cattle to help you make fodder, and no fodder for your cattle, here's something for a cow," said Nekhliudof, reddening, and fetching forth from his pocket a packet of crumpled bank-notes and untying it. "Buy you a cow at my expense, and get some fodder from the granary; I will give orders. See to it that you have a cow by next Sunday. I shall come to see."

Churis hesitated long; and when he made no motion to take the money, Nekhliudof laid it down on the end of the table, and a still deeper flush spread over his face.

"Many thanks for your kindness," said Churis, with his ordinary smile, which was somewhat sarcastic.

The old woman sighed heavily several times as she stood under the loft, and seemed to be repeating a prayer.

The situation was embarrassing for the young prince; he hastily got up from the bench, went out into the entry, and called to Churis to follow him. The sight of the man whom he had been befriending was so pleasant that he found it hard to tear himself away.

"I am glad to help you," said he, halting by the well. "It's in my power to help you, because I know that you are not lazy. You will work, and I will assist you; and, with God's aid, you will come out all right."

[1] Churis calls this little piece of land *ocminnik*. In the government of Tula, where Count Tolstoï lives, the *ocminnik* (from *vosem*, eight) is a measure equaling one-eighth of a *desyatín*, or 2.7 acres.

"There's no hope of coming out all right, your excellency," said Churis, suddenly assuming a serious and even stern expression of countenance, as if the young man's assurance that he would come out all right had awakened all his opposition. "In my father's time my brothers and I did not see any lack; but when he died, we broke all up. It kept going from bad to worse. It all comes from living alone."

"Why did you break up?"

"All on account of the women, your excellency. It was just after your grandfather died; when he was alive, we should not have ventured to do it; then the present order of things came in. He was just like you, he took an interest in everything; and we should not have dared to separate. The late master did not like to look after the peasants; but after your grandfather's time, Andreï Ilyitch took charge. God forgive him! he was a drunken, careless man. We came to him once and again with complaints, — no living on account of the women, — begged him to let us separate. Well, he put it off, and put it off; but at last things came to such a pass, the women kept each to their own part; we began to live apart; and of course, what could a single peasant do? Well, there was no law or order. Andreï Ilyitch managed simply to suit himself. 'Take all you can get.' And whatever he could extort from a peasant, he took without asking. Then the poll-tax was raised, and they began to exact more provisions, and we had less and less land, and the grain stopped growing. Well, when the new allotment was made, then he took away from us our manured land, and added it to the master's, the villain, and ruined us entirely. He ought have been hung. Your father — the kingdom of heaven be his! — was a good barin, but it was rarely enough that we ever had sight of him; he always lived in Moscow. Well, of course they used to drive the carts in pretty often. Sometimes it would be the season of bad roads,[1] and no fodder; but no matter! The barin couldn't get along without it. We did not dare to complain at this, but

---

[1] *Rasputitsa*, the breaking up of the winter.

there was n't system. But now your grace [1] lets any
of us peasants see your face, and so a change has come
over us; and the overseer is a different kind of man.
Now we know for sure that we have a barin. And it is
impossible to say how grateful your peasants are for
your kindness. But before you came, there was n't any
real barin; every one was barin. Ilyitch was barin,
and his wife put on the airs of a lady,[2] and the scribe
from the police-station was barin. Too many of 'em!
ukh! the peasants had to put up with many trials."

Again Nekhliudof experienced a feeling akin to shame
or remorse. He put on his hat, and went on his way.

CHAPTER VI

"YUKHVANKA the clever [3] wants to sell a horse," was
what Nekhliudof next read in his note-book; and he
proceeded along the street to Yukhvanka's place.[4]
Yukhvanka's izba was carefully thatched with straw
from the threshing-floor of the estate; the framework
was of new light gray aspen wood (also from stock
belonging to the estate), had two handsome painted
shutters for the window, and a porch with eaves and
ingenious balustrades cut out of deal planks.

The narrow entry and the summer-room were also in
perfect order; but the general impression of sufficiency
and comfort given by this establishment was somewhat
injured by a barn inclosed in the gates, which had a
dilapidated hedge and a sagging pent-roof appearing
from behind it.

Just as Nekhliudof approached the steps from one
side, two peasant women came up on the other, carrying
a tub full of water. One was Yukhvanka's wife, the
other his mother.

The first was a robust, healthy-looking woman, with
an extraordinarily exuberant bosom, and wide, fat
cheeks. She wore a clean shirt embroidered on the

---

[1] *Vasha milost,* your mercy. [3] *Yukhvanka-Mudr'yonui.*
[2] *Baruinya.* [4] *Dvor.*

sleeves and collar, an apron of the same material, a new linen skirt, peasants' shoes, a string of beads, and an elegant four-cornered head-dress of embroidered red paper and spangles.

The end of the water-yoke was not in the least unsteady, but was firmly settled on her wide and solid shoulder. Her easy forcefulness, manifested in her rosy face, in the curvature of her back, and the measured swing of her arms and legs, made it evident that she had splendid health and a man's strength.

Yukhvanka's mother, bearing the other end of the yoke, was, on the contrary, one of those elderly women who seem to have reached the final limit of old age and decrepitude. Her bony frame, clad in a black, dilapidated shirt and a faded linen skirt, was bent so that the water-yoke rested rather on her back than on her shoulder. Her two hands, whose distorted fingers seemed to clutch the yoke, were of a strange dark chestnut color, and were convulsively cramped. Her drooping head, wrapped up in some sort of clout, bore the most repulsive evidences of indigence and extreme old age.

From under her narrow brow, perfectly covered with deep wrinkles, two red eyes, unprotected by lashes, gazed with leaden expression to the ground. One yellow tooth protruded from her sunken upper lip, and, constantly moving, sometimes came in contact with her sharp chin. The wrinkles on the lower part of her face and neck hung down like little bags, quivering at every motion.

She breathed heavily and hoarsely; but her bare, distorted legs, though it seemed as if they would have barely strength to drag along over the ground, moved with measured steps.

CHAPTER VII

Almost stumbling against the prince, the young wife precipitately set down the tub, showed a little embarrassment, dropped a courtesy, and then with shining eyes glanced up at him, and, endeavoring to hide a slight smile behind the sleeve of her embroidered shirt, ran up the steps, clattering in her wooden shoes.

"Mother,[1] you take the water-yoke to Aunt Nastasia," said she, pausing at the door, and addressing the old woman.

The modest young proprietor looked sternly but scrutinizingly at the rosy woman, frowned, and turned to the old dame, who, seizing the yoke with her crooked fingers, submissively lifted it to her shoulder, and was about to direct her steps to the adjacent izba.

"Is your son at home?" asked the prince.

The old woman, her bent form bent more than usual, made an obeisance, and tried to say something in reply, but, suddenly putting her hand to her mouth, was taken with such a fit of coughing, that Nekhliudof without waiting went into the hut.

Yukhvanka, who had been sitting on the bench in the "red corner,"[2] when he saw his barin, threw himself on the oven, apparently anxious to hide from him, hastily thrust something away in the loft, and, with mouth and eyes twitching, squeezed himself close to the wall, as if to make way for the prince.

Yukhvanka was a light-complexioned fellow, thirty years of age, spare, with a young, pointed beard. He was well proportioned, and rather handsome, save for the unpleasant expression of his hazel eyes, under his knitted brow, and for the lack of two front teeth, which immediately attracted one's attention because his lips were short and constantly parted.

He wore a Sunday shirt with bright red gussets, striped print drawers, and heavy boots with wrinkled legs.

The interior of Vanka's hut was not so narrow and gloomy as that of Churis's, though it was fully as stifling, as redolent of smoke and sheepskin, and showed as disorderly an array of peasant garments and utensils.

Two things here strangely attracted the attention, —

---

[1] *Matushka.*
[2] Where the holy images and lighted taper are to be found.

a small damaged samovar standing on the shelf, and a
black frame near the ikon, with the remains of a dirty
mirror and the portrait of some general in a red
uniform.

Nekhliudof looked with distaste on the samovar, the
general's portrait, and the loft, where stuck out, from
under some rags, the end of a copper-mounted pipe.
Then he turned to the peasant.

"How do you do, Yepifan?" said he, looking into his
eyes.

Yepifan bowed low, and mumbled, "Good-morning,
'slency," [1] with a peculiar abbreviation of the last word,
while his eyes wandered restlessly from the prince to
the ceiling, and from the ceiling to the floor, and not
pausing on anything.   Then he hastily ran to the loft,
dragged out a coat, and began to put it on.

"Why are you putting on your coat?" asked Nekhliudof, sitting down on the bench, and evidently endeavoring to look at Yepifan as sternly as possible.

"How can I appear before you without it, 'slency?
You see we can understand...."

"I have come to find out why you need to sell a
horse? Have you many horses? What horse do you
wish to sell?" said the prince, without wasting words,
but propounding questions that he had evidently pre-
considered.

"We are greatly beholden to you, 'slency, that you
do not think it beneath you to visit me, your muzhik,"
replied Yukhvanka, casting hasty glances at the general's portrait, at the stove, at the prince's boots, and
everything else except Nekhliudof's face. "We always
pray God for your 'slency."

"Why sell the horse?" repeated Nekhliudof, raising
his voice, and coughing.

Yukhvanka sighed, tossed back his hair, — again his
glance roved about the hut, — and noticing the cat, which
lay on the bench contentedly purring, he shouted out
to her, "Scat, you rubbish!" [2] and quickly addressed

---

[1] *Vasiaso* for *vashe siatelstvo* (your excellency).
[2] *Bruis', podlaya!*

himself to the barin. "A horse, 'slency, which ain't worth anything. If the beast was good for anything, I should n't think of selling him, 'slency."

"How many horses have you in all?"

"Three horses, 'slency."

"No colts?"

"Of course, 'slency. There is one colt."

CHAPTER VIII

"COME, show me your horses. Are they in the yard?"[1]

"Indeed they are, 'slency. I have done as I was told, 'slency. Could we fail to heed you, 'slency? Yakof Ilyitch told me not to send the horses out to pasture. 'The prince,' says he, 'is coming to look at them,' and so we did n't send them. For, of course, we should n't dare to disobey you, 'slency."

While Nekhliudof was on his way to the door, Yukhvanka snatched down his pipe from the loft, and flung it into the stove. His lips were still drawn in with the same expression of constraint even when the prince was not looking at him.

A wretched little gray mare, with thin tail, all stuck up with burrs, was sniffing at the filthy straw under the pent-roof. A long-legged colt two months old, of some nondescript color, with bluish hoofs and nose, followed close behind her.

In the middle of the yard stood a pot-bellied brown gelding with closed eyes and thoughtfully pendent head. It was apparently an excellent little horse for a peasant.

"So these are all your horses?"

"No, indeed, 'slency. Here's still another mare, and here's the little colt," replied Yukhvanka, pointing to the horses, which the prince could not help seeing.

"I see. Which one do you propose to sell?"

"This here one, 'slency," he replied, waving his jacket

[1] *Dvor.*

in the direction of the somnolent gelding, and constantly winking and sucking in his lips.

The gelding opened his eyes, and lazily switched his tail.

"He does not seem to be old, and he's fairly plump," said Nekhliudof. "Bring him up, and show me his teeth. I can tell if he's old."

"You can't tell by one indication, 'slency. The beast is n't worth a farthing. He's peculiar. You have to judge both by tooth and limb, 'slency," replied Yukhvanka, smiling very gayly, and letting his eyes rove in all directions.

"What nonsense! Bring him here, I tell you."

Yukhvanka stood, still smiling, and made a deprecatory gesture; and it was only when Nekhliudof cried angrily, "Well, what are you up to?" that he moved toward the shed, seized the halter, and began to pull at the horse, scaring him, and getting farther and farther away as the horse resisted.

The young prince was evidently vexed to see this, and perhaps, also, he wished to show his own shrewdness.

"Give me the halter," he cried.

"Excuse me. It's impossible for you, 'slency, — don't...."

But Nekhliudof went straight up to the horse's head, and, suddenly seizing him by the ears, bent it down to the ground with such force, that the gelding, who, as it seems, was a very peaceful peasant steed, began to kick and strangle in his endeavors to get away.

When Nekhliudof perceived that it was perfectly useless to exert his strength so, and looked at Yukhvanka, who was still smiling, the thought most maddening at his time of life occurred to him, — that Yukhvanka was laughing at him, and regarding him as a mere child.

He reddened, let go of the horse's ears, and, without making use of the halter, opened the creature's mouth, and looked at his teeth: they were sound, the crowns full, so far as the young man had time to make his observations. No doubt the horse was in his prime.

Meantime Yukhvanka came to the shed, and, seeing that the harrow was lying out of its place, seized it, and stood it up against the wattled hedge.

"Come here," shouted the prince, with an expression of childish annoyance in his face, and almost with tears of vexation and wrath in his voice. "What! call this horse old?"

"Excuse me, 'slency, very old, twenty years old at least. A horse that ...."

"Silence! You are a liar and a good-for-nothing. No decent peasant will lie, there's no need for him to," said Nekhliudof, choking with the angry tears that filled his throat.

He stopped speaking, lest he should be detected in weeping before the peasant. Yukhvanka also said nothing, and had the appearance of a man who was almost on the verge of tears, blew his nose, and slowly shook his head.

"Well, how are you going to plow when you have disposed of this horse?" continued Nekhliudof, calming himself with an effort, so as to speak in his ordinary voice. "You are sent out into the field on purpose to drive the horses for plowing, and you wish to dispose of your last horse? And I should like to know why you need to lie about it."

In proportion as the prince calmed down, Yukhvanka also calmed down. He straightened himself up, and, while he sucked in his lips constantly, he let his eyes rove about from one object to another.

"Lie to you, 'slency? We are no worse off than others in going to work."

"But what will you go on?"

"Don't worry. We will do your work, 'slency," he replied, starting up the gelding, and driving him away. "Even if we didn't need money, I should want to get rid of him."

"Why do you need money?"

"Have no grain, 'slency; and besides, we peasants have to pay our debts, 'slency."

"How is it you have no grain? Others, who have

families, have corn enough; but you have no family, and you are in want. Where is it all gone?"

"Ate it up, 'slency, and now we have n't a bit. I will buy a horse in the autumn, 'slency."

"Don't for a moment dare to think of selling your horse."

"But if we don't then what'll become of us, 'slency? No grain, and forbidden to sell anything," he replied, turning his head to one side, sucking in his lips, and suddenly glancing boldly into the prince's face. "Of course we shall die of starvation."

"Look here, brother," cried Nekhliudof, paling, and experiencing a feeling of righteous indignation against the peasant. "I can't endure such peasants as you are. It will go hard with you."

"Just as you will, 'slency," he replied, shutting his eyes with an expression of feigned submission; "I should not think of disobeying you. But it comes not from any fault of mine. Of course, I may not please you, 'slency; at all events, I can do as you wish; only I don't see why I deserve to be punished."

"This is why: because your yard is exposed, your manure is not plowed in, your hedges are broken down, and yet you sit at home smoking your pipe, and don't work; because you don't give a crust of bread to your mother, who gave you your whole place, [1] and you let your wife beat her, and she has to come to me with her complaints."

"Excuse me, 'slency, I don't know what you mean by smoking your pipe," replied Yukhvanka, in a constrained tone, showing beyond peradventure that the complaint about his smoking touched him to the quick. "It is possible to say anything about a man."

"Now you're lying again! I myself saw...."

"How could I venture to lie to you, 'slency?"

Nekhliudof made no answer, but bit his lip, and began to walk back and forth in the yard. Yukhvanka, standing in one place and not lifting his eyes, followed the prince's legs.

[1] *Khozyaïstvo.*

"See here, Yepifan," said Nekhliudof, in a childishly gentle voice, coming to a pause before the peasant, and endeavoring to hide his vexation, "it is impossible to live so, and you are working your own destruction. Just think. If you want to be a good peasant, then turn over a new leaf, cease your evil courses, stop lying, don't get drunk any more, honor your mother. You see, I know all about you. Take hold of your work; don't steal from the crown woods, for the sake of going to the tavern. Think how well off you might be. If you really need anything, then come to me; tell me honestly what you need and why you need it; and don't tell lies, but tell the whole truth, and then I won't refuse you anything that I can possibly grant."

"Excuse me, 'slency; I think I understand you, 'slency," said Yukhvanka, smiling as if he comprehended the entire significance of the prince's words.

That smile and answer completely disenchanted Nekhliudof as far as he had any hope of reforming the man, and of turning him into the path of virtue by means of moral suasion. It seemed to him hard that it should be wasted energy when he had the power to warn the peasant, and that all he had said was exactly what he should not have said.

He shook his head gravely, and went to the entry. The old woman was sitting on the threshold and groaning heavily, as it seemed to the young proprietor as a sign of approbation of his words, which she had overheard.

"Here's something for you to get bread with," said Nekhliudof in her ear, pressing a bank-note into her hand. "But keep it for yourself, and don't give it to Yepifan, else he'll drink it up."

The old woman with her distorted hand laid hold of the door-post, and tried to get up. She began to pour out her thanks to the prince; her head began to wag, but Nekhliudof was already on the other side of the street when she got to her feet.

CHAPTER IX

"Davuidka Byelui[1] asks for grain and posts," was what followed Yukhvanka's case in the note-book.

After passing by a number of yards, Nekhliudof came to a turn in the lane, and there fell in with his overseer Yakof Alpatuitch, who, while the prince was still at a distance, took off his oiled cap, and, pulling out a crumpled, foulard handkerchief began to wipe his fat red face.

"Cover yourself, Yakof! Yakof, cover yourself, I tell you."....

"Where have you been, if I may ask your excellency?" asked Yakof, using his cap to shield his eyes from the sun, but not putting it on.

"I have been at Yukhvanka's. Now please tell me, why does he act so?" asked the prince, as he walked along the street.

"Why, indeed, your excellency!" echoed the overseer, as he followed behind the prince in a respectful attitude. He put on his cap, and began to twist his mustache.

"What's to be done with him? He's thoroughly good for nothing, lazy, thievish, a liar; he persecutes his mother, and to all appearances he is such a confirmed good-for-nothing that there is no reforming him."

"I didn't know, your excellency, that he displeased you so."....

"And his wife," continued the prince, interrupting the overseer, "seems like a bad woman. The old mother is dressed worse than a beggar, and has nothing to eat; but she wears all her best clothes, and so does he. I really don't know what is to be done with them."

Yakof knit his brows thoughtfully when Nekhliudof spoke of Yukhvanka's wife.

"Well, if he behaves so, your excellency," began the overseer, "then it will be necessary to find some way to correct things. He is in abject poverty like all the peasants who have no assistance, but he seems to manage his affairs quite differently from the others. He's a

[1] Little David White.

clever fellow, knows how to read, and he's far from being a dishonest peasant. At the collection of the poll-taxes he was always on hand. And for three years, while I was overseer he was bailiff, and no fault was found with him. In the third year the warden took it into his head to depose him, so he was obliged to take to farming. I believe when he lived in town at the station he got drunk sometimes, so they had to devise some means. They used to threaten him, in fun, and he came to his senses again. He was good-natured, and got along well with his family. But as it does not please you to use these means, I am sure I don't know what we are to do with him. He has really got very low. He can't be sent into the army, because, as you may be pleased to remember, two of his teeth are missing. Yes, and there are others besides him, I venture to remind you, who absolutely have no fear...."

"Enough of that, Yakof," interrupted Nekhliudof, smiling shrewdly. "You and I have discussed that again and again. You know what ideas I have on this subject; and, whatever you may say to me, I still remain of the same opinion."

"Certainly, your excellency, you understand it all," said Yakof, shrugging his shoulders, and looking askance at the prince as if what he saw were worthy of no consideration. "But as far as the old woman is concerned, I beg you to see that you are disturbing yourself to no purpose," he continued. "Certainly it is true that she has brought up the orphans, she has fed Yukhvanka, and got him a wife, and so forth; but you know that it is common enough among peasants, when the mother or father has transferred the property [1] to the son, then the son and daughter-in-law get control, and the old mother is obliged to work for her own living to the utmost of her strength. Of course they are lacking in delicate feelings, but this is common enough among the peasantry; and so I take the liberty of explaining to you that you are stirred up about the old woman all for nothing. She is a clever old woman, and a good house-

[1] *Khozyaïstvo.*

wife;[1] is there any reason for a gentleman to worry over her? Well, she quarreled with her daughter-in-law; maybe the young woman struck her; that's like a woman, and they would make up again while you torment yourself. You really take it all too much to heart," said the overseer, looking with a certain expression of fondness mingled with condescension at his barin, who was walking silently with long strides before him up the street.

"Will you go home now?" he added.

"No, to Davuidka Byelui's or Kazyol's — what is his name?"

"Well, he's a good-for-nothing, I assure you. All the race of the Kazyols are of the same sort. I haven't had any success with him; he cares for nothing. Yesterday I rode past the peasant's field, and his buckwheat wasn't even sowed yet. What do you wish done with such people? The old man taught his son, but still he's a good-for-nothing just the same; whether for himself or for the estate, he makes a bungle of everything. Neither the warden nor I have been able to do anything with him; we've sent him to the station-house, and we've punished him at home, because you are pleased now to like...."

"Who? the old man?"

"Yes, the old man. The warden more than once has punished him before the whole assembly, and, would you believe it? he would shake himself, go home, and be as bad as ever. And Davuidka, I assure your excellency, is a law-abiding peasant, and a quick-witted peasant; that is he doesn't smoke and doesn't drink," explained Yakof; "and yet he's worse than the other, who gets drunk. There's nothing else to do with him than to make a soldier of him or send him to Siberia. All the Kazyols are the same; and Matriushka, who lives in the village, belongs to their family, and is the same sort of cursed good-for-nothing. Don't you care to have me here, your excellency?" inquired the overseer, perceiving that the prince did not heed what he was saying.

[1] *Khozyaïka.*

"No, go away," replied Nekhliudof, absent-mindedly, and turned his steps toward Davuidka Byelui's.

Davuidka's hovel [1] stood askew and alone at the very edge of the village. It had neither yard, nor corn-kiln, nor barn. Only some sort of dirty stalls for cattle were built against one side. On the other, a heap of brushwood and logs was piled up, in imitation of a yard. [2]

Tall, green steppe-grass was growing in the place where the courtyard should have been.

There was no living creature to be seen near the hovel, except a sow lying in the mire at the threshold, and grunting.

Nekhliudof tapped at the broken window; but, as no one made answer, he went into the entry and shouted, "Halloa there!" [3]

This also brought no response. He passed through the entry, peered into the empty stalls, and entered the open hut.

An old red cock and two hens with ruffs were scratching with their claws, and strutting about over the floor and benches. When they saw a man, they spread their wings, and, cackling with terror, flew against the walls, and one took refuge on the oven.

The whole hut, which was not quite fourteen feet [4] square, was occupied by the oven with its broken pipe, a loom, which, in spite of its being summer-time, was not taken down, and a most filthy table made of split and uneven plank.

Although it was a dry situation, there was a filthy puddle at the door, caused by the recent rain, which had leaked through roof and ceiling. Loft there was none. It was hard to realize that this was a human habitation, such decided evidence of neglect and disorder was impressed on both the exterior and the interior of the hovel; nevertheless, in this hovel lived Davuidka Byelui and all his family.

At the present moment, notwithstanding the heat of

[1] *Izba.* [2] *Dvor.*
[3] *Khozyaeva*, literally, master and mistress.
[4] Six *arshin.*

the June day, Davuidka, with his head covered by his sheepskin,[1] was fast asleep, curled up on one corner of the oven. The panic-stricken hen, skipping up on the oven, and growing more and more agitated, took up her position on Davuidka's back, but did not awaken him.

Nekhliudof, seeing no one in the hovel, was about to go, when a prolonged humid sigh betrayed the sleeper.[2]

"Eí! who's there?" cried the prince.

A second prolonged sigh was heard from the oven. "Who's there? Come here!"

Still another sigh, a sort of a bellow, and a heavy yawn responded to the prince's call.

"Well, what do you want?"

Something moved slowly on the oven. The skirt of a torn sheepskin[3] was lifted; one huge leg in a dilapidated boot was put down, then another, and finally Davuidka's entire figure emerged. He sat up on the oven, and rubbed his eyes drowsily and morosely with his fist.

Slowly shaking his head, and yawning, he looked into the hut, and, seeing the prince, began to make greater haste than before; but still his motions were so slow that Nekhliudof had time to walk back and forth three times from the puddle to the loom before Davuidka got down from the oven.

Davuidka, called *Byelui*, — White, — was white in reality; his hair and his body and his face were all perfectly white.

He was tall, and very stout, but stout as peasants are wont to be, that is, not in the waist alone, but in the whole body. His stoutness, however, was of a peculiar flabby, unhealthy kind. His rather comely face, with pale blue, good-natured eyes and a wide-trimmed beard, bore the impress of ill-health. There was not the slightest trace of tan or blood; it was of a uniform yellowish ashen tint, with pale livid circles under the eyes, quite as if his face were stuffed with fat or bloated.

His hands were puffy and yellow, like the hands of men afflicted with dropsy, and they were covered with

---

[1] *Polushubok.*   [2] *Khozyaïn.*   [3] *Tulup.*

a growth of fine white hair. He was so drowsy that he could scarcely open his eyes or cease from staggering and yawning.

"Well, are n't you ashamed of yourself," began Nekhliudof, "sleeping in the very best part of the day,[1] when you ought to be attending to your work, when you have n't any corn?"

As Davuidka little by little shook off his drowsiness, and began to realize that it was his barin who was standing before him, he folded his arms across his stomach, hung his head, inclining it a trifle to one side, and did not move a limb or say a word; but the expression of his face and the pose of his whole body seemed to say, "I know, I know; it is an old story with me. Well, strike me, if it must be; I will endure it."

He evidently was anxious for the prince to get through speaking and give him his thrashing as quickly as possible, even if he struck him severely on his swollen cheeks, and then leave him in peace.

Perceiving that Davuidka did not understand him, Nekhliudof endeavored by various questions to rouse the peasant from his vexatiously obstinate silence.

"Why have you asked me for wood when you have enough to last you a whole month here, and you have n't had any anything to do? What?"

Davuidka still remained silent, and did not move.

"Well, answer me."

Davuidka muttered something, and blinked his white eyelashes.

"You must go to work, brother. What will become of you if you don't work? Now you have no grain, and what's the reason of it? Because your land is badly plowed, and not harrowed, and no seed put in at the right time, — all from laziness. You asked me for grain; well, let us suppose that I gave it to you, so as to keep you from starving to death, still it is not becoming to do so. Whose grain do I give you? whose do you think? Answer me, — whose grain do I give you?" insisted Nekhliudof.

---

[1] Literally, middle of the white day.

"The master's,"[1] muttered Davuidka, raising his eyes timidly and questioningly.

"But where did the master's grain come from? Think for yourself, who plowed for it? who harrowed? who planted it? who harvested it? The peasants, hey? Just look here: if the master's grain is given to the peasants, then those peasants who work most will get most; but you work less than anybody. You are complained about on all sides. You work less than all the others, and yet you ask for more of the master's grain than all the rest. Why should it be given to you, and not to the others? Now, if all, like you, lay on their backs, it would not be long before everybody in the world died of starvation. Brother, you've got to work. This is disgraceful. Do you hear, Davuid?"

"I hear you," said the other, slowly, through his teeth.

CHAPTER X

At this moment, the window was darkened by the head of a peasant woman who passed, carrying some linen on a yoke, and presently Davuidka's mother came into the izba. She was a tall woman, fifty years old, very fresh and lively. Her ugly face was covered with pock-marks and wrinkles; but her straight, firm nose, her delicate, compressed lips, and her keen gray eyes gave witness to her mental strength and energy.

The angularity of her shoulders, the flatness of her chest, the thinness of her hands, and the solid muscles of her black bare legs, made it evident that she had long ago ceased to be a woman, and had become a mere drudge.

She came hurrying into the hovel, shut the door, set down her linen, and looked angrily at her son.

Nekhliudof was about to say something to her, but she turned her back on him, and began to cross herself before the black wooden ikon, which was visible behind the loom.

---

[1] *Gospodski-to*: belonging to the lord of the estate.

When she had thus done, she adjusted the dirty checkered handkerchief which was tied around her head, and made a low obeisance to the prince.

"A pleasant Lord's day to you, excellency,"[1] she said. "God spare you; you are our father."

When Davuidka saw his mother, he grew confused, bent his back a little, and hung his head still lower.

"Thanks, Arina," replied Nekhliudof. "I have just been talking with your son about your affairs."[2]

Arina, or Arishka-Burlak,[8] as the peasants called her even when she was a girl, rested her chin on the clenched fist of her right hand, which she supported with the palm of the left, and, without waiting for what her barin might say, began to talk so sharply and loud that the whole hovel was filled with the sound of her voice; and from outside it might have been concluded that several women had suddenly begun to talk together.

"What, my father, what is then to be said to him? You can't talk to him as to a man. Here he stands, the lout," she continued, contemptuously wagging her head in the direction of Davuidka's woe-begone, stolid form.

"How are *my* affairs, sir, your excellency? We are poor. In your whole village there are none so bad off as we are, either for our own work or for yours. It's a shame! And it's all his fault. I bore him, fed him, gave him to drink. Did n't expect to have such a lubber. This is what we've come to: the grain is all gone, and no more work is to be got out of him than from that piece of rotten wood. All he can do is to lie on top of the oven, or else he stands here, and scratches his empty pate," she said, mimicking him.

"If you could only frighten him, father! I myself beseech you; punish him, for the Lord God's sake! send him off as a soldier .... it's all one. But he's no good to me .... that's the way it is."

"Now, are n't you ashamed, Davuidka, to bring your

---

[1] *S prasnikom Khristovuim, vashe siyatelstvo;* literally, with Christ's holiday.   [2] *Khozyaistvo.*

[8] Clodhopper; *burlak* is the term by which the boatmen on the Volga are known.

mother to this?" said Nekhliudof, reproachfully, addressing the muzhik.

Davuidka did not move.

"One might think that he was a sick peasant," continued Arina, with the same eagerness and the same gestures; "but only to look at him you can see he's fatter than the pig at the mill. It would seem as if he might have strength enough to work on something, the lubber! But no, not he! He prefers to curl himself up on top of the oven. And even when he undertakes to do anything, it would make you sick even to look at him, the way he goes about the work! He wastes time when he gets up, when he moves, when he does anything," said she, dwelling on the words, and awkwardly swaying from side to side with her angular shoulders.

"Now, here to-day my old man himself went to the forest after wood, and told him to dig a hole; but he did not even put his hand to the shovel." ....

She paused for a moment.

"He has killed me," she suddenly hissed, gesticulating with her arms, and advancing toward her son with threatening gestures. "Curse your smooth, bad face!"

She scornfully, and at the same time despairingly, turned from him, spat, and again addressed the prince with the same animation, still swinging her arms, but with tears in her eyes.

"I am the only one, benefactor. My old man is sick, old; yes, and I get no help out of him; and I am the only one at all. And this fellow hangs around my neck like a stone. If he would only die, then it would be easier; that would be the end of it. He lets me starve, the coward. You are our father. There's no help for me. My daughter-in-law died of work, and I shall too."

CHAPTER XI

"How did she die?" inquired Nekhliudof, somewhat skeptically.

"She died of hard work, as God knows, benefactor.

We brought her last year from Baburino," she continued, suddenly changing her wrathful expression to one of tearfulness and grief. "Well, the woman was young, fresh, obliging, good stuff. As a girl, she lived at home with her father in clover, never knew want; and when she came to us, then she learned to do our work.... for the estate and at home and everywhere..... She and I.... that was all to do it. What was it to me? I was used to it. She was going to have a baby, good father; and she began to suffer pain; and all because she worked beyond her strength. Well, she did herself harm, the poor little sweetheart. Last summer, about the time of the feast of Peter and Paul, she had a poor little boy born. But there was no bread. We ate whatever we could get, my father. She went to work too soon; her milk all dried up. The baby was her first-born. There was no cow, and we were mere peasants. She had to feed him on rye. Well, of course, it was sheer folly. It kept pining away on this. And when the child died, she became so down-spirited, — she would sob and sob, and howl and howl; and then it was poverty and work, and all the time going from bad to worse. So she passed away in the summer, the sweetheart, at the time of the feast of St. Mary's Intercession. He brought her to it, the beast," she cried, turning to her son with wrathful despair..... "I wanted to ask your excellency a favor," she continued, after a short pause, lowering her voice and making an obeisance.

"What?" asked Nekhliudof, absent-mindedly, but still moved by her story.

"You see he's a young peasant still. He demands so much work of me. To-day I am alive, to-morrow I may die. How can he live without a wife? He won't be any good to you at all. Help us to find some one for him, good father."

"That is, you want to get a wife for him? Is that it? What an idea!"

"God's will be done! You are in the place of parent. to us."[1]

---

[1] *Vui nashi otsui-materi:* you are our fathers-mothers.

And, after making a sign to her son, she and the man threw themselves on the floor at the prince's feet.

"Why do you stoop to the ground?" asked Nekhliudof, peevishly, taking her by the shoulder. "Don't you know it is impossible to speak so? You know I don't like this sort of thing. Marry your son, of course, if you have a girl in view. I should be very glad if you had a daughter-in-law to help you."

The old woman got up, and began to rub her dry eyes with her sleeves. Davuidka followed her example, and, rubbing his eyes with his weak fist, with the same patiently submissive expression, continued to stand, and listen to what Arina said.

"Plenty of brides, certainly. Here's Vasiutka Mikherkin's daughter, and a right good girl she is; but the girl would not come to us without your consent."

"Isn't she willing?"

"No, benefactor, she isn't."

"Well, what is to be done? I can't compel her. Select some one else. If you can't find one at home, go to another village. I will pay for her, only she must come of her own free will. It is impossible to marry her by force. There's no law allows that; that would be a great sin."

"E-e-kh! benefactor! Is it possible that any one would come to us of her own accord, seeing our way of life, our wretchedness? Not even the wife of a soldier would like to undergo such want. What muzhik would let us have his girl? It is not to be expected. You see we're in the very depths of poverty. They will say, 'Since you starved one to death, it will be the same with mine.' Who is to give her?" she added, shaking her head dubiously. "Give us your advice, excellency."

"Well, what can I do?"

"Think of some one for us, kind sir," repeated Arina, urgently. "What are we to do?"

"How can I think of any one? I can't do anything at all for you as things are."

"Who will help us if you do not?" said Arina, drooping her head, and spreading her palms with an expression of melancholy discontent.

"Here you have asked for grain, and so I will give orders for some to be delivered to you," said the prince, after a short silence, during which Arina sighed, and Davuidka imitated her. "But I cannot do anything more."

Nekhliudof went into the entry. Mother and son with low bows followed their barin.

CHAPTER XII

"O-okh! alas for my wretchedness!" exclaimed Arina, sighing deeply.

She paused, and looked angrily at her son. Davuidka immediately turned around, and, clumsily lifting his stout leg, incased in a huge dirty boot, over the threshold, took refuge in the opposite door.

"What shall I do with him, father?" continued Arina, turning to the prince. "You yourself see what he is. He is not a bad muzhik; does n't get drunk, and is peaceable; would n't hurt a little child. It 's a sin to say hard things of him. There 's nothing bad about him, and God knows what has taken place in him to make him so bad to himself. You see he himself does not like it. Would you believe it, father,[1] my heart bleeds when I look at him, and see what suffering he undergoes. You see, whatever he is, he is my son. I pity him. Oh, how I pity him!.... You see, it is n't as if he had done anything against me or his father or the authorities. But, no; he 's a bashful man, almost like a child. How can he bear to be a widower? Help us out, benefactor," she said once more, evidently desirous of removing the unfavorable impression which her bitter words might have left on the prince. "Father, your excellency, I...." she went on to say in a confidential whisper, "my wit does not go far enough to explain him. It seems as if bad men had spoiled him."

[1] *Batyushka.*

She paused for a moment.

"If we could find the man, we might cure him."

"What nonsense you talk, Arina! How can he be spoiled?"

"My father,[1] they spoil him so that we can never make a man of him! Many bad people in the world! Out of ill-will they take a handful of earth from out of one's path, or something of that sort; and one is made a no-man forever after. Isn't that a sin? I think to myself, Might I not go to the old man Dunduk, who lives at Vorobyevka? He knows all sorts of words; and he knows herbs, and he can make charms; and he finds water with a cross. Wouldn't he help me?" said the woman. "Maybe he will cure him."

"What abjectness and superstition!" thought the young prince, shaking his head gloomily, and walking back with long strides through the village.

"What's to be done with him? To leave him in this situation is impossible, both for myself and for the others and for him, — impossible," he said to himself, counting off on his fingers these reasons.

"I cannot bear to see him in this plight; but how extricate him? He renders nugatory all my best plans for the management of the estate. If such peasants are allowed, none of my dreams will ever be realized," he went on, experiencing a feeling of despite and anger against the peasant in consequence of the ruin of his plans. "To send him to Siberia, as Yakof suggests, against his will, would that be good for him? or to make him a soldier? That is best. At least I should be quit of him, and I could replace him by a decent muzhik."

Such was his decision.

He thought about this with satisfaction; but at the same time something obscurely told him that he was thinking with only one side of his mind, and not wholly right.

He paused.

"I will think about it some more," he said to himself. "To send him off as a soldier .... why? He is a good

---

[1] *Atyets tiu moï:* thou my father.

man, better than many; and I know .... Shall I free him?" he asked himself, putting the question from a different side of his mind. "It would n't be fair. Yes, it's impossible."

But suddenly a thought occurred to him that greatly pleased him. He smiled with the expression of a man who has decided a difficult question.

"I will take him to the house," he said to himself. "I will look after him myself; and by means of kindness and advice, and selecting his employment, I will teach him to work, and reform him."

CHAPTER XIII

"THAT's what I'll do," said Nekhliudof to himself, with a pleasant self-consciousness; and then, recollecting that he had still to go to the rich muzhik Dutlof, he directed his steps to a lofty and ample establishment, with two chimneys, standing in the midst of the village.

As he passed a neighboring cottage on his way thither, he stopped to speak with a tall, slatternly peasant-woman of forty summers, who came to meet him.

"Good-morning, father," [1] she said, with some show of assurance, stopping at a little distance from him with a pleased smile and a low obeisance.

"Good-morning, nurse. How are you? I was just going to see your neighbor."

"Pretty well, sir, your excellency. It's a good thing. But won't you come in? I beg you to. My old man would be very pleased."

"Well, I'll come; and we'll have a little talk together, nurse. Is this your house?"

"It is, sir."

And the nurse led the way into the izba. Nekhliudof followed her into the entry, and sat down on a tub, and began to smoke a cigarette.

"It's hot inside. It's better to sit down here and

---

[1] *Spraznikom, batyushka:* with a holiday, little father.

have our talk," he said, in reply to the woman's invitation to go into the izba.

The nurse was a well-preserved and handsome woman. In the features of her countenance, and especially in her big black eyes, there was a strong resemblance to the prince himself. She folded her hands under her apron, and, looking fearlessly at him, and incessantly moving her head, began to talk with him.

"Why is it, father? Why do you wish to visit Dutlof?"

"Oh, I am anxious for him to take thirty desyatins[1] of land of me, and enlarge his domain; and moreover I want him to join me in buying some wood also. You see, he has money, so why should it be idle? What do you think about it, nurse?"

"Well, what can I say? Of course, the Dutlofs are strong people; he's the leading muzhik in the whole estate," replied the nurse, shaking her head. "Last summer he built another building out of his own lumber. He did not demand anything at all of the estate. They have horses, and yearling colts besides, at least six troikas, and cattle, cows, and sheep; so that it is a sight worth seeing when they are driven along the street from pasture, and the women of the house come out to get them into the yard. There is such a crush of animals at the gate that they can scarcely get through, so many of them there are. And two hundred beehives at the very least. He is a strong peasant, and must have money."

"But what do you think, — has he much money?" asked the prince.

"Men say, out of spite of course, that the old man has no little money. But he does not go round talking about it, and he does not tell even his sons, but he must have. Why shouldn't he take hold of the woodland? Perhaps he is afraid of getting a reputation for letting money go. Five years ago he and Shkalik the dvornik[2]

[1] Eighty-one acres.
[2] *Dvornik* sometimes means the owner as well as the caretaker of a *dvor*, or house and grounds.

went shares in getting a bit of meadow-land; and this
Shkalik, some way or other, cheated him, so that the old
man was three hundred rubles out of pocket. And from
that time he has given it up. How can he help being fore-
handed, your excellency, father?" continued the nurse.
"He has three farms, a big family, all workers; and
besides, the old man — what harm in saying so? — is a
capital manager. He is lucky in everything; it is sur-
prising, — in his grain and in his horses and in his cattle
and in his bees, and he's lucky in his children. Now
he has got them all married off. He has found hus-
bands for his daughters; and he has just married
Ilyushka, and given him his freedom. He himself
bought the letter of enfranchisement. And so a fine
woman has come into his house."

"Well, do they live harmoniously?" asked the prince.

"As long as there's the right sort of a head to the
house, they get along. Yet even the Dutlofs .... but of
course that's among the women. The daughters-in-law
bark at each other a little behind the oven, but the old
man generally holds them in hand; and the sons live
harmoniously."

The nurse was silent for a little.

"Now, the old man, we hear, wants to leave his eldest
son, Karp, as master of the house. 'I am getting old,'
says he. 'It's my business to attend to the bees.'
Well, Karp is a good muzhik, a careful muzhik; but he
does n't manage to please the old man in the least.
There's no sense in it."

"Well, perhaps Karp wants to speculate in land and
wood. What do you think about it?" pursued the
prince, wishing to learn from the woman all that she
knew about her neighbors.

"Scarcely, sir,"[1] continued the nurse. "The old man
has n't disclosed his money to his son. As long as he
lives, of course, the money in the house will be under
the old man's control; and it will increase all the time
too."

"But is n't the old man willing?"

[1] *Batyushka.*

"He is afraid."

"What is he afraid of?"

"How is it possible, sir, for a seignorial peasant [1] to make a show of his money? And it's a hard question to decide what to do with money anyway. Here he went into business with the dvornik, and was cheated. Where was he to get redress? And so he lost his money. But with the proprietor he would have any loss made good immediately, of course."

"Yes, hence...." said Nekhliudof, reddening. "But good-by, nurse."

"Good-by, sir, your excellency. Greatly obliged to you."

CHAPTER XIV

"HADN'T I better go home?" mused Nekhliudof, as he strode along toward the Dutlof inclosure, and felt a boundless melancholy and moral weariness.

But at this moment the new deal gates were thrown open before him with a creaking sound, and a handsome, light-haired ruddy fellow of eighteen in wagoner's attire appeared, leading a troïka of powerful-limbed, shaggy, and still sweaty horses. He hastily brushed back his blond hair, and bowed to his barin.

"Tell me, is your father at home, Ilya?" asked Nekhliudof.

"At the beehouse, back of the yard," replied the youth, driving the horses, one after the other, through the half-opened gates.

"I will not give it up. I will make the proposal. I will do the best I can," reflected Nekhliudof; and, after waiting till the horses had passed on, he entered Dutlof's spacious yard.

It was plain to see that the manure had only recently been carried away. The ground was still black and damp; and in places, particularly in the hollows, were left red fibrous clots.

[1] *Muzhik gospodsky.*

In the yard and under the high sheds, many carts stood in orderly rows, together with plows, sledges, harrows, barrels, and all sorts of farming implements. Doves were flitting about, cooing in the shadows under the broad solid rafters. There was an odor of manure and tar.

In one corner Karp and Ignat were fitting a new cross-bar to a large iron-mounted, three-horse *telyega*, or wagon.

All three of Dutlof's sons bore a strong family resemblance. The youngest, Ilya, who had met Nekhliudof at the gate, was beardless, of smaller stature, ruddier complexion, and more neatly dressed, than the others. The second, Ignat, was rather taller and darker. He had a wedge-shaped beard; and, though he wore boots, a driver's shirt, and a lambskin cap, he had not such a festive, holiday appearance as his brother had.

The eldest, Karp, was still taller. He wore clogs, a gray kaftan, and a shirt without gussets. He had a reddish beard, trimmed; and his expression was serious, even to severity.

"Do you wish my father sent for, your excellency?" he asked, coming to meet the prince, and bowing slightly and awkwardly.

"No, I will go to him at the hives; I wish to see what he's building there. But I should like a talk with you," said Nekhliudof, drawing him to the other side of the yard, so that Ignat might not overhear what he was about to talk about with Karp.

The self-confidence and degree of pride noticeable in the deportment of the two peasants, and what the nurse had told the young prince, so troubled him, that it was difficult for him to make up his mind to speak with them about the matter proposed.

He had a sort of guilty feeling, and it seemed to him easier to speak with one brother out of the hearing of the other. Karp seemed surprised that his barin took him to one side, but he followed him.

"Listen," began Nekhliudof, awkwardly, "I wished to inquire of you if you had many horses."

"We have about five troïkas, also some colts," replied Karp, in a free-and-easy manner, scratching his back.

"Tell me, are your brothers going to take out relays of horses for the post?"

"We shall send out three troïkas to carry the mail. And there's Ilyushka, he has been off with his team; but he's just come back."

"Well, is that profitable for you? How much do you earn that way?"

"What do you mean by profit, your excellency? We at least get enough to live on and bait our horses; thank God for that!"

"Then, why don't you take hold of something else? You see, you might buy wood, or take more land."

"Of course, your excellency; we might rent some land if there were any convenient."

"I wish to make a proposition to you. Since you only make enough out of your teaming to live on, you had better take thirty desyatins of land from me. All that strip behind Sapovo I will let you have, and you can carry on your farming better."

And Nekhliudof, carried away by his plan for a peasant farm, which more than once he had proposed to himself, and deliberated about, began fluently to explain to the peasant his proposition about it.

Karp listened attentively to the prince's words.

"We are very grateful for your kindness," said he, when Nekhliudof stopped, and looked at him in expectation of his answer. "Of course here there's nothing very bad. To occupy himself with farming is better for a peasant than to go off as a whip. He goes among strangers; he sees all sorts of men; he gets wild. It's the very best thing for a peasant, to occupy himself with land."

"You think so, do you?"

"As long as my father is alive, how can I think, your excellency? It's as he wills."

"Take me to the beehives. I will talk with him."

"Come with me this way," said Karp, slowly directing himself to the shed back of the house. He opened a low gate which led to the apiary, and, after letting the prince pass through, he shut it, and returned to Ignat, and silently took up his interrupted labors.

CHAPTER XV

NEKHLIUDOF, stooping low, passed through the low gate, under the gloomy shed, to the apiary, which was situated back of the *dvor*, or yard.

A small space, surrounded by straw and a wattled hedge, through the chinks of which the light streamed, was filled with beehives symmetrically arranged, and covered with shavings, while the golden bees were humming around them. Everything was bathed in the warm and brilliant rays of the June sun.

From the gate a well-trodden footway led through the middle to a wooden side building, with a tin-foil image on it gleaming brightly in the sun.

A regular row of young lindens, lifting, above the thatched roof of the neighboring courtyard, their bushy tops, almost audibly rustled their dark green, fresh foliage, in unison with the sound of the buzzing bees. All the shadows from the covered hedge, from the lindens, and from the beehives fell dark and short on the delicate curling grass springing up between the catkins.

The bent, small figure of the old man, with his gray hair and bald spot shining in the sun, was visible near the door of a straw-thatched structure situated among the lindens. When he heard the creaking of the gate, the old man looked up, and, wiping his heated, sweaty face with the flap of his shirt, and smiling with pleasure, came to meet the prince.

In the apiary it was so comfortable, so pleasant, so warm, so free! The figure of the gray-haired old man, with thick wrinkles radiating from his eyes, and wearing wide shoes on his bare feet, as he came waddling along, good-naturedly and contentedly smiling, to welcome the prince to his own private possessions, was so ingenuously soothing that Nekhliudof for a moment forgot the

trying impressions of the morning, and his cherished
dream came vividly up before him. He already saw all
his peasants just as prosperous and contented as the
old man Dutlof, and all smiling soothingly and pleasantly upon him, because to him alone they were in-
debted for their prosperity and happiness.

"Would you like a net, your excellency? The bees
are angry now," said the old man, taking down from
the fence a dirty gingham bag fragrant of honey, and
handing it to the prince. "The bees know me, and
don't sting," he added, with the pleasant smile that
rarely left his handsome sunburned face.

"I don't need it either. Well, are they swarming
yet?" asked Nekhliudof, also smiling, though without
knowing why.

"Yes, they are swarming, Father Mitri Mikolayevitch,"[1] replied the old man, throwing an expression of
peculiar endearment into this form of addressing his
barin by his name and patronymic. "They have only
just begun to swarm; it has been a cold spring, you
know."

"I have just been reading in a book," began Nekhliudof, defending himself from a bee which had got
entangled in his hair, and was buzzing under his ear,
"that if the wax stands straight on the bars, then the
bees swarm earlier. Therefore such hives as are made
of boards .... with cross-b...."

"You don't want to wave your arms; that makes it
worse," said the little old man. "Now don't you think
you had better put on the net?"

Nekhliudof felt a sharp pain, but by some sort of
childish egotism he did not wish to acknowledge it; and
so, once more refusing the bag, continued to talk with
the old man about the construction of hives, about which
he had read in the "Maison Rustique," and which, according to his idea, ought to be made twice as large.
But another bee stung him in the neck, and he lost the
thread of his discourse, and stopped short in the midst
of it.

[1] *Batyushka* Mitri Mikolayevitch, rustic for Dmitri Nikolayevitch.

"That's well enough, Father Mitri Mikolayevitch," said the old man, looking at the prince with paternal protection; "that's well enough in books, as you say. Yes; maybe the advice is given with some deceit, with some hidden meaning; but only just let him do as he advises, and we shall be the first to have a good laugh at his expense. And this happens! How are you going to teach the bees where to deposit their wax? They themselves put it on the cross-bar, sometimes straight and sometimes aslant. Just look here!" he continued, opening one of the nearest hives, and gazing at the entrance-hole blocked by a bee buzzing and crawling on the crooked comb. "Here's a young one. It sees; at its head sits the queen, but it lays the wax straight and sideways, both according to the position of the block," said the old man, evidently carried away by his interest in his occupation, and not heeding the prince's situation. "Now, to-day, it will fly with the pollen. To-day is warm; it's on the watch," he continued, again covering up the hive and pinning down with a cloth the crawling bee; and then brushing off into his rough palm a few of the insects from his wrinkled neck.

The bees did not sting him; but as for Nekhliudof, he could scarcely refrain from the desire to beat a retreat from the apiary. The bees had already stung him in three places, and were buzzing angrily on all sides around his head and neck.

"You have many hives?" he asked, as he retreated toward the gate.

"What God has given," replied Dutlof, sarcastically. "It is not necessary to count them, father; the bees don't like it. Now, your excellency, I wanted to ask a favor of you," he went on to say, pointing to the small posts standing by the fence. "It was about Osip, the nurse's husband. If you would only speak to him. In one village it's not right for one to treat a neighbor in such a mean way; it's not good."

"What has he done that's mean?.... Ah, how they sting!" exclaimed the prince, already seizing the latch of the gate.

"Every year now, he lets his bees out among my young ones. We could stand it, but strange bees get away their comb and kill them," said the old man, not heeding the prince's grimaces.

"Very well, by and by; at once," said Nekhliudof. And, having no longer strength of will to endure, he hastily beat a retreat through the gate, fighting his tormentors with both hands.

"Rub it with dirt. It's nothing," said the old man, coming to the dvor after the prince. The prince took some earth, and rubbed the spot where he had been stung, and reddened as he cast a quick glance at Karp and Ignat, who did not deign to look at him. Then he frowned angrily.

CHAPTER XVI

"I WANTED to ask you something about my sons, your excellency," said the old man, either pretending not to notice, or really not noticing, the prince's angry face.

"What?"

"Well, we are well provided with horses, praise the Lord! And that's our trade, and so we don't have to work on your land."

"What do you mean?"

"If you would only be kind enough to let my sons have leave of absence, then Ilyushka and Ignat would take three troïkas, and go out teaming for all summer. Maybe they'd earn something."

"Where would they go?"

"Just as it happened," replied Ilyushka, who, at this moment, having put the horses under the shed, joined his father. "The Kadminski boys went with eight horses to Romen. They not only earned their own living, they say, but brought back a gain of more than three hundred per cent. Fodder, they say, is cheap at *Odest*."

"Well, that's the very thing I wanted to talk with you about," said the prince, addressing the old man, and anxious to draw him shrewdly into a talk about the farm. "Tell me, please, if it would be more profitable to go to teaming than farming at home?"

"Why not more profitable, your excellency?" said Ilyushka, again putting in his word, and at the same time quickly shaking back his hair. "There's no way of keeping horses at home."

"Well, how much do you earn in the summer?"

"Since spring, as feed was high, we went to Kief with merchandise, and to Kursk, and back again to Moscow with grits; and in that way we earned our living. And our horses had enough, and we brought back fifteen rubles in money."

"There's no harm in taking up with an honorable profession, whatever it is," said the prince, again addressing the old man. "But it seems to me that you might find another form of activity. And besides, this work is such that a young man goes everywhere. He sees all sorts of people, — may get wild," he added, quoting Karp's words.

"What can we peasants take up with, if not teaming?" objected the old man, with his sweet smile. "If you are a good driver, you get enough to eat, and so do your horses; but, as regards mischief, they are just the same as at home, thank the Lord![1] It isn't the first time that they have been. I have been myself, and never saw any harm in it, nothing but good."

"How many other things you might find to do at home! with fields and meadows ...."

"How is it possible?" interrupted Ilyushka, with animation. "We were born for this. All the regulations are at our fingers' ends. We like the work. It's the most enjoyable we have, your excellency. How we like to go teaming!"

"Your excellency, will you not do us the honor of coming into the house? You have not yet seen our

[1] *Slava-ti Gospodi*, glory to thee, O Lord.

new izba," said the old man, bowing low, and winking to his son.

Ilyushka hastened into the house, and Nekhliudof and the old man followed after him.

CHAPTER XVII

As soon as he got into the house, the old man bowed once more; then, using his coat-tail to dust the bench in the front room, he smiled, and said: —

"What do you want of us, your excellency?"

The hut was white and roomy, with a chimney; and it had a loft and berths. The fresh aspen-wood beams, between which could be seen the moss, scarcely withered, were as yet not turned dark. The new benches and the loft were not polished smooth, and the floor as yet showed no marks of wear. One young peasant woman, rather lean, with a serious oval face, was sitting on a berth, and using her foot to rock a hanging cradle that was suspended from the ceiling by a long hook. This was Ilya's wife.

In the cradle slept a suckling child, very quietly breathing, with closed eyes, and with his arms and legs sprawled out.

Another young woman, robust and rosy-cheeked, — Karp's wife, — with her sleeves rolled up above her elbows, showing strong arms and hands red even higher than her wrists, was standing in front of the oven, and mincing onions in a wooden dish.

A pock-marked woman, showing signs of pregnancy, which she tried to conceal, was standing near the oven. The room was hot, not only from the summer sun, but from the heat of the oven; and there was a strong smell of baking bread.

Two flaxen-headed little boys and a girl gazed down from the loft upon the prince, with faces full of curiosity. They had come in, expecting something to eat.

Nekhliudof was delighted to see this happy household; and at the same time he felt a sense of constraint

in the presence of these women and children, all looking at him. He flushed a little as he sat down on the
bench.

"Give me a crust of hot bread; I am fond of it,"
said he, and the flush deepened.

Karp's wife cut off a huge slice of bread, and handed
it on a plate to the prince. Nekhliudof said nothing,
not knowing what to say. The women also were silent;
the old man smiled benevolently.

"Well, now, why am I so awkward? as if I were to
blame for something," thought Nekhliudof. "Why
shouldn't I make my proposition about the farm?
What stupidity!"

Still he remained silent.

"Well, Father Mitri Mikolayevitch, what are you
going to say about my boys' proposal?" asked the old
man.

"I should absolutely advise you not to send them
away, but to have them stay at home, and work," said
Nekhliudof, suddenly collecting his wits. "You know
what I have proposed to you. Go in with me, and
buy some of the crown woods, and some more land...."

"But how are we going to get money to buy it, your
excellency?" Dutlof asked, interrupting the prince.

"Why, it isn't very much wood, only two hundred
rubles' worth," replied Nekhliudof.

The old man gave an indignant laugh.

"Very good, if that's all. Why not buy it?" said
he.

"Haven't you money enough?" asked the prince,
reproachfully.

"Okh, sir, your excellency!" replied the old man,
with grief expressed in his tone, looking apprehen-
sively toward the door. "Only enough to feed my
family, not enough to buy woodland."

"But you know you have money,—what do you do
with it?" insisted Nekhliudof.

The old man suddenly fell into a terrible state of excitement; his eyes flashed, his shoulders began to
twitch.

"Wicked men may say all sorts of things about me,"
he muttered in a trembling voice. "But, so may God
be my witness!" he said, growing more and more animated, and turning his eyes toward the ikon, "may my
eyes crack, may I perish with all my family, if I have
anything more than the fifteen silver rubles which
Ilyushka brought home; and we have to pay the poll-
tax, you yourself know that. And we built the hut...."

"Well, well, all right," said the prince, rising from
the bench. "Good-by, friends."[1]

CHAPTER XVIII

"My God! my God!" was Nekhliudof's mental exclamation, as with long strides he hastened home through
the shady alleys of his weed-grown garden, and, absent-
mindedly, snapped off the leaves and branches which
came in his way.

"Is it possible that my dreams about the ends and
duties of my life are all idle nonsense? Why is it hard
for me, and mournful, as if I were dissatisfied with
myself because I imagined that, having once begun this
course, I should constantly experience the fullness of the
morally pleasant feeling which I had when, for the first
time, these thoughts came to me?"

And with extraordinary vividness and distinctness he
saw in his imagination that happy moment which he
had experienced a year before.

He had arisen very early, before every one else in the
house, and feeling painfully those secret, indescribable
impulses of youth, he had gone aimlessly out into the
garden, and from there into the woods; and, amid the
energetic, but tranquil, nature pulsing with the new
life of Maytime, he had wandered long alone, without
thought, and suffering from the exuberance of some
feeling, and not finding any expression for it.

[1] *Proshchaïte, khozyaeva; khozyaeva* includes all the adult members
of the family.

Then, with all the allurement of what is unknown, his youthful imagination brought up before him the voluptuous form of a woman; and it seemed to him that was the object of his indescribable longing. But another, deeper sentiment said, *Not that*, and impelled him to search and be disturbed in mind.

Without thought or desire, as always happens after extra activity, he lay on his back under a tree, and looked at the diaphanous morning clouds drifting over him across the deep, endless sky.

Suddenly, without any reason, the tears sprang to his eyes, and God knows in what way the thought came to him with perfect clearness, filling all his soul and giving him intense delight, — the thought that love and righteousness are the same as truth and enjoyment, and that there is only one truth, and only one possible happiness, in the world.

The deeper feeling this time did not say, *Not that*. He sat up, and began to verify this thought.

"That is it, that is it," said he to himself, in a sort of ecstasy, measuring all his former convictions, all the phenomena of his life, by the truth just discovered to him, and as it seemed to him absolutely new.

"What stupidity! All that I knew, all that I believed in, all that I loved," he had said to himself. "Love is self-denying; this is the only true happiness independent of chance," he had said over and over again, smiling and waving his hands.

Applying this thought on every side to life, and finding in it confirmation both of life and that inner voice which told him that this was *it*, he had experienced a new feeling of pleasant agitation and enthusiasm.

"And so I ought to do good if I would be happy," he thought; and all his future vividly came up before him, not as an abstraction, but imaged in the form of the life of a proprietor.

He saw before him a huge field, conterminous with his whole life, which he was to consecrate to the good, and in which really he should find happiness. There was no need for him to search for a sphere of activity;

it was all ready. He had one out-and-out obligation:
he had his serfs. ....

And what comfortable and beneficent labor lay before
him! "To work for this simple, impressionable, incor-
ruptible class of people; to lift them from poverty;
to give them pleasure; to give them education, which,
fortunately, I will turn to use in correcting their faults,
which arise from ignorance and superstition; to develop
their morals; to induce them to love the right. .... What
a brilliant, happy future! And, besides all this, I, who
am going to do this for my own happiness, shall take
delight in their appreciation, shall see how every day I
shall go farther and farther toward my predestined end.
A wonderful future! Why could I not have seen this
before ?

"And besides," so he had thought at the same time,
"who will hinder me from being happy in love for a
woman, in enjoyment of family ?"

And his youthful imagination portrayed before him a
still more bewitching future.

"I and my wife, whom I shall love as no one ever
loved a wife before in the world, we shall always live
amid this restful, poetical, rural nature, with our children, maybe, and with my old aunt. We have our love
for each other, our love for our children; and we shall
both know that our aim is the right. We shall help
each other in pressing on to this goal. I shall make
general arrangements; I shall give general aid when it
is right; I shall carry on the farm, the savings-bank,
the workshop. And she, with her dear little head, and
dressed in a simple white dress, which she lifts above
her dainty ankle as she steps through the mud, will go
to the peasants' school, to the hospital, to some unfortunate peasant who in truth does not deserve help, and
everywhere carry comfort and aid. .... Children, old men,
women, will wait for her, and look on her as some
angel, as on Providence. Then she will return, and
hide from me the fact that she has been to see the
unfortunate peasant, and given him money; but I shall
know all, and give her a hearty hug, and rain kisses

thick and fast on her lovely eyes, her modestly blushing cheeks, and her smiling, rosy lips."

*   *   *   *   *

CHAPTER XIX

"WHERE are those dreams?" the young man now asked himself as he walked home after his round of visits. "Here more than a year has passed since I have been seeking for happiness in this course, and what have I found? It is true, I sometimes feel that I can be contented with myself; but this is a dry, doubtful kind of content. Yet, no; I am simply dissatisfied! I am dissatisfied because I find no happiness here; and I desire, I passionately long for, happiness. I have not experienced delight, I have cut myself off from all that gives it. Wherefore? for what end? Does that make it easier for any one?

"My aunt was right when she wrote that it is easier to find happiness than to give it to others. Have my peasants become any richer? Have they learned anything? or have they shown any moral improvement? Not the least. They are no better off, but it grows harder and harder every day for me. If I saw any success in my undertakings, if I saw any signs of gratitude, ... but, no! I see falsely directed routine, vice, untruthfulness, helplessness. I am wasting the best years of my life."

Thus he said to himself, and he recollected that his neighbors, as he heard from his nurse, called him "a mere boy"; that he had no money left in the counting-room; that his new threshing-machine, which he had invented, much to the amusement of the peasants, only made a noise, and did not thresh anything when it had been set in motion for the first time in presence of numerous spectators, who had gathered at the threshing-floor; that from day to day he had to expect the coming of the district judge for the list of goods and chattels, which he had neglected to make out, having been engrossed in various new enterprises on his estate.

And suddenly there arose before him, just as vividly as before that walk through the forest and his ideal of rural life had arisen, — just as vividly there appeared his little university room at Moscow, where he used to sit half the night before a solitary candle, with his chum and his favorite boy friend.

They used to read for five hours on a stretch, and study such stupid lessons in civil law; and when they were done with them, they would send for supper, open a bottle of champagne, and talk about the future which awaited them.

How entirely different the young student had thought the future would be! Then the future was full of enjoyment, of varied occupation, brilliant with success, and beyond a peradventure sure to bring them both to what seemed to them the greatest blessing in the world, — to fame.

"He will go on, and go on rapidly, in that path," thought Nekhliudof of his friend; "but I ...."

But by this time he was already mounting the steps to his house; and near it were standing a score of peasants and house-servants, waiting for their barin with various requests. And this brought him back from dreams to the reality.

Among the crowd was a ragged and blood-stained peasant-woman, who was lamenting and complaining of her father-in-law, who had been beating her. There were two brothers, who for two years past had been going on shares in their domestic arrangements, and now looked at each other with hatred and despair. There was also an unshaven, gray-haired domestic serf, with hands trembling from the effects of intoxication; and this man was brought to the prince by his son, a gardener, who complained of his disorderly conduct. There was a peasant, who had driven his wife out of the house because she had not worked any all the spring. There was also the wife, a sick woman, who sobbed, but said nothing, as she sat on the grass by the

steps,—only showed her inflamed and swollen leg, carelessly wrapped up in a filthy rag.

Nekhliudof listened to all the petitions and complaints; and after he had given advice to one, blamed
others, and replied to still others, he began to feel a sort
of whimsical sensation of weariness, shame, weakness,
and regret. And he went to his room.

CHAPTER XX

IN the small room occupied by Nekhliudof stood
an old leather divan decorated with copper nails, a
few chairs of the same description, an old-fashioned
inlaid extension-table with scallops and brass mount-
ings, and strewn with papers, and an old-fashioned
English grand piano with narrow keys, broken and
twisted.

Between the windows hung a large mirror with an
old carved frame gilded. On the floor, near the table,
lay packages of papers, books, and accounts.

This room, on the whole, had a characterless and
disorderly appearance; and this lively disorder presented a sharp contrast with the affectedly aristocratic
arrangement of the other rooms of the great mansion.

When Nekhliudof reached his room, he flung his
hat angrily on the table, and sat down in a chair
which stood near the piano, crossed his legs, and
shook his head.

"Will you have lunch, your excellency?" asked a
tall, thin, wrinkled old woman, who entered just at
this instant, dressed in a cap, a great kerchief, and
a print dress.

Nekhliudof looked at her for a moment or two in
silence, as if collecting his thoughts.

"No, I don't wish anything, nurse," said he, and
again fell into thought.

The nurse shook her head at him in some vexation,
and sighed.

"Eh! Father Dmitri Nikolayevitch, are you melancholy? Such tribulation comes, but it will pass away. God knows...."

"I am not melancholy. What have you brought, Malanya Finogenovna?" replied Nekhliudof, endeavoring to smile.

"Ain't melancholy! can't I see?" the nurse began to say with warmth. "The whole livelong day to be all sole alone![1] And you take everything to heart so, and look out for everything; and besides, you scarcely eat anything. What's the reason of it? If you'd only go to the city, or visit your neighbors, as others do! You are young, and the idea of bothering over things so! Pardon me, little father, I will sit down," pursued the nurse, taking a seat near the door. "You see, we have got into such a habit that we lose fear. Is that the way gentlemen do? There's no good in it. You are only ruining yourself, and the people are spoiled. That's just like our people; they don't understand it, that's a fact. You had better go to your auntie. What she wrote was good sense," said the nurse, admonishing him.

Nekhliudof kept growing more and more dejected. His right hand, resting on his knee, lazily struck the piano, making a chord, a second, a third....

Nekhliudof moved nearer, drew his other hand from his pocket, and began to play. The chords which he made were sometimes not premeditated, were occasionally not even according to rule, often remarkable for absurdity, and did not show that he had any musical talent; but the exercise gave him a certain undefinable melancholy enjoyment.

At every modification in the harmony, he waited with muffled heart-beat for what would come out of it; and when anything came, he, in a dark sort of way, completed with his imagination what was missing.

It seemed to him that he heard a hundred melodies, and a chorus, and an orchestra simultaneously joining in with his harmony. But his chief pleasure was in the powerful activity of his imagination; confused and

[1] *Dyen dyenskoï adin-adinyoshenek.*

broken, but bringing up with striking clearness before him the most varied, mixed, and absurd images and pictures from the past and the future.

Now it presents the puffy figure of Davuidka Byelui, timidly blinking his white eyelashes at the sight of his mother's black fist with its network of veins; his bent back, and huge hands covered with white hairs, exhibiting a uniform patience and submission to fate, sufficient to overcome torture and deprivation.

Then he saw the brisk, presuming nurse, and somehow seemed to picture her going through the villages, and announcing to the peasants that they ought to hide their money from the proprietors; and he unconsciously said to himself, "Yes, it is necessary to hide money from the proprietors."

Then suddenly there came up before him the fair head of his future wife, for some reason weeping, and leaning on his shoulder in deep grief.

Then he seemed to see Churis's kindly blue eyes looking affectionately at his pot-bellied little son. Yes, he saw in him a helper and savior, apart from his son. "That is love," he whispered.

Then he remembered Yukhvanka's mother, remembered the expression of patience and conciliation which, notwithstanding her prominent teeth and her irregular features, he recognized on her aged face.

"It must be that I have been the first during her seventy years of life to recognize her good qualities," he said to himself, and whispered, "Strange"; but he continued still to drum on the piano, and to listen to the sounds.

Then he vividly recalled his retreat from the bees, and the expressions on the faces of Karp and Ignat, who evidently wanted to laugh, though they made believe not look at him. He reddened, and involuntarily glanced at the nurse, who still remained sitting by the door, looking at him with silent attention, occasionally shaking her gray head.

Here, suddenly, he seemed to see a troïka of sleek horses, and Ilyushka's handsome, robust form, with bright curls, gayly shining, narrow blue eyes, fresh complexion, and delicate down just beginning to appear on lip and chin.

He remembered how Ilyushka was afraid that he would not be permitted to go teaming, and how eagerly he argued in favor of the work that he liked so well. And he sees the gray, early, misty morning, and the smooth paved road, and the long line of three-horse wagons, heavily laden and protected by mats, and marked with big black letters. The stout, contented, well-fed horses, thundering along with their bells, arching their backs, and tugging on the traces, pull in unison up the hill, forcibly straining on their long-nailed shoes over the smooth road.

And coming toward the train of wagons down the hill dashes the postman, with jingling bells, which are echoed far and wide by the great forest extending along on both sides of the road.

"*A-a-aï!*" in a loud, boyish voice, shouts the *yamshchik*, or head driver, who has a badge on his lambskin cap, and swings his whip around his head.

Beside the front wheel of the front team, the red-headed, cross-looking Karp is walking heavily in huge boots. From behind the mat in the second team Ilyushka shows his handsome head, as he sits on the driver's seat gloriously playing the bugle. Three troïka-wagons loaded with boxes, with creaking wheels, with the sound of bells and shouts, file by. Ilyushka once more hides his handsome face under the matting, and falls off to sleep.

Now it is a fresh, clear evening. The deal gates open for the weary horses as they halt in front of the tavern yard; and one after the other, the high mat-covered teams roll in across the planks that lie at the gates, and come to rest under the wide sheds.

Ilyushka gayly exchanges greetings with the light-complexioned, wide-bosomed landlady, who asks, "Have you come far? and will there be many of you to supper?" and at the same time looks with pleasure on the handsome lad, with her bright, kindly eyes.

And now, having unharnessed the horses, he goes into the warm house [1] crowded with people, crosses himself, sits down at the generous wooden bowl, and enters into lively conversation with the landlady and his companions.

And then he goes to bed in the open air under the stars which gleam down into the shed. His bed is fragrant hay, and he is near the horses, which, stamping and snorting, eat their fodder in the wooden cribs. He goes to the shed, turns toward the east, and after crossing himself thirty times in succession on his broad brawny chest, and throwing back his bright curls, he repeats "Our Father" and "Lord have mercy" a score of times, and wrapping himself, head and all, in his cloak, sleeps the healthy, dreamless sleep of strong, fresh manhood.

And here he sees in his vision the city of Kief, with its saints and throngs of priests, Romen, with its merchants and merchandise; he sees *Odest*, and the distant blue sea studded with white sails, and the city of Tsargrad,[2] with its golden palaces, and the white-breasted, black-eyed Turkish maidens; and thither he flies, lifting himself on invisible wings.

He flies freely and easily, always farther and farther away, and sees below him golden cities bathed in clear effulgence, and the blue sky with bright stars, and a blue sea with white sails; and smoothly and pleasantly he flies, always farther and farther away. ....

"Splendid!" whispers Nekhliudof to himself; and the thought, "Why am I not Ilyushka?" comes to him.

[1] *Izba.*   [2] Constantinople.

LUCERNE

FROM THE RECOLLECTIONS OF PRINCE NEKHLIUDOF

JULY 20, 1857.

YESTERDAY evening I arrived at Lucerne, and put up at the best inn there, the Schweitzerhof.

"Lucerne, the chief city of the canton, situated on the shore of the Vierwaldstätter See," says Murray, "is one of the most romantic places of Switzerland: here cross three important highways, and it is only an hour's distance by steamboat to Mount Righi, from which is obtained one of the most magnificent views in the world."

Whether that be true or no, other Guides say the same thing, and consequently at Lucerne there are throngs of travelers of all nationalities, especially the English.

The magnificent five-storied building of the Hotel Schweitzerhof is situated on the quay, at the very edge of the lake, where in olden times there used to be the crooked covered wooden bridge[1] with chapels on the corners and pictures on the roof. Now, thanks to the tremendous inroad of Englishmen, with their necessities, their tastes, and their money, they have torn down the old bridge, and in its place erected a granite quay, straight as a stick. On the quay they have built straight, quadrangular five-storied houses; in front of the houses they have set out two rows of lindens and provided them with supports, and between the lindens is the usual supply of green benches.

This is the promenade; and here back and forth

---

[1] Hofbrück, torn down in 1852.

stroll the Englishwomen in their Swiss straw hats, and
the Englishmen in simple and comfortable attire, and
rejoice in their work. Possibly these quays and houses
and lindens and Englishmen would be excellent in their
way anywhere else, but here they seem discordant amid
this strangely magnificent, and at the same time inde-
scribably harmonious and smiling nature.

As soon as I went up to my room, and opened the
window facing the lake, the beauty of the sheet of
water, of the mountains, and of the sky, at the first
moment literally dazzled and overwhelmed me. I experienced an inward unrest, and the necessity of expressing in some manner the feelings that suddenly filled my
soul to overflowing. I felt a desire to embrace, powerfully to embrace, some one, to tickle him, or to pinch
him ; in short, to do to him and to myself something
extraordinary.

It was seven o'clock in the evening. The rain had
been falling all day, but now it had cleared.

The lake, iridescent as melted sulphur, and dotted with
boats, which left behind them vanishing trails, spread
out before my windows smooth, motionless as it were,
between the variegated green shores. Farther away it
was contracted between two monstrous headlands, and,
darkling, set itself against and disappeared behind a
confused pile of mountains, clouds, and glaciers. In
the foreground stretched a panorama of moist, fresh
green shores, with reeds, meadows, gardens, and villas.
Farther away, the dark green wooded heights, crowned
with the ruins of feudal castles ; in the background, the
rolling, pale lilac-colored vista of mountains, with fantastic peaks built up of crags and pallid snow-capped
summits. And everything was bathed in a fresh,
transparent azure atmosphere, and kindled by the warm
rays of the setting sun, bursting forth through the riven
skies.

Not on the lake or on the mountains or in the skies
was there a single completed line, a single unmixed
color, a single moment of repose ; everywhere motion,
irregularity, fantasy, endless conglomeration and variety

of shades and lines; and above all, a calm, a softness, a unity, and the inevitability of beauty.

And here amid this indeterminate, kaleidoscopic, unfettered loveliness, before my very window, stretched stupidly, compelling the gaze, the white line of the quay, the lindens with their supports, and the green seats, — miserable, tasteless creations of human ingenuity, not subordinated, like the distant villas and ruins, to the general harmony of the beautiful scene, but on the contrary brutally opposed to it. ....

Constantly, though against my will, my eyes were attracted to that horribly straight line of the quay; and mentally I should have liked to get rid of it, to demolish it like a black spot which should disfigure the nose beneath one's eye.

But the quay with the sauntering Englishmen remained where it was, and I involuntarily tried to find a point of view where it would be out of my sight. I succeeded in finding such a view; and till dinner was ready I took delight, alone by myself, in this incomplete and therefore the more enjoyable feeling of oppression that one experiences in the solitary contemplation of natural beauty.

About half-past seven I was called to dinner. Two long tables, accommodating at least a hundred persons, were spread in the great, magnificently decorated dining-room on the first floor. The silent gathering of the guests lasted three minutes, — the rustle of women's gowns, the soft steps, the softly spoken words addressed to the courtly and elegant waiters. And all the places were occupied by ladies and gentlemen dressed elegantly, even richly, and for the most part in perfect taste.

As is apt to be the case in Switzerland, the majority of the guests were English, and this gave the ruling characteristics of the common table: that is, a strict decorum regarded as an obligation, a reserve founded not in pride but in the absence of any necessity for social relationship, and finally a uniform sense of satisfaction felt by each in the comfortable and agreeable gratification of his wants.

On all sides gleamed the whitest laces, the whitest collars, the whitest teeth, — natural and artificial, — the whitest complexions and hands. But the faces, many of which were very handsome, bore the expression merely of individual prosperity, and absolute absence of interest in all that surrounded them unless it bore directly on their own individual selves; and the white hands, glittering with rings or protected by mitts, moved only for the purpose of straightening collars, cutting meat, or filling wine-glasses; no soul-felt emotion was betrayed in these actions.

Occasionally members of some one family would exchange remarks in subdued voices, about the excellence of such and such a dish or wine, or about the beauty of the view from Mount Righi.

Individual tourists, whether men or women, sat beside one another in silence, and did not even seem to see one another. If it happened occasionally that, out of this five-score human beings, two spoke to each other, the topic of their conversation was certain to be the weather, or the ascent of the Righi.

Knives and forks scarcely rattled on the plates, so perfect was the observance of propriety; and no one dared to convey pease and vegetables to the mouth otherwise than on the fork. The waiters, involuntarily subdued by the universal silence, asked in a whisper what wine you would be pleased to order.

Such dinners always depress me: I dislike them, and before they are over I become blue. It always seems to me as if I had done something wrong; just as when I was a boy I was set upon a chair in consequence of some naughtiness, and bidden ironically, "Now rest a little while, my dear young fellow." And all the time my young blood was pulsing through my veins, and in the other room I could hear the merry shouts of my brothers.

I used to try to rebel against this feeling of being choked down, which I experienced at such dinners, but in vain. All these dead-and-alive faces have an irresistible influence over me, and I myself become also as one dead. I have no desires, I have no thoughts; I do not even observe.

At first I attempted to enter into conversation with my neighbors; but I got no response beyond the phrases which had probably been repeated in that place a hundred thousand times, a hundred thousand times by the same persons.

And yet these people were by no means all stupid and feelingless; but evidently many of them, though they seemed so dead, led self-centered lives, just as I did, and in many cases far more complicated and interesting ones than my own. Why, then, should they deprive themselves of one of the greatest enjoyments of life, — the enjoyment that comes from the intercourse of man with man?

How different it used to be in our *pension* at Paris, where twenty of us, belonging to as many different nationalities, professions, and individualities, met together at a common table, and, under the influence of the Gallic sociability, found the keenest zest!

There, immediately, from one end of the table to the other, the conversation, sandwiched with witticisms and puns, though often in a broken speech, became general. There every one, without being solicitous for the proprieties, said whatever came into his head. There we had our own philosopher, our own disputant, our own *bel esprit*, our own butt, — all common property.

There, immediately after dinner, we would move the table to one side, and, without paying too much attention to rhythm, take to dancing the polka on the dusty carpet, and often keep it up till evening. There, though we were rather flirtatious, and not overwise or dignified, still we were human beings.

And the Spanish countess with romantic proclivities, and the Italian *abbate* who insisted on declaiming from the "Divine Comedy" after dinner, and the American doctor who had the *entrée* into the Tuileries, and the young dramatic author with his long hair, and the pianist who, according to her own account, had composed the best polka in existence, and the unhappy widow who was a beauty, and wore three rings on every finger, — all of us enjoyed this society, which, though somewhat superficial, was human and pleasant. And we each carried away from it hearty recollections of the others, superficial or serious, as the case might be.

But at these English *table-d'hôte* dinners, as I look at all these laces, ribbons, jewels, pomaded locks, and silken gowns, I often think how many living women would be happy, and would make others happy, with these adornments.

Strange to think how many friends and lovers — most fortunate friends and lovers — are, perhaps, sitting side by side without knowing it! And God knows why they never come to this knowledge, and never give each other this happiness, which they might so easily give, and which they so long for.

I began to feel depressed, as usual, after such a dinner; and, without waiting for dessert, I sallied out in the most gloomy frame of mind for a constitutional through the city. My melancholy frame of mind was not relieved, but was rather confirmed, by the narrow, muddy streets without lanterns, the shuttered shops, the encounters with drunken workmen, and with women hastening after water, or in bonnets, glancing around them as they glided down the alleys or along the walls.

It was perfectly dark in the streets when I returned to the hotel without casting a glance about me, or having an idea in my head. I hoped that sleep would put an end to my melancholy. I experienced that horrible spiritual chill, loneliness, and heaviness, which sometimes, without any reason, beset those who are just arrived in any new place.

Looking down at my feet, I walked along the quay to the Schweitzerhof, when suddenly my ear was struck by the strains of a peculiar but thoroughly agreeable and sweet music.

These strains had an immediately enlivening effect on me. It was as if a bright, cheerful light had poured into my soul. I felt contented, gay. My slumbering attention was awakened again to all surrounding objects ; and the beauty of the night and the lake, to which, till then, I had been indifferent, suddenly came over me with quickening force like something new.

I involuntarily took in at a glance the dark sky with gray clouds flecking its deep blue, now lighted by the rising moon, the glassy, dark green lake, with its surface reflecting the lighted windows, and far away the snowy mountains ; and I heard the croaking of the frogs over on the Froschenburg shore, and the dewy fresh call of the quail.

Directly in front of me, in the spot whence the sounds of music had first come, and which still especially attracted my attention, I saw, amid the semi-darkness on the street, a throng of people standing in a semicircle, and in front of the crowd, at a little distance, a small man in dark clothes.

Behind the throng and the man, there stood out harmoniously against the blue, ragged sky, gray and blue, the black tops of a few Lombardy poplars in some garden, and, rising majestically on high, the two stern spires that stand on the towers of the ancient cathedral.

I drew nearer, and the strains became more distinct. At some distance I could clearly distinguish the full accords of a guitar, sweetly swelling in the evening air, and several voices, which, while taking turns with one another, did not sing any definite theme, but gave suggestions of one in places wherever the melody was most pronounced.

The theme was in somewhat the nature of a mazurka, sweet and graceful. The voices sounded now near at hand, now far distant; now a bass was heard, now a tenor, now a falsetto such as the Tyrolese warblers are wont to sing.

It was not a song, but the graceful, masterly sketch of a song. I could not comprehend what it was, but it was beautiful.

Those voluptuous, soft chords of the guitar, that sweet, gentle melody, that solitary figure of the man in black, amid the fantastic environment of the dark lake.

the gleaming moon, and the twin spires of the cathedral rising in majestic silence, and the black tops of the poplars, — all was strange and perfectly beautiful, or at least seemed so to me.

All the confused, arbitrary impressions of life suddenly became full of meaning and beauty. It seemed to me as if a fresh fragrant flower had sprung up in my soul. In place of the weariness, dullness, and indifference toward everything in the world, which I had been feeling the moment before, I experienced a necessity for love, a fullness of hope, and an unbounded enjoyment of life.

"What dost thou desire, what dost thou long for?" an inner voice seemed to say. "Here it is. Thou art surrounded on all sides by beauty and poetry. Breathe it in, in full, deep draughts, as long as thou hast strength. Enjoy it to the full extent of thy capacity. 'T is all thine, all blessed!"....

I drew nearer. The little man was, as it seemed, a traveling Tyrolese. He stood before the windows of the hotel, one leg advanced, his head thrown back; and, as he thrummed on the guitar, he sang his graceful song in all those different voices.

I immediately felt an affection for this man, and a gratefulness for the change which he had brought about in me.

The singer, as far as I was able to judge, was dressed in an old black coat. He had short black hair, and he wore a civilian's hat which was no longer new. There was nothing artistic in his attire, but his clever and youthfully gay motions and pose, together with his diminutive stature, formed a pleasing and at the same time pathetic spectacle.

On the steps, in the windows, and on the balconies of the brilliantly lighted hotel, stood ladies handsomely decorated and attired, gentlemen with polished collars, porters and lackeys in gold-embroidered liveries; in the street, in the semicircle of the crowd, and farther along on the sidewalk, among the lindens, were gathered groups of well-dressed waiters, cooks in white caps and aprons, and young girls wandering about with arms about each others' waists.

All, it seemed, were under the influence of the same feeling as I myself experienced. All stood in silence around the singer, and listened attentively. Silence reigned, except in the pauses of the song, when there came from far away across the waters the regular click of a hammer, and from the Fröschenburg shore rang in fascinating monotone the voices of the frogs, interrupted by the mellow, monotonous call of the quail.

The little man in the darkness, in the midst of the street, poured out his heart like a nightingale, in couplet after couplet, song after song. Though I had come close to him, his singing continued to give me greater and greater gratification.

His voice, which was of great power, was extremely pleasant and tender; the taste and feeling for rhythm which he displayed in the control of it were extraordinary, and proved that he had great natural gifts.

After he sung each couplet, he invariably repeated the theme in variation, and it was evident that all his graceful variations came to him at the instant, spontaneously.

Among the crowd, and above on the Schweitzerhof, and near by on the boulevard, were heard frequent murmurs of approval, though generally the most respectful silence reigned.

The balconies and the windows kept filling more and more with handsomely dressed men and women leaning on their elbows, and picturesquely illuminated by the lights in the house.

Promenaders came to a halt, and in the darkness on the quay stood men and women in little groups. Near me, at some distance from the common crowd, stood an aristocratic cook and lackey, smoking their cigars. The cook was forcibly impressed by the music, and at every high falsetto note enthusiastically nodded his head to the lackey, and nudged him with his elbow with an expression of astonishment which seemed to say, "How he sings! hey?"

The lackey, by whose undissimulated smile I could mark the depth of feeling he experienced, replied to the cook's nudges by shrugging his shoulders, as if to show that it was hard enough for him to be made enthusiastic, and that he had heard much better music.

In one of the pauses of his song, while the minstrel was clearing his throat, I asked the lackey who he was, and if he often came there.

"Twice in the summer he comes here," replied the lackey. "He is from Aargau; he gets his livelihood by begging."

"Tell me, do many like him come round here?" I asked.

"Oh, yes," replied the lackey, not comprehending the full force of what I asked; but, immediately after, recollecting himself, he added, "Oh, no. This one is the only one I ever heard here. No one else."

At this moment the little man had finished his first song, was briskly twanging his guitar, and said something in his German *patois*, which I could not understand, but which brought forth a hearty round of laughter from the surrounding throng.

"What was that he said?" I asked.

"He said his throat is dried up, he would like some wine," replied the lackey, who was standing near me.

"What? is he rather fond of the glass?"

"Yes, all that sort of people are," replied the lackey, smiling and pointing at the minstrel.

The minstrel took off his cap, and swinging his guitar went toward the hotel. Raising his head, he addressed the ladies and gentlemen standing by the windows and on the balconies, saying in a half-Italian, half-German accent, and with the same intonation as jugglers use in speaking to their audiences : —

"*Messieurs et mesdames, si vous croyez que je gagne quelque chose, vous vous trompez : je ne suis qu'un pauvre tiaple.*"

He stood in silence a moment, but as no one gave him anything, he once more took up his guitar, and said : —

"*A présent, messieurs et mesdames, je vous chanterai l'air du Righi.*"

His hotel audience made no response, but stood in expectation of the coming song. Below on the street a laugh went round, probably in part because he had expressed himself so strangely, and in part because no one had given him anything.

I gave him a few centimes, which he deftly changed from one hand to the other, and bestowed them in his vest-pocket; and then, replacing his cap, began once more to sing; it was the graceful, sweet Tyrolese melody which he had called *l'air du Righi.*

This song, which formed the last on his programme, was even better than the preceding, and from all sides in the wondering throng were heard sounds of approbation.

He finished. Again he swung his guitar, took off his cap, held it out in front of him, went two or three steps nearer to the windows, and again repeated his stock phrase: "*Messieurs et mesdames, si vous croyez que je gagne quelque chose,*" which he evidently considered to be very shrewd and witty; but in his voice and motions I perceived now a certain irresolution and childish timidity which were especially touching in a person of such diminutive stature.

The elegant public, still picturesquely grouped in the lighted windows and on the balconies, were shining in their rich attire; a few conversed in soberly discreet tones, apparently about the singer who was standing there below them with outstretched hand; others gazed down with attentive curiosity on the little black figure; on one balcony could be heard a young girl's merry, ringing laughter.

In the crowd below the talk and laughter kept growing louder and louder.

The singer for the third time repeated his phrase, but in a still weaker voice, and did not even end the sentence; and again he stretched his hand with his cap, but instantly drew it back. Again, not one of those brilliantly dressed scores of people standing to listen to him threw him a penny.

The crowd laughed heartlessly.

The little singer, so it seemed to me, shrunk more into himself, took his guitar into his other hand, lifted his cap, and said : —

"*Messieurs et mesdames, je vous remercie, et je vous souhais une bonne nuit.*"

Then he put on his hat.

The crowd cackled with laughter and satisfaction. The handsome ladies and gentlemen, calmly exchanging remarks, withdrew gradually from the balconies. On the boulevard the promenading began once more. The street, which had been still during the singing, assumed its wonted liveliness ; a few men, however, stood at some distance, and, without approaching the singer, looked at him and laughed.

I heard the little man muttering something between his teeth, as he turned away ; and I saw him, apparently growing more and more diminutive, start toward the city with brisk steps. The promenaders, who had been looking at him, followed him at some distance, still making merry at his expense. ....

My mind was in a whirl ; I could not comprehend what it all meant ; and still standing in the same place, I gazed abstractedly into the darkness after the little man, who was fast disappearing, as he went with ever increasing swiftness with long strides into the city, followed by the merrymaking promenaders.

I was overmastered by a feeling of pain, of bitterness, and, above all, of shame for the little man, for the crowd, for myself, as if it were I who had asked for money and received none ; as if it were I who had been turned to ridicule.

Without looking any longer, feeling my heart oppressed, I also hurried with long strides toward the entrance of the Schweitzerhof. I could not explain the feeling that overmastered me ; only there was something like a stone, from which I could not free myself, weighing down my soul and oppressing me.

At the stately, well-lighted entrance I met the Swiss, who politely made way for me. An English family was also at the door.   A portly, handsome, tall gentleman, with black side-whiskers, in a black hat, and with a plaid on one arm, while in his hand he carried a costly cane, came out slowly, and full of importance.   Leaning on his arm was a lady, who wore a raw silk gown and a bonnet with bright ribbons and the most charming laces. With them was a pretty, fresh-looking young lady, in a graceful Swiss hat, with a feather, *à la mousquetaire ;* from under it escaped long, light yellow curls, softly encircling her fair face.   In front of them skipped a buxom girl of ten, with round, white knees which showed from under her thin embroideries.   "What a lovely night !" the lady was saying in a sweet, happy voice, as I passed them.

"Oh, yes," growled the Englishman, lazily ; and it was evident that he found it so enjoyable to be alive in the world, that it was too much trouble even to speak.

And it seemed as if all of them alike found it so comfortable and easy, so light and free, to be alive in the world, their faces and motions expressed such perfect indifference to the lives of every one else, and such absolute confidence, that it was to them that the Swiss made way, and bowed so profoundly, and that when they returned they would find clean, comfortable beds and rooms, and that all this was bound to be, and was their indefeasible right, that I could not help contrasting them with the wandering minstrel, who, weary, perhaps hungry, full of shame, was retreating before the laughing crowd.   And then, suddenly, I comprehended what it was that oppressed my heart with such a load of heaviness, and I felt an indescribable anger against these people.

Twice I walked up and down past the Englishman, and each time, without turning out for him, my elbow punched him, which gave me a feeling of indescribable satisfaction ; and then, darting down the steps, I hastened through the darkness in the direction taken by the little man on his way to the city.

Overtaking three men, walking together, I asked them where the singer was ; they laughed, and pointed straight ahead. There he was, walking alone with brisk steps; no one was with him; all the time, as it seemed to me, he was indulging in bitter monologue.

I caught up with him, and proposed to him to go somewhere with me and drink a bottle of wine. He kept on with his rapid walk, and looked at me indignantly; but when it dawned on him what I meant, he halted.

"Well, I will not refuse, if you are so kind," said he; "here is a little *café*, we can go in there. It's very ordinary," he added, pointing to a drinking-saloon that was still open.

His expression "very ordinary" involuntarily suggested to my mind the idea of not going to a very ordinary *café*, but to go to the Schweitzerhof, where those who had been listening to him were. Notwithstanding the fact that several times he showed a sort of timid disquietude at the idea of going to the Schweitzerhof, declaring that it was too fashionable for him there, still I insisted on carrying out my purpose; and he, already pretending that he was not in the least abashed, and gayly swinging his guitar, went back with me across the quay.

A few loiterers who had happened along as I was talking with the minstrel, and had stopped to hear what I had to say, now, after arguing among themselves, followed us to the very entrance of the hotel, evidently expecting from the Tyrolese some further demonstration.

I ordered a bottle of wine of a waiter whom I met in the hall. The waiter smiled and looked at us, and went by without answering. The head waiter, to whom I addressed myself with the same order, listened to me and, measuring the minstrel's modest little figure from head to foot, sternly ordered the waiter to take us to the room at the left.

The room at the left was a bar-room for simple people. In the corner of this room a hunchbacked maid was washing dishes. The whole furniture consisted of bare wooden tables and benches.

The waiter who came to serve us looked at us with a supercilious smile, thrust his hands in his pockets, and exchanged some remarks with the humpbacked dishwasher. He evidently tried to give us to understand that he felt himself immeasurably higher than the minstrel, both in dignity and social position, so that he considered it not only an indignity, but actually ridiculous, that he was called on to serve us.

"Do you wish *vin ordinaire?*" he asked, with a knowing look, winking toward my companion and switching his napkin from one hand to the other.

"Champagne, and your very best," said I, endeavoring to assume my haughtiest and most imposing appearance.

But neither my champagne, nor my endeavor to look haughty and imposing, had the least effect on the servant; he smiled incredulously, loitered a moment or two gazing at us, took time enough to glance at his gold watch, and with leisurely steps, as if going out for a walk, left the room.

Soon he returned with the wine, bringing two other waiters with him. These two sat down near the dishwasher, and gazed at us with amused attention and a bland smile, just as parents gaze at their children when they are gently playing. Only the humpbacked dishwasher, it seemed to me, did not look at us scornfully but sympathetically.

Though it was trying and awkward to lunch with the minstrel, and to play the entertainer, under the fire of all these waiters' eyes, I tried to do my duty with as little constraint as possible. In the lighted room I could see him better. He was a small but symmetrically built and muscular man, though almost a dwarf in stature; he had bristly black hair, teary big black eyes, bushy eyebrows, and a thoroughly pleasant, attractively shaped mouth. He had little side-whiskers, his hair was short, his attire was very simple and mean. He was not over-clean, was ragged and sunburnt, and in general had the look of a laboring-man. He was far more like a poor tradesman than an artist.

Only in his ever humid and brilliant eyes, and in his

firm mouth, was there any sign of originality or genius.
By his face it might be conjectured that his age was
between twenty-five and forty; in reality, he was
thirty-seven.

Here is what he related to me, with good-natured
readiness and evident sincerity, of his life. He was a
native of Aargau. In early childhood he had lost father
and mother; other relatives he had none. He had never
owned any property. He had been apprenticed to a
carpenter; but twenty-two years previously one of his
arms had been attacked by caries, which had prevented
him from ever working again.

From childhood he had been fond of singing, and he
began to be a singer. Occasionally strangers had given
him money. With this he had learned his profession,
bought his guitar, and now for eighteen years he had
been wandering about through Switzerland and Italy,
singing before hotels. His whole luggage consisted of
his guitar, and a little purse in which, at the present
time, there was only a franc and a half. That would
have to suffice for supper and lodgings this night.

Every year now for eighteen years he had made the
round of the best and most popular resorts of Switzerland, — Zurich, Lucerne, Interlaken, Chamounix, etc.;
by the way of the St. Bernard he would go down into
Italy, and return over the St. Gotthard, or through
Savoy. Just at present it was rather hard for him to
walk, as he had caught a cold, causing him to suffer
from some trouble in his legs, — he called it *Gliederzucht*,
or rheumatism, — which grew more severe from year to
year; and, moreover, his voice and eyes had grown
weaker. Nevertheless, he was on his way to Interlaken,
Aix-les-Bains, and thence over the little St. Bernard to
Italy, which he was very fond of. It was evident that
on the whole he was well content with his life.

When I asked him why he returned home, if he had
any relatives there, or a house and land, his mouth
parted in a gay smile, and he replied, "*Oui, le sucre
est bon, il est doux pour les enfants!*" and he winked at
the servants.

I did not catch his meaning, but the group of servants burst out laughing.

"No, I have nothing of the sort, but still I should always want to go back," he explained to me. "I go home because there is always a something that draws one to one's native place."

And once more he repeated with a shrewd, self-satisfied smile, his phrase, "*Oui, le sucre est bon,*" and then laughed good-naturedly.

The servants were very much amused, and laughed heartily; only the hunchbacked dish-washer looked earnestly from her big kindly eyes at the little man, and picked up his cap for him, when, as we talked, he once knocked it off the bench. I have noticed that wandering minstrels, acrobats, even jugglers, delight in calling themselves artists, and several times I hinted to my comrade that he was an artist; but he did not at all accept this designation, but with perfect simplicity looked on his work as a means of existence.

When I asked him if he had not himself written the songs which he sang, he showed great surprise at such a strange question, and replied that the words of whatever he sang were all of old Tyrolese origin.

"But how about that song of the Righi? I think that cannot be very ancient," I suggested.

"Oh, that was composed about fifteen years ago. There was a German in Basle; he was a clever man; it was he who composed it. A splendid song. You see he composed it especially for travelers."

And he began to repeat the words of the Righi song, which he liked so well, translating them into French as he went along.

> "*If you wish to go to Righi,*
> *You will not need shoes to Wegis*
> *(For you go that far by steamboat),*
> *But from Wegis take a stout staff,*
> *Also on your arm a maiden;*
> *Drink a glass of wine on starting,*
> *Only do not drink too freely,*
> *For if you desire to drink here,*
> *You must earn the right to, first.*"

"Oh! a splendid song!" he exclaimed, as he finished.

The servants, evidently, also found the song much to their mind, because they came up closer to us.

"Yes, but who was it composed the music?" I asked.

"Oh, no one at all; you know you must have something new when you are going to sing for strangers."

When the ice was brought, and I had given my comrade a glass of champagne, he seemed somewhat ill at ease, and, glancing at the servants, he turned and twisted on the bench.

We touched our glasses to the health of all artists; he drank half a glass, then he seemed to be collecting his ideas, and knit his brows in deep thought.

"It is long since I have tasted such wine, *je ne vous dis que ça*. In Italy the *vino d'Asti* is excellent, but this is still better. Ah! Italy; it is splendid to be there!" he added.

"Yes, there they know how to appreciate music and artists," said I, trying to bring him round to the evening's mischance before the Schweitzerhof.

"No," he replied. "There, as far as music is concerned, I cannot give anybody satisfaction. The Italians are themselves musicians, — none like them in the world; but I know only Tyrolese songs. They are something of a novelty to them, though."

"Well, you find rather more generous gentlemen there, don't you?" I went on to say, anxious to make him share in my resentment against the guests of the Schweitzerhof. "There it would not be possible to find a big hotel frequented by rich people, where, out of a hundred listening to an artist's singing, not one would give him anything."

My question utterly failed of the effect that I expected. It did not enter his head to be indignant with them; on the contrary, he saw in my remark an implied slur on his talent which had failed of its reward, and he hastened to set himself right before me. "It is not every time that you get anything," he remarked; "sometimes one is n't in good voice, or you are tired;

now to-day I have been walking ten hours, and singing almost all the time. That is hard. And these important aristocrats do not always care to listen to Tyrolese songs."

"But still, how can they help giving?" I insisted. He did not comprehend my remark.

"That's nothing," he said; "but here the principal thing is, *on est tres serré pour la police*, that's what's the trouble. Here, according to these republican laws, you are not allowed to sing; but in Italy you can go wherever you please, no one says a word. Here, if they want to let you, they let you; but if they don't want to, then they can throw you into jail."

"What? That's incredible!"

"Yes, it is true. If you have been warned once, and are found singing again, they may put you in jail. I was kept there three months once," he said, smiling as if that were one of his pleasantest recollections.

"Oh! that is terrible!" I exclaimed. "What was the reason?"

"That was in consequence of one of the new laws of the republic," he went on to explain, growing animated. "They cannot comprehend here that a poor fellow must earn his living somehow. If I were not a cripple, I would work. But what harm do I do to any one in the world by my singing? What does it mean? The rich can live as they wish, but *un pauvre tiaple* like myself can't live at all. What does it mean by laws of the republic? If that is the way they run, then we don't want a republic. Isn't that so, my dear sir? We don't want a republic, but we want.... we simply want.... we want".... he hesitated a little, ... "we want natural laws."

I filled up his glass.

"You are not drinking," I said.

He took the glass in his hand, and bowed to me.

"I know what you wish," he said, blinking his eyes at me, and threatening me with his finger. "You wish to make me drunk, so as to see what you can get out of me; but no, you shan't have that gratification."

"Why should I make you drunk?" I inquired. "All I wished was to give you a pleasure."

He seemed really sorry that he had offended me by interpreting my insistence so harshly. He grew confused, stood up, and touched my elbow.

"No, no," said he, looking at me with a beseeching expression in his moist eyes. "I was only joking."

And immediately after he made use of some horribly uncultivated slang expression, intended to signify that I was, nevertheless, a fine young man.

"*Je ne vous dis que ça*," he said in conclusion.

In this fashion the minstrel and I continued to drink and converse; and the waiters continued to stare at us unceremoniously, and, as it seemed, to ridicule us.

In spite of the interest which our conversation aroused in me, I could not avoid taking notice of their behavior; and I confess I began to grow more and more angry.

One of the waiters arose, came up to the little man, and, looking at the top of his head, began to smile. I was already full of wrath against the inmates of the hotel, and had not yet had a chance to pour it out on any one; and now I confess I was in the highest degree irritated by this audience of waiters.

The Swiss, not removing his hat, came into the room, and sat down near me, leaning his elbows on the table. This last circumstance, which was so insulting to my dignity or my vainglory, completely enraged me, and gave an outlet for all the wrath which the whole evening long had been boiling within me. Why had he so humbly bowed when he had met me before, and now, because I was sitting with the traveling minstrel, did he come and take his place near me so rudely? I was entirely overmastered by that boiling, angry indignation which I enjoy in myself, which I sometimes endeavor to stimulate when it comes over me, because it has an exhilarating effect on me, and gives me, if only for a short time, a certain extraordinary flexibility, energy, and strength in all my physical and moral faculties.

I leaped to my feet.

"Whom are you laughing at?" I screamed at the waiter; and I felt my face turn pale, and my lips involuntarily set together.

"I am not laughing, I only...." replied the waiter, moving away from me.

"Yes, you are; you are laughing at this gentleman. And what right have you to come, and to take a seat here, when there are guests? Don't you dare to sit down!"

The Swiss, muttering something, got up and turned to the door.

"What right have you to make sport of this gentleman, and to sit down by him, when he is a guest, and you are a waiter? Why didn't you laugh at me this evening at dinner, and come and sit down beside me? Because he is meanly dressed, and sings in the streets? Is that the reason? and because I have better clothes? He is poor, but he is a thousand times better than you are; that I am sure of, because he has never insulted any one, but you have insulted him."

"I didn't mean anything," replied my enemy, the waiter. "Did I disturb him by sitting down?"

The waiter did not understand me, and my German was wasted on him. The rude Swiss was about to take the waiter's part; but I fell upon him so impetuously that the Swiss pretended not to understand me, and waved his hand.

The hunchbacked dish-washer, either because she perceived my wrathful state, and feared a scandal, or possibly because she shared my views, took my part, and, trying to force her way between me and the porter, told him to hold his tongue, saying that I was right, but at the same time urging me to calm myself.

"*Der Herr hat Recht; Sie haben Recht,*" she said over and over again. The minstrel's face presented a most pitiable, terrified expression; and evidently he did not understand why I was angry, and what I wanted; and he urged me to let him go away as soon as possible.

But the eloquence of wrath burned within me more and more. I understood it all, — the throng that had made merry at his expense, and his auditors who had not given him anything; and not for all the world would I have held my peace.

I believe that, if the waiters and the Swiss had not been so submissive, I should have taken delight in having a brush with them, or striking the defenseless English girl on the head with a stick. If at that moment I had been at Sevastopol, I should have taken delight in devoting myself to slaughtering and killing in the English trench.

"And why did you take this gentleman and me into this room, and not into the other? What?" I thundered at the Swiss, seizing him by the arm so that he could not escape from me. "What right had you to judge by his appearance that this gentleman must be served in this room, and not in that? Have not all guests who pay equal rights in hotels? Not only in a republic, but in all the world! Your scurvy republic! .... Equality, indeed! You would not dare to take an Englishman into this room, not even those Englishmen who have heard this gentleman free of cost; that is, who have stolen from him, each one of them, the few centimes which ought to have been given to him. How did you dare to take us to this room?"

"That room is closed," said the porter.

"No," I cried, "that isn't true; it isn't closed."

"Then you know best."

"I know .... I know that you are lying."

The Swiss turned his back on me.

"Eh! What is to be said?" he muttered.

"What is to be said?" I cried. "Now conduct us instantly into that room!"

In spite of the dish-washer's warning, and the entreaties of the minstrel, who would have preferred to go home, I insisted on seeing the head waiter, and went with my guest into the big dining-room. The head waiter, hearing my angry voice, and seeing my menacing face, avoided a quarrel, and, with contemptuous servility, said that I might go wherever I pleased. I could not prove to the Swiss that he had lied, because he had hastened out of sight before I went into the hall.

The dining-room was, in fact, open and lighted; and at one of the tables sat an Englishman and a lady, eating their supper. Although we were shown to a special table, I took the dirty minstrel to the very one where the Englishman was, and bade the waiter bring to us there the unfinished bottle.

The two guests at first looked with surprised, then with angry, eyes at the little man, who, more dead than alive, was sitting near me. They talked together in a low tone; then the lady pushed back her plate, her silk dress rustled, and both of them left the room. Through the glass doors I saw the Englishman saying something in an angry voice to the waiter, and pointing with his hand in our direction. The waiter put his head through the door, and looked at us. I waited with pleasurable anticipation for some one to come and order us out, for then I could have found a full outlet for all my indignation. But fortunately, though at the time I felt injured, we were left in peace. The minstrel, who before had fought shy of the wine, now eagerly drank all that was left in the bottle, so that he might make his escape as quickly as possible.

He, however, expressed his gratitude with deep feeling, as it seemed to me, for his entertainment. His teary eyes grew still more humid and brilliant, and he made use of a most strange and complicated phrase of gratitude. But still very pleasant to me was the sentence in which he said that if everybody treated artists as I had been doing, it would be very good, and ended by wishing me all manner of happiness. We went out into the hall together. There stood the servants, and my enemy the Swiss apparently airing his grievances against me before them. All of them, I thought, looked at me as if I were a man who had lost his wits. I treated the little man exactly like an equal, before all that audience of servants; and then, with all the respect that I was able to express in my behavior, I took off my

hat, and pressed his hand with its dry and hardened
fingers.

The servants pretended not to pay the slightest attention to me. Only one of them indulged in a sarcastic
laugh.

As soon as the minstrel had bowed himself out, and
disappeared in the darkness, I went up-stairs to my
room, intending to sleep off all these impressions and
the foolish, childish anger which had come upon me so
unexpectedly. But, finding that I was too much excited
to sleep, I once more went down into the street with the
intention of walking until I should have recovered my
equanimity, and, I must confess, with the secret hope
that I might accidentally come across the porter or the
waiter or the Englishman, and show them all their rude-
ness, and, most of all, their unfairness. But beyond the
Swiss, who when he saw me turned his back, I met no
one; and I began to promenade in absolute solitude
back and forth along the quay.

"This is an example of the strange fate of poetry,"
said I to myself, having grown a little calmer. "All
love it, all are in search of it; it is the only thing in life
that men love and seek, and yet no one recognizes its
power, no one prizes this best treasure of the world, and
those who give it to men are not rewarded. Ask any
one you please, ask all these guests of the Schweitzerhof,
what is the most precious treasure in the world, and all,
or ninety-nine out of a hundred, putting on a sardonic
expression, will say that the best thing in the world is
money.

"'Maybe, though, this does not please you, or coin-
cide with your elevated ideas,' it will be urged; 'but what
is to be done if human life is so constituted that money
alone is capable of giving a man happiness? I cannot
force my mind not to see the world as it is,' it will be
added, 'that is, to see the truth.'

"Pitiable is your intellect, pitiable the happiness
which you desire! And you yourselves, unhappy creatures, not knowing what you desire, ... why have you all
left your fatherland, your relatives, your money-making

trades and occupations, and come to this little Swiss city of Lucerne? Why did you all this evening gather on the balconies, and in respectful silence listen to the little beggar's song? And if he had been willing to sing longer, you would have been silent and listened longer. What! could money, even millions of it, have driven you all from your country, and brought you all together in this little nook of Lucerne? Could money have gathered you all on the balconies to stand for half an hour silent and motionless? No! One thing compels you to do it, and will forever have a stronger influence than all the other impulses of life: the longing for poetry which you know, which you do not realize, but feel, always will feel as long as you have any human sensibilities. The word 'poetry' is a mockery to you; you make use of it as a sort of ridiculous reproach; you regard the love for poetry as something meet for children and silly girls, and you make sport of them for it. For yourselves you must have something more definite.

"But children look upon life in a healthy way; they recognize and love what man ought to love, and what gives happiness. But life has so deceived and perverted you, that you ridicule the only thing that you really love, and you seek for what you hate and for what gives you unhappiness.

"You are so perverted that you did not perceive what obligations you were under to the poor Tyrolese who rendered you a pure delight; but at the same time you feel needlessly obliged to humiliate yourselves before some lord, which gives you neither pleasure nor profit, but rather causes you to sacrifice your comfort and convenience. What absurdity! what incomprehensible lack of reason!

"But it was not this that made the most powerful impression on me this evening. This blindness to all that gives happiness, this unconsciousness of poetic enjoyment, I can almost comprehend, or at least I have become wonted to it, since I have almost everywhere met with it in the course of my life; the harsh, unconscious churlishness of the crowd was no novelty to me; whatever those who argue in favor of popular sentiment may say, the throng is a conglomeration of very possibly good people, but of people who touch each other only on their coarse animal sides, and express only the weakness and harshness of human nature. But how was it that you, children of a free, humane people, you Christians, you simply as human beings, repaid with coldness and ridicule the poor beggar who gave you a pure enjoyment? But no, in your country there are asylums for beggars. There are no beggars, there must be none; and there must be no feelings of sympathy, since that would be a confession that beggary existed.

"But he labored, he gave you enjoyment, he besought you to give him something of your superfluity in payment for his labor of which you took advantage. But you looked on him with a cool smile as on one of the curiosities in your lofty brilliant palaces; and though there were a hundred of you, favored with happiness and wealth, not one man or one woman among you gave him a *sou*. Abashed he went away from you, and the thoughtless throng, laughing, followed and ridiculed not you, but him, because you were cold, harsh, and dishonorable; because you robbed him in receiving the entertainment which he gave you; for this you jeered *him*.

"'*On the* 19*th of July,* 1857, *in Lucerne, before the Schweitzerhof Hotel, in which were lodging very opulent people, a wandering beggar minstrel sang for half an hour his songs, and played his guitar. About a hundred people listened to him. The minstrel thrice asked all to give him something. No one person gave him a thing, and many made sport of him.*'

"This is not an invention, but an actual fact, as those who desire can find out for themselves by consulting the papers for the list of those who were at the Schweitzerhof on the 19th of July.

"This is an event which the historians of our time ought to describe in letters of inextinguishable flame. This event is more significant and more serious, and fraught with far deeper meaning, than the facts that are printed in newspapers and histories. That the English have killed several thousand Chinese because the Chinese would not sell them anything for money while their land is overflowing with ringing coins; that the French have killed several thousand Kabyles because the wheat grows well in Africa, and because constant war is essential for the drill of an army; that the Turkish ambassador in Naples must not be a Jew; and that the Emperor Napoleon walks about in Plombières, and gives his people the express assurance that he rules only in direct accordance with the will of the people, — all these are words which darken or reveal something long known. But the episode that took place in Lucerne on the 19th of July seems to me something entirely novel and strange, and it is connected not with the everlastingly ugly side of human nature, but with a well-known epoch in the development of society. This fact is not for the history of human activities, but for the history of progress and civilization.

"Why is it that this inhuman fact, impossible in any German, French, or Italian country, is quite possible here where civilization, freedom, and equality are carried to the highest degree of development, where there are gathered together the most civilized travelers from the most civilized nations? Why is it that these cultivated human beings, generally capable of every honorable human action, had no hearty, human feeling for one good deed? Why is it that these people who, in their palaces, their meetings, and their societies, labor warmly for the condition of the celibate Chinese in India, about the spread of Christianity and culture in Africa, about the formation of societies for attaining all perfection, — why is it that they should not find in their souls the simple, primitive feeling of human sympathy? Has such a feeling entirely disappeared, and has its place been taken by vainglory, ambition, and cupidity, governing these men in their palaces, meetings, and societies? Has the spreading of that reasonable, egotistical association of people, which we call civilization, destroyed and rendered nugatory the desire for instinctive and loving association? And is this that boasted equality for which so much innocent blood has been shed, and so many crimes have been perpetrated? Is it possible that nations, like children, can be made happy by the mere sound of the word 'equality'?

"Equality before the law? Does the whole life of a people revolve within the sphere of law? Only the thousandth part of it is subject to the law; the rest lies outside of it, in the sphere of the customs and intuitions of society.

"But in society the lackey is better dressed than the minstrel, and insults him with impunity. I am better dressed than the lackey, and insult him with impunity. The Swiss considers me higher, but the minstrel lower, than himself; when I made the minstrel my companion, he felt that he was on an equality with us both, and behaved rudely. I was impudent to the Swiss, and the Swiss acknowledged that he was inferior to me. The waiter was impudent to the minstrel, and the minstrel accepted the fact that he was inferior to the waiter.

"And is that government free, even though men seriously call it free, where a single citizen can be thrown into prison, because, without harming any one, without interfering with any one, he does the only thing he can to prevent himself from dying of starvation?

"A wretched, pitiable creature is man with his craving for positive solutions, thrown into this everlastingly tossing, limitless ocean of *good* and *evil*, of facts, of combinations and contradictions. For centuries men have been struggling and laboring to put the *good* on one side, the *evil* on the other. Centuries will pass, and no matter how much the unprejudiced mind may strive to decide where the balance lies between the *good* and the *evil*, the scales will refuse to tip the beam, and there will always be equal quantities of the *good* and the *evil* on each scale.

"If only man would learn to form judgments, and not indulge in rash and arbitrary thoughts, and not to make reply to questions that are propounded merely to remain forever unanswered! If only he would learn that every thought is both a lie and a truth!— a lie from the one-sidedness and inability of man to recognize all truth ; and true because it expresses one side of mortal endeavor. There are divisions in this everlastingly tumultuous, end- less, endlessly confused chaos of the *good* and the *evil*. They have drawn imaginary lines over this ocean, and they contend that the ocean is really thus divided.

"But are there not millions of other possible subdi- visions from absolutely different standpoints, in other planes ? Certainly these novel subdivisions will be made in centuries to come, just as millions of different ones have been made in centuries past.

"Civilization is *good*, barbarism is *evil;* freedom, *good*, slavery, *evil*. Now this imaginary knowledge annihilates the instinctive, beatific, primitive craving for the *good* which is in human nature. And who will ex- plain to me what is freedom, what is despotism, what is civilization, what is barbarism ?

"Where are the boundaries that separate them ? And whose soul possesses so absolute a standard of good and evil as to measure these fleeting, complicated facts ? Whose intellect is so great as to comprehend and weigh all the facts in the irretrievable past ? And who can find any circumstance in which *good* and *evil* do not exist together ? And because I know that I see more of one than of the other, is it not because my standpoint is wrong ? And who has the ability to separate himself so absolutely from life, even for a moment, as to look upon it independently from above ?

"One, only one infallible Guide we have, — the uni- versal Spirit which penetrates all collectively and as units, which has endowed each of us with the craving for the right; the Spirit which commands the tree to grow toward the sun, which commands the flower in autumn-tide to scatter its seed, and which commands each one of us unconsciously to draw closer together. And this one unerring, inspiring voice rings out louder than the noisy, hasty development of civilization.

"Who is the greater man, and who the greater bar- barian, — that lord, who, seeing the minstrel's well-worn clothes, angrily left the table, who gave him not the millionth part of his possessions in payment of his labor, and now lazily sitting in his brilliant, comfortable room, calmly expresses his opinion about the events that are happening in China, and justifies the massacres that have been done there; or the little minstrel, who, risking imprisonment, with a franc in his pocket, and doing no harm to any one, has been going about for a score of years, up hill and down dale, rejoicing men's hearts with his songs, though they have jeered at him, and almost cast him out of the pale of humanity; and who, in weariness and cold and shame, has gone off to sleep, no one knows where, on his filthy straw?"

At this moment, from the city, through the dead silence of the night, far, far away, I caught the sound of the little man's guitar and his voice.

"No," something involuntarily said to me, "you have no right to commiserate the little man, or to blame the lord for his well-being. Who can weigh the inner happiness which is found in the soul of each of these men? There he stands somewhere in the muddy road, and gazes at the brilliant moonlit sky, and gayly sings amid the smiling, fragrant night; in his soul there is no reproach, no anger, no regret. And who knows what is transpiring now in the hearts of all these men within those opulent, brilliant rooms? Who knows if they all have as much unencumbered, sweet delight in life, and as much satisfaction with the world, as dwells in the soul of that little man?

"Endless are the mercy and wisdom of Him who has permitted and formed all these contradictions. Only to thee, miserable little worm of the dust, audaciously, lawlessly attempting to fathom His laws, His designs, — only to thee do they seem like contradictions.

"Full of love He looks down from His bright, immeasurable height, and rejoices in the endless harmony in which you all move in endless contradictions. In thy pride thou hast thought thyself able to separate thyself from the laws of the universe. No, thou also, with thy petty, ridiculous anger against the waiters, — thou also hast disturbed the harmonious craving for the eternal and the infinite." ....

RECOLLECTIONS OF A
BILLIARD–MARKER

A STORY

WELL, it happened about three o'clock. The gentlemen were playing. There was the tall visitor, as our men called him. The prince was there, — the two are always together. The mustached barin was there; also the little hussar, Oliver, who was an actor; there was the Polish *pan*.[1] It was a pretty good crowd.

The tall visitor and the prince were playing together. Now, here I was walking up and down around the billiard-table with my stick, keeping tally, — ten and forty-seven, twelve and forty-seven.

Everybody knows it's our business to score. You don't get a chance to get a bite of anything, and you don't get to bed till two o'clock o' nights, but you're always being screamed at to bring the balls.

I was keeping tally; and I look, and see a new barin comes in at the door. He gazed and gazed, and then sat down on the divan. Very good!

"Now, who can that be?" thinks I to myself. "He must be somebody."

His dress was neat, — neat as a pin, — checkered tricot pants, stylish little short coat, plush vest, and gold chain and all sorts of trinkets dangling from it.

He was dressed neat; but there was something about the man neater still; slim, tall, his hair brushed forward in style, and his face fair and ruddy, — well, in a word, a fine young fellow.

---

[1] Polish name for lord or gentleman.

You must know our business brings us into contact with all sorts of people. And there's many that ain't of much consequence, and there's a good deal of poor trash. So, though you're only a scorer, you get used to telling folks; that is, in a certain way you learn a thing or two.

I looked at the barin. I see him sit down, modest and quiet, not knowing anybody; and the clothes on him are so brand-new that, thinks I, "Either he's a foreigner, — an Englishman maybe, — or some count just come. And though he's so young, he has an air of some distinction."

Oliver sat down next him, so he moved along a little.

They began a game. The tall man lost. He shouts to me. Says he, "You're always cheating. You don't count straight. Why don't you pay attention?"

He scolded away, then threw down his cue, and went out. Now, just look here! Evenings, he and the prince plays for fifty silver rubles a game; and here he only lost a bottle of Makon wine, and got mad. That's the kind of a character he is.

Another time he and the prince plays till two o'clock. They don't bank down any cash; and so I know neither of them's got any cash, but they are simply playing a bluff game.

"I'll go you twenty-five rubles," says he.

"All right."

Just yawning, and not even stopping to place the ball, — you see, he was not made of stone, — now just notice what he said. "We are playing for money," says he, "and not for chips."

But this man puzzled me worse than all the rest. Well, then, when the big man left, the prince says to the stranger, "Wouldn't you like," says he, "to play a game with me?"

"With pleasure," says he.

He sat there, and looked rather foolish, indeed he did. He may have been courageous in reality; but, at all events, he got up, went over to the billiard-table, and did not seem flustered as yet. But whether he was flustered or not, you couldn't help seeing that he was not quite at his ease.

Either his clothes were a little too new, or he was embarrassed because everybody was looking at him; at any rate, he seemed to have no energy. He sort of sidled up to the table, caught his pocket on the edge, began to chalk his cue, dropped his chalk.

Whenever he hit the ball, he always glanced around, and reddened. Not so the prince. He was used to it; he chalked and chalked his hand, tucked up his sleeve; he goes and sits down when he pockets the ball, even though he is such a little man.

They played two or three games; then I notice the prince puts up the cue, and says, "Would you mind telling me your name?"

"Nekhliudof," says he.

Says the prince, "Was your father commander in the corps of cadets?"

"Yes," says the other.

Then they began to talk in French, and I could not understand them. I suppose they were talking about family affairs.

"*Au revoir*," says the prince. "I am very glad to have made your acquaintance."

He washed his hands, and went to get a lunch; but the other stood by the billiard-table with his cue, and was knocking the balls about.

It's our business, you know, when a new man comes along, to be rather sharp; it's the best way. I took the balls, and went to put them up. He reddened, and says, "Can't I play any longer?"

"Certainly you can," says I. "That's what billiards is for." But I don't pay any attention to him. I straighten the cues.

"Will you play with me?"

"Certainly, sir," says I.

I place the balls.

"Shall we play for odds?"

"What do you mean, — 'play for odds'?"

"Well," says I, "you give me a half-ruble, and I crawl under the table."

Of course, as he had never seen that sort of thing, it seemed strange to him; he laughed.

"Go ahead," says he.

"Very well," says I, "only you must give me odds."

"What!" says he, "are you a worse player than I am?"

"Most likely," says I. "We have few players who can be compared with you."

We began to play. He certainly had the idea that he was a crack shot. It was a caution to see him shoot; but the Pole sat there, and kept shouting out every time: —

"Ah, what a chance! ah, what a shot!"

But what a man he was! His ideas were good enough, but he didn't know how to carry them out. Well, as usual I lost the first game, crawled under the table, and grunted.

Thereupon Oliver and the Pole jumped down from their seats, and applauded, thumping with their cues.

"Splendid! Do it again," they cried, "once more."

Well enough to cry "once more," especially for the Pole. That fellow would have been glad enough to crawl under the billiard-table, or even under the Blue bridge, for a half-ruble! Yet he was the first to cry, "Splendid! but you haven't wiped off all the dust yet."

I, Petrushka the marker, was pretty well known to everybody.

Only, of course, I did not care to show my hand yet. I lost my second game.

"It does not become me at all to play with you, sir," says I.

He laughed. Then, as I was playing the third game, he stood forty-nine and I nothing. I laid the cue on the billiard-table, and said, "Barin, shall we play off?"

"What do you mean by playing off?" says he. "How would you have it?"

"You make it three rubles or nothing," says I.

"Why," says he, "have I been playing with you for money?" The fool!

He turned rather red.

Very good. He lost the game. He took out his pocket-book, — quite a new one, evidently just from the English shop, — opened it; I see he wanted to make a little splurge. It was stuffed full of bills, — nothing but hundred-ruble notes.

"No," says he, "there's no small stuff here."

He took three rubles from his purse.

"There," says he, "there's your two rubles; the other pays for the games, and you keep the rest for vodka."

"Thank you, sir, most kindly."

I see that he is a splendid fellow. For such a one I would crawl under anything. For one thing, it's a pity that he won't play for money. For then, thinks I, I should know how to work him for twenty rubles, and maybe I could stretch it out to forty.

As soon as the Pole saw the young barin's money, he says, "Wouldn't you like to try a little game with me? You play so admirably."

Such sharpers prowl around.

"No," says he, "excuse me; I have not the time."

And he went out.

I don't know who that man was, that Pole. Some one called him *Pan*, and it stuck to him. Every day he used to sit in the billiard-room, and always look on. He was no longer allowed to take a hand in any game whatever; but he always sat by himself, and got out his pipe, and smoked. But then he could play well.

Very good. Nekhliudof came a second time, a third time; he began to come frequently. He would come morning and evening. He learned to play French carom and pyramid pool, — everything, in fact. He became less bashful, got acquainted with everybody, and played tolerably well. Of course, being a young man of a good family, with money, everybody liked him. The only exception was the "tall visitor"; he quarreled with him.

And the whole thing grew out of a trifle.

They were playing pool, — the prince, the "tall visitor," Nekhliudof, Oliver, and some one else. Nekhliudof was standing near the stove talking with some one. When it came the big man's turn to play, it happened that his ball was just opposite the stove. There was very little space there, and he liked to have elbow-room.

Now, either he did n't see Nekhliudof, or he did it on purpose; but, as he was flourishing his cue, he hit Nekhliudof in the chest, a tremendous rap. It actually made him groan. What then? He did not think of apologizing, he was so boorish. He even went farther: he did n't look at him; he walks off grumbling : —

"Who 's jostling me there? It made me miss my shot. Why can't we have some room?"

Then the other went up to him, pale as a sheet, but quite self-possessed, and says so politely : —

"You ought first, sir, to apologize; you struck me," says he.

"Catch me apologizing now! I should have won the game," says he, "but now you have spoiled it for me."

Then the other one says : —

"You ought to apologize."

"Get out of my way! I insist upon it, I won't."

And he turned away to look after his ball.

Nekhliudof went up to him, and took him by the arm.

"You 're a boor," says he, "my dear sir."

Though he was a slender young fellow, almost like a girl, still he was all ready for a quarrel. His eyes flashed fire; he looked as if he could eat him alive. The big guest was a strong, tremendous fellow, no match for Nekhliudof.

"Wha-at!" says he, "you call me a boor?"

Yelling out these words, he raises his hand to strike him.

Then everybody there rushed up, and seized them both by the arms, and separated them.

After much talk, Nekhliudof says : —

"Let him give me satisfaction; he has insulted me."

"Not at all," said the other. "I don't care a whit

about any satisfaction. He's nothing but a boy, a mere nothing. I'll pull his ears for him."

"If you are n't willing to give me satisfaction, then you are no gentleman."

And, saying this, he almost cried.

"Well, and you, you are a little boy; nothing you say or do can offend me."

Well, we separated them, — led them off, as the custom is, to different rooms. Nekhliudof and the prince had become friends.

"Go," says the former; "for God's sake make him listen to reason."....

The prince went. The big man says : —

"I'm not afraid of any one," says he. "I am not going," says he, "to have any explanation with such a baby. I won't do it, and that's the end of it."

Well, they talked and talked, and then the matter died out, only the "tall visitor" ceased to come to us any more.

As a result of this, — this row, I might call it, — he was regarded as quite the cock of the walk. He was quick to take offense, — I mean Nekhliudof ; — as to so many other things, however, he was as unsophisticated as a new-born babe.

I remember once, the prince says to Nekhliudof, "Whom do you keep here?"

"No one," says he.

"What do you mean, — 'no one'!"

"Why should I?" says Nekhliudof.

"How so, — why should you?"

"I have always lived thus. Why should n't I continue to live the same way?"

"You don't say so! It is incredible!"

And saying this, the prince burst into a peal of laughter, and the mustached barin also roared. They could n't get over it.

"What, never?" they asked.

"Never!"

They were dying with laughter. Of course I understood well enough what they were laughing at him for.

I keep my eyes open. "What," thinks I, "will come of it?"

"Come," says the prince, "come with me now."

"No; not for anything," was his answer.

"Now, that is absurd," says the prince. "Come along!"

They went out.

They came back at one o'clock. They sat down to supper; quite a crowd of them were assembled. Some of our very best customers, — Atanof, Prince Razin, Count Shustakh, Mirtsof. And all congratulated Nekhliudof, laughing as they did so. They called me in; I saw that they were pretty jolly.

"Congratulate the barin," they shout.

"What on?" I ask.

How did he call it? His initiation or his enlightenment;[1] I can't remember exactly.

"I have the honor," says I, "to congratulate you."

And he sits there very red in the face, yet he smiles. Did n't they have fun with him, though!

Well and good. They went afterward to the billiardroom, all very gay; and Nekhliudof went up to the billiard-table, leaned on his elbow, and said: —

"It's amusing to you, gentlemen," says he, "but it's sad for me. Why," says he, "why did I do it? Prince," says he, "I shall never forgive you or myself as long as I live."

And he actually burst into tears. Evidently he did not know himself what he was saying. The prince went up to him with a smile.

"Don't talk nonsense," says he. "Let's go home, Anatoli."

"I won't go anywhere," says the other. "Why did I do that?"

And the tears poured down his cheeks. He would not leave the billiard-table, and that was the end of it. That's what it means for a young and inexperienced man to ....

In this way he used often to come to us. Once he

---

[1] *S posvyashcheniem-li, s prosvyashcheniem-li.*

came with the prince, and the mustached man who
was the prince's crony; the gentlemen always called
him "Fedotka." He had prominent cheek-bones, and
was homely enough, to be sure; but he used to dress
neatly and drove in a carriage. Why did the gentlemen
like him so well? I really could not tell.

"Fedotka! Fedotka!" they'd call, and ask him to
eat and to drink, and they'd spend their money paying
up for him; but he was a thoroughgoing beat. If ever
he lost, he would be sure not to pay; but if he won,
you bet he wouldn't fail to collect his money. Often,
too, he came to grief; yet there he was, walking arm in
arm with the prince.

"You are lost without me," he would say to the
prince.

"I am, Fedot,"[1] says he; "but not a Fedot of that
sort."

And what jokes he used to crack, to be sure! Well,
as I said, they had already arrived that time, and one
of them says, "Let's have the balls for three-handed
pool."

"All right," says the other.

They began to play at three rubles a stake. Nekhliudof and the prince chat about all sorts of things.

"Ah!" says one of them, "you mind only what a
neat little ankle she has."

"Oh," says the other, "her ankle is well enough;
but what beautiful hair."

Of course they paid no attention to the game, only
kept on talking to one another.

As to Fedotka, that fellow was alive to his work; he
played his very best, but they didn't do themselves
justice at all.

And so he won six rubles from each of them. God
knows how many games he had won from the prince,
yet I never knew them to pay each other any money;
but Nekhliudof took out two greenbacks, and handed
them over to him.

"No," says he, "I don't want to take your money.

---

[1] *Fedot, da nye tot,* an untranslatable play on the word.

Let's square it: play 'quits or double,'[1]— either double
or nothing."

I set the balls. Fedotka began to play the first hand.
Nekhliudof seemed to play only for fun; sometimes he
would come very near winning a game, yet just fail of
it. Says he, "It would be too easy a move, I won't
have it so." But Fedotka did not forget what he was
up to. Carelessly he proceeded with the game, and
thus, as if it were unexpectedly, won.

"Let us play double stakes once more," says he.

"All right," says Nekhliudof.

Once more Fedotka won the game.

"Well," says he, "it began with a mere trifle. I
don't wish to win much from you. Shall we make it
once more or nothing?"

"Yes."

Say what you may, but fifty rubles is a pretty sum,
and Nekhliudof himself began to propose, "Let us make
it double or quit." So they played and played.

It kept growing worse and worse for Nekhliudof.
Two hundred and eighty rubles were written up against
him. As to Fedotka, he had his own method; he would
lose a simple game, but when the stake was doubled, he
would win sure.

But the prince sits by and looks on. He sees that
the matter is growing serious.

"Enough!"[2] says he, "hold on."

My! they keep increasing the stake.

At last it went so far that Nekhliudof was in for more
than five hundred rubles. Fedotka laid down his cue,
and said:—

"Aren't you satisfied for to-day? I'm tired," says
he.

Yet I knew he was ready to play till dawn of day,
provided there was money to be won. Stratagem, of
course. And the other was all the more anxious to go
on. "Come on! Come on!"

"No,—by God, I'm tired. Come," says Fedot;
"let's go up-stairs; there you shall have your *revanche*."

---

[1] *Kitudubl* = Fr. *quitte ou double*.　　　　[2] *ase = assez*.

Up-stairs with us meant the place where the gentlemen used to play cards.

From that very day, Fedotka wound his net round
him so that he began to come every day. He would
play one or two games of billiards, and then proceed
up-stairs, — every day up-stairs.

What they used to do there, God only knows; but it
is a fact that from that time he began to be an entirely
different kind of man, and seemed hand in glove with
Fedotka. Formerly he used to be stylish, neat in his
dress, with his hair slightly curled even; but now it
would be only in the morning that he would be anything like himself; but as soon as he had paid his visit
up-stairs, he would not be at all like himself.

Once he came down from up-stairs with the prince,
pale, his lips trembling, and talking excitedly.

"I cannot permit such a one as *he* is," says he, "to
say that I am not...." How did he express himself? I
cannot recollect, something like "not defined [1] enough,"
or what, — "and that he won't play with me any more.
I tell you I have paid him ten thousand, and I should
think that he might be a little more considerate, before
others, at least."

"Oh, bother!" says the prince, "is it worth while to
lose one's temper with Fedotka?"

"No," says the other, "I will not let it go so."

"Why, old fellow, how can you think of such a thing
as lowering yourself to have a row with Fedotka?"

"That is all very well; but there were strangers
there, mind you."

"Well, what of that?" says the prince; "strangers?
Well, if you wish, I will go and make him ask your
pardon."

"No," says the other.

And then they began to chatter in French, and I
could not understand what it was they were talking about.

And what would you think of it? That very evening
he and Fedotka ate supper together, and they became
friends again.

---

[1] *Velikaten* for *delikaten.*

Well and good. At other times again he would come alone.

"Well," he would say, "do I play well?"

It's our business, you know, to try to make everybody contented, and so I would say, "Yes, indeed;" and yet how could it be called good play, when he would poke about with his cue without any sense whatever.

And from that very evening when he took in with Fedotka, he began to play for money all the time. Formerly he didn't care to play for stakes, even for a dinner or for champagne. Sometimes the prince would say:—

"Let's play for a bottle of champagne."

"No," he would say. "Let us rather have the wine by itself. Hollo, there! bring a bottle!"

And now he began to play for money all the time; he used to spend his entire days in our establishment. He would either play with some one in the billiard-room, or he would go "up-stairs."

Well, thinks I to myself, every one else gets something from him, why don't I get some advantage out of it?

"Well, sir," says I, one day, "it's a long time since you have had a game with me."

And so we began to play. Well, when I won ten half-rubles of him, I says:—

"Don't you want to make it double or quit, sir?"

He said nothing. Formerly, if you remember, he would call me *durak*, fool, for such a boldness. But now we went to playing "quit or double."

I won eighty rubles of him.

Well, what would you think? Since that first time he used to play with me every day. He would wait till there was no one about, for of course he would have been ashamed to play with a mere marker in presence of others. Once he had got rather warmed up by the play (he already owed me sixty rubles), and so he says:—

"Do you want to stake all you have won?"

"All right," says I.

I won. "One hundred and twenty to one hundred and twenty?"

"All right," says I.

Again I won. "Two hundred and forty against two hundred and forty?"

"Isn't that too much?" I ask.

He made no reply. We played the game. Once more it was mine. "Four hundred and eighty against four hundred and eighty?"

I says, "Well, sir, I don't want to wrong you. Let us make it a hundred rubles that you owe me, and call it square."

You ought to have heard how he yelled at this, and yet he was not a proud man at all.

"Either play, or don't play!" says he.

Well, I see there's nothing to be done. "Three hundred and eighty, then, if you please," says I.

I really wanted to lose. I allowed him forty points in advance. He stood fifty-two to my thirty-six. He began to cut the yellow one, and missed eighteen points; and I was standing just at the turning-point. I made a stroke so as to knock the ball off of the billiard-table. No — so luck would have it. Do what I might, he even missed the doublet. I had won again.

"Listen," says he. "Piotr," — he did not call me *Petrushka* then, — "I can't pay you the whole on the spot. In a couple of months I can pay three thousand even, if it were necessary."

And there he stood just as red, and his voice kind of trembled.

"Very good, sir," says I.

With this he laid down the cue. Then he began to walk up and down, up and down, the sweat running down his face.

"Piotr," says he, "let's try it again, double or quit."

And he almost burst into tears.

"What, sir, what! would you play against such luck?"

"Oh, let us play, I beg of you."

And he brought the cue, and put it in my hand.

I took the cue, and I threw the balls on the table so that they bounced over on to the floor; I could not help showing off a little, naturally. I say, "All right, sir."

But he was in such a hurry that he went and picked up the balls himself, and I thinks to myself, "Anyway, I'll never be able to get the seven hundred rubles from him, so I can lose them to him all the same."

I began to play carelessly on purpose. But no — he won't have it so.

"Why," says he, "you are playing badly on purpose."

But his hands trembled, and when the ball went toward a pocket, his fingers would spread out and his mouth would screw up to one side, as if he could by any means force the ball into the pocket. Even I couldn't stand it, and I say : —

"That won't do any good, sir."

Very well. As he won this game, I says : —

"This will make it one hundred and eighty rubles you owe me, and fifty games; and now I must go and get my supper."

So I put up my cue, and went off.

I went and sat down all by myself, at a small table opposite the door; and I look in and see, and wonder what he will do. Well, what would you think? He began to walk up and down, up and down, probably thinking that no one's looking at him; and then he would give a pull at his hair, and then walk up and down again, and keep muttering to himself; and then he would pull his hair again.

After that he wasn't seen for a week. Once he came into the dining-room as gloomy as could be, but he didn't enter the billiard-room.

The prince caught sight of him.

"Come," says he, "let's have a game."

"No," says the other, "I am not going to play any more."

"Nonsense! come along."

"No," says he, "I won't come, I tell you. For you it's all one whether I go or not, yet for me it's no good to come here."

And so he did not come for ten days more. And then, it being the holidays, he came dressed up in a dress suit: he'd evidently been into company. And he was here all day long; he kept playing, and he came the next day, and the third. ....

And it began to go in the old style, and I thought it would be fine to have another trial with him.

"No," says he, "I'm not going to play with you; and as to the one hundred and eighty rubles that I owe you, if you'll come at the end of a month, you shall have it."

Very good. So I went to him at the end of a month.

"By God," says he, "I can't give it to you; but come back on Thursday."

Well, I went on Thursday. I found that he had a splendid suite of apartments.

"Well," says I, "is he at home?"

"He hasn't got up yet," I was told.

"Very good, I will wait."

For a body-servant he had one of his own serfs, such a gray-haired old man! That servant was perfectly single-minded, he didn't know anything about beating about the bush. So we got into conversation.

"Well," says he, "what is the use of our living here, master and I? He's squandered all his property, and it's mighty little honor or good that we get out of this Petersburg of yours. When he started from the country, he thought it would be as it was with the last barin (the kingdom of heaven be his!), I shall go about with princes and counts and generals; he thought to himself, 'I'll find a countess for a sweetheart, and she'll have a big dowry, and we'll live on a big scale.' But it's quite a different thing from what he expected; here we are, running about from one tavern to another as bad off as we could be! The Princess Rtishcheva, you know, is his own aunt, and Prince Borotintsef is his godfather. What do you think? He went to see them only once, that was at Christmas time; he never shows his nose there. Yes, and even their people laugh about it to me. 'Why,' says they, 'your barin is not a bit like his father!' And once I take it upon myself to say to him:—

"'Why wouldn't you go, sir, and visit your aunt? They are feeling bad because you haven't been for so long.'

"'It's stupid there, Demyanitch,' says he. Just to think, he found his only amusement here in the saloon! If he only would enter the service! yet, no; he has got entangled with cards and all the rest of it. When men get going that way, there's no good in anything; nothing comes to any good. ..... *E-ekh!* we are going to the dogs, and no mistake. ..... The late mistress (the kingdom of heaven be hers!) left us a rich inheritance: no less than a thousand souls, and about three hundred thousand rubles worth of timber lands. He has mortgaged it all, sold the timber, let the estate go to rack and ruin, and still no money on hand. When the master is away, of course, the overseer is more than the master. What does he care? He only cares to stuff his own pockets.

"A few days ago a couple of peasants brought complaints from the whole estate. 'He has wasted all the property,' they say. What do you think? he pondered over the complaints, and gave the peasants ten rubles apiece. Says he, 'I'll be there very soon. I shall have some money, and I will settle all accounts when I come,' says he.

"But how can he settle accounts when we are getting into debt all the time? Money or no money, yet the winter here has cost eighty thousand rubles, and now there isn't a silver ruble in the house. And allowing to his kind-heartedness. You see, he's such a simple barin that it would be hard to find his equal; that's the very reason that he's going to ruin,—going to ruin, all for nothing."

And the old man almost wept.

Nekhliudof woke up about eleven, and called me in.

"They have n't sent me any money yet," says he. "But it is n't my fault. Shut the door," says he.

I shut the door.

"Here," says he, "take my watch or this diamond pin, and pawn it. They will give you more than one hundred and eighty rubles for it, and when I get my money I will redeem it," says he.

"No matter, sir," says I. "If you don't happen to have any money, it 's no consequence; let me have the watch, if you don't mind. I can wait for your convenience."

I can see that the watch is worth more than three hundred.

Very good. I pawned the watch for a hundred rubles, and carried him the ticket.

"You will owe me eighty rubles," says I, "and you had better redeem the watch."

And so it happened that he still owed me eighty rubles.

After that he began to come to us again every day. I don't know how matters stood between him and the prince, but at all events he kept coming with him all the time, or else they would go and play cards up-stairs with Fedotka. And what queer accounts those three men kept between them! this one would lend money to the other, the other to the third, yet who it was that owed the money you never could find out.

And in this way he kept on coming our way for well-nigh two years; only it was to be plainly seen that he was a changed man, such a devil-may-care manner he assumed at times. He even went so far at times as to borrow a ruble of me to pay a hack-driver; and yet he would still play with the prince for a hundred rubles' stake.

He grew gloomy, thin, sallow. As soon as he came he used to order a little glass of absinthe, take a bite of something, and drink some port wine, and then he would grow more lively.

He came one time before dinner; it happened to be carnival time, and he began to play with a hussar.

Says he, "Do you want to play for a stake?"

"Very well," says he. "What shall it be?"

"A bottle of Claude Vougeaux? What do you say?"

"All right."

Very good. The hussar won, and they went off for their dinner. They sat down at table, and then Nekhliudof says, "Simon, a bottle of Claude Vougeaux, and see that you warm it to the proper point."

Simon went out, brought in the dinner, but no wine.

"Well," says he, "where's the wine?"

Simon hurried out, brought in the roast.

"Let us have the wine," says he.

Simon makes no reply.

"What's got into you? Here we've almost finished dinner, and no wine. Who wants to drink with dessert?"

Simon hurried out.

"The landlord," says he, "wants to speak to you."

Nekhliudof turned scarlet. He sprang up from the table.

"What's the need of calling me?"

The landlord is standing at the door.

Says he, "I can't trust you any more, unless you settle my little bill."

"Well, didn't I tell you that I would pay the first of the month?"

"That will be all very well," says the landlord, "but I can't be all the time giving credit, and having no settlement. There are more than ten thousand rubles of debts outstanding now," says he.

"Well, that'll do, *monshoor*, you know that you can trust me! Send the bottle, and I assure you that I will pay you very soon."

And he hurried back.

"What was it? why did they call you out?" asked the hussar.

"Oh, some one wanted to ask me a question."

"Now it would be a good time," says the hussar, "to have a little warm wine to drink."

"Simon, hurry up!"

Simon came back, but still no wine, nothing. Too bad! He left the table, and came to me.

"For God's sake," says he, "Petrushka, let me have six rubles!"

He was pale as a sheet.

"No, sir," says I; "by God, you owe me quite too much now."

"I will give forty rubles for six, in a week's time."

"If only I had it," says I, "I should not think of refusing you, but I haven't."

What do you think! He rushed away, his teeth set, his fist doubled up, and ran down the corridor like one mad, and all at once he gave himself a knock on the forehead.

"O my God!" says he, "what has it come to?"

But he did not return to the dining-room; he jumped into a carriage, and drove away. Did n't we have our laugh over it! The hussar asks:—

"Where is the gentleman who was dining with me?"

"He has gone," said some one.

"Where has he gone? What message did he leave?"

"He did n't leave any; he just took to his carriage, and went off."

"That 's a fine way of entertaining a man!" says he.

Now, thinks I to myself, it 'll be a long time before he comes again after this; that is, on account of this scandal. But no. On the next day he came about evening. He came into the billiard-room. He had a sort of a box in his hand. Took off his overcoat.

"Now, let us have a game," says he.

He looked out from under his eyebrows, rather fierce like.

We played one game.

"That 's enough now," says he; "go and bring me a pen and paper; I must write a letter."

Not thinking anything, not suspecting anything, I bring some paper, and put it on the table in the little room.

"It 's all ready, sir," says I.

"Very good."

He sat down at the table. He kept on writing and writing, and muttering to himself all the time; then he jumps up, and, frowning, says:—

"Look and see if my carriage has come yet."

It was on a Friday, during carnival time, and so there were n't any of the customers on hand; they were all at some ball. I went to see about the carriage, and just as I was going out of the door, "Petrushka! Petrushka!" he shouted, as if something suddenly frightened him.

I turn round. I see he's pale as a sheet, standing there, and looking at me.

"Did you call me, sir?" says I.

He made no reply.

"What do you want?" says I.

He says nothing.

"Oh, yes!" says he. "Let's have another game."

Then, says he:—

"Have n't I learned to play pretty well?"

He had just won the game. "Yes," says I.

"All right," says he; "go now, and see about my carriage."

He himself walked up and down the room.

Without thinking anything, I went down to the door. I did n't see any carriage at all. I started to go up again.

Just as I was going up, I heard what sounded like the thud of a billiard-cue. I went into the billiard-room. I noticed a peculiar smell.

I looked around; and there he was, lying on the floor, in a pool of blood, with a pistol beside him. I was that scared that I could not speak a word.

He kept twitching, twitching his leg, and stretched himself a little. Then he sort of snored, and stretched out his full length in such a strange way.

And God knows why such a sin came about,—how it was that it occurred to him to ruin his own soul,—but as to what he left written on this paper, I don't understand it at all.

Truly, you can never account for what is going on in the world.

———

"God gave me all that a man can desire, — wealth, name, intellect, noble aspirations. I wanted to enjoy myself, and I trod in the mire all that was best in me.

"I have done nothing dishonorable, I am not unfortunate, I have not committed any crime; but I have done worse: I have destroyed my feelings, my intellect, my youth.

"I became entangled in a filthy net, from which I cannot escape, and to which I cannot accustom myself. I feel that I am falling lower and lower every moment, and I cannot stop my fall.

———

"And what ruined me? Was there in me some strange passion which I might plead as an excuse? No!

".... My recollections are pleasant.

"One fearful moment of forgetfulness, which can never be erased from my mind, led me to come to my senses. I shuddered when I saw what a measureless abyss separated me from what I desired to be, and might have been. In my imagination arose the hopes, the dreams, and the thoughts of my youth.

"Where are those lofty thoughts of life, of eternity, of God, which at times filled my soul with light and strength? Where that aimless power of love which kindled my heart with its comforting warmth?

———

".... But how good and happy I might have been, had I trodden that path which, at the very entrance of life, was pointed out to me by my fresh mind and true feelings! More than once did I try to go from the ruts in which my life ran, into that sacred path.

"I said to myself, Now I will use my whole strength of will; and yet I could not do it. When I happened to be alone, I felt awkward and timid. When I was with others, I no longer heard the inward voice; and I fell all the time lower and lower.

"At last I came to a terrible conviction that it was impossible for me to lift myself from this low plane. I ceased to think about it, and I wished to forget all; but hopeless repentance worried me still more and more. Then, for the first time, the thought of suicide occurred to me.

"I once thought that the nearness of death would rouse my soul. I was mistaken. In a quarter of an hour I shall be no more, yet my view has not in the least changed. I see with the same eyes, I hear with the same ears, I think the same thoughts; there is the same strange incoherence, unsteadiness, and lightness in my thoughts."

ALBERT

A STORY

(1857)

CHAPTER I

FIVE rich young men went at three o'clock in the morning to a ball in Petersburg to have a good time.

Much champagne was drunk; a majority of the gentlemen were very young; the girls were pretty; a pianist and a fiddler played indefatigably one polka after another; there was no cessation to the noise of conversation and dancing. But there was a sense of awkwardness and constraint; every one felt somehow or other — and this is not unusual — that all was not as it should be.

There were several attempts made to make things more lively, but the simulated liveliness was much worse than melancholy.

One of the five young men, who was more discontented than any one else, with himself and with the others, and with the whole evening, got up with a feeling of disgust, took his hat, and went out noiselessly, intending to go home.

There was no one in the anteroom, but in the next room at the door he heard two voices disputing. The young man paused, and lisened.

"It is impossible, there are guests in there," said a woman's voice.

"Come, let me in, please. I will not do any harm," urged a man, in a gentle voice.

"Indeed, I will not let you in without the madame's permission," said the woman. "Where are you going? Oh, what a man you are!" ....

The door was flung open, and on the threshold appeared the figure of a strange-looking man. Seeing a guest, the maid ceased to detain him; and the stranger, timidly bowing, with a somewhat unsteady gait, came into the room.

He was a man of medium stature, with a lank, crooked back, bow legs, and long disheveled hair. He wore a short paletot, and tight ragged trousers over coarse dirty boots. His necktie, twisted into a string, exposed his long white neck. His shirt was filthy, and the sleeves came down over his lean hands.

But, notwithstanding his excessively emaciated body, his face was attractive and fair; and a fresh color even mantled his cheeks under his thin dark beard and side-whiskers. His disheveled locks, thrown back, exposed a low and remarkably pure forehead. His dark, languid eyes looked unswervingly forward with an expression of serenity, submission, and sweetness, which made a fascinating combination with the expression of his fresh, curved lips, visible under his thin mustache.

Advancing a few steps, he paused, turned to the young man, and smiled. He found it apparently rather hard to smile. But his face was so lighted up by it, that the young man, without knowing why, smiled in return.

"Who is that man?" he asked of the maid in a whisper, as the stranger walked toward the room where the dancing was going on.

"A crazy musician from the theater," replied the maid. "He sometimes comes to call upon the madame."

"Where are you going, Delyesof?" some one at this moment called from the drawing-room.

The young man who was called Delyesof returned to the drawing-room. The musician was now standing at the door; and, as his eyes fell on the dancers, he showed by his smile and by the beating of his foot how much pleasure this spectacle afforded him.

"Won't you come and have a dance, too?" said one of the guests to him.

The musician bowed, and looked at the madame inquiringly.

"Come, come. Why not, since the gentlemen have invited you?" said the madame.

The musician's thin, weak features suddenly began to work; and smiling and winking, and shuffling his feet, he awkwardly, clumsily, proceeded to prance through the room.

In the midst of a quadrille a jolly officer, who was dancing very beautifully and with great liveliness, accidentally hit the musician in the back. His weak, weary legs lost their equilibrium; and the musician,[1] staggering several steps to one side, measured his length on the floor.

Notwithstanding the sharp, hard sound made by his fall, almost every one at the first moment laughed.

But the musician did not rise. The guests grew silent, even the piano ceased to sound. Delyesof and the madame were the first to reach the prostrate musician. He was lying on his elbow, and gloomily looking down. When he had been lifted to his feet, and set in a chair, he threw back his hair from his forehead with a quick motion of his bony hand, and began to smile without replying to the questions that were put.

"Mr. Albert! Mr. Albert!" exclaimed the madame. "Were you hurt? Where? Now, I told you that you had better not try to dance. ..... He is so weak," she added, addressing her guests. "It takes all his strength."

"Who is he?" some one asked the madame.

"A poor man, an artist. A very nice young fellow; but he's a sad case, as you can see."

She said this undeterred by the musician's presence. He suddenly opened his eyes, and, as if he were frightened at something, shrank away, and pushed aside those who were standing about him.

[1] *Khozyaïka.*

"It's nothing at all," said he, suddenly, arising from the chair with evident effort.

And in order to show that he had suffered no injury, he went into the middle of the room, and was going to dance; but he tottered, and would have fallen again, had he not been supported.

Everybody felt awkward. All looked at him, and no one spoke.

The musician's glance again lost its vivacity; and, apparently forgetting that any one was looking, he began to rub his knee with his hand. Suddenly he raised his head, advanced one faltering foot, and, with the same awkward gesture as before, tossed back his hair, and went to a violin-case, and took out the instrument.

"It was nothing at all," said he again, waving the violin. "Gentlemen, we will have a little music."

"What a strange face!" said the guests among themselves.

"Maybe there is great talent lurking in that unfortunate creature," said one of them.

"Yes; it's a sad case, — a sad case," said another.

"What a lovely face! .... There is something extraordinary about it," said Delyesof. "Let us have a look at him." ....

CHAPTER II

ALBERT by this time, not paying attention to any one, had raised his violin to his shoulder, and was slowly crossing over to the piano, and tuning his instrument. His lips were drawn into an expression of indifference, his eyes were almost shut; but his lank, bony back, his long white neck, his crooked legs, and shaggy black hair presented a strange but somehow not entirely ridiculous spectacle. After he had tuned the violin, he struck a quick chord, and, throwing back his head, turned to the pianist, who was waiting to accompany him.

"*Mélancolie*, G *dur*," he said, turning to the pianist with a peremptory gesture.

And immediately after, as if in apology for his peremptory gesture, he smiled sweetly, and with the same smile turned to his audience again.

Tossing back his hair with his right hand, Albert stood at one side of the piano, and, with a flowing motion of his arm, drew the bow across the strings. Through the room there swept a pure, harmonious sound, which instantly brought absolute silence.

At first there seemed to be a clear light. The notes of the theme poured forth in full abundance and exquisitely beautiful, after the dawn of the first light so unexpectedly clear and serene, suddenly illuminating the inner world of each hearer's consciousness.

Not one discordant or imperfect note distracted the attention. All the tones were clear, beautiful, and full of meaning. All silently, with trembling expectation, followed the development of the theme. From the state of tedium, of noisy gayety, or of spiritual drowsiness, into which these people had fallen, they were suddenly transported to a world the existence of which they had wholly forgotten.

There arose in their souls, now a sense of quiet contemplation of the past, now of passionate remembrance of some happiness, now the boundless longing for power and glory, now feelings of humility, of unsatisfied love, and of melancholy.

Now bitter-sweet, now vehemently despairing, the notes, freely intermingling, poured forth and poured forth, so sweetly, so powerfully, and so spontaneously, that it was not so much that sounds were heard, as that some sort of beautiful stream of poetry, long known, but now for the first time expressed, gushed through the soul.

At each note he played, Albert grew taller and taller. At a little distance, he had no appearance of being either crippled or peculiar. Pressing the violin to his chin, and with an expression of listening with passionate attention to the tones he produced, he convulsively moved his feet. Now he straightened himself up to his full height, now eagerly bent his back.

His left hand, bent intensely over the strings, seemed as it had swooned in its position, while only the bony fingers changed about spasmodically; the right hand moved smoothly, gracefully, without effort.

His face shone with absolute, enthusiastic delight; his eyes gleamed with a radiant, steely light; his nostrils quivered, his red lips were parted in rapture.

Sometimes his head bent down closer to his violin, his eyes almost closed, and his face, half shaded by his long locks, lighted up with a smile of genuine bliss. Sometimes he quickly straightened himself up, changed from one leg to the other, and his pure forehead and the radiant look which he threw around the room were alive with pride, greatness, and the consciousness of power.

Once the pianist made a mistake and struck a false chord. Physical pain was apparent in the whole form and face of the musician. He paused for a second, and with an expression of childish anger stamped his foot, and cried, " *Moll, ce moll!* " The pianist corrected his mistake; Albert closed his eyes, smiled, and, again forgetting himself and every one else and the whole world, gave himself up with beatitude to his work.

All who were in the room while Albert was playing preserved an attentive silence, and seemed to live and breathe only in the music.

The gay officer sat motionless in a chair by the window, with his lifeless eyes fixed on the floor, and breathing slowly and heavily long, heavy sighs. The girls, in perfect silence, sat along by the walls, only occasionally exchanging glances expressive of approval, or occasionally becoming perplexity.

The madame's fat, smiling face was radiant with happiness. The pianist kept his eyes fixed on Albert's face, and while his whole figure from head to foot showed his solicitude lest he should make some mistake, he did his best to follow him. One of the guests, who had been drinking more heavily than the rest, lay at full length on a divan, and tried not to move lest he should betray his emotion.

Delyesof experienced an unusual sensation. It seemed as if an icy band, now contracting, now expanding, were pressed on his head. The roots of his hair seemed endued with consciousness; the cold shivers ran down his back, something rose higher and higher in his throat, his nose and palate were full of little needles, and the tears stole down his cheeks.

He shook himself, tried to swallow them back and wipe them away without attracting attention, but fresh tears followed and streamed down his face. By some sort of strange association of impressions, the first tones of Albert's violin carried Delyesof back to his early youth.

Old before his time, weary of life, a broken man, he suddenly felt as if he were a boy of seventeen again, self-satisfied and handsome, blissfully dull, unconsciously happy. He remembered his first love for his cousin who wore a pink dress; he remembered his first confession of it in the linden alley; he remembered the warmth and the inexpressible charm of the fortuitous kiss; he remembered the immensity and enigmatical mystery of Nature as it surrounded them then.

In his imagination, as it went back in its flight, *she* gleamed in a mist of indefinite hopes, of incomprehensible desires, and the indubitable faith in the possibility of impossible happiness. All the priceless moments of that time, one after the other, arose before him, not like unmeaning instants of the fleeting present, but like the immutable, full-formed, reproachful images of the past.

He contemplated them with rapture, and wept, — wept not because the time had passed and he might have spent it more profitably (if that time had been given to him again, he would not have spent it any more profitably), but he wept because it had passed and would never return. His recollections evolved themselves without effort, and Albert's violin was their interpreter. It said, "They have passed, forever passed, the days of thy strength, of love, and of happiness; passed forever, and never will return. Weep for them, shed all thy tears, let thy life pass in tears for these days; this is the only and best happiness that remains to thee."

At the end of the next variation, Albert's face grew serene, his eyes flushed, great, clear drops of perspiration poured down his cheeks. The veins swelled on his forehead; his whole body swayed more and more; his lips had grown pale and were parted, and his whole figure expressed an enthusiastic craving for enjoyment.

Despairingly swaying with his whole body, and throwing back his hair, he laid down his violin, and with a smile of proud satisfaction and happiness gazed at his audience. Then his back assumed its ordinary curve, his head sank, his lips grew set, his eyes lost their fire; and, as if he were ashamed of himself, timidly glancing round, and stumbling, he went into the next room.

CHAPTER III

SOMETHING strange came over all the audience, and something strange was noticeable in the dead silence that succeeded Albert's playing. Apparently, each desired, and yet was not able, to express what it all meant.

What did it mean, — this brightly lighted, warm room, these brilliant women, the dawn just appearing at the windows, these hurrying pulses, and the pure impressions made by the fleeting sounds? But no one attempted to acknowledge the meaning of it all; on the contrary, almost all, feeling incapable of going wholly in the direction of that which the new impression concealed from them, rebelled against it.

"Well, now, he plays mighty well," said the officer.

"Wonderfully," replied Delyesof, stealthily wiping his cheek with his sleeve.

"One thing sure, it's time to be going, gentlemen," said he who had been lying on the divan, straightening himself up a little. "We'll have to give him something, gentlemen. Let us make a collection."

At this time, Albert was sitting alone in the next room on a divan. As he leaned his elbows on his bony knees, he smoothed his face with his dirty, sweaty hands, tossed back his hair, and smiled at his own happy thoughts.

A large collection was taken up, and Delyesof was chosen to present it.

Aside from this, Delyesof, who had been so keenly and unusually affected by the music, had conceived the thought of conferring some benefit on this man.

It came into his head to take him home with him, to feed him, to establish him somewhere, — in other words, to lift him from his vile position.

"Well, are you tired?" asked Delyesof, approaching him. Albert replied with a smile. "You have creative talent; you ought seriously to devote yourself to music, to play in public."

"I should like to have something to drink," exclaimed Albert, as if suddenly waking up.

Delyesof brought him some wine, and the musician greedily drained two glasses.

"What splendid wine!" he exclaimed.

"What a lovely thing that *Mélancolie* is!" said Delyesof.

"Oh, yes, yes," replied Albert, with a smile. "But pardon me, I do not know with whom I have the honor to be talking; maybe you are a count or a prince. Couldn't you let me have a little money?" He paused for a moment. "I have nothing — I am a poor man; I couldn't pay it back to you."

Delyesof flushed, grew embarrassed, and hastily handed the musician the money that had been collected for him.

"Very much obliged to you," said Albert, seizing the money. "Now let us have some more music; I will play for you as much as you wish. Only let me have something to drink, something to drink," he repeated, as he started to his feet.

Delyesof gave him some more wine, and asked him to sit down by him.

"Pardon me if I am frank with you," said Delyesof. "Your talent has interested me so much. It seems to me that you are in a wretched position."

Albert glanced now at Delyesof, now at the madame, who just then came into the room.

"Permit me to help you," continued Delyesof. "If you need anything, then I should be very glad if you would come and stay with me for a while. I live alone, and maybe I could be of some service to you."

Albert smiled, and made no reply.

"Why don't you thank him?" said the madame. "It seems to me that this would be a capital thing for you. —Only I would advise you not," she continued, turning to Delyesof, and shaking her head warningly.

"Very much obliged to you," said Albert, seizing Delyesof's hand with both his moist ones. "Only now let us have some music, please."

But the rest of the guests were already making their preparations to depart; and as Albert had not addressed them, they came out into the anteroom.

Albert bade the madame farewell; and, having put on his worn hat with wide brim, and a last summer's *alma viva*, which composed his only protection against the winter, he went with Delyesof down the steps.

As soon as Delyesof took his seat in his carriage with his new friend, and became conscious of that unpleasant odor of intoxication and filthiness exhaled by the musician, he began to repent of the step he had taken, and to curse himself for his childish softness of heart and lack of reason. Moreover, all that Albert said was so foolish and in such bad taste, and now that he was out in the open air he seemed suddenly so disgustingly intoxicated, that Delyesof was disgusted.

"What shall I do with him?" he asked himself.

After they had been driving for a quarter of an hour, Albert relapsed into silence, his hat slipped off his head and fell to his feet, he himself sprawled out in a corner of the carriage, and began to snore.

The wheels crunched monotonously over the frozen snow, the feeble light of dawn scarcely made its way through the frosty windows.

Delyesof glanced at his companion. His long body, wrapped in his mantle, lay almost lifeless near him. It seemed to him that a long head with large black nose was swaying on his trunk; but on examining more closely he perceived that what he took to be nose and face was the man's hair, and that his actual face was lower down.

He bent over and studied the features of Albert's face. Then the beauty of his brow and of his peace-fully closed mouth once more charmed him. Under the influence of nervous excitement caused by the sleepless hours of the long night and the music, Delyesof, as he looked at that face, was once more carried back to the blessed world of which he had caught a glimpse once before that night; again he remembered the happy and *magnanimous* time of his youth, and he ceased to repent of his impulsive act. At that moment he loved Albert truly and warmly, and firmly resolved to be a benefactor to him.

CHAPTER IV

THE next morning, when Delyesof was awakened to go to his office, he saw, with an unpleasant feeling of surprise, his old screen, his old servant, and his clock on the table.

"What did I expect to see if not the usual objects that surround me?" he asked himself.

Then he recollected the musician's black eyes and happy smile; the motive of the *Mélancolie* and all the strange experiences of the night came back into his consciousness. It was never his way, however, to re-consider whether he had done wisely or foolishly in taking the musician home with him. After he had dressed, he carefully laid out his plans for the day; he took some paper, wrote out some necessary direc-tions for the house, and hastily put on his cloak and galoshes.

As he went by the dining-room he glanced in at the door. Albert, with his face buried in the pillow and lying at full length in his dirty, tattered shirt, was buried in the profoundest slumber on the morocco

divan, where in absolute unconsciousness he had been
deposited some hours before.

Delyesof could not help feeling that something was
not right.

"Please go for me to Boriuzovsky, and borrow his
violin for a day or two," said he to his man; "and when
he wakes up, bring him some coffee, and get him some
clean linen and some old suit or other of mine. Fit him
out as well as you can, please."

When he returned home in the afternoon, Delyesof,
to his surprise, found that Albert was not there.

"Where is he?" he asked of his man.

"He went out immediately after dinner," replied the
servant. "He took the violin, and went out, saying
that he would be back again in an hour; but since that
time we have not seen him."

"Ta, ta! how provoking!" said Delyesof. "Why
did you let him go, Zakhar?"

Zakhar was a Petersburg lackey, who had been in
Delyesof's service for eight years. Delyesof, as a
bachelor, living alone, could not help intrusting him
with his plans, and liked to get his judgment in regard
to each of his undertakings.

"How should I have ventured to detain him?" replied Zakhar, playing with his watch-charms. "If you
had intimated, Dmitri Ivanovitch, that you wished me
to keep him here, I might have kept him at home.
But you only spoke of his wardrobe."

"Ta! how vexatious! Well, what has he been doing
while I was out?"

Zakhar smiled.

"Indeed, he's a real artist, as one may say, Dmitri
Ivanovitch. As soon as he woke up he asked for some
Madeira; then he began to keep the cook and me pretty
busy. Such an absurd.... However, he's a very interesting character. I brought him some tea, got some
dinner ready for him; but he would not eat alone, so
he asked me to sit down with him. But when he began
to play on the fiddle, then I knew that you would not
find many such artists at Izler's. One might well

keep such a man. When he played 'Down the Little Mother Volga' for us, why, it was enough to make a man weep. It was too good for anything! The people from the floors came down into our entry to listen." ....

"Well, did you give him some clothes?" asked the barin, interrupting.

"Certainly I did; I gave him your night-shirt, and I put on him a paletot of my own. You want to help such a man as that, he 's a fine fellow." Zakhar smiled. "He kept asking me what rank you were, and if you had important acquaintances, and how many souls of peasantry you had."

"Very good; but now we must send and find him; and henceforth don't give him anything to drink, otherwise you 'll do him more harm than good."

"That is true," said Zakhar, in assent. "He does n't seem in very robust health; my former barin used to have an overseer who, like him...."

Delyesof, who had already long ago heard the story of the drunken overseer, did not give Zakhar time to finish, but bade him make everything ready for the night, and then go out and bring the musician back.

He threw himself down on his bed, and put out the candle; but it was long before he fell asleep, for thinking about Albert.

"This may seem strange to some of my friends," said Delyesof to himself, "but it is so seldom I can do anything for any one besides myself, that I ought to thank God for a chance when one presents itself, and I will not lose it. I will do everything. I certainly will do everything I can to help him. Maybe he is not absolutely crazy, but only inclined to get drunk. It certainly will not cost me very much. Where one is, there is always enough to satisfy two. Let him live with me awhile, and then we will find him a place, or get him up a concert; we 'll help him off the shoals, and then there will be time enough to see what will come of it."

An agreeable sense of self-satisfaction came over him after making this resolution.

"Certainly I am not a bad man; I might say I am far from being a bad man," he thought. "I might go so far as to say that I am a good man, when I compare myself with others." ....

He had just dropped off to sleep when the sound of opening doors, and steps in the anteroom, roused him again.

"Well, shall I treat him rather severely?" he asked himself; "I suppose that is best, and I ought to do it."

He rang.

"Well, did you find him?" he asked of Zakhar, who answered his call.

"He's a poor, wretched fellow, Dmitri Ivanovitch," said Zakhar, shaking his head significantly, and closing his eyes.

"What! is he drunk?"

"Very weak."

"Had he the violin with him?"

"I brought it; the lady gave it to me."

"All right. Now please don't bring him to me to-night; let him sleep it off; and to-morrow don't under any circumstances let him out of the house."

But before Zakhar had time to leave the room, Albert came in.

CHAPTER V

"You don't mean to say that you've gone to bed at this time!" said Albert, with a smile. "I was there again, at Anna Ivanovna's. I spent a very pleasant evening. We had music, — fine sport; there was a very pleasant company there. Please let me have a glass of something to drink," he added, seizing a carafe of water that stood on the table, "only not water."

Albert was just as he had been the night before, — the same lovely, smiling eyes and lips, the same fresh, inspired brow, and weak features. Zakhar's paletot fitted him as if it had been made for him, and the clean, wide, unstarched collar of the night-shirt pic-

turesquely fitted around his slender white neck, giving
him a peculiarly childlike and innocent appearance.

He sat down on Delyesof's bed, smiling with pleasure
and gratitude, and looked at him without speaking.
Delyesof gazed into Albert's eyes, and suddenly felt himself once more under the sway of that smile. All desire
for sleep vanished from him, he forgot his resolution to
be stern; on the contrary, he felt like having a gay
time, to hear some music, and to talk confidentially with
Albert till morning.

Delyesof bade Zakhar bring a bottle of wine, cigarettes, and the violin.

"This is excellent," said Albert. "It's early yet,
we'll have a little music. I will play whatever you
like."

Zakhar, with evident satisfaction, brought a bottle
of Lafitte, two glasses, some mild cigarettes such as
Albert smoked, and the violin. But, instead of going
off to bed as his barin bade him, he lighted a cigar, and
sat down in the next room.

"Let us talk instead," said Delyesof to the musician,
who was beginning to tune the violin.

Albert sat down submissively on the bed, and smiled
pleasantly.

"Oh, yes!" said he, suddenly striking his forehead
with his hand, and putting on an expression of anxious
curiosity. The expression of his face always gave an
intimation of what he was going to say. "I wanted to
ask you," — he hesitated a little, — "that gentleman
who was there with you last evening..... You called him
N. Was he the son of the celebrated N.?"

"His own son," replied Delyesof, not understanding
at all what Albert could find of interest in him.

"Indeed!" he exclaimed, smiling with satisfaction.
"I instantly noticed that there was something peculiarly
aristocratic in his manners. I love aristocrats. There
is something splendid and elegant about an aristocrat.
And that officer who danced so beautifully," he went on
to ask. "He also pleased me very much, he was so gay
and noble-looking. He is called Adjutant N. N."

"Who?" asked Delyesof.

"The one who ran into me when we were dancing. He must be a splendid man."

"No, he is a silly fellow," replied Delyesof.

"Oh, no! it can't be," rejoined Albert, hotly. "There's something very, very pleasant about him. And he's a glorious musician," he added. "He played something from an opera. It's a long time since I have seen any one who pleased me so much."

"Yes, he plays very well; but I don't like his playing," said Delyesof, wishing to bring his companion to talk about music. "He does not understand classic music, but only Donizetti and Bellini; and that's no music, you know. You agree with me, don't you?"

"Oh, no, no! Pardon me," replied Albert, with a gentle expression of opposition. "The old music is music; but modern music is music, too. And in the modern music there are extraordinarily beautiful things. Now, 'Somnambula,' and the *finale* of 'Lucia,' and Chopin, and 'Robert'! I often think," — he hesitated, apparently collecting his thoughts, — "that if Beethoven were alive, he would weep tears of joy to hear 'Somnambula.' It's so beautiful all through. I heard 'Somnambula' first when Viardot and Rubini were here. That was something worth while," he said, with shining eyes, and making a gesture with both hands, as if he were casting something from his breast. "I'd give a good deal, but it would be impossible, to bring it back."

"Well, but how do you like the opera nowadays?" asked Delyesof.

"Bosio is good, very good," was his reply, "exquisite beyond words; but she does not touch me here," he said, pointing to his sunken chest. "A singer must have passion, and she has n't any. She is enjoyable, but she does n't torture you."

"Well, how about Lablache?"

"I heard him in Paris, in 'The Barber of Seville.' Then he was the only one, but now he is old. He can't be an artist, he is old."

"Well, supposing he is old, still he is fine in *mor-*

ceaux d'ensemble," said Delyesof, still speaking of Lablache.

"How can he be old?" said Albert, severely. "He can't be old. The artist can never be old. Much is needed in an artist, the fire most of all," he declared with glistening eyes, and raising both hands in the air. And, indeed, a terrible inner fire seemed to glow throughout his whole frame. "Ah, my God!" he exclaimed suddenly. "You don't know Petrof, do you, — Petrof, the artist?"

"No, I don't know him," replied Delyesof, with a smile.

"How I wish that you and he might become acquainted! You would enjoy talking with him. How he does understand art! He and I often used to meet at Anna Ivanovna's, but now she is vexed with him for some reason or other. But I really wish that you might make his acquaintance. He has great, great talent."

"Oh! Does he paint pictures?" asked Delyesof.

"I don't know. No, I think not; but he was an artist of the Academy. What thoughts he had! Whenever he talks, it is wonderful. Oh, Petrof has great talent, only he leads a very gay life!.... It's too bad," said Albert, with a smile. The next moment he got up from the bed, took the violin, and began to tune it.

"Have you been at the opera lately?" asked Delyesof.

Albert looked round and sighed.

"Ah, I have not been able to!" he said, clutching his head. Again he sat down by Delyesof. "I will tell you," he went on to say, almost in a whisper. "I can't go; I can't play there. I have nothing, nothing at all .... no clothes, no home, no violin. It's a wretched life .... a wretched life!" he repeated several times. "Yes, and why have I got into such a state? Why, indeed? It ought not to have been," said he, smiling. "*Akh! Don Juan.*"

And he struck his head.

"Now let us have something to eat," said Delyesof.

Albert, without replying, sprang up, seized the violin, and began to play the *finale* of the first act of "Don Juan," accompanying it with a description of the scene in the opera.

Delyesof felt the hair stand up on his head, when he played the voice of the dying commander.

"No, I cannot play to-night," said Albert, laying down the instrument. "I have been drinking too much."

But, immediately afterward, he went to the table, poured out a brimming glass of wine, drank it at one gulp, and again sat down on the bed near Delyesof.

Delyesof looked steadily at Albert. The latter occasionally smiled, and Delyesof returned his smile. Neither of them spoke, but the glance and smile brought them close together into a reciprocity of affection. Delyesof felt that he was growing constantly fonder and fonder of this man, and he experienced an inexpressible pleasure.

"Were you ever in love?" he asked suddenly. Albert remained sunk in thought for a few seconds, then his face lighted up with a melancholy smile. He bent over toward Delyesof, and gazed straight into his eyes.

"Why did you ask me that question?" he whispered. "But I will tell you all about it. — I like you," he added, after a few moments of thought, and glancing around. "I will not deceive you, I will tell you all, just as it was, from the beginning." He paused, and his eyes took on a strange, wild appearance. "You know that I am weak in judgment," he said suddenly. "Yes, yes," he continued. "Anna Ivanovna has told you about it. She tells everybody that I am crazy. It is n't true, she says it for a joke; she is a good woman, but I really have not been quite well for some time." Albert paused again, and stood up, gazing with wide-opened eyes at the dark door. "You asked me if I had ever been in love. Yes, I have been in love," he whispered, raising his brows. "That happened long ago; it was at a time when I still had a place at the theater. I went to play second violin at the opera, and she came into a parquet box at the left."

Albert stood up, and bent over to Delyesof's ear.
"But no," said he, "why should I mention her name?
You probably know her, everybody knows her. I said
nothing, but simply looked at her; I knew that I was a
poor artist, and she an aristocratic lady. I knew that
very well. I only looked at her, and had no thoughts."

Albert paused for a moment, as if making sure of his
recollections.

"How it happened, I know not, but I was invited
once to accompany her on my violin..... Now I was
only a poor artist!" he repeated, shaking his head, and
smiling. "But no, I cannot tell you, I cannot!" he exclaimed, again clutching his head. "How happy I
was!"

"What? did you go to her house often?" asked
Delyesof.

"Once, only once..... But it was my own fault; I
wasn't in my right mind. I was a poor artist, and she
an aristocratic lady. I ought not to have spoken to her.
But I lost my senses, I committed a folly. Petrof told
me the truth: 'It would have been better only to have
seen her at the theater.'"

"What did you do?" asked Delyesof.

"Ah! wait, wait, I cannot tell you that.".

And, hiding his face in his hands, he said nothing for
some time.

"I was late at the orchestra. Petrof and I had been
drinking that evening, and I was excited. She was sitting in her box, and talking with a general. I don't
know who that general was. She was sitting at the very
edge of the box, with her arm resting on the rim. She
wore a white dress, with pearls on her neck. She was
talking with him, but she looked at me. Twice she
looked at me. She had arranged her hair in such a becoming way! I stopped playing, and stood near the
bass, and gazed at her. Then, for the first time, something strange took place in me. She smiled on the general, but she looked at me. I felt certain that she was
talking about me; and suddenly, I seemed to be not in
my place in the orchestra, but was standing in her box,

and seizing her hand in that place. What was the meaning of that?" asked Albert, after a moment's silence.

"That is the power of the imagination," said Delyesof.

"No, no, ... I cannot tell," said Albert, frowning. "Even then I was poor. I had no home; and when I went to the theater, I sometimes used to sleep there."

"What, in the theater? in the dark, empty auditorium?" asked Delyesof.

"Ah! I am not afraid of these stupid things. Ah! just wait a moment. As soon as everybody was gone, I went to that box where she had been sitting, and slept there. That was my only pleasure. How many nights I spent there! Only once again did I have that experience. At night many things seemed to come to me. But I cannot tell you much about them." Albert squinted his eyes, and looked at Delyesof. "What did it mean?" he asked.

"It was strange," replied the other.

"No, wait, wait!" He bent over to his ear, and said in a whisper: —

"I kissed her hand, wept there before her, and said many things to her. I heard the fragrance of her sighs, I heard her voice. She said many things to me that one night. Then I took my violin, and began to play softly. And I played beautifully. But it became terrible to me. I am not afraid of such stupid things, and I don't believe in them, but my head felt terribly," he said, smiling sweetly, and moving his hand over his forehead. "It seemed terrible to me on account of my poor mind; something happened in my head. Maybe it was nothing; what do you think?"

Neither spoke for several minutes.

> "*Und wenn die Wolken sie verhüllen,*
> *Die Sonne bleibt doch ewig klar.*"[1]

hummed Albert, smiling gently. "That is true, is n't it?" he asked.

[1] E'en though the clouds may veil it,
The sun shines ever clear.

"Ich auch habe gelebt und genossen." [1]

"Ah, old man Petrof! how this would have made things clear to you!"

Delyesof, in silence and with dismay, looked at his companion's excited and colorless face.

"Do you know the Juristen waltzes?" suddenly asked Albert, in a loud voice; and, without waiting for an answer, jumped up, seized the violin, and began to play the lively waltz. In absolute self-forgetfulness, and evidently imagining that a whole orchestra was playing for him, Albert smiled, danced, shuffled his feet, all the time playing admirably.

"Hey, we will have some sport!" he exclaimed, as he ended, and waved his violin. "I am going," said he, after sitting down in silence for a little. "Won't you come along, too?"

"Where?" asked Delyesof, in surprise.

"Let us go to Anna Ivanovna's again. It's gay there, — bustle, people, music."

Delyesof for a moment was almost persuaded. However, coming to his senses, he tried to prevent Albert from going that day.

"I should like to go this minute."

"Indeed, I wouldn't go."

Albert sighed, and laid down the violin.

"Shall I stay, then?"

He looked over at the table, but the wine was gone; and so, wishing him good-night, he left the room.

Delyesof rang.

"See here," said he to Zakhar, "don't let Mr. Albert go anywhere without asking me about it first."

CHAPTER VI

THE next day was a holiday. Delyesof, on waking, sat in his parlor, drinking his coffee and reading a book. Albert, who was in the next room, had not yet moved.

[1] I also have lived and enjoyed.

Zakhar discreetly opened the door, and looked into the dining-room.

"Would you believe it, Dmitri Ivanovitch, there he lies asleep on the bare divan. I would not send him away for anything, God knows. He's like a little child. Indeed, he's an artist!"

At twelve o'clock, there was a sound of yawning and coughing on the other side of the door.

Zakhar again went into the dining-room; and Delyesof heard his wheedling voice, and Albert's gentle, beseeching voice.

"Well, how is he?" asked Delyesof, when Zakhar came out.

"He is in low spirits, Dmitri Ivanovitch. He doesn't want to get dressed. He's so cross. All he asks for is something to drink."

"Now, if we are to get hold of him, we must strengthen his character," said Delyesof, to himself. And, forbidding Zakhar to give him any wine, he again devoted himself to his book; in spite of himself, however, listening all the time to what was going on in the dining-room.

But there was no movement there, only occasionally were heard a heavy chest cough and spitting. Two hours passed. Delyesof, after dressing to go out, resolved to look in upon his guest. Albert was sitting motionless at the window, leaning his head on his hands.

He looked round. His face was sallow, morose, and not only melancholy but deeply unhappy. He tried to welcome his host with a smile, but his face assumed a still more woebegone expression. It seemed as if he were on the point of tears.

With effort he stood up and bowed.

"If I might have just a little glass of simple vodka," he exclaimed, with a supplicating expression. "I am so weak. If you please!"

"Coffee will be more strengthening, I would advise you."

Albert's face instantly lost its childish expression; he

gazed coldly, sadly, out of the window, and fell back feebly into the chair.

" Would n't you like some breakfast ? "

" No, thank you, I have n't any appetite."

" If you want to play on the violin, you will not disturb me," said Delyesof, laying the instrument on the table.

Albert looked at the violin with a contemptuous smile.

" No, I am too weak, I cannot play," he said, and pushed the instrument from him.

After that, in reply to all Delyesof's propositions to go to walk, to go to the theater in the evening, or anything else, he only shook his head mournfully, and preserved an obstinate silence.

Delyesof went out, made a few calls, dined with some friends, and before the theater hour, he returned to his rooms to change his attire and find out how the musician was getting along.

Albert was sitting in the dark anteroom, and, with his head resting on his hand, was gazing at the heated stove. He was neatly dressed, washed, and combed ; but his eyes were sad and vacant, and his whole form expressed even more weakness and debility than in the morning.

" Well, have you had dinner, Mr. Albert ? " asked Delyesof.

Albert nodded his head affirmatively, and, after looking with a terrified expression at Delyesof, dropped his eyes. It made Delyesof feel uncomfortable.

" I have been talking to-day with a manager," said he, also dropping his eyes. " He would be very glad to make terms with you, if you would like to accept an engagement."

" I thank you, but I cannot play," said Albert, almost in a whisper ; and he went into his room, and closed the door as softly as possible. After a few minutes, lifting the latch as softly as possible, he came out of the room, bringing the violin. Casting a sharp, angry look at Delyesof, he laid the instrument on the table, and again disappeared.

Delyesof shrugged his shoulders, and smiled.

"What am I to do now? Wherein am I to blame?" he asked himself.

"Well, how is the musician?" was his first question when he returned home late that evening.

"Bad," was Zakhar's short and ringing reply. "He sighs all the time, and coughs, and says nothing at all, only he has asked for vodka four or five times, and once I gave him some. We shall be killing him this way, Dmitri Ivanovitch. That was the way the overseer ...."

"Well, hasn't he played on the fiddle?"

"Didn't even touch it. I carried it to him twice .... Well, he took it up slowly, and brought it out," said Zakhar, with a smile. "Do you still bid me refuse him something to drink?"

"Don't give him anything to-day; we'll see what'll come of it. What is he doing now?"

"He has shut himself into the drawing-room."

Delyesof went into his library, took down a few French books and the Testament in German.

"Put these books to-morrow in his room; and look out, don't let him get away," said he to Zakhar.

The next morning Zakhar informed his barin that the musician had not slept a wink all night. "He kept walking up and down his rooms, and going to the sideboard to try to open the cupboard and door; but everything, in spite of his efforts, remained locked."

Zakhar told how, while pretending to go to sleep, he heard Albert muttering to himself in the darkness and gesticulating.

* * * * *

Each day Albert grew more gloomy and taciturn. It seemed as if he were afraid of Delyesof, and his face expressed painful terror whenever their eyes met. He did not touch either book or violin, and made no replies to the questions put to him.

On the third day after the musician came to stay with him, Delyesof returned home late in the evening, tired

and worried. He had been on the go all day, attending
to his duties. Though they had seemed very simple and
easy, yet, as is often the case, he had not made any progress at all, in spite of his strenuous endeavors. Afterward he had stopped at the club, and lost at whist. He
was out of spirits.

"Well, God be with him," he replied to Zakhar, who
had been telling him of Albert's pitiable state. "To-
morrow I shall be really worried about him. Is he willing or not to stay with me, and follow my advice? No?
Then it's idle. I have done the best that I could."

"That's what comes of trying to be a benefactor to
people," said he to himself. "I am putting myself to
inconvenience for him. I have taken this filthy creature
into my rooms, which keeps me from receiving strangers
in the morning; I work and am kept on the run; and
yet he looks on me as some enemy who, against his will,
would keep him in pound. But the worst is that he is
not willing to take a step in his own behalf. That's the
way with them all."

That word *all* referred to people in general, and especially to those with whom he had been associated in business that day. "But what is to be done for him now?
What is he contemplating? Why is he melancholy? Is
he melancholy because of the debauch from which I
rescued him? on account of the degradation in which
he has been? the humiliation from which I saved him?
Can it be that he has fallen so low that it is a burden for
him to look on a pure life?....

"No, this was a childish action," reasoned Delyesof.
"Why should I undertake to direct others, when it is as
much as I can do to manage my own affairs?"

The impulse came over him to let him go immediately,
but after a little deliberation he postponed it till the
morning.

During the night Delyesof was aroused by the noise
of a falling table in the anteroom, and the sound of
voices and stamping feet. He lighted a candle, and
began to listen with amazement.

"Just wait a little, I will tell Dmitri Ivanovitch," said

Zakhar's voice; Albert's voice replied passionately and incoherently.

Delyesof leaped up, and went with his candle into the anteroom. Zakhar, in his night-dress, was standing against the door; Albert, in cap and *alma viva*, was trying to pull him away, and was screaming at him in a pathetic voice: —

"You have no right to detain me; I have a passport; I have not stolen anything from you. You must let me go. I will go to the police."

"I beg of you, Dmitri Ivanovitch," said Zakhar, turning to his barin, and continuing to stand guard at the door. "He got up in the night, found the key in my paletot, and he has drunk up the whole decanter of sweet vodka. Was that good? And now he wants to go. You ordered me not to let him out, and so I could not let him go."

Albert, seeing Delyesof, began to pull still more violently on Zakhar.

"No one has the right to detain me! He cannot do it," he screamed, raising his voice more and more.

"Let him go, Zakhar," said Delyesof. "I do not wish to detain you, and I have no right to, but I advise you to stay till to-morrow," he added, addressing Albert.

"No one has the right to detain me. I am going to the police," screamed Albert, more and more furiously, addressing only Zakhar, and not heeding Delyesof. "Guard!" he suddenly shouted at the top of his voice.

"Now, what are you screaming like that for? You see you are free to go," said Zakhar, opening the door.

Albert ceased screaming.

"How did they dare? They were going to murder me! No!" he muttered to himself, as he put on his galoshes. Not bidding them good-by, and still muttering something unintelligible, he went out of the door. Zakhar accompanied him to the gate, and came back.

"Thank the Lord, Dmitri Ivanovitch! Any longer would have been a sin," said he to his barin. "And now we must verify the silver."

Delyesof only shook his head, and made no reply.

There came over him a lively recollection of the first two evenings which he and the musician had spent together; he remembered the last wretched days which Albert had spent there; and, above all, he remembered the sweet but absurd sentiment of wonder, of love, and of sympathy which had been aroused in him by the very first sight of this strange man; and he began to pity him.

"What will become of him now?" he asked himself. "Without money, without warm clothing, alone at midnight!"

He thought of sending Zakhar after him, but now it was too late.

"Is it cold outdoors?" he asked.

"A healthy frost, Dmitri Ivanovitch," replied the man. "I forgot to tell you that you will have to buy some more firewood to last till spring."

"But what did you mean by saying that it would last?"

CHAPTER VII

OUT of doors it was really cold; but Albert did not feel it, he was so excited by the wine that he had taken and by the quarrel.

As he entered the street, he looked around him, and rubbed his hands with pleasure. The street was empty, but the long lines of lights were still brilliantly gleaming; the sky was clear and beautiful. "What!" he cried, addressing the lighted window in Delyesof's apartments; and then, thrusting his hands into his trousers pockets under his paletot, and looking straight ahead, he walked with heavy and uncertain steps straight up the street.

He felt an extraordinary heaviness in his legs and abdomen, something hummed in his head, some invisible power seemed to hurl him from side to side; but he still plunged ahead in the direction of where Anna Ivanovna lived.

Strange, disconnected thoughts rushed through his head. Now he remembered his quarrel with Zakhar, now something recalled the sea, and his first voyage in the steamboat to Russia; now the merry night that he had spent with some friend in the wine-shop by which he was passing; then suddenly there came to him a familiar air, singing itself in his recollections, and he seemed to see the object of his passion and the terrible night in the theater.

But notwithstanding their incoherence, all these recollections presented themselves before his imagination with such distinctness that when he closed his eyes he could not tell which was nearer to the reality, — what he was doing, or what he was thinking. He did not realize and he did not feel how his legs moved, how he staggered and hit against a wall, how he looked around him, and how he made his way from street to street. He realized and felt only that which presented itself to him, fantastically changing and confusing him.

As he went along the Little Morskaya, Albert tripped and fell. Collecting himself in a moment, he saw before him a huge and magnificent edifice, and he went toward it.

In the sky not a star was to be seen, nor sign of dawn, nor moon, neither were there any street-lights there; but all objects were perfectly distinguishable. The windows of the edifice, which loomed up at the corner of the street, were brilliantly lighted, but the lights wavered like reflections. The building kept coming nearer and nearer, clearer and clearer, to Albert.

But the lights vanished the moment Albert entered the wide portals. Inside it was dark. He took a few steps under the vaulted ceiling, and something like shadows glided by and fled at his approach.

"Why did I come here?" wondered Albert; but some irresistible power dragged him forward into the depths of the immense hall. ....

There stood some lofty platform, and around it in silence stood what seemed like little men. "Who is going to speak?" asked Albert. No one answered, but some one pointed to the platform. There stood now on the platform a tall, thin man, with bushy hair and dressed in a variegated khalat. Albert immediately recognized his friend Petrof.

"How strange! what is he doing here?" said Albert to himself.

"No, brethren," said Petrof, pointing to something, "you did not appreciate the man while he was living among you; you did not appreciate him! He was not a cheap artist, not a merely mechanical performer, not a crazy, ruined man. He was a genius, a great musical genius, who perished among you unknown and unvalued."

Albert immediately understood of whom his friend was speaking; but not wishing to interrupt him, he hung his head modestly.

"He, like a sheaf of straw, was wholly consumed by the sacred fire which we all serve," continued the voice. "But he has completely fulfilled all that God gave him; therefore he ought to be considered a great man. You may despise him, torture him, humiliate him," continued the voice, more and more energetically, "but he has been, is, and will be immeasurably higher than you all. He is happy, he is good. He loved you all alike, or cared for you, it is all the same; but he has served only that with which he was so highly endowed. He loved one thing, — beauty, the only infinite good in the world. Oh, yes, what a man he is! Fall all of you before him. On your knees!" cried Petrof, in a thundering voice.

But another voice mildly answered from another corner of the hall. "I do not wish to bow my knee before him," said the voice.

Albert instantly recognized that it was Delyesof's voice.

"Why is he great? And why should we bow before him? Has he conducted himself in an honorable and righteous manner? Has he brought society any advantage? Do we not know how he borrowed money, and never returned it; how he carried off a violin that belonged to a brother artist, and pawned it?"....

"My God! how did he know all that?" said Albert to himself, drooping his head still lower.

"Do we not know," the voice went on, "how he pandered to the lowest of the low, pandered to them for money?" continued Delyesof. "Do we not know how he was driven out of the theater? How Anna Ivanovna threatened to hand him over to the police?"

"My God! that is all true, but protect me," cried Albert. "You are the only one who knows why I did so."

"Stop, for shame!" cried Petrof's voice again. "What right have you to accuse him? Have you lived his life? Have you experienced his enthusiasms?"

"Right! right!" whispered Albert.

"Art is the highest manifestation of power in man. It is given only to the favored few, and it lifts the chosen to such an eminence that the head swims, and it is hard to preserve its integrity. In art, as in every struggle, there are heroes who bring all under subjection to them, and perish if they do not attain their ends."

Petrof ceased speaking; and Albert lifted his head, and tried to shout in a loud voice, "Right! right!" but his voice died without a sound.

"That is not the case with you. This does not concern you," sternly said the artist Petrof, addressing him. "Yes, humble him, despise him," he continued, "for he is better and happier than all the rest of you."

Albert, with rapture in his heart at hearing these words, could not contain himself, but went up to his friend, and was about to kiss him.

"Get you gone, I do not know you," replied Petrof. "Go your own way, you cannot come here."

"Here, you drunken fellow, you cannot come here," cried a policeman at the crossing.

Albert hesitated, then collected all his forces, and, endeavoring not to stumble, crossed over to the next street.

It was only a few steps to Anna Ivanovna's. From the hall of her house a stream of light fell on the snowy dvor, and at the gate stood sledges and carriages.

Clinging with both hands to the balustrade, he made his way up the steps, and rang the bell.

The maid's sleepy face appeared at the open door, and looked angrily at Albert.

"It is impossible," she cried; "I have been forbidden to let you in," and she slammed the door.

The sounds of music and women's voices floated down to him.

Albert sat down on the ground, and leaned his head against the wall, and shut his eyes. At that very instant a throng of indistinct but correlated visions took possession of him with fresh force, mastered him, and carried him off into the beautiful and free domain of fancy.

"Yes! he is better and happier," involuntarily the voice repeated in his imagination.

From the door were heard the sounds of a polka. These sounds also told him that he was better and happier. In a neighboring church was heard the sound of a prayer bell; and the prayer bell also told him that he was better and happier.

"Now I will go back to that hall again," said Albert to himself. "Petrof must have many things still to tell me."

There seemed to be no one now in the hall; and, in the place of the artist Petrof, Albert himself stood on the platform, and was playing on his violin all that the voice had said before.

But his violin was of strange make: it was composed of nothing but glass, and he had to hold it with both hands, and slowly rub it on his breast to make it give out sounds. The sounds were so sweet and delicious, that Albert felt he had never before heard anything like them. The more tightly he pressed the violin to his breast, the more sweet and consoling they became. The louder the sounds, the more swiftly the shadows vanished, and the more brilliantly the walls of the hall were illuminated. But it was necessary to play very cautiously on the violin, lest it should break.

Albert played on the instrument of glass cautiously

and well. He played things the like of which he felt
no one would ever hear again.

He was growing tired, when a heavy distant sound
began to annoy him. It was the sound of a bell, but
this sound seemed to have a language.

"Yes," said the bell, with its notes coming from
somewhere far off and high up, "yes, he seems to you
wretched; you despise him, but he is better and happier than you. No one ever will play more on that
instrument!"

These words which he understood seemed suddenly
so wise, so novel, and so true to Albert, that he stopped
playing, and, while trying not to move, lifted his eyes
and his arms toward heaven. He felt that he was
beautiful and happy. Although no one was in the hall,
Albert expanded his chest, and proudly lifted his head,
and stood on the platform so that all might see him.

Suddenly some one's hand was gently laid on his
shoulder; he turned around, and in the half-light saw
a woman. She looked pityingly at him, and shook her
head. He immediately became conscious that what he
was doing was wrong, and a sense of shame came over
him.

"Where shall I go?" he asked her.

Once more she gazed long and fixedly at him, and
bent her head pityingly. She was the one, the very one
whom he loved, and her dress was the same; on her full
white bosom was the pearl necklace, and her lovely arms
were bare above the elbows.

She took him in her arms, and bore him away from
the hall. "The exit is on that side," said Albert, but
she, not answering, smiled, and bore him away from the
hall. At the entrance of the hall, Albert saw the moon
and water. But the water was not below as is usually
the case, and the moon was not above; there was a white
circle in one place as sometimes happens. The moon
and the water were together, — everywhere, above and
below, and on all sides and around them both. Albert
and his love darted off toward the moon and the water,
and he now realized that she whom he loved more than all

in the world was in his arms: he embraced her, and felt inexpressible felicity.

"Is not this a dream?" he asked himself. But no, it was the reality, it was more than reality; it was reality and recollection combined.

Then he felt that the indescribable pleasure which he had felt during the last moment was gone, and would never be renewed.

"Why am I weeping?" he asked of her. She looked at him in silence, with pitying eyes. Albert understood what she desired to say in reply. "Just as when I was alive," he went on to say. She, without replying, looked straight forward.

"This is terrible! How can I explain to her that I *am* alive?" he asked himself in horror. "My God, I am alive! Do understand me," he whispered.

"He is better and happier," said a voice.

But something kept oppressing Albert ever more powerfully. Whether it was the moon or the water, or her embrace or his tears, he could not tell, but he was conscious that he could not say all that he ought to say, and that all would be quickly over.

* * * * * *

Two guests coming out from Anna Ivanovna's rooms stumbled against Albert lying on the threshold. One of them went back to Anna Ivanovna, and called her. "That was heartless," he said. "You might let a man freeze to death that way."

"Why, that is my Albert. See where he was lying!" exclaimed the madame. "Annushka, have him brought into the room; find a place for him somewhere," she added, addressing the maid.

"Oh! I am alive, why do you bury me?" muttered Albert, as they brought him unconscious into the room.

TWO HUSSARS

A TALE

(1856)

> Jomini, ay, Jomini,
> But not a half a word of vodka.[1]
>
> —D. Davuidof.

AT the very beginning of this century, when there were no railways, no macadamized roads, no gas-light or stearine candles, no low and springy divans, no furniture without veneer, no disillusionized young men with eye-glasses, no female philosophers of liberal tendencies, no pretty *dames aux Camélias*, such as our time has produced in abundance; in those innocent days when travelers made the journey from Moscow to Petersburg by stage or carriage, and took with them all the appurtenances of a domestic kitchen, and traveled for a week, night and day, over soft roads, muddy or dusty as the case might be, pinned their faith to Pozharsky cutlets, Valdaï bluebells, and rolls; when during the long autumn evenings tallow candles burned till they had to be snuffed, and cast their rays on family circles of twenty or thirty people — at balls, wax or spermaceti candles were set up in candelabra; when furniture was placed with stiff precision; when our fathers were still young, not merely by the absence of wrinkles and gray hair, but fought duels for women,

---

[1] From the poem entitled, "The Song of an Old Hussar," in which a veteran contrasts the mighty days of the past with the trivial present. Denis Vasilyevitch Davuidof, who was an officer of hussars, died in 1839. —Ed.

and would rush from one end of a room to the other to pick up a handkerchief dropped accidentally or otherwise, and our mothers wore short waists and huge sleeves, and decided family affairs by the drawing of lots; when the charming *dames aux Camélias* avoided the light of day; in the naïve period of Masonic lodges, of Martinists, and of the *Tugendbund;* at the time of the Miloradovitches, Davuidofs, and Pushkins, — a meeting of landed proprietors took place in the governmental city of K., and the election of the college of nobles was drawing to a close.

CHAPTER I

"WELL, it's all the same, be it in the hall," said a young officer dressed in a shuba, and wearing a hussar's helmet, as he dismounted from a traveling sledge in front of the best hotel of the city of K.

"The house is full, little father, your excellency,[1] — a tremendous crowd," said the hall-boy, who had already learned from the officer's man that it was Count Turbin, and therefore dignified him with the title of "your excellency." "Madame Afremof and her daughters have expressed the intention of going away this evening; you can be accommodated with their room as soon as it is vacated, — No. 11," the hall-boy went on to say, noiselessly showing the count the way, and constantly turning round to look at him.

In the general "hall," at a small table under a blackened full-length portrait of the Emperor Alexander, sat a number of men, evidently belonging to the local aristocracy, drinking champagne; and on one side were some traveling merchants in blue shubas.

The count entered the room, and calling Blücher, a huge gray boarhound which accompanied him, he threw off his cloak, the collar of which was covered with frost, and, after ordering vodka, sat down at the table in a

---

[1] *Batyushka vashe Siatyelstvo;* the *yamshchik* (postilion or driver) shortens this title into *vasyaso.*

short blue satin jacket, and entered into conversation
with the gentlemen sitting there. The latter, attracted
toward the newcomer by his handsome and frank exterior, offered him a glass of champagne.

The count had begun to drink his glass of vodka;
but now he also ordered a bottle of champagne, in
order to return the courtesy of his new companions.

The driver came in to ask for vodka money.

"Sashka,"[1] cried the count, "give it to him."

The driver went out with Sashka, but quickly returned, holding the money in his hands.

"What! little father, 'slency, is that right? I did
my best for you. You promised me a half-ruble, and
he has only given me a quarter!"

"Sashka, give him a ruble."

Sashka, hanging down his head, gazed at the driver's
feet.

"He will have enough," said he, in his deep voice.
"Besides, I haven't any more money."

The count drew from his pocket-book the two solitary
blue notes[2] which were in it, and gave one to the driver,
who kissed his hand, and went off. "I have come to
the end," said the count, "my last five rubles."

"True hussar style, count," said one of the nobles,
whose mustaches, voice, and a certain energetic freedom
in the use of his legs proclaimed him, beyond peradventure, to be a retired cavalryman. "Are you going
to spend some time here, count?"

"I must have some money if I stay, otherwise I should
not be very likely to. Besides, there are no spare rooms,
the devil take it, in this cursed tavern."

"I beg of you, count," pursued the cavalryman,
"wouldn't you like to come in with me? My room is
No. 7. If you wouldn't object to sleeping there for the
present. You might stay on with us for three days at
least. To-night there's to be a ball at the marshal's;
how glad he would be to see you!"

"That's right, count, stay with us," urged another of

---

[1] Diminished diminutive of Aleksandr.
[2] Blue notes were five rubles.

the table companions, a handsome young man. "What is your hurry? And besides, this happens only once in three years, — these elections. We might get a glimpse of some of our girls, count!"

"Sashka, get me some clean linen. I am going to have a bath," said the count, rising. "And then we will see; perhaps I may decide to pay my respects to the marshal."

Then he called the waiter, and said something to him in an undertone. The waiter replied, with a laugh, "That is within human possibility," and went out.

"Well, then, batyushka, I have given orders to have my trunk taken to your room," cried the count, as he went out of the door.

"I shall consider it a favor; it delights me," replied the cavalryman, as he hastened to the door, and cried, "No. 7; don't forget!"

When the count's steps could no longer be heard, the cavalryman returned to his place, and drawing his chair nearer to a functionary, and looking directly at him with smiling eyes, said: —

"Well, he's the very one."

"What one?"

"I tell you that he's that very same hussar duelist, — let me see, the famous Turbin. He knew me. I'll wager he knew me. I assure you, at Lebedyan' he and I were on a spree for three weeks, and were never sober once. That was when I was after a remount. There was one little affair at that time, — we were engaged in it together. Ah, he is a gay lad! isn't he, though?"

"Indeed he is. What pleasant manners he has! There's no fault to be found with him," replied the handsome young man. "How quickly we became acquainted!.... He isn't more than twenty-five, is he?"

"He certainly would not seem so, would he?.... But he's really more than that. Well, now you want to know who he is, don't you? Who carried off the Migunova? He did. He killed Sablin. He kicked Matnyef out of the window. He 'did' Prince Nesterof out of three hundred thousand rubles. He's a regular madcap, you must know, — a gambler, duelist, seducer, but a whole-souled fellow, a genuine hussar. We got talked about a good deal, but if any one really understood what it meant to be a genuine hussar! Those were great times."

And the cavalryman began to tell his comrade of a drinking-bout with the count at Lebedyan' which had never taken place, nor could have taken place. It could not have taken place, first because he had never seen the count before, and had retired from the service two years before the count had entered it; and secondly, because this cavalryman had never served in the cavalry, but had served four years as a very insignificant yunker in the Bielevsky regiment; and just as soon as he was promoted to be ensign, he retired.

But ten years before he had received an inheritance, and actually went to Lebedyan'; and there he spent seven hundred rubles with the cavalry officers, and had had made for him an uhlan's uniform with orange lapels, with the intention of entering the uhlans. His thought of entering the cavalry, and his three weeks spent with the officers at Lebedyan', made the very happiest and most brilliant period of his life; so that he began to transfer his thought into a reality. Then, as he added remembrance to it, he began actually to believe in his military past, — but this did not prevent him from being a genuinely worthy man through his kindness of heart and uprightness.

"Yes, any one who has never served in the cavalry," he went on to say, "will never understand us fellows."

He sat astride of his chair, and, thrusting out his lower jaw, went on in a deep voice: "It happens you are riding along in front of the battalion. A devil is under you, not a horse, prancing along; thus you sit on this perfect devil. The battalion commander comes along. 'Lieutenant,' says he, 'I beg of you — your service is absolutely indispensable. You must lead the battalion for the parade.' Very well, and so it goes. You look around, you give a shout, you lead the brave fellows who are under your command. .... Ah! the deuce take it! 't was a glorious time!"

The count came back from the bath, all ruddy, and with his hair wet, and went directly to No. 7, where the cavalryman was already sitting in his *khalat*, or dressing-gown, with his pipe, and thinking with delight and some little anxiety of the good fortune that had befallen him in sharing his room with the famous Turbin.

"Well, now," the thought came into his head, "suppose he should take me, and strip me naked, and carry me outside the town limits, and set me down in the snow .... or smear me with tar .... or simply .... But, no; he would not do such a thing to a comrade," he said, trying to comfort himself.

"Sashka, give Blücher something to eat," cried the count.

Sashka made his appearance. He had been drinking glasses of vodka ever since his arrival, and was beginning to be genuinely tipsy.

"You have not been able to control yourself. You have been getting drunk, you scoundrel![1] .... Feed Blücher."

"It won't kill him to fast. .... You see, ... he's so plump," replied Sashka, caressing the dog.

"Now, none of your impudence. Go and feed him."

"All you care for is to have your dog fat; but if a man drinks a little glass, then you pitch into him."

"Hey! I'll beat you!" cried the count, with a voice which made the window-panes rattle, and even to the cavalryman seemed rather terrible.

"You'd better ask if *Sashka* has had anything to eat to-day. All right, strike away, if a dog is more to you than a man," continued Sashka.

But at this he received such a violent blow of the fist across the face that he staggered, struck his head against the partition, and, clutching his nose, leaped through the door, and threw himself down on a chest in the corridor.

"He has broken my teeth," he growled, wiping his

[1] *Kanal'ya* from French *canaille*.

bloody nose with one hand, and with the other scratching Blücher's back, as the dog licked him. "He has broken my teeth, Blüchka; and yet he is my count, and I would jump into the fire for him, that's a fact. Because he's my count, do you understand, Blüchka? And do you want something to eat?"

After lying there awhile he got up, gave the dog his dinner, and, almost sobered, went to serve his count, and get him his tea.

"You would simply offend me," said the cavalryman, timidly, standing in front of the count, who was lying on the bed with his feet propped against the partition. "Now, you see, I am an old soldier and comrade, I may say; instead of letting you borrow of any one else, it would give me great pleasure to let you have two hundred rubles. I haven't them with me now, — only a hundred, — but I can get the rest to-day; don't refuse, you would simply offend me, count!"

"Thanks, old fellow,"[1] said Turbin, instantly perceiving what sort of relationship would exist between them, and slapping the cavalryman on the shoulder. "Thanks. Well, then, we'll go to the ball if you say so. But now what shall we do? Tell me what you have in your city: any pretty girls? any one ready for a spree? any one play cards?"

The cavalryman explained that there would be plenty of pretty girls at the ball; that the *ispravnik*, or district police, Captain Kolkoff, who had just been reëlected, was the greatest hand for sprees, only he lacked the spirit of a genuine hussar, but still was a first-rate fellow; that Ilyushka's chorus of gipsies had been singing at K. ever since the elections began; that Stioshka[2] was the soloist, and that after the marshal's reception every one was going there that evening.

"And the stakes are pretty high. Lukhnof, a visitor here," he said, "is sweeping in the money; and Ilyin, a cornet of uhlans, who rooms in No. 8, has already lost a pile. The game has already begun there. They play

[1] *Batyushka.*
[2] Diminutive of Stepanida, Stephanie.

there every evening; and he's a wonderfully fine young
fellow, I tell you, count, this Ilyin is. There's nothing
mean about him — he'd give you his last shirt."

"Then let us go to his room. We will see what sort
of men you have," said the count.

"Come on! come on! they will be awfully glad."

CHAPTER II

ILYIN, the cornet of uhlans, had not long been awake.
The evening before, he had sat down at the gambling-
table at eight o'clock, and lost for fifteen hours running
till eleven o'clock that day. He had lost a great
amount, but exactly how much he did not know, because
he had had three thousand rubles of his own money,
and fifteen thousand belonging to the treasury, which
he had long ago mixed up with his own, and he dared
not make a reckoning lest his anticipations that even
the public money would not be sufficient to settle his
debt should be confirmed.

He went to sleep about noon, and slept that heavy,
dreamless sleep peculiar to very young men who have
been losing heavily. Waking at six, about the time
Count Turbin had arrived at the hotel, and seeing cards
and chalk scattered around him on the floor, and the
soiled tables in confusion in the room, he remembered
with horror the evening's games, and the last card, a
knave, which had lost him five hundred rubles; but,
still scarcely believing in the reality, he drew out from
under his pillow his money, and began to count it. He
recognized a few bank-notes which, with corners turned
down and indorsements, had gone from hand to hand
around the table; he remembered all the particulars.
He had lost his own three thousand rubles, and twenty-
five hundred belonging to the treasury had disappeared.

The uhlan had been playing for four nights in succession.

He had come from Moscow, where the public money
had been put into his hands. At K. the post-superin-

tendent had detained him under the pretext that there were no post-horses, but in reality in accordance with his agreement with the hotel-keeper to detain all visitors for a day.

The uhlan, who was a gay young fellow, and had just received from his parents at Moscow three thousand rubles for his military equipment, was glad to spend a few days in the city of K. during the elections, and counted on having a good time.

He knew a landed proprietor who lived there with his family, and he was preparing to call on him and pay his respects to his daughters, when the cavalryman appeared, made his acquaintance, and that very evening, without malice prepense, took him down into the parlor, and introduced him to his friends, Lukhnof and several other gamblers. From that time, the uhlan had kept steadily at gaming, and not only had not called on the proprietor, but had not thought of inquiring farther for horses, and for four days had not left his room.

After he had dressed, and taken his tea, he went to the window. He felt an inclination to go out, so as to dispel the importunate recollections of the game. He put on his cloak and went into the street.

The sun had just sunk behind the white houses with their red roofs. It was already twilight. It was mild. The snow was softly falling in big, damp flakes, into the muddy streets. His mind suddenly became filled with unendurable melancholy at the thought that he had wasted all that day in sleep, and now the day was done. "This day which has gone will never come back again," he said to himself.

"I have ruined my youth," he suddenly exclaimed, not because he really felt that he had ruined his youth, — he did not think about it at all, — but simply this phrase came into his head.

"What shall I do now?" he reasoned; "borrow of some one, and go away?"

A lady was passing along the sidewalk.

"What a stupid woman!" he said to himself, for some unaccountable reason.

"There 's no one I can borrow of. I have ruined my youth."

He came to a block of stores. A merchant in a fox-skin shuba was standing at the door of his shop, and inviting custom.

"If I had n't taken the eight, I should have won."

A little old beggar-woman followed him, sniveling.

"I have no one to borrow of."

A gentleman in a bearskin shuba passed him. A policeman was standing on the corner.

"What can I do that will make a sensation? Fire a pistol at them? No! That would be stupid. I have ruined my youth. Oh! what a splendid harness that is hanging in that shop! I should like to be riding behind a troĭka!.... Ekh! you fine fellows![1] I am going back. Lukhnof will be there pretty soon, and we 'll have a game."

He returned to the hotel, and once more counted his money. No, he had not been mistaken the first time; twenty-five hundred rubles of the public funds were missing, just as before.

"I will put up twenty-five rubles first; the next time, a quarter stake; then on seven, on fifteen, on thirty, and on sixty.... three thousand. I will buy that harness, and start. He won't give me any odds, the villain! I have ruined my youth!"

This was what was passing through the uhlan's mind just as Lukhnof came into the room.

"Well, have you been up long, Mikhaĭlo Vasilyitch?" inquired Lukhnof, deliberately removing from his thin nose his gold eye-glasses, and carefully wiping them with a red silk handkerchief.

"No, only just this minute. I had a splendid sleep!"

"A new hussar has just come. He is staying with Zavalshevsky. Had you heard about it?"

"No, I had n't. Well, no one seems to be here yet."

"I believe they have gone to Priakhin's. They 'll be here very soon."

In fact, shortly after there came into the room an

---

[1] *Galubchiki,* little pigeons.

officer of the garrison, who was always hovering round Lukhnof; a Greek merchant with a huge hooked nose, cinnamon complexion, and deep-set black eyes; a stout, puffy proprietor, a brandy-distiller who gambled all night long, and always made his stakes on the basis of half a ruble. All of these wished to begin playing as promptly as possible, but the more daring players said nothing about it; Lukhnof, in particular, with perfect equanimity, told stories of rascality in Moscow.

"Just think of it," said he, " Moscow, the metropolis, the capital; and there they go out at night with crooks, dressed like demons; and they scare the stupid people, and rob pedestrians, and that is the end of it. Do the police notice it? No! It is astonishing!"

The uhlan listened attentively to the tales of these highwaymen, but finally got up and unobtrusively ordered cards to be brought. The stout proprietor was the first to express himself.

"Well, gentlemen, we are wasting golden moments. To work, let us to work!"

"Yes, you won by the half-ruble last evening, and so you like it," exclaimed the Greek.

"It's a good time to begin," said the garrison officer.

Ilyin looked at Lukhnof. Lukhnof, returning his gaze, went on calmly with his story of the robbers who dressed themselves up like devils with claws.

"Will you start the bank?" asked the uhlan.

"Is n't it rather early?"

"Byelof!" cried the uhlan, reddening for some reason or other, " bring me something to eat..... I have n't had any dinner to-day, gentlemen. Bring some champagne, and deal the cards."

At this moment, the count and Zavalshevsky entered. Turbin and Ilyin proved to be in the same division. They immediately struck up an acquaintance, drank some champagne together, clinking their glasses, and in five minutes were calling each other "thou."

It was evident that Ilyin made a very pleasant impression on the count. The count smiled whenever he looked at him, and was amused at his freshness.

"What a fine young uhlan!" he said, "what a mustache! what a splendid mustache!"

Ilyin's upper lip bore the first down of a mustache, which was as yet almost white.

"You were preparing to play, were you not?" asked the count. "Well, I should like to win from you, Ilyin. I think that you must be a master," he added, smiling.

"Yes, we were just starting in," replied Lukhnof, opening a pack of cards. — "Aren't you going to join us, count?"

"No, I won't to-night. If I did there wouldn't be anything left of any of you! When I take a hand I always break the bank. But I haven't any money just now. I lost at Volotchok, at the station-house. It was by some sort of infantryman who wore rings; what a cheat he was! and he cleaned me out completely."

"Were you long there at the station?" asked Ilyin.

"I stayed there twenty-two hours. I shall not forget that station, curse it! and the superintendent won't forget it either."

"Why?"

"I got there, you see; out came the superintendent, rascally face, the liar! 'There are no horses,' said he. Well, now I must tell you, I have made a rule in such cases: when there are no horses, I keep on my shuba, and go straight to the superintendent's room, — not the office, mind you, but the superintendent's own room, — and I have all the windows and doors opened, as if it were stifling. Well, that's what I did here. Cold! you remember how cold it has been this last month; twenty degrees below. The superintendent began to remonstrate. I knock his teeth in for him. There was some old woman there; and some young girls and peasant-women set up a piping, were going to seize their pots and fly to the village. .... I go to the door, and say, 'Let me have horses, and I'll go away: if you don't, I won't let you out, I'll freeze you all to death.'"

"What an admirable way!" said the puffy proprietor, bursting out into a laugh. "That's the way one would freeze out cockroaches."

"But I wasn't sufficiently on my guard: the superintendent and all his women managed to get out and run away. Only the old woman remained on the oven as my hostage. She kept sniffing, and offering prayers to God. Then we entered into negotiations. The supertendent came back, and, standing at a distance, tried to persuade me to let the old woman go. But I set Blucher on him: Blücher is a magnificent dog to take care of superintendents. Even then the rascal did not let me have horses till the next morning. And then came along that footpad! I went into the next room, and began to play. Have you seen Blücher? — Blücher! Fiu!"

Blücher came running in. The players received him with flattering attention, although it was evident that they were anxious to get to work at entirely different matters.

"By the way, gentlemen, why don't you begin your game? I beg of you, don't let me interfere with you. You see I am a chatterbox," said Turbin. "*Whether you love or not*, 't is an excellent thing."

CHAPTER III

LUKHNOF took two candles, brought out a huge dark-colored pocket-book full of money; slowly, as if performing some sacrament, opened it on the table; took out two one-hundred-ruble notes, and placed them under the cards.

"There, just the same as last evening; the bank begins with two hundred," said he, adjusting his glasses, and opening a pack of cards.

"Very good," said Ilyin, not glancing at him, or interrupting his conversation with Turbin.

The game began. Lukhnof kept the bank with mechanical regularity, occasionally pausing, and deliberately writing down something, or looking sternly over his glasses, and saying in a weak voice, "Throw."

The stout proprietor talked more noisily than the rest, making various calculations aloud, while he wet his clumsy fingers and bent down the corners of his cards.

The garrison officer silently wrote in a fine hand his account on a card, and under the table turned down small corners.

The Greek sat next the banker, attentively following the game with his deep black eyes, apparently waiting for something.

Zavalshevsky, as he stood by the table, would suddenly become all of a tremble, draw from his trousers pocket a red note or a blue,[1] lay a card on it, pound on it with his palm, and say, " Bring me luck, little seven !" Then he would bite his mustache, change from one leg to the other, and remain in a continual state of excitement until the card came out.

Ilyin, who had been eating veal and cucumbers placed near him on the haircloth divan, briskly wiped his hands on his coat, and began to put down one card after another.

Turbin, who had taken his seat at first on the divan, immediately noticed that something was wrong. Lukhnof did not look at the uhlan, or say anything to him; but occasionally his eyes for an instant rested on the uhlan's hands. The most of his cards lost.

"If I could only trump that little card," exclaimed Lukhnof in reference to a card played by the stout proprietor, who was still making half-ruble wagers.

" Trump Ilyin's instead; what would be the use of trumping mine ?" replied the proprietor.

And, in point of fact, Ilyin's cards were trumped oftener than the others'. He nervously tore up his losing card under the table, and with trembling hands chose another.

Turbin arose from the divan, and asked the Greek to give him his place next the banker. The Greek changed places; and the count, taking his chair, and not moving his eyes, began to watch Lukhnof's hands attentively.

" Ilyin," said he, suddenly, in his ordinary voice, which,

[1] The five-ruble assignat was blue, the ten-ruble one was red, the twenty-five-ruble note was white. — ED.

without his intending to do so, drowned out the others,
"why do you stick to those routine cards? You don't
know how to play!"

"Supposing I don't, it's all the same."

"You'll lose that way surely. Let me play against
the bank for you."

"No, excuse me, I beg of you. I always play for
myself. Play for yourself if you like."

"I have told you that I am not going to play. But I
should like to play for you. I hate to see you losing so."

"Ah, well! you see it's my luck."

The count said nothing more, and, leaning on his
elbow, began once more to watch the banker's hand just
as attentively as before.

"Shameful!" he suddenly cried in a loud voice,
dwelling on the word.

Lukhnof glared at him.

"Shameful, shameful!" he repeated still louder,
staring straight into Lukhnof's eyes.

The game continued.

"That — is — not — right!" said Turbin again, as
Lukhnof trumped one of Ilyin's high cards.

"What displeases you, count?" politely asked the
banker, with an air of indifference.

"Because you give Ilyin a simplum, and turn down
your corners. That's what is shameful!"

Lukhnof made a slight motion with his shoulders and
brows, signifying that he was resigned to any fate, and
then he went on with the game.

"Blücher, fiu!" cried the count, rising; "over with
him!" he added quickly.

Blücher, bumping against the divan with his back,
and almost knocking the garrison officer from his feet,
came leaping toward his master, looking at every one
and wagging his tail as if asking, "Who is misbehaving
here, hey?"

Lukhnof laid down the cards, and moved his chair
away.

"This is no way to play," said he. "I detest dogs.

What kind of a game can you have if a whole pack of hounds is to be brought in?"

"Especially that kind of dog; they are called blood-suckers, if I am not mistaken," suggested the garrison officer.

"Well, are we to play or not, Mikhaïlo Vasilyitch?" asked Lukhnof, addressing the uhlan.

"Don't bother us, count, I beg of you," said Ilyin, turning to Turbin.

"Come here for a moment," said Turbin, taking Ilyin's arm, and drawing him behind the partition.

Even then the count's words were perfectly audible, though he spoke in his ordinary tone. But his voice was so powerful that it could always be heard three rooms off.

"Are you beside yourself? Don't you see that that man with the glasses is a cheat of the worst order?"

"Hey? Nonsense! Be careful what you say."

"No nonsense! but quit it, I tell you. It makes no difference to me. Another time I myself would have plucked you; but now I am sorry to see you ruining yourself. Have you any public money left?"

"No. What makes you think so about him?"

"Brother, I have been over this same road, and I know the ways of these professional gamblers. I tell you that the man in the glasses is a cheat. Quit, please. I ask you as a comrade."

"All right; I'll have just one more hand, and then have done with it."

"I know what that 'one more' means; very well, we will see."

They returned to the gaming-table. In one deal he laid down so many cards, and so many of them were trumped, that he lost a large amount.

Turbin rested his hand in the middle of the table:—

"That's enough! now let us be going."

"No, I can't go yet; leave me, please," said Ilyin, in vexation, shuffling the bent cards and not looking at Turbin.

"All right! the devil be with you! Lose all you've

got, if that please you; but it's time for me to be going.
— Come, Zavalshevsky, let us go to the marshal's."

And they went out. No one spoke, and Lukhnof did
not make the bank until the noise of their feet and of
Blücher's paws had died away down the corridor.

"That's a madcap," said the proprietor, smiling.

"Well, now he won't bother us any more," said the
garrison officer, in a hurried whisper.

And the game went on.

CHAPTER IV

THE band, composed of the marshal's domestic serfs,
were stationed in the butler's pantry, which had been
put in order on account of the ball, and, having turned
up the sleeves of their coats, had begun at the signal of
their leader to play the ancient polonaise, " Aleksandr,
Yelisavieta"; and under the soft, brilliant light of the
wax candles, the couples were just beginning to move
in tripping measure through the great ball-room; a gov-
ernor-general of Catherine's time, with a star, taking out
the gaunt wife of the marshal, the marshal with the governor's wife, and so on throughout all the hierarchy of
the government in various combinations and variations,
— when Zavalshevsky, in a blue coat with a huge collar,
and epaulets on his shoulders, and wearing stockings
and pumps, and exhaling about him an odor of jasmine
with which he had plentifully drenched his mustaches,
the facings of his coat, and his handkerchief, entered
with the handsome count, who wore tight-fitting blue
trousers and a red pelisse embroidered with gold, and
wearing on his breast the cross of Vladimir and a medal
of 1812.

The count was of medium height, but had an extremely handsome figure. His clear blue eyes of remarkable brilliancy, and dark reddish hair which was
rather long and fell in thick ringlets, gave his beauty
a peculiar character.

The count was expected at the ball. The handsome young man who had seen him at the hotel had already spoken of him to the marshal.

The impressions made by this announcement were of various kinds, but on the whole were not altogether pleasant.

" I suppose this young man will turn us into ridicule," was what the old women and the men said to themselves.

"Suppose he should carry me off," was what the wives and young ladies thought, with more or less apprehension.

As soon as the polonaise was finished, and the couples had made each other low bows, once more the women formed little groups by themselves, and the men by themselves. Zavalshevsky, proud and happy, led the count up to the hostess.

The marshal's wife, conscious of a certain inward trepidation lest this hussar should make her the cause of some scandal before everybody, said proudly and scornfully, as she turned away, "Very glad to see you. I hope that you will dance." And then she looked at the count mistrustfully, with a peculiar expression, as much as to say, " Now, if you insult any woman, then you are a perfect scoundrel after this."

The count, however, quickly overcame this prejudice by his amiability, his politeness, and his handsome jovial appearance; so that in five minutes the expression on the face of the marshal's wife plainly declared to all who stood around her, " I know how to manage all these men. He immediately realized whom he was talking with. And now he will be charming to me all the rest of the evening."

Moreover, just then the governor, who had known his father, came up to the count, and very graciously drew him to one side, and entered into conversation with him, which still more pleased the fashionable society of the town, and raised the count in their estimation.

Then Zavalshevsky presented the count to his sister, a plump young widow, who, ever since the count entered the room, had kept her big black eyes fastened on him.

The count asked the little widow for the waltz which at that moment the musicians had struck up, and his artistic dancing conquered the last vestiges of the popular prejudice.

"Ah, he's a master at dancing!" said a stout lady, following the legs in blue trousers which were flashing through the ball-room, and mentally counting, "One, two, three; one, two, three, — he's a master."

"How gracefully he moves his feet! how gracefully!" said another woman, who did not stand very high in the governmental society. "How does he manage to not hit any one with his spurs? Wonderful, very skilful!"

The count, by his skill in dancing, eclipsed the three best dancers of the city. These were, a governor's aide, a tall man with white eyebrows famous for his rapid dancing and because he held the lady pressed very close to his breast; secondly, the cavalryman, who was famous for his graceful swaying during the waltz, and for his frequent but light tapping with his heels; and thirdly, a civilian of whom everybody said that, though intellectually he was a light-weight, yet he was an admirable dancer and the life of all balls.

In point of fact, this civilian from the beginning to the end of a ball invariably invited all the ladies in the order in which they sat, did not cease for a moment to dance, and only occasionally paused to wipe his weary but radiant face with his cambric handkerchief, which would become wet through.

The count had surpassed them all, and had danced with the three principal ladies, — with the stout one, who was rich, handsome, and stupid; with the middle-sized one, who was lean, and not particularly good-looking, but handsomely dressed; and with the little one, who was not pretty, but very witty.

He had danced also with others, — with all the pretty women, and there were many pretty women there.

But the little widow, Zavalshevsky's sister, pleased the

count more than all the rest; with her he danced a
quadrille and a schottische and a mazurka.

At first, when they took their places for the quadrille,
he overwhelmed her with compliments, comparing her
to Venus and Diana, and to a rose bush, and to some
other flower besides.

To all these amenities the little widow only bent her
white neck, modestly dropped her eyes, looking at her
white muslin gown, or changing her fan from one hand
to the other.

When, at last, she said, "This is too much, count; you
are jesting," or words to that effect, her voice, which
was rather guttural, betrayed such naïve simplicity of
heart and amusing stupidity, that the count, as he looked
at her, actually imagined that she was not a woman but
a flower, not a rose, but some kind of a pinkish-white
wild-flower, exuberant and odorless, growing alone on a
virgin snowdrift in some far, far-distant land.

Such a strange impression was made on the count by
this union of *naïveté* and unconventionality, together
with fresh beauty, that several times, in the pauses of
the conversation, when he looked silently into her eyes
or contemplated the loveliness of her arms and neck,
the desire came over him with such vehemence to take
her into his arms and kiss her again and again, that he
was really obliged to restrain himself.

The little widow was quite satisfied with the impression which she perceived that she had made; but there
was something in the count's behavior that began to dis-
quiet her and fill her with apprehensions, though the
young hussar was not only flatteringly amiable, but even
— as we nowadays should regard it — mawkishly polite
to her.

He ran to get orgeat for her, picked up her handkerchief, snatched a chair from the hands of a scrofulous
young proprietor, who also desired to pay her attention
and who was not quick enough. But perceiving that
such assiduities as were fashionable at that period had
little effect on his lady, he began to amuse her by telling
her ludicrous anecdotes: he assured her that if she would

bid him he was ready instantly to stand on his head, or
to crow like a cock, or to jump out of the window, or to
fling himself into a hole in the ice.

This procedure was a brilliant success: the little
widow became very gay; she rippled with laughter,
displaying her marvelous white teeth, and was entirely
satisfied with her cavalier. The count each moment
grew more and more enchanted with her, so that at the
end of the quadrille he was genuinely in love with her.

After the quadrille, when she was approached by her
former adorer, a young man of eighteen, the son of a
very rich proprietor, the same scrofulous young man
from whom Turbin had snatched away the chair, she
received him with perfect coolness, and not one-tenth
part of the constraint was noticeable in her which she
felt when she was with the count.

"You are very kind," she said, all the time gazing at
Turbin's back, and unconsciously reckoning how many
yards of gold lace were used for his whole jacket. "You
are very kind; you promised to come to take me for a
walk, and to bring me some comfits."

"Well, I did come, Anna Feodorovna, but you were
not at home, and I left the very best comfits for you,"
said the young man, in a voice which was very thin,
considering his height.

"You are always provided with excuses; I don't need
your comfits. Please do not think ...."

"I begin to see, Anna Feodorovna, how you have
changed toward me, and I know why. But it is not
right," he added, but without finishing his remark, evidently owing to some powerful interior emotion, which
caused his lips to tremble strangely.

Anna Feodorovna did not heed him, and continued to
follow Turbin with her eyes.

The marshal, at whose house the ball was given, — a
stout but toothless old man, — majestically came up to
the count, and, taking him by the arm, invited him into
his library to smoke and drink if he so desired.

As soon as Turbin disappeared, Anna Feodorovna
felt that there was absolutely nothing for her to do in

the ball-room, and, slipping her hand through the arm of a dried-up old maid, who was a friend of hers, went with her into the dressing-room.

"Well, what do you think of him? Is he nice?" asked the old maid.

"Only it's terrible — the way he follows you up!" said Anna Feodorovna, going to the mirror, and contemplating herself in it.

Her face was aglow, her eyes were full of mischief, her color was heightened; then suddenly imitating the ballet-dancers whom she had seen during election time, she pirouetted round on one toe, and, laughing her guttural but sweet laugh, she leaped up in the air, crossing her knees.

"What a man he is! he even asked me for a *souvenir*," she confided to her friend. "But he will ne-e-ver get one," she said, singing the last words, and lifting one finger in the kid glove which reached to her elbow. ....

In the library where Turbin was conducted by the marshal stood various kinds of vodka, liqueurs, edibles,[1] and champagne. In a cloud of tobacco-smoke the nobility were sitting, or walking up and down, talking about the elections.

"When the whole of the high nobility of our district has honored him with an election," exclaimed the newly elected ispravnik, who was already tolerably tipsy, "he certainly ought not to fail in his duties toward society in general." ....

The conversation was interrupted by the count's coming. All were presented to him, and the ispravnik especially pressed his hand long between both of his, and asked him several times to go with him after the ball to the new tavern, where he would treat the gentlemen of the nobility, and where they would hear the gipsies sing.

The count accepted his invitation, and drank with him several glasses of champagne.

"Why aren't you dancing, gentlemen?" he asked, as he was about to leave the library.

---

[1] *Zakuski.*

"We are n't dancers," replied the ispravnik, laughing. "We prefer the wine, count.... and besides, all these young ladies have grown up under my eyes, count. But still, I do sometimes take part in a schottische, count.... I can do it, count."....

"Come on then for a while," said Turbin. "Let us have some sport before we go to the gipsies."

"What say you, gentlemen? Let us come! Let us delight our host!"

And the three gentlemen who, since the beginning of the ball, had been drinking in the library and had very red faces, began to draw on their gloves, some of black kid, another of knit silk, and were just going with the count to the ball-room, when they were detained by the scrofulous young man, who, pale as a sheet, and scarcely able to refrain from tears, came straight up to Turbin.

"You have an idea, because you are a count, you can run into people as if you were at a fair," said he, with difficulty drawing his breath; "hence it is n't fitting...."

Once more the stream of his speech was interrupted by the involuntary trembling of his lips.

"What?" cried Turbin, frowning suddenly, "what? .... You're a baby," he cried, seizing him by the arm, and squeezing it so that the blood rushed to the young man's head, not so much from vexation as from fright. "What is it? Do you want to fight? If so, I am at your service."

Turbin had scarcely let go of his arm, which he had squeezed so powerfully, when two nobles seized the young man by the sleeve, and carried him off through a back door.

"What! have you lost your wits? You've surely been drinking too much. We shall have to tell your papa. What's the matter with you?" they asked.

"No, I have n't been drinking; but he ran into me, and did not apologize. He's a hog, that's what he is," whined the young man, now actually in tears.

Nevertheless they did not heed him, but carried him off home.

"Never mind, count," said the ispravnik and Zavalshevsky, assuringly. "He's a mere child. They still whip him; he's only sixteen years old. It's hard to tell what is to be done with him. What fly stung him? And his father is such an honorable man! He's our candidate."

"Well, the devil take him if he refuses."....

And the count returned to the ball-room, and, as gayly as before, danced the schottische with the pretty little widow, and laughed heartily when he saw the antics of the gentlemen who had come with him out of the library, and he joined in the general burst of merriment all through the ball-room when the ispravnik tripped and measured his length on the floor in the midst of the dancers.

CHAPTER V

ANNA FEODOROVNA, while the count was in the library, went to her brother, and, for the very reason of her conviction that she ought to pretend to feel very little interest in the count, she began to question him : —

"Who is this hussar that has been dancing with me? Tell me, brother."

The cavalryman explained, to the best of his ability, what a great man this hussar was, and in addition he told his sister that the count had stopped there simply because his money had been stolen on the route; he himself had loaned him a hundred rubles, but that was not enough. Couldn't his sister let him have two hundred more? Zavalshevsky asked her not to say anything about this to any one, and, above all, not to the count.

Anna Feodorovna promised to send the money the next day, and to keep it a secret; but somehow or other, during the schottische, she had a terrible desire to offer the count as much money as he needed.

She deliberated long, blushed, and at last, mastering her confusion, thus addressed herself to the task : —

"My brother told me, count, that you met with a misfortune on the road, and hadn't any money. Now, if you need some, wouldn't you take some of me? I should be awfully glad."

But after she had thus spoken, Anna Feodorovna was suddenly overcome with fright, and blushed. All the gayety had instantly vanished from the count's face.

"Your brother is a fool!" said he, in a cutting tone. "You know, when a man insults a man, then they fight a duel; but when a woman insults a man, then what do they do? Do you know?"

Poor Anna Feodorovna blushed to her ears with confusion. She dropped her eyes, and made no reply.

"They kiss the woman in public," said the count, softly, bending over to whisper in her ear. "Permit me, however, to kiss your little hand," he added, almost inaudibly, after a long silence, having some pity on his lady's confusion.

"Ah! only not quite yet," urged Anna Feodorovna, with a deep sigh.

"But when, then? To-morrow I am going away early..... But really, you owe it to me."

"Well, then of course it is impossible," said Anna Feodorovna, smiling.

"Only give me a chance to see you before to-morrow, so that I may kiss your hand. I will find one."

"How will you find one?"

"That is not your affair. I can do anything to see you..... Is it agreed?"

"Agreed."

The schottische came to an end; they danced through the mazurka, and in it the count did marvels, purloining handkerchiefs, bending on one knee, and clinking his spurs in an extraordinary manner, after the Warsaw style, so that all the old men came from their boston to look into the ball-room; and the cavalryman, who was the best dancer, confessed himself outdone. After they had eaten supper, they danced till the *Grossvater*, and began to disperse.

The count, all this time, did not take his eyes from the little widow. He had not been insincere when he declared his readiness to throw himself into a hole in the ice.

Whether it was caprice, or love, or stubbornness, but that evening all the strength of his mind had been concentrated into one desire, — to see her, and to make love to her.

As soon as he perceived that Anna Feodorovna was taking her farewell of the hostess, he hastened to the servants' quarters, and thence, without his shuba, to the place where the carriages were drawn up.

"Anna Feodorovna Zaïtsova's equipage," he cried.

A high, two-seated coach with lanterns moved out, and started to drive up to the doorstep.

"Stop!" shouted the count to the coachman, wading out to the carriage through snow that was knee-deep.

"What is wanted?" called the driver.

"I want to get into the carriage," replied the count, opening the door as the carriage moved, and trying to climb in.

"Stop, you devil! stupid! Vaska! stop!" cried the coachman to the postilion, and reining in the horses. "What are you getting into another person's carriage for? This belongs to the Lady Anna Feodorovna, and not to your grace."

"Hush up, blockhead! Here! there's a ruble for you; now come down and shut the door!" said the count.

But as the coachman did not move, he lifted the steps himself, and, opening the window, managed to pull the door to.

In this, as in all ancient carriages, especially those upholstered in yellow galloon, there was an odor of mustiness and burnt bristles.

The count's legs were wet to the knees from melting snow, and almost freezing in his thin boots and trousers; and his whole body was penetrated by a cold like that of winter.

The coachman was grumbling on his box, and seemed to be preparing to get down. But the count heard nothing and felt nothing. His face was aglow, his heart was beating violently. He convulsively clutched the yellow strap, thrust his head out of the side window, and his whole being was concentrated in the expectation of one thing.

He was not doomed to wait long. At the doorsteps, they shouted, "Zaïtsova's carriage!" The coachman shook his reins, the carriage swung on its high springs; the lighted windows of the house passed one after another by the carriage windows.

"See here, rogue, if you tell the lackey that I am here," said the count, thrusting his head through the front window, and addressing the coachman, "you'll feel my whip; but if you hold your tongue, I will give you ten rubles more."

He had scarcely time to shut the window, when the carriage shook again still more violently, and then the wheels came to a stop.

He drew back as far as possible into the corner; he ceased to breathe; he even shut his eyes, so apprehensive was he that his passionate expectation would be disappointed.

The door was opened; one after the other, with a creak, the steps were let down; a woman's dress rustled, and the close atmosphere of the carriage was impregnated by the odor of jasmine; a woman's dainty feet hurried up the steps, and Anna Feodorovna, brushing against the count's leg with the skirt of her cloak, which was loosely thrown about her, silently, and with a deep sigh, took her place on the cushioned seat next him.

Whether she saw him or not, no one could decide, not even Anna Feodorovna herself; but when he took her hand, and said, "Now I will kiss your little hand anyway," she evinced very little dismay. She said nothing, but let him take her hand, and he covered it with kisses, even her arm above the glove.

The carriage rolled away.

"Tell me something. You are not angry?" said he to her.

She silently sank back into her corner, but suddenly, for some reason or other, burst into tears, and let her head fall on his breast.

CHAPTER VI

THE newly elected ispravnik, with his company, the cavalryman, and other members of the nobility, had already been listening for some time to the gipsies, and drinking at the new tavern, when the count, in a blue-lined bearskin shuba which had belonged to Anna Feodorovna's late husband, joined them.

"Little father, your excellency! we had almost given up expecting you," said a squint-eyed black gipsy who displayed a set of brilliant teeth, as he met him in the entry and hastened to divest him of his shuba. "We have n't met since we were at Lebedyan'.....Stioshka has pined away on account of you."

Stioshka, a slender young gipsy girl[1] with a cherry red bloom on her cinnamon-colored cheeks, with brilliant deep black eyes, shaded by long eyelashes, also hurried to meet him.

"Ah! dear little count![2] my sweetheart! This is a pleasure," she exclaimed through her teeth, with a joyous smile.

Ilyushka himself came to greet Turbin, pretending that he was very glad to see him. The old women, the wives, the young girls, hastened to the spot and surrounded the guest.

One would have said that he was a relative or a god-brother to them.

Turbin kissed all the young gipsy girls on the lips; the old women and the men kissed him on the shoulder or on the hand.

The gentlemen were also very glad of the count's arrival; the more because the festivity, having passed its apogee, was now becoming tame; every one began to feel a sense of satiety. The wine, having lost its exhilarating effect on the nerves, only served to load the stomach. Every one had discharged the last cartridge of his wildness, and was looking around moodily. All

[1] *Tsiganotchka.*
[2] *Grafchik! galubchik!*

the songs had been sung, and ran in the heads of each, leaving a mere impression of noise and confusion.

Even if any one did something strange and wild, the rest seemed to look on it as nothing very entertaining or amusing.

The ispravnik, stretched out on the floor in shameless fashion at the feet of an old gipsy woman, was kicking his legs in the air, and crying : —

"Champagne!.... The count has come!....Champagne! .... He has come!.... Now give us champagne!.... I will make a bath of champagne, and swim in it! Gentlemen of the nobility, I love your admirable society!.... Stioshka, sing 'The Narrow Road.'"

The cavalryman was also tipsy, but in a different fashion. He was sitting in the corner of a divan with a tall, handsome gipsy woman, Liubasha; and with the consciousness that intoxication was beginning to cloud his eyes, he kept blinking them, and swinging his head, and repeating the same words over and over again; he was proposing in a whisper to the gipsy to fly with him somewhere.

Liubasha, smiling, listened to him as if what he said were very amusing to her, and at the same time rather melancholy. Occasionally she cast her glances at her husband, the squint-eyed Sashka, who was standing behind a chair near her. In reply to the cavalryman's declaration of love, she bent over to his ear, and begged him to buy her some perfume and a ribbon without any one knowing it, so that the others should not see it.

"Hurrah!" cried the cavalryman when the count came in.

The handsome young man, with an expression of anxiety, was walking up and down the room with solicitously steady steps, and humming an air from the " Revolt in the Seraglio."

An old *paterfamilias*, dragged out to see the gipsies through the irresistible entreaties of the gentlemen of the nobility, who had told him that if he stayed away everything would go to pieces, and in that case they had better not go, was lying on a divan where he had stretched himself out immediately on his arrival; and no one paid any attention to him.

A functionary, who had been there before, had taken off his coat, was sitting with his legs on the table, and was rumpling up his hair, and thus proving that he understood how to be dissipated. As soon as the count came in, he unbuttoned his shirt-collar, and lifted his legs still higher. The count's arrival gave new life generally to the festivities.

The gipsy girls, who had been scattered about the room, again formed their circle. The count seated Stioshka, the soloist, on his knee, and ordered more champagne to be brought. Ilyushka, with his guitar, stood in front of the soloist, and began the *plyaska*, that is, the gipsy song and dance. He played, "When I walk along the Street," "Hey! you Hussars," "Do you hear, do you understand?" and others of the usual order.

Stioshka sang splendidly. Her flexible, sonorous contralto, with its deep chest notes, her smiles while she was singing, her mischievous, passionate eyes, and her little foot which involuntarily kept time to the measure of the song, her despairing wail at the end of each couplet, — this all touched some resonant but tender chord. It was evident that she lived only in the song that she was singing.

Ilyushka, in his smile, his back, his legs, his whole being, carrying out in pantomime the idea expressed in the song, accompanied it on his guitar, and, fixing his eyes on her as if he were hearing her for the first time, attentively and carefully lifted and drooped his head with the rhythm of the song.

Then he suddenly straightened himself up as the singer sang the last note, and, apparently feeling himself superior to every one else in the world, with proud deliberation kicked the guitar, turned it over, stamped his foot, tossed back his locks, and looked at the chorus with a frown.

All his body, from his neck to his toes, began to dance in every sinew.

And twenty powerful, energetic voices, each trying

to outdo the other in making strange and extraordinary noises, were lifted in union.

The old women sprang down from their chairs, waving their handkerchiefs, and showing their teeth, and crying in rhythmic measure, each louder than the other. The bassos, leaning their heads on one side, and swelling their necks, bellowed from behind their chairs.

When Stioshka emitted her high notes, Ilyushka brought his guitar nearer to her as if he were trying to aid her; and the handsome young man, in his enthusiasm, cried out that now they struck B-flat.

When they came to the national dance, the *Plyasovaya*, and Duniasha, with shoulders and bosom shaking, stepped in front of the count, and was passing on, Turbin leaped from his place, took off his uniform, and, remaining only in his red shirt, boldly joined her, keeping up the same measure, and cutting with his feet such antics, that the gipsies laughed and exchanged glances of approval.

The ispravnik, who was sitting Turkish fashion, pounded his chest with his fist, and cried " *Vivat !*" and then, seizing the count by the leg, began to tell him that out of two thousand rubles, he had only five hundred left, and that it was at the count's disposal if only he would give him that pleasure.

The old *paterfamilias* woke up, and wanted to go home, but they would not let him. The handsome young man asked a gipsy girl to waltz with him. The cavalryman, anxious to exalt himself by his friendship with the count, got up from his corner, and embraced Turbin.

"Ah, my turtle-dove!" he cried. "Why did you leave us so soon? ha?"

The count said nothing, being evidently absorbed in thought.

"Where did you go? Ah, count, you rascal, I know where you went!"

This familiarity somehow displeased Count Turbin. Without smiling, he looked in silence into the cavalryman's face, and suddenly gave him such a terrible and

grievous affront that the cavalryman was mortified, and
for some time did not know how to take such an insult,
whether as a joke or not as a joke. At last he made
up his mind that it was a joke; he smiled, and returned
to his gipsy, assuring her that he would really marry
her after Easter.

Another song was sung, a third, they danced again;
the round of gayety was kept up, and every one
continued to feel gay. There was no end to the
champagne.

The count drank a great deal. His eyes seemed to
grow rather moist, but he did not grow dizzy; he
danced still better than the rest, spoke without any
thickness, and even joined in a chorus, and supported
Stioshka when she sang "The sweet emotion of
friendship."

In the midst of the dance and song the merchant
who kept the hotel came to beg the guests to go home,
as it was three o'clock in the morning.

The count took the landlord by the throat, and
ordered him to dance the prisiadka. The merchant
refused. The count snatched a bottle of champagne,
and standing the merchant on his head, ordered him to
stay so, and then amid general hilarity slowly poured
the whole bottle over him.

The dawn was already breaking. All were pale and
weary except the count.

"At all events, I must be getting back to Moscow,"
said he, suddenly rising. "Come with me, all of you, to
my room, boys. .... See me off, and let us have some tea."

All accompanied him with the exception of the sleeping proprietor, who still remained there; they piled into
three sledges that were waiting at the door, and drove
off to the hotel.

CHAPTER VII

"HAVE the horses put in!" cried the count, as he entered the sitting-room of the hotel with all his friends, including the gipsies.

"Sashka, — not the gipsy Sashka, but mine, — tell the superintendent that if the horses are poor I will flog him. Now, give us some tea. Zavalshevsky, make some tea; I am going to Ilyin's; I want to find how things have gone with him," added Turbin; and he went out into the corridor, and directed his steps to the uhlan's room.

Ilyin had just finished playing, and, having lost all his money down to his last kopek, had thrown himself face down on the worn-out haircloth divan, and was picking the hairs out one by one, sticking them into his mouth, biting them in two, and spitting them out again.

Two tallow candles, one of which was already burnt down to the paper, stood on the card-cluttered ombre-table, and mingled their feeble rays with the morning light which was beginning to shine through the window.

The uhlan's mind was vacant of all thought; that strange, thick fog of the gambling passion muffled all the capabilities of his mind, so that there was not even room for regret.

Once he endeavored to think what was left for him to do, how he should get away without a kopek, how he should pay back the fifteen thousand rubles of public money that he had lost in gambling, what his colonel would say, what his mother would say, what his comrades would say; and such fear came over him, and such disgust at himself, that, in his anxiety to rid himself of the thought of it, he arose and began to walk up and down through the room, trying only to walk on the cracks of the floor; and then once more he began to recall all the least details of the evening.

He vividly imagined that he was winning the whole back again; he takes a nine, and lays down a king of spades on two thousand rubles; a queen lies at the right, at the left an ace, at the right a king of diamonds — and all was lost! But if he had had a six at the right and a king of diamonds at the left, then he would have won it all back, he would have staked all again on P, and would have won back his fifteen thousand rubles; then he would have bought a good pacer of the regimental commander, an extra pair of horses, and a phaéton. And what else besides? Ah! indeed, it would have been a splendid, splendid thing!

Again he threw himself down on the divan, and began to bite the hairs once more.

"Why are they singing songs in No. 7?" he wondered. "It must be they are having a jollification in Turbin's room. I'm of a good mind to go there and have a good drink."

Just at this moment the count came in.

"Tell me, have you been cleaned out, brother, hey?" he cried.

"I will pretend to be asleep, otherwise I shall have to talk with him, and I really want to sleep now."

Nevertheless, Turbin went up to him, and laid his hand caressingly on his head. ....

"Well, my dear little friend, have you been cleaned out? have you had bad luck? Tell me."

Ilyin made no reply.

The count took him by the arm.

"I have been losing. What is it to you?" muttered Ilyin, in a sleepy voice expressing indifference and vexation; he did not change his position.

"Everything?"

"Well, yes. What harm is there in it? All! What is it to you?"

"Listen: tell me the truth, as to a comrade," said the count, who, under the influence of the wine that he had been drinking, was disposed to be tender, and continued to smooth the other's hair. "You know I have taken a fancy to you. Tell me the truth. If you have lost the public money, I will help you out; if you don't, it will be too late. .... Was it public money?"

Ilyin leaped up from the sofa.

"If you wish me to tell you, don't speak to me so, because.... and I beg of you don't speak to me.... I will blow my brains out.... that's the only thing that's left for me now!" he exclaimed with genuine despair, letting his head sink into his hands, and bursting into tears, although but the moment before he had been calmly thinking about his horses.

"Ekh! you're a pretty young girl! Well, who might not have the same thing happen to him? It isn't so bad as it might be; perhaps we can straighten things out; wait for me here."

The count hastened from the room.

"Where is the pomyeshchik[1] Lukhnof's room?" he demanded of the hall-boy.

The hall-boy offered to show the count the way. The count forced his way into Lukhnof's room, in spite of the objections of the lackey, who said that his master had only just come in, and was preparing to retire.

Lukhnof in his dressing-gown was sitting in front of a table, counting over a number of packages of banknotes piled up before him. On the table was a bottle of Rheinwein, of which he was very fond. He had procured himself this pleasure from his winnings.

Coldly, sternly, Lukhnof looked at the count over his glasses, affecting not to recognize him.

"It seems that you do not know me," said the count, approaching the table with resolute steps.

Lukhnof recognized the count, and asked:—

"What do you want?"

"I wish to play with you," said Turbin, sitting down on the divan.

"Now?"

"Yes."

"Another time I should be most happy, count; but now I am tired, and am getting ready to go to bed. Won't you have some wine? It is excellent wine."

"But I wish to play with you for a little while *now*."

"I am not prepared to play any more. Maybe some

---

[1] Landed proprietor.

of the other guests will. *I will not*, count! I beg of you to excuse me."

"So you will not?"

Lukhnof shrugged his shoulders as if to express his regret at not being able to fulfil the count's desires.

"Will you not play under any consideration?"

The same gesture.

"I am very desirous of playing with you. .... Say, will you play, or not?"

Silence.

"Will you play?" asked the count a second time.

The same silence, and a quick glance over his glasses at the count's face, which was beginning to grow dark.

"Will you play?" cried the count in a loud voice, striking his hand on the table so violently that the bottle of Rheinwein toppled over and the wine ran out. "You have been cheating, have you not? Will you play? I ask you for the third time."

"I have told you, no! This is truly strange, count, ... perfectly unjustifiable, to come this way, and put your knife at a man's throat," remarked Lukhnof, not lifting his eyes.

A brief silence followed, during which the count's face grew paler and paler. Suddenly Lukhnof received a terrible blow on the head, which stunned him. He fell back on the divan, trying to grasp the money, and screamed in a penetratingly despairing tone, such as was scarcely to be expected from him, he was always so calm and imposing in his deportment.

Turbin gathered up the remaining bank-notes that were lying on the table, pushed away the servant who had come to his master's assistance, and with quick steps left the room.

"If you wish satisfaction, I am at your service; I shall be in my room for half an hour yet, — No. 7," added the count, turning back as he reached the door.

"Villain! thief!" cried a voice from within the room. .... "I will have satisfaction at law!"

Ilyin, who had not paid any heed to the count's

promise to help him, was still lying on the divan in his room, drowned in tears of despair.

The count's caresses and sympathy had awakened him to a consciousness of the reality, and now, amidst the fog of strange thoughts and recollections which filled his mind, it made itself more and more felt.

His youth, rich in hopes, honor, his social position, the dreams of love and friendship, were all destroyed forever. The fountain of his tears began to run dry, a too calm feeling of hopelessness took possession of him; and the thought of suicide, now bringing no sense of repulsion or terror, more and more frequently recurred to him.

At this moment the count's firm steps were heard.

On Turbin's face were still visible the last traces of his recent wrath, his hands trembled slightly; but in his eyes shone a kindly gayety and self-satisfaction.

"There! It has been won back for you!" he cried, tossing on the table several packages of bank-notes. "Count them; are they all there? Then come as soon as possible to the sitting-room; I am going away immediately," he added, pretending not to perceive the tremendous revulsion of joy and gratefulness which rushed over the uhlan's face. Then, humming a gipsy song, he left the room.

CHAPTER VIII

SASHKA, tightening his girdle, was waiting for the horses to be harnessed, but insisted on going first to get the count's cloak, which, with the collar, must have been worth three hundred rubles, and return that miserable blue-lined shuba to that rascally man who had exchanged with the count at the marshal's. But Turbin said that it was not necessary, and went to his room to change his clothes.

The cavalryman kept hiccoughing as he sat silently by his gipsy girl. The ispravnik called for vodka, and invited all the gentlemen to come and breakfast with him, promising them that his wife would, without fail, dance the national dance with the gipsies.

The handsome young man was earnestly arguing with Ilyushka that there was more soul in the piano-forte, and that it was impossible to take B-flat on the guitar. The functionary was gloomily drinking tea in one corner, and apparently the daylight made him feel ashamed of his dissipation.

The gipsies were conversing together in Romany, and urging that they should once more enliven the gentlemen; to which Stioshka objected, declaring that it would only vex the barorai.[1]

For all concerned, the last spark of the orgy was dying out.

"Well, then, one more song for a farewell, and then home with you," exclaimed the count, fresh, gay, and radiant above all the others, as he came into the room dressed in his traveling attire.

The gipsies had again formed their circle, and were just getting ready to sing, when Ilyin came in with a package of bank-notes in his hand, and drew the count to one side.

"I had only fifteen thousand rubles of public money, but you gave me sixteen thousand three hundred," said the uhlan; "this is yours, of course."

"That's a fine arrangement. Let me have it."

Ilyin handed him the money, looking timidly at the count, and opened his mouth to say something; but then he reddened so painfully that the tears came into his eyes, and he seized the count's hand, and began to squeeze it.

"Away with you, Ilyushka.... listen to me! Now, here's your money, but you must accompany me with your songs to the city limits!"

And he flung on the gipsy's guitar the thirteen hundred rubles which Ilyin had brought him. But the count had forgotten to repay the cavalryman the one hundred rubles which he had borrowed of him the evening before.

[1] *Barorai*, in Romany, count or prince, or more correctly great barin. — AUTHOR'S NOTE IN TEXT.

It was now ten o'clock in the morning. The little sun was rising above the housetops, the streets were beginning to fill with people, the merchants had long ago opened their shops, nobles and functionaries were riding up and down through the streets, and ladies were out shopping, when the band of gipsies, the ispravnik, the cavalryman, the handsome young fellow, Ilyin, and the count, who was wrapped up in his blue-lined bearskin shuba, came out on the door-steps of the hotel.

It was a sunny day, and it thawed. Three hired troïkas, with their tails knotted, and splashing through the liquid mud, pranced up to the steps; and the whole jolly company prepared to take their places. The count, Ilyin, Stioshka, Ilyushka, and Sashka, the count's man, mounted the first sledge.

Blücher was beside himself with delight, and, wagging his tail, barked at the shaft-horse.

The other gentlemen, together with the gipsies, men and women, climbed into the other sledges. From the very hotel the sledges flew off side by side, and the gipsies set up a merry chorus and song.

The troïkas with the songs and jingling bells dashed through the whole length of the city to the gates, compelling all the equipages which they met to rein up on the very sidewalks.

Merchants and passers-by who did not know them, and especially those who did, were filled with astonishment to see nobles of high rank in the midst of "the white day," dashing through the streets with intoxicated gipsies and gipsy girls singing at the tops of their voices.

When they reached the city limits, the troïkas stopped, and all the party took farewell of the count.

Ilyin, who had imbibed a good deal at the leave-taking, and had insisted on driving the horses, suddenly became melancholy, and began to urge the count to stay just one day more; but when he was assured that this was impossible, quite unexpectedly threw himself into his arms, and began to kiss his new friend, and promised him that as soon as he got to camp, he would petition to be transferred into the regiment of hussars in which Turbin served.

The count was extraordinarily hilarious; he tipped into a snowdrift the cavalryman, who, since morning, had definitely taken to saying *thou* to him; he set Blücher on the ispravnik; he took Stioshka into his arms, and threatened to carry her off with him to Moscow; but at last he tucked himself into the sledge, and stationed Blücher by his side, who was always ready to ride. Sashka took his place on the box, after once more asking the cavalryman to secure the count's cloak from *them*, and to send it to him. The count cried "Go on,"[1] took off his cap, waved it over his head, and whistled in post-boy fashion to the horses. The troïkas parted company.

As far as the eye could see stretched a monotonous snow-covered plain, over which wound the yellowish muddy ribbon of the road.

The bright sunlight, dancing, glistened on the melting snow, which was covered with a thin transparent crust, and pleasantly warmed the face and back.

The steam arose from the sweaty horses. The bells jingled.

A muzhik with a creaking sledge, heavily loaded, slowly turned out of the road, twitching his hempen reins, and tramping through the slushy snow with his well-soaked linden-bark lapti.

A stout, handsome peasant woman, with a child wrapped in a sheepskin on her lap, who was seated on another load, used the end of her reins to whip up a white mangy-tailed old nag.

Suddenly the count remembered Anna Feodorovna.

"Back!" he cried.

The driver did not understand at first.

"Turn round and drive back; back to the city! Be quick about it."

The troïka again passed the city gate, and quickly drew up in front of the boarded steps of Mrs. Zaïtsof's dwelling.

---

[1] *Pashol.*

The count briskly mounted the steps, passed through the vestibule and the drawing-room, and, finding the widow still asleep, he took her in his arms, lifting her from her bed, and kissed her sleeping eyes again and again, and then darted back to the sledge.

Anna Feodorovna awoke from her slumber, and demanded, "What has happened?"

The count sprang into his sledge, shouted to the driver, and now no longer delaying, and thinking, not of Lukhnof, or of the little widow, or of Stioshka, but only of what was awaiting him in Moscow, rapidly left the city of K. behind him.

CHAPTER IX

A SCORE of years had passed. Much water had run since then, many men had died, many children had been born, many had grown up and become old; still more thoughts had been born and perished. Much that was beautiful and much that was ugly in the past had disappeared; much that was beautiful in the new had been brought forth, and still more that was incomplete and abortive of the new had appeared in God's world.

Count Feodor Turbin had long ago been killed in a duel with some foreigner whom he struck on the street with his long whip. His son, as like him as two drops of water, had already reached the age of two or three and twenty, and was a lovely fellow, already serving in the cavalry.

Morally the young Count Turbin was entirely different from his father. There was not a shadow of those fiery, passionate, and, in truth be it said, corrupt inclinations, peculiar to the last century.

Together with intelligence, cultivation, and inherited natural gifts, a love for the proprieties and amenities of life, a practical view of men and circumstances, wisdom and forethought, were his chief characteristics.

The young count made admirable progress in his profession; at twenty-three he was already lieutenant.

When war broke out, he came to the conclusion that it would be more for his interests to enter the regular army; and he joined a regiment of hussars as captain of cavalry, where he was soon given command of a battalion.

In the month of May, 1848, the S. regiment of hussars was on its way through the government of K., and the very battalion which the young Count Turbin commanded was obliged to be quartered for one night at Morozovka, Anna Feodorovna's village. Anna Feodorovna was still alive, but was now so far from being young that she no longer called herself young, which, for a woman, means much.

She had grown very stout, and this, it is said, makes a woman young. But this was not the worst of it; over her pallid, stout flesh was a network of coarse, flabby wrinkles. She no longer went to the city, she even found it hard to mount into her carriage; but still she was just as good-natured and as completely vacant-minded as ever, — the truth may be told, now that she no longer bribes it by her beauty.

Under her roof lived her daughter Liza, a rustic Russian belle of twenty-three summers, and her brother, our acquaintance the cavalryman, who had good-naturedly spent all his patrimony, and now, in his old age, had taken refuge with Anna Feodorovna.

The hair on his head had become perfectly gray; his upper lip was sunken, but the mustache that it wore was carefully dyed. Wrinkles covered not only his brow and cheeks, but also his nose and neck; and yet his weak bow-legs gave evidence of the old cavalryman.

Anna Feodorovna's whole family and household were gathered in the small drawing-room of the ancient house. The balcony door and windows, looking out into a star-shaped linden park, were open. The gray-haired Anna Feodorovna, in a lilac-colored gown,[1] was sitting on the divan, before a small round mahogany table, shuffling cards. The old brother, dressed in spruce white panta-

[1] *Katsaveïka.*

loons and a blue coat, had taken up his position near the window, and was weaving a band of white paper with a fork, an occupation which his niece had taught him, and which gave him great enjoyment, as he had nothing else to do, his eyes not being strong enough to enable him to read newspapers, which was his favorite occupation. Near him Pimotchka, a *protégée* of Anna Feodorovna, was studying her lessons under the guidance of Liza, who, with wooden knitting-needles, was knitting goat-wool stockings for her uncle.

The last rays of the setting sun, as always at this time, threw under the linden alley their soft reflections on the last window-panes and the little *étagère* which stood near it.

In the garden it was so still that one could hear the swift rush of a swallow's wings, and so quiet in the room that Anna Feodorovna's gentle sigh, or the old man's cough as he kept changing the position of his legs, was the only sound.

"How does this go, Lizanka? show me, please. I keep forgetting," said Anna Feodorovna, pausing in the midst of her game of patience.

Liza, without stopping her work, went over to her mother, and, glancing at the cards, "Oh! you have mixed them all up, dear mamasha," said she, arranging the cards. "That is the way they should be placed. Now they come as you desired," she added, secretly withdrawing one card.

"Now you are always managing to deceive me! You said that it would go."

"No, truly; it goes, I assure you. It has come out right."

"Very well, then; very well, you rogue! But is n't it time for tea?"

"I have just ordered the samovar heated. I will go and see about it immediately. Shall we have it brought here?.... Now, Pimotchka, hasten and finish your lessons, and we will go and take a run."

And Liza started for the door.

"Lizotchka! Lizanka!" cried her uncle, steadfastly

regarding his fork, "it seems to me I have dropped another stitch. Arrange it for me, my darling."[1]

"In a moment, in a moment. First I must have the sugar broken up."

And in point of fact, within three minutes, she came running into the room, went up to her uncle, and took him by the ear.

"That's to pay you for dropping stitches," said she, laughing. "You have not been knitting as I taught you."

"Now, that'll do, that'll do, adjust it for me; there seems to be some sort of a knot."

Liza took the fork, pulled out a pin from her kerchief, which now, being loosened, was blown back a little by the breeze coming through the window, pretended to pick out a knot, and then, after taking a stitch or two, handed it back to her uncle.

"Now you must kiss me for that," said she, putting up her rosy cheek toward him, and readjusting her kerchief. "You shall have rum in your tea to-day. To-day is Friday, you see."

And again she went to the tea-room.

"Uncle dear, come and look! some hussars are riding up toward the house!" her ringing voice was heard to say.

Anna Feodorovna and her brother hastened into the tea-room, the windows of which faced the village, and looked at the hussars. Very little was to be seen; through the cloud of dust it could be judged only that a body of men was advancing.

"What a pity, sister," remarked the uncle to Anna Feodorovna, "what a pity that we are so cramped, and the wing is not built yet, so that we might invite the officers here. Officers of the hussars! they are such glorious, gay young fellows! I should like to have a glimpse at them."

"Well, I should be heartily glad, but you know yourself that there is nowhere to put them; my sleeping-room, Liza's room, the parlor, and then your room, —

[1] *Galubchik.*

that's all there is. Where could we put them? Judge for yourself. Mikhaïlo Matveyef has put the village elder's house[1] in order for them; he says it will be nice there."

"But we must find you a husband, Lizotchka, among them, — a glorious hussar!" said the uncle.

"No, I do not want a hussar; I want a uhlan. Let me see, you served in the uhlans, did n't you, uncle? .... I don't care to know these hussars. They say they are all desperate fellows."

And Liza blushed a little, and then once more her ringing laugh was heard.

"Here's Ustiushka running; we must ask her what she saw," said she.

Anna Feodorovna sent to have Ustiushka brought in.

"She has no idea of sticking to her work, she must always be running off to look at the soldiers," said Anna Feodorovna. ..... "Now, tell me, where have they lodged the officers?"

"With the Yeremkins, your ladyship. There are two of them, such lovely men! One of them is a count, they tell me."

"What's his name?"

"Kazarof or Turbinof. I don't remember, excuse me."

"There now, you're a goose, you don't know how to tell anything at all. You might have remembered his name!"

"Well, I'll run and find out."

"I know that you are quite able to do that. But no, let Danilo go. — Brother, go and tell him to go; have him ask if there is not something which the officers may need; everything must be done in good form; have them understand that it is the lady of the house who has sent to find out."

The old people sat down again in the tea-room, and Liza went to the servants' room to put the lumps of sugar in the sugar-bowl. Ustiushka was there telling about the hussars.

[1] *Starostina izba.*

"Oh, my dear young lady, what a handsome man he is! that count!" she said, "absolutely a little cherubim,[1] with black eyebrows. You ought to have such a husband as that; what a lovely little couple you would make!"

The other maids smiled approvingly; the old nurse, sitting by the window with her stocking, sighed, and drawing a long breath, murmured a prayer.

"It seems to me that the hussars have given you a great deal of pleasure," said Liza. "You are a master hand at description. Bring me the mors,[2] Ustiushka, please; we must give the officers something sour to drink."

And Liza, laughing, went out with the sugar-bowl.

"But I should like to see what sort of a man this hussar is," she said to herself, — "whether he is brunette or blond. And I imagine he would not object to making our acquaintance. But he will go away, and never know that I was here and was thinking about him. And how many have passed by me in this way! No one ever sees me except uncle and Ustiusha! How many times I have arranged my hair, how many pairs of cuffs I have put on, and yet no one ever sees me or falls in love with me," she thought, with a sigh, contemplating her white, plump arm.

"He must be tall, and have big eyes, and a nice little black mustache. .... No! I am already over twenty-two, and no one has ever fallen in love with me except the pock-marked Ivan Ipatuitch. And four years ago I was still better-looking; and so my girlhood has gone, and no one is the better for it. Ah! I am a wretched, wretched country girl!"

Her mother's voice, calling her to pour the tea, aroused the country girl from this momentary reverie.

She shook her little head, and went into the tea-room.

The best things always happen unexpectedly; and the more you try to force them, the worse they come out. In the country, it is rare that any attempt is made

---

[1] *Kherubimchik.*
[2] A sour beverage made of cranberries.

to impart education, and therefore when a good one is found it is generally a surprise. And thus it happened, in a notable degree, in the case of Liza.

Anna Feodorovna, through her own lack of intelligence and natural laziness, had not given Liza any education at all; had not taught her music or the French language which is so indispensable. But the girl whom she had unexpectedly had by her late husband, had proved to be a healthy, bright little child; she had intrusted her to a wet-nurse and a day-nurse; she had fed her, and dressed her in print dresses and goatskin shoes, and let her run wild and gather mushrooms and berries; had her taught reading and arithmetic by a resident seminarist. And thus, as fate would have it, when her daughter had reached the age of sixteen, she found in her a companion, a soul who was always cheerful and good-natured and the actual mistress of the house.

Through her goodness of heart, Anna Feodorovna always had in her house some *protégée*, either a serf or some foundling. Liza, from the time she was ten years old, had begun to take care of these; to teach them, clothe them, take them to church, and keep them still when they were inclined to be mischievous.

Then her old broken-down but good-natured uncle made his appearance, and he had to be taken care of like a child. Then the domestic servants and the peasants began to come to the young mistress with their desires and their ailments; and she treated them with elderberry, mint, and spirits of camphor. Then the domestic management of the house fell into her hands entirely. Then came the unsatisfied craving for love, which found expression only in nature and religion.

Thus Liza, by chance, grew into an active, good-naturedly cheerful, self-poised, pure, and deeply religious young woman.

To be sure, she had her little fits of jealousy and envy when she saw, all around her in church, her neighbors dressed in new, fashionable hats which came from K.; she was sometimes vexed to tears by her old,

irritable mother, and her caprices; she had her dreams
of love in the most absurd and even the crudest forms,
but her healthy activity, which she could not shirk,
drove them away; and now, at twenty-two, not a single
spot, not a single compunction, had touched the fresh,
calm soul of this maiden, now developed into the fullness of perfect physical and moral beauty.

Liza was of medium height, rather plump than lean;
her eyes were brown, small, with a soft dark shade on
the lower lid; she wore her flaxen hair in a long braid.

In walking she took long steps, and swayed like a
duck, as the saying is.

The expression of her face, when she was occupied
with her duties, and nothing especially disturbed her,
seemed to say to all who looked into it, " Life in this
world is good and pleasant to one who has a heart
full of love, and a pure conscience."

Even in moments of vexation, of trouble, of unrest,
or of melancholy, in spite of her tears, of the draw-
ing-down of the left brow, of the compressed lips, of
the petulance of her desires, even then in the dimples
of her cheeks, in the corners of her mouth, and in her
brilliant eyes, so used to smile and rejoice in life,—
even then there shone a heart good and upright, and
unspoiled by knowledge.

CHAPTER X

It was still rather warm, though the sun was already
set, when the battalion arrived at Morozovka.   In front
of them, along the dusty village street, trotted a
brindled cow, separated from the herd, bellowing, and
occasionally stopping to look round, and never once
perceiving that all she had to do was to turn out and
let the battalion pass.

Peasants, old men, women, children, and domestic
serfs, crowding both sides of the road, gazed curiously
at the hussars.

Through a thick cloud of dust the hussars rode

along on raven-black horses, curveting and occasionally snorting.

At the right of the battalion, gracefully mounted on
beautiful black steeds, rode two officers. One was the
commander, Count Turbin; the other a very young
man, who had recently been promoted from the yunk-
ers; his name was Polozof.

A hussar, in a white kitel, came from the best of
the cottages, and, taking off his cap, approached the
officers.

"What quarters have been assigned to us?" asked
the count.

"For your excellency?" replied the quartermaster,
his whole body shuddering. "Here at the starosta's; I
have put his cottage in order. I tried to get a room at
the mansion,[1] but they said no; the proprietress is so
ill-tempered."

"Well, all right," said the count, dismounting and
stretching his legs as he reached the starosta's cottage.
"Tell me, has my carriage come?"

"It has deigned to arrive, your excellency," replied
the quartermaster, indicating with his cap the leathern
carriage-top which was to be seen inside the gate, and
then hastening ahead into the entry of the cottage,
which was crowded with the family of serfs, gathered to
have a look at the officer.

He even tripped over an old woman, as he hastily
opened the door of the neatly cleaned cottage, and stood
aside to let the count pass.

The cottage was large and commodious, but not perfectly clean. The German body-servant, dressed like a
gentleman,[2] was standing in the cottage, and, having
just finished setting up the iron bed, was taking out
clean linen from a trunk.

"Phu! what a nasty lodging!" exclaimed the count,
in vexation. "Diadenko! Is it impossible to find me
better quarters at the proprietor's or somewhere?"

"If your excellency command, I will go up to the
mansion," replied Diadenko; "but the house is small

---

[1] *Barsky dvor.*   [2] *Barin.*

and wretched, and seems not much better than the cottage."

"Well, that's all now. You can go."

And the count threw himself down on the bed, supporting his head with his hands.

"Johann!" he cried to his body-servant; "again you have made a hump in the middle. Why can't you learn to make a bed decently?"

Johann wanted to make it over again.

"No, you need not trouble about it now! .... Where's my khalat?" he asked, in a petulant voice. The servant gave him the garment.

The count, before he put it on, examined the skirt. "There it is! You have not taken that spot out! Could it be possible for any one to be a worse servant than you are?" he added, snatching the khalat from the servant's hands and putting it on. "Now tell me, do you do this way on purpose? .... Is tea ready?" ....

"I have n't had time to make it," replied Johann.

"Durak .... fool!"

After this, the count took a French novel which was at hand, and read for some time without speaking; but Johann went out into the entry to blow up the coals in the samovar.

It was plain to see that the count was in a bad humor; it must have been owing to weariness, to the dust on his face, to his tightly fitting clothes, and to his empty stomach.

"Johann!" he cried again, "give me an account of those ten rubles. What did you get in town?"

The count looked over the account which the servant handed him, and made some dissatisfied remarks about the high prices paid.

"Give me the rum for the tea."

"I did not get any rum," said Johann.

"Delightful! How many times have I told you always to have rum?"

"I did n't have money enough."

"Why did n't Polozof buy it? You might have got some from his man."

"The cornet Polozof? I do not know. He bought tea and sugar."

"Beast!.... Get you gone. ..... You are the only man who has the power to exhaust my patience! You know that I always take rum in my tea when I am on the march."

"Here are two letters brought for you from head-quarters," said the body-servant.

The count, as he lay on the bed, tore open the letters, and proceeded to read them. At this moment the cornet came in with gay countenance, having quartered the battalion.

"Well, how is it, Turbin? It's first-rate here, it seems to me. I am tired out, I confess it. It has been a warm day."

"First-rate! I should think so! A dirty, stinking hut! and no rum, thanks to you. Your stupid did not buy any, nor this one either. You might have said something, anyway!"

And he went on with his reading. After he had read the letter through, he crumpled it up, and threw it on the floor.

"*Why* didn't you buy some rum?" the cornet in a whisper demanded of his servant in the entry. "Didn't you have any money?"

"Well, why should we be always the ones to spend the money? I have enough to spend for without that, and *his* German does nothing but smoke his pipe, — that's all."

The second letter was evidently not disagreeable, because the count smiled as he read it.

"Who's that from?" asked Polozof, returning to the room, and trying to arrange for himself a couch on the floor near the oven.

"From Mina," replied the count, gayly, handing him the letter. "Would you like to read it? What a lovely woman she is!.... Now, she's better than our fine young ladies, that's a fact. .... Just see what feeling and what wit in that letter! There's only one thing that I don't like, — she asks me for money!"

"No, that's not pleasant," replied the cornet.

"Well, it's true I promised to give her some; but this expedition .... and besides, if I am commander of the battalion, at the end of three months I will send some to her. I should not regret it; she's really a charmer! Isn't she?" he asked, with a smile, following with his eyes Polozof's expression as he read the letter.

"Horribly illiterate, but sweet; it seems to me she really loves you," replied the cornet.

"Hm! I should think so! Only these women truly love when they do love."

"But who was the other from?" asked the cornet, handing back the letter which he had just read.

"That? Oh, that's from a certain man, very ugly, to whom I owe a gambling debt, and this is the third time he's reminded me of it. ..... I can't pay it to him now. ..... It's a stupid letter," replied the count, evidently nettled by the recollection of it.

The two officers remained silent for some little time. The cornet, who, it seemed, had come under Turbin's influence, drank his tea without speaking, though he occasionally cast a glance at the clouded face of the handsome count, who gazed steadily out of the window. He did not venture to renew the conversation.

"Well, then, I think it can be accomplished without difficulty," suddenly exclaimed the count, turning to Polozof, and gayly nodding his head. "If we who are in the line get promoted this year, yes, and if we take part in some engagement, then I can overtake my former captains of the guard."

They were still talking on this theme over their second glass of tea, when the old Danilo came with the message from Anna Feodorovna.

"And she would also like to know whether you are not pleased to be the son of Count Feodor Ivanovitch Turbin," Danilo added, on his own responsibility, as he had found out the officer's name, and still remembered the late count's visit to the city of K. "Our mistress,[1] Anna Feodorovna, used to be very well acquainted with him."

---

[1] *Baruinya.*

"He was my father. Now tell the lady that I am very much obliged, but that I need nothing; only, if it would not be possible to give me a cleaner room in the mansion, say, or somewhere."

"Now, why did you do that?" asked Polozof, after Danilo had gone. "Isn't it just the same thing? For one night isn't it just as well here? And it will put them to inconvenience."

"There it is again! It seems to me we have had enough of being sent round among these smoky hovels.[1] .... It's easy enough to see that you are not a practical man. .... Why shouldn't we seize the opportunity of sleeping when we can, like decent men, even if it's for only one night? And they, contrary to what you think, will be awfully glad. There's only one thing objectionable. If this lady used to know my father," continued the count, with a smile which discovered his white gleaming teeth, — "somehow I always feel a little ashamed of my late papasha; there's always some scandalous story, or some debt or other. And so I can't endure to meet any of my father's acquaintances. However, that was an entirely different age," he added seriously.

"Oh! I did not tell you," rejoined Polozof. "I recently met Ilyin, the brigade commander of uhlans. He is very desirous of seeing you; he is passionately fond of your father."

"I think that he is terrible trash, that Ilyin. But the worst is that all these gentlemen who imagine that they knew my father in order to make friends with me, insist upon telling me, as if it were very pleasant for me to hear, about escapades of his which make me blush. It is true I am not impulsive, and I look on things dispassionately; while he was too hot-spirited a man, and sometimes he played exceedingly reprehensible tricks. However, that was all due to his time. In our day and generation, maybe, he would have been a very sensible man, for he had tremendous abilities; one must give him credit for that."

[1] *Kurnaya izba*, a peasant's hut without chimney.

In a quarter of an hour the servant returned, and brought an invitation for them to come and spend the night at the mansion.

CHAPTER XI

As soon as Anna Feodorovna learned that the officer of hussars was the son of Count Feodor Turbin, she was thrown into a great state of excitement.

"Oh! great heavens![1] he is my darling!.... Danilo! run, hurry, tell them the lady invites them to stay at her house," she cried, in great agitation, and hastening to the servants' room. "Lizanka! Ustiushka! You must have your room put in order, Liza. You can go into your uncle's room; and you, brother.... brother, you can sleep to-night in the drawing-room. It's for only one night."

"That's nothing, sister! I would sleep on the floor."

"He must be a handsome fellow, I think, if he's like his father. Only let me see him, the turtle-dove!.... You shall see for yourself, Liza. Ah! his father was handsome!.... Where shall we put the table? Let it go there," said Anna Feodorovna, fidgeting about. "There now, bring in two beds; take one from the overseer's, and get from the *étagère* the glass candlestick which my brother gave me for my birthday, and put in a wax candle."

At last all was ready. Liza, in spite of her mother's interference, arranged her room in her own way for the two officers.

She brought out clean linen sheets, fragrant of mignonette, and had the beds made; she ordered a carafe of water, and candles to be placed near it on the little table. She burned scented paper in the girls' room, and moved her own little bed into her uncle's chamber.

Anna Feodorovna gradually became calm, and sat

[1] *Batyushki moï !*

down again in her usual place; she even took out her cards; but, instead of shuffling them, she leaned on her fat elbow, and gave herself up to her thoughts.

"How time has gone! how time has gone!" she exclaimed, in a whisper. "It is long! long! isn't it? I seem to see him now! Oh! he was a scamp!"—And the tears came into her eyes.—"Now here is Lizanka, but she isn't at all what I was at her age. She is a nice girl; but no, not quite...."

"Lizanka, you had better wear your mousseline-delaine dress this evening."

"Why, are you going to invite them down-stairs, mamasha? You had better not do it," rejoined Liza, with a feeling of invincible agitation at the thought of seeing the officers. "You had better not, mamasha!"

In point of fact, much as she desired to see them, she felt even more apprehensive of some painful pleasure awaiting her, as it seemed to her.

"Perhaps they themselves would like to make our acquaintance, Lizotchka," said Anna Feodorovna, smoothing her daughter's hair, and at the same time thinking, "No, not such hair as I had at her age. No, Lizotchka, how much I could wish for you that...."

And she really wished something very excellent for her daughter, but she could scarcely look forward to a match with the count; she could not desire such a relationship as she herself had formed with his father; but that something good would come of it, she wished very, very much for her daughter. She possibly had the desire to live over again in her daughter's happiness all the life which she lived with the late lamented.

The old cavalryman was also somewhat excited by the count's coming. He went to his room, and shut himself up in it. At the end of a quarter of an hour, he reappeared dressed in a Hungarian coat and blue pantaloons; and, with anxiously happy expression of countenance, such as a girl wears when she puts on her first ball-gown, he started for the room assigned to the guests.

"I shall have a glimpse of some of the hussars of

to-day, sister. The late count was indeed a genuine hussar. We shall see! we shall see!"

The officers had by this time come in by the back entrance, and were in the room that had been put at their service.

"There, now," said the count, stretching himself out in his dusty boots on the bed which had just been made for him, "see how much better off we are here than we were there in that hovel with the cockroaches!"

"Better? of course; but think what obligations we are putting ourselves under to the people here." ....

"What rubbish! One must always be a practical man. They are awfully glad to have us, of course. .... Fellow!" cried the count, "ask some one to put a curtain up at this window, else there'll be a draught in the night."

Just at this moment the old man came in to make the acquaintance of the officers. Though he grew rather red in the face, of course, he did not fail to tell how he had been a comrade of the late count's, how he had enjoyed his society, and he even went so far as to say that more than once he had been under obligations to the late count. Whether he meant, in speaking of the obligations to the late count, a reference to the hundred rubles which the count had borrowed and never returned, or to his throwing him into the snowdrift, or to his grossly insulting him, the old man entirely failed to explain.

However, the count was very urbane with the old cavalryman, and thanked him for his hospitality.

"You must excuse us if it is not very luxurious, count," — he almost said "your excellency," as he had got out of the habit of meeting with men of rank. "My sister's house is rather small. As for the window here, we will immediately find something to serve as a curtain, and it will be first-rate," added the little old man; and, under the pretext of going for a curtain, but chiefly because he wanted to give his report about the officers as quickly as possible, he left the room.

The pretty little Ustiusha came, bringing her mistress's shawl to serve as a curtain. She was also com-

missioned to ask if the gentlemen would not like some
tea.

This pleasant hospitality had a manifestly beneficent influence on the count's spirits. He laughed gayly, and jested
with Ustiusha so that she even called him a bad man;
he asked her if her mistress was pretty, and in reply to
her question whether he would like some tea, declared
that she might please bring him some, but above all,
as his supper was not ready, he would like some vodka
now, a bite of something to eat, and some sherry if there
was any.

The old uncle was in raptures over the young count's
politeness, and praised to the skies the young generation of officers, saying that the men of the present day
were incomparably superior to those of the past.

Anna Feodorovna could not agree to that, — no one
could be any better than Count Feodor Ivanovitch, —
and she was beginning to grow seriously angry, and remarked dryly : —

"For you, brother, the one who flatters you last is
the best! Without any question, the men of our time
are better educated; but still Feodor Ivanovitch could
dance the schottische, and was so amiable that everybody
in his day, you might say, was crazy over him! only he
did not care for any one except me. Oh, certainly there
were fine men in the old time!"

At this moment came the message requesting the
vodka, the lunch, and the sherry.

"There now, just like you, brother! You never do
things right. We ought to have ordered supper. ..... Liza,
attend to it, that's a darling."

Liza hastened to the storeroom for mushrooms and
fresh cream butter, and told the cook to prepare beef
cutlets.

"How much sherry is there? Have n't you any left,
brother?"

"No, sister, I have not had any."

"What! no sherry? but what is it you drink in your
tea?"

"That is rum. Anna Feodorovna."

"Isn't that the same thing? Give them some of that. It is all the same, rum! Or would it not be better to invite them down here, brother? You know all about it. They would not be offended, I imagine, would they?"

The cavalryman assured her that he would answer for it that the count, in his goodness of heart, would not decline, and that he would certainly bring them.

Anna Feodorovna went off to put on, for some unknown reason, her grosgrain gown and a new cap; but Liza was so busy that she had no time to take off her pink gingham frock with wide sleeves. Moreover, she was terribly wrought up; it seemed to her that something astonishing, like a very low black cloud, was sweeping down on her soul.

This count-hussar, this handsome fellow, she imagined as an absolutely novel and to her incomprehensible but beautiful creature. His character, his habits, his words, it seemed to her, must be something extraordinary, such as had never come into the range of her experience. All that he thought and said must be wise and true; all that he did must be honorable; his whole appearance must be beautiful. She could have no doubt of that. If he had demanded not merely a lunch and sherry, but even a bath in spirits of salvia, she would not have been surprised, she would not have blamed him, and she would have been convinced that this was just and reasonable.

The count immediately accepted when the cavalryman brought him his sister's invitation; he combed his hair, put on his coat, and took his cigar-case.

"Let us come!" he said to Polozof.

"Indeed, we had better not go," replied the cornet; "*ils feront des frais pour nous recevoir.*"

"Rubbish! it will make them happy. Besides, I have been making inquiries .... there's a pretty daughter here. .... Come along," said the count in French.

"*Je vous en prie, messieurs,*" said the cavalryman, merely for the sake of giving them to understand that he also could speak French, and understood what the officers were saying.

CHAPTER XII

Liza, red in the face and with downcast eyes, was ostensibly occupied with filling up the teapot, and did not dare to look at the officers as they entered the room.

Anna Feodorovna, on the contrary, briskly jumped up and bowed, and, without taking her eyes from the count's face, began to talk to him, now finding an extraordinary resemblance to his father, now presenting her daughter, now offering him tea, preserves, or jelly-cakes.

No one paid any attention to the cornet, owing to his modest appearance; and he was very glad of it, because it gave him a chance, within the limits of propriety, to observe and study the details of Liza's beauty, which had evidently come over him with the force of a surprise.

The uncle, listening to his sister's conversation, had a speech ready on his lips, and was waiting for a chance to relate his cavalry experiences.

The count smoked his cigar over his tea, so that Liza had great difficulty in refraining from coughing, but he was very talkative and amiable; at first, in the pauses of Anna Feodorovna's interminable speeches, he introduced his own anecdotes, and finally he took the conversation into his own hands.

One thing struck his listeners as rather strange: in his talk he often used words which, though not considered reprehensible in his own set, were here rather audacious, so that Anna Feodorovna was somewhat abashed, and Liza blushed to her ears. But the count did not notice this, and continued to be just as natural and amiable as ever.

Liza filled the glasses in silence, not putting them into the hands of the guests, but setting them down near them; she had not entirely recovered from her agitation, but listened eagerly to what the count was saying.

His tales, which were not characterized by wit or cleverness, and the hesitancies in the conversation, grad-

ually reassured her. The very bright things she had
expected from him were not forthcoming, nor did she
discover any of that surpassing elegance which she had
confusedly hoped to find in him. Even over the third
glass of tea, when her timid eyes once encountered his,
and he did not avoid them, but continued almost too
boldly to stare at her, with a lurking smile, she became
conscious of a certain feeling of hostility against him;
and she soon discovered that there was not only nothing
out of the ordinary in him, but that he was very little
different from those whom she had already seen, so
that there was no reason to be afraid of him. Except
that he had long and neat finger-nails, there was no
mark of special beauty about him.

Liza suddenly, not without some inward sorrow, re-
nouncing her dream, regained her self-possession; and
only the undemonstrative cornet's eyes, which she felt
fixed upon her, disquieted her.

"Perhaps it is not the count, but the other," she said
to herself.

CHAPTER XIII

AFTER tea, the old lady invited her guests into the
other room, and again sat down in her usual place.

"But perhaps you would like to rest, count?" she
asked. "Well, then, what will you amuse yourselves
with, my dear guests?" she proceeded to ask, after she
had been assured to the contrary. "Do you play cards,
count?—Here, brother, you might take a hand in some
game or other."....

"Why, you yourself can play *préférence*," replied the
cavalryman. "You had better take a hand, then.
Count, will you play? And you?"

The officers were agreeable to everything that might
satisfy their amiable hosts.

Liza brought from her room her old cards which she
used for divining whether her mother would speedily
recover of a cold, or whether her uncle would return on

such and such a day from the city if he chanced to
have gone there, or whether her neighbor would be in
during the day, and other like things. These cards,
though they had been in use for two months, were less
soiled than those which Anna Feodorovna used for the
same purpose.

"Perhaps you are not accustomed to playing for
small stakes," suggested the uncle. "Anna Feodorovna
and I play for half-kopeks, ... and then she always gets
the better of all of us."

"Oh! make your own arrangements. I shall be
perfectly satisfied," said the count.

"Well, then, be it in paper kopeks for the sake of
our dear guests; only let me gain, as I am an old
woman," said Anna Feodorovna, settling herself in her
chair, and adjusting her mantilla.

"Maybe I shall win a ruble of them," thought Anna
Feodorovna, who in her old age felt a little passion for
cards.

"If you would like, I will teach you to play with tablets," said the count, "and with the *miseries*. It is very
jolly."

They were all delighted with this new Petersburg
fashion. The uncle went so far as to assert that he
knew it, and that it was just the same thing as boston,
but that he had forgotten somewhat about it.

Anna Feodorovna did not comprehend it at all; and
it took her so long to get into it, that she felt under the
necessity of smiling and nodding her head assuringly,
to give the impression that she now understood, and
that it was all perfectly clear to her. But there was no
little amusement created when in the midst of the game
Anna Feodorovna, with ace and king blank, called
"misery," and remained with the six. She even began
to grow confused, smiled timidly, and hastened to assure
them that she had not as yet become accustomed to the
new way.

Nevertheless they put down the points against her,
and many of them too; the more because the count,
through his practice of playing on large stakes, played

carefully, led very prudently, and entirely ignored what the cornet meant by various thumps with his foot under the table, or why he made such stupid blunders in playing.

Liza brought in more jelly-cakes, three kinds of preserves, and large apples cooked in a peculiar way; and then, standing behind her mother's chair, she looked on at the game, and occasionally watched the officers, and especially the count's white hands with their delicate long pink nails, as he, with such skill, assurance, and grace, threw the cards, and took the tricks.

Once more Anna Feodorovna, with some show of temper, going beyond the others, bid as high as seven, and lost three points; and when, at her brother's instigation, she set some wild figure, she was utterly lost and flustered.

"It's nothing, mamasha; you'll win it back again," said Liza, with a smile, anxious to rescue her mother from her ridiculous position. "Sometime you'll put a fine on uncle; then he will be caught."

"But you might help me, Lizotchka," cried Anna Feodorovna, looking with an expression of dismay at her daughter; "I don't know how this ...."

"But I don't know how to play this either," rejoined Liza, mentally calculating her mother's losses. "But if you go on at this rate, mamasha, you will lose a good deal, and Pimotchka will not have her new gown," she added in jest.

"Yes, in this way it is quite possible to lose ten silver rubles," said the cornet, looking at Liza, and wishing to draw her into conversation.

"Aren't we playing for paper money?" asked Anna Feodorovna, gazing round at the others.

"I don't know, I am sure," replied the count. "But I don't know how to reckon in bank-notes. What are they? what do you mean by bank-notes?"[1]

"Why, no one nowadays reckons in bank-notes," explained the cavalryman, who was playing like a hero and was on the winning side.

[1] *Assignatsii.*

The old lady ordered some sparkling beverage called *shiputchki*, drank two glasses herself, grew quite flushed, and seemed to abandon all hope. One braid of her gray hair escaped from under her cap, and she did not even put it up. It was evident that she thought herself losing millions, and that she was entirely ruined. The cornet kept nudging the count's leg more and more emphatically. The count was noting down the old lady's losses.

At last the game came to an end. In spite of Anna Feodorovna's efforts to bring her reckoning higher than it should be, and to pretend that she had been cheated in her account, and that it could not be correct, in spite of her dismay at the magnitude of her losses, at last when the account was made out, she was found to have lost nine hundred and twenty points.

"Isn't that equal to nine paper rubles?" she asked again and again; and she did not begin to realize how great her forfeit was, until her brother, to her horror, explained that she was "out" thirty-two and a half paper rubles, and that it was absolutely necessary for her to pay it.

The count did not even sum up his gains, but, as soon as the game was over, arose and went over to the window where Liza was arranging the zakushka, and putting potted mushrooms on a plate for their supper. There he did with perfect calmness and naturalness what the cornet had been anxious and yet unable to effect all the evening, — he engaged her in conversation about the weather.

The cornet at this time was brought into a thoroughly unpleasant predicament. Anna Feodorovna, in the absence of the count and Liza, who had managed to keep her in a jovial frame of mind, became really angry.

"Indeed, it is too bad that we have caused you to lose so heavily," said Polozof, in order to say something. "It is simply shameful."

"I should think these tablets and *miseries* were something of your own invention. I don't know anything about them. How many paper rubles does the whole amount to?" she demanded.

"Thirty-two rubles, thirty-two and a half," insisted the cavalryman, who, from the effect of having been on the winning side, was in a very waggish frame of mind. "Give him the money, sister. ..... Give it to him."

"I will give all I owe, only you must not ask for any more. No, I shall never win it back in my life."

And Anna Feodorovna went to her room, all in excitement, hurried back, and brought nine paper rubles. Only on the old man's strenuous insistence she was induced to pay the whole sum.

Polozof had some fear that the old lady would pour out on him the vials of her wrath if he entered into conversation with her. He silently, without attracting attention, turned away, and rejoined the count and Liza, who were talking at the open window.

On the table, which was now spread for the supper, stood two tallow candles, the flames of which occasionally flared in the gentle breeze of the mild May night. Through the window, opening into the garden, came a very different light from that which filled the room. The moon, almost at its full, already beginning to lose its golden radiance, was pouring over the tops of the lofty lindens, and making brighter and brighter the delicate fleecy clouds that occasionally overcast it.

From the pond, the surface of which, silvered in one place by the moon, could be seen through the trees, came the voices of the frogs. In the sweet-scented lilac bush under the very window, which from time to time slowly shook its heavy-laden blossoms, birds were darting and fluttering.

"What marvelous weather!" said the count, as he joined Liza, and sat down on the low window-seat. "I suppose you go to walk a good deal, don't you?"

"Yes," rejoined Liza, not experiencing the slightest embarrassment in the count's company. "Every morning, at seven o'clock, I make the tour of the estate, and sometimes I take a walk with Pimotchka, — mamma's *protégée*."

"It's pleasant living in the country," cried the count, putting his monocle to his eye, and gazing first at the garden, and then at Liza. "But don't you like to take a walk on moonlight nights?"

"No. Three years ago my uncle and I used to go out walking every moonlight night. He had some sort of strange illness,—insomnia. Whenever there was a full moon, he could not sleep. His room, you see, opens into the garden, and the window is low. The moon shines right into it."

"Strange," remarked the count. "Then this is your room."

"No, I only sleep there for this one night. You occupy my room."

"Is it possible?.... oh, good heavens![1] I shall never in the world forgive myself for the trouble that I have caused," said the count, casting the monocle from his eye as a sign of sincerity..... "If I had only known that I was going to...."

"How much trouble was it? On the contrary, I am very glad. My uncle's room is so nice and jolly; there's a low window there. I shall sit down in it before I go to bed, or perhaps I shall go down, out into the garden, and take a little walk."

"What a glorious girl!" said the count to himself, replacing the monocle, and staring at her, and while pretending to change his seat in the window, trying to touch her foot with his. "And how shrewdly she gave me to understand that I may meet her in the garden at the window, if I wish!"

Liza even lost in the count's eyes a large share of her charm, so easy did the conquest of her seem to him.

"And how blissful it must be," said the count, dreamily, gazing into the shadow-haunted alley, "to spend such a night in the garden, with the object of one's love!"

Liza was somewhat abashed by these words, and by a second unexpected pressure upon her foot. Before she thought, she made some remark for the sake of dissimulating her embarrassment.

She said, "Yes, it is splendid to walk in the moonlight."

[1] *Okh! Bozhe moï!*

There was something disagreeable about the whole conversation. She put the cover on the jar from which she had been taking the mushrooms, and was just turning from the window, when the cornet came toward her, and she felt a curiosity to know what kind of a man he was.

"What a lovely night!" said he.

"They can only talk about the weather," thought Liza.

"What a wonderful view!" continued the cornet, "only I should think it would be tiresome," he added, through a strange propensity, peculiar to him, of saying things sure to offend the people who pleased him very much.

"Why should you think so? Always the same cooking and always the same gown might become tiresome; but a lovely garden can never be tiresome when you enjoy walking, and especially when there's a moon rising higher and higher. From my uncle's room you can see the whole pond. I shall see it from there to-night."

"And you have n't any nightingales at all, have you?" asked the count, very much put out because Polozof had come and prevented him from learning the exact conditions of the rendezvous.

"Oh, yes, we always have them; last year the hunters caught one; and only last week one was singing beautifully, but the district inspector[1] came along with his bells, and scared him away. Three years ago my uncle and I used to sit out in the covered alley, and listen to one for two hours at a time."

"What is this chatterbox telling you about?" inquired the old uncle, joining the trio. "Are n't you ready for something to eat?"

At supper, the count, by his reiterated praise of the viands, and by his appetite, succeeded in bringing his hostess into a somewhat happier frame of mind. Afterward the officers made their adieux, and went to their room. The count shook hands with the old cavalier,

[1] *Stanovoï.*

and, to Anna Feodorovna's surprise, with her, without
offering to kiss her hand; and he also shook hands with
Liza, at the same time looking straight into her eyes
and craftily smiling his pleasing smile. This glance
again somewhat disconcerted the maiden.

"He is very handsome," she said to herself, "only he
is quite too conceited."

CHAPTER XIV

"WELL, now, are n't you ashamed?" exclaimed Polozof, when the two officers had returned to their chamber.
"I tried to lose, and I kept nudging you under the table.
Now does n't your conscience prick you? The poor old
lady was quite beside herself."

The count burst into a terrible fit of laughter.

"A most comical dame! How abused she felt!"

And again he began to laugh so heartily that even
Johann, who was standing in front of him, cast down
his eyes to conceal a smile.

"And here is the son of an old family friend! Ha,
ha, ha!" continued the count, in a gale of laughter.

"No, indeed, it is not right. I felt really sorry for
her," said the cornet.

"What rubbish! How young you are! What! did
you think I was going to lose? Why should I lose? I
only lose when I don't know any better. Ten rubles,
brother, will come in handy. You must look on life in
a practical way, or else you will always be a fool."

Polozof said nothing more: in the first place, he
wanted to think by himself about Liza, who seemed
to him to be an extraordinarily pure and beautiful
creature.

He undressed, and lay down on the clean, soft bed
which had been made ready for him.

"How absurd all these honors and the glory of war!"
he thought to himself, gazing at the window shaded by
the shawl, through the interstices of which crept the

pale rays of the moon. "Here is happiness — to live in a quiet nook, with a gentle, bright, simple-hearted wife; that is enduring, true happiness."

But somehow he did not communicate these imaginations to his friend; and he did not even speak of the rustic maiden, though he felt sure that the count was also thinking about her.

"Why don't you undress?" he asked the count, who was walking up and down the room.

"Oh, I don't feel like sleeping! Put out the candle if you like," said he. "I can undress in the dark."

And he continued to walk back and forth.

"He does not feel sleepy," repeated Polozof, who after the evening's experiences felt more than ever dissatisfied with the count's influence on him, and disposed to revolt against it. "I imagine," he reasoned, mentally addressing Turbin, "what thoughts are now trooping through that well-combed head of yours. And I saw how she pleased you. But you are not the kind to appreciate that simple-hearted, pure-minded creature. Mina is the one for you; you want the epaulets of a colonel. Indeed, I have a mind to ask him how he liked her."

And Polozof was about to address him, but he hesitated; he felt that not only he was not in the right frame of mind to discuss with him if the count's views of Liza were what he interpreted them to be, but that he should not have the force of mind necessary for him to disagree with him, so accustomed was he to submit to an influence which for him grew each day more burdensome and unrighteous.

"Where are you going?" he asked, as the count took his cap and went to the door.

"I am going to the stable; I wish to see if everything is all right."

"Strange!" thought the cornet; but he blew out the candle, and, trying to dispel the absurdly jealous and hostile thoughts that arose against his former friend, he turned over on the other side.

Anna Feodorovna, meantime, having crossed herself,

as usual, and kissed her brother, her daughter, and her *protégée* affectionately, also retired to her room.

Long had it been since the old lady had experienced in a single day such powerful sensations. She could not even say her prayers in tranquillity; all the melancholy but vivid remembrances of the late count, and of this young dandy who had so ruthlessly taken advantage of her, kept coming up in her mind.

Nevertheless, she undressed as usual, and drank a half-glass of kvas which stood ready on the little table near the bed, and lay down. Her beloved cat came softly into the room. Anna Feodorovna called her, and began to stroke her fur, and listen to her purring; but still she could not go to sleep.

"It is the cat that disturbs me," she said to herself, and pushed her away. The cat fell to the floor softly, and, slowly waving her bushy tail, got up on the oven;[1] and then the maid, who slept in the room on the floor, brought her felt and spread it down, put out the candle, and lighted the night-lamp.

At last the maid began to snore; but sleep still refused to come to Anna Feodorovna, and calm her excited imagination. The face of the hussar kept arising before her mental vision, when she shut her eyes; and it seemed to her that it appeared in various strange guises in her room, when she opened her eyes and looked at the commode, at the table, and her white raiment hanging up in the feeble light of the night-lamp. Then it seemed hot to her in the feather-bed, and the ticking of the watch on the table became unendurable; exasperating to the last degree, the snoring of the maid. She wakened her, and bade her cease snoring.

Again the thoughts of her daughter, the old count, and of the young count, and of the game of *préférence*, became strangely mixed in her mind. Now she seemed to see herself waltzing with the former count; she saw her own plump, white shoulders, she felt on them some one's kisses, and then she saw her daughter in the young count's embrace.

[1] The *lezhanka*, a part of the oven built out as a sort of couch.

Once more Ustiushka began to snore. ....

"No, it's somehow different now, the men aren't the same. *He* was ready to fling himself into the fire for my sake. Yes, I was worth doing it for! But this one, have no fear, is sound asleep like a goose,[1] happy because he won the game, and with never a thought of wooing. How his father fell on his knees, and said, 'Whatever you desire I will do; I would kill myself in a moment for you; what do you desire?' And he would have killed himself, if I had bade him!" ....

Suddenly the sound of bare feet was heard in the corridor; and Liza, with a handkerchief thrown over her head, came in, pale and trembling, and almost fell on her mother's bed. ....

After saying good-night to her mother, Liza had gone alone to the room that had been her uncle's. Putting on a white jacket, throwing a handkerchief round her thick, long braids, she put out the light, opened the window, and curled up in a chair, turning her dreamy eyes to the pond, which was now all shining with silver brilliancy.

All her ordinary occupations and interests came up before her now in an entirely different light; her capricious old mother, unreasoning love for whom had become a part of her very soul, her feeble but amiable old uncle, the domestics, the peasants, who worshiped their young mistress, the milch cows and the calves; all this nature which was forever the same in its continual death and resurrection, amid which she had grown up, with love for others, and with the love of others for her, — all this, which had hitherto given her such a gentle, agreeable peace of mind, suddenly seemed to her something different; it all seemed to her dismal, superfluous.

It was as if some one said to her, "Fool, fool! For twenty years you have been occupied in trivialities, you have been serving others without reason, and you have not known what life, what happiness, were!"

This was what she thought now as she gazed down into the depths of the motionless moonlit garden, and the thought came over her with vastly more force than

---

[1] *Durak durakom*, a downright fool.

ever before. And what was it induced this train of
thought? It was not in the least a sudden love for the
count, as might easily be supposed. On the contrary,
he did not please her. It might rather have been the
cornet of whom she was thinking; but he was homely,
poor, and taciturn. She naturally enough forgot him,
and with indignation and annoyance recalled to her
memory the features of the count.

" No, he is not the one," she said to herself.

Her ideal was so charming! It was an ideal which
might have been loved in the midst of this night, in the
midst of this nature, without infringing its supernal
beauty; an ideal not in the least circumscribed by the
necessity of reducing it to coarse reality.

In days gone by her lonely situation, and the absence
of men who might have attracted her, caused all the
strength of the love which Providence has implanted
impartially in the hearts of each one of us, to be still
intact and potential in her soul. But now she had been
living so long with the pathetic happiness of feeling
that she possessed in her heart this something, and occasionally opening the mysterious chalice of her heart,
of rejoicing in the contemplation of its riches, ready to
pour out without stint on some one all that it contained!

God grant that she may not have to take this melancholy delight with her to the tomb! Who knows if
there be any better and more powerful delight, or if it
is not the only true and possible one?

" O Father in heaven," she thought, "is it possible
that I have lost my youth and my happiness, and that
they will never return?.... Will they never return again?
Can it be really true?"

She gazed in the direction of the moon at the bright,
far-off sky, studded with white wavy clouds, which were
sweeping on toward the moon, blotting out the little
stars.

" If the moon seizes that topmost little cloud, then it
means that it is true," she thought.

A thin, smokelike ribbon of cloud passed over the
lower half of the brilliant orb, and gradually the light

grew fainter on the turf, on the linden tops, on
the pond: the black shadows of the trees grew less
distinct. And as if to harmonize with the gloomy
shade that was enveloping nature, a gentle breeze stirred
through the leaves, and brought to the window the dewy
fragrance of the leaves, the moist earth, and the bloom-
ing lilacs.

"No, it is not true!" she said, trying to console herself; "but if the nightingale should sing this night,
then I should take it to mean that all my forebodings
are nonsense, and that there is no need of losing hope."

And long she sat in silence, as if expecting some one,
while once more all grew bright and full of life; and
then again and again the clouds passed over the moon,
making everything somber.

She was even beginning to grow drowsy, as she sat
there by the window, when she was aroused by the
nightingale's melodious trills clearly echoing across the
pond.

The rustic maiden opened her eyes. Once more,
with a new enjoyment, her whole soul was dedicated to
that mysterious union with the nature which so calmly
and serenely spread out before her.

She leaned on both elbows. A certain haunting sensation of gentle melancholy oppressed her heart; and
tears of pure, deep love, burning for satisfaction, good
consoling tears, sprang to her eyes.

She leaned her arms on the window-sill, and rested
her head on them. Her favorite prayer seemed of its
own accord to arise in her soul, and thus she fell asleep
with moist eyes.

The pressure of some one's hand awakened her. She
started up. But the touch was gentle and pleasant.
The hand squeezed hers with a stronger pressure.

Suddenly she realized the true state of things,
screamed, tore herself away; and, trying to make herself believe that it was not the count who, bathed in
the brilliant moonlight, was standing in front of her
window. she ran from the room. ....

CHAPTER XV

IT was indeed the count. When he heard the maiden's shriek, and the cough of the watchman who was coming from the other side of the fence to investigate, he had the sensation of being a thief caught in the act, and darted across the dew-drenched grass, to hide in the depths of the park.

"Oh, what a fool I was!" he said instinctively. "I frightened her. I ought to have been more gentle, to have wakened her by gentle words. Oh, I am a beast, a blundering beast."

He paused and listened. The watchman had come through the wicket-gate into the park, dragging his cane along the sanded walk.

It was necessary for him to hide. He went toward the pond. The frogs made him tremble as they hastily sprang from under his very feet into the water. There, notwithstanding his wet feet, he crouched down on his heels, and proceeded to recall all he had done, — how he had crept through the hedge, found her window, and at last caught a glimpse of a white shadow; how several times, while on the watch for the least noise, he had crept up to her window, and then hastened away again; how at one moment it seemed to him that doubtless she was waiting for him with vexation in her heart that he was so dilatory; and at the next how impossible it seemed that she would so easily make an assignation with him; and how, finally coming to the conclusion that, through the embarrassment naturally felt by a country maiden, she was only pretending to be asleep, he had resolutely gone up to the window, and seen clearly her position, and then suddenly, for some occult reason, had run away again; and only after a powerful effort of self-control, being ashamed of his cowardice, he had gone boldly up to her and touched her on the hand.

The watchman again coughed, and, shutting the squeaky gate, went out of the park. The window in the young girl's room was shut, and the wooden shutters inside were drawn.

The count was awfully vexed to see this. He would have given a good deal for the chance to begin it all over again; he would not have acted so stupidly. ....

"A marvelous girl! what freshness! simply charming! And so I lost her. .... Stupid beast that I was."

However, as he was not in the mood to go to sleep yet, he walked, as chance should lead, along the path, through the linden alley, with the resolute steps of a man who has been angry.

And now for him also this night brought, as its gifts of reconciliation, a strange, calming melancholy, and a craving for love.

The clay path, here and there dotted with sprouting grass or dry twigs, was flecked with patches of pale light where the moon sent its direct rays through the thick foliage of the lindens. Here and there a bending bough, as if loaded down with gray moss, gleamed on one side. The silvered foliage occasionally rustled.

At the house there was no light in the windows; all sounds were hushed, only the nightingale filled with his song all the immensity of silent and glorious space.

"God! what a night, what a marvelous night!" thought the count, breathing in the cool fragrance of the park. "Somehow I feel melancholy, as if I were dissatisfied with myself and with others, and dissatisfied with my whole life. But what a splendid, sweet girl! Perhaps she was really offended."

Here his fancies changed. He imagined himself there in the garden with this country maiden in various and most remarkable situations; then his mistress Mina supplanted the maiden's place.

"What a fool I am! I ought simply to have put my arm around her waist, and kissed her."

And with this regret the count returned to his room. The cornet was not yet asleep. He immediately turned over in bed, and looked at the count.

"Aren't you asleep?" asked the count.

"No."

"Shall I tell you what happened?"

"Well."

"No, I'd better not tell you. .... Yes, I will too. Move your legs over a little."

And the count, who had already given up vain regret for his unsuccessful intrigue, sat down with a gay smile on his comrade's bed.

"Could you imagine that the young lady of the house gave me a rendezvous?"

"What is that you say?" screamed Polozof, leaping out of bed.

"Well, now listen."

"But how? When? It cannot be!"

"See here; while you were making out your accounts in *préférence*, she told me that she would this night be sitting at the window, and that it was possible to get in at that window. Now, this is what it means to be a practical man; while you were there reckoning up with the old woman, I was arranging this little affair. You yourself heard her say openly in your presence, that she was going to sit at the window to-night, and look at the pond."

"Yes; but she said that without any meaning in it."

"I am not so sure whether she said it purposely or otherwise. Maybe she did not wish to come at it all at once, only it looked like that. But a wretched piece of work came out of it. Like a perfect fool I spoilt the whole thing," he added, scornfully smiling at himself.

"Well, what is it? Where have you been?"

The count told him the whole story, with the exception of his irresolute and repeated advances.

"I spoilt it myself; I ought to have been bolder. She screamed and ran away from the window."

"So she screamed and ran away?" repeated the cornet, replying with a constrained smile to the count's smile, which had such a long and powerful influence on him.

"Yes, but now it's time to go to sleep."

Polozof again turned his back to the door, and lay in silence for ten minutes. God knows what was going on in his soul; but when he turned over again, his face was full of passion and resolution.

"Count Turbin," said he, in a broken voice.

"Are you dreaming, or not?" replied the count, calmly. "What is it, Cornet Polozof?"

"Count Turbin, you are a cowardly scoundrel," cried Polozof, and he sprang from the bed.

CHAPTER XVI

THE next day the battalion departed. The officers did not see any of the household, or bid them farewell. Neither did they speak together.

It was understood that they were to fight their duel when they came to the next halting-place. But Captain Schultz, a good comrade, an admirable horseman, who was loved by everybody in the regiment, and had been chosen by the count for his second, succeeded in arranging the affair in such a manner that not only they did not fight, but that no one in the regiment knew about the matter; and Turbin and Polozof, though their old relations of friendship were never restored, still said "thou," and met at meals and at the gaming-table.

FAMILY HAPPINESS

(1859)

PART FIRST

CHAPTER I

SONYA and I were in mourning for our mother, who had died in the autumn, and we had spent the whole winter in the country alone with Katya.

Katya was an old family friend, our governess, who had brought all of us up, and whom I had known and loved ever since my memory began. Sonya was my younger sister.

The winter at our old house at Pokrovskoye had been dreary and forlorn. The weather had been cold and windy, so that the snowdrifts were heaped high above our windows; the panes had been almost constantly covered with frost, so that nothing could be seen out of them, and we had been kept housed almost all the time. It was rare that any friends came to see us, and, if they did, they brought no increase of joy or cheer to our home. All wore long faces, and spoke with sub-dued voices, as if afraid of awakening some one; all refrained from laughing, but they sighed, and often shed tears and looked solemnly at me, and especially at little Sonya, in her black frock.

The presence of death still seemed to be felt in the house; the grief and horror of death were in the very atmosphere.

Mamma's chamber was shut up, and I felt a sensation

of pain, and also a strange impulse to look into that cold and empty chamber, when I passed by it on my way to bed.

At that time I was seventeen, and mamma, the very year that she died, was intending to move to the city for the sake of "bringing me out."

The loss of my mother was a terrible grief for me; but I must confess that there was associated with it the feeling that I was young and pretty — for everybody told me so — and that it was a pity to have wasted another winter alone in the country. Before the end of the winter this painful sense of loneliness and tedium increased to such a degree that I refused to leave my room, I kept the piano shut, and never took up a book.

When Katya advised me to do this thing or that, I replied: "I don't wish to, I can't," and the question arose in my soul, "Why? Why do anything, when the best days of my life are thus going to waste? Why?"

And to this question there was no other answer than tears.

They told me that I was growing thin, and losing my beauty, but even that made no difference to me.

Why? Who was to see?

It seemed to me that my whole life was destined to be spent in this dull solitude and helpless gloom, from which I had no power or even desire to make my escape.

Toward the end of the winter, Katya began to worry about me, and resolved, when the opportunity offered, to take me abroad. But in order to do this we needed money; and we had a very dim idea of what our mother had left us, and therefore we waited from day to day for our guardian to come and settle up our affairs.

In March he came.

"Now, thank the Lord!" said Katya to me, one day, as I was wandering about, from room to room, like a shadow, idle, listless, aimless; "Sergyeï Mikhaïluitch has come; he sends to inquire after us, and will be here to dinner. Come, now! show a little energy, my dear Masha," she added. "Otherwise, what will he think of you? He is so fond of you both!"

Sergyeï Mikhaïluitch was a near neighbor of ours, and a friend of our late father, though he was much his junior. Not only would his coming change all our plans, and enable us to leave the country, but from childhood I had been accustomed to love and honor him; and so, when Katya advised me to "show a little energy," she knew very well that it would mortify me more to appear in an unfavorable light before him than before any other of our friends. Moreover, not only did I share the traditional attachment for him felt by every one in the house, from Katya and Sonya (whose godfather he was) down to the stable-boy, but in my eyes he had a special interest, owing to a word which mamasha had dropped in my hearing. She said that she would like to find such a man as a husband for me.

At that time her words struck me as strange and disagreeable, for my hero was a quite different sort of man. My ideal was graceful, slender, pale, and melancholy, while Sergyeï Mikhaïluitch was no longer young, was tall and stout, and, as it seemed to me, always cheerful; but nevertheless those words of mamasha's had struck my imagination, and, as long as six years before, when I was eleven and he had addressed me by the familiar *tui*, thou, had romped with me, and called me "little maid-violet," [1] I had asked myself, not without dread, what I should do if he suddenly asked me to become his wife.

Before dinner, for which Katya had prepared a cream pie and a spinach sauce, Sergyeï Mikhaïluitch arrived. From the window I saw him drive up toward the house, in his light sleigh; but, as soon as he disappeared around the corner, I hastened into the drawing-room, wishing to make it appear that I was not too eagerly expecting him.

But as soon as I heard the sound of his feet in the anteroom, and his hearty voice and Katya's steps, I could not restrain myself, but ran out to meet him. He was holding Katya by the hand, and talking in his deep voice. A smile was on his face.

When he saw me, he paused and gazed at me for

---

[1] *Dyevotchka-fiyalka.*

some little time without bowing. I felt awkward, and was conscious that the color was rising in my face.

"Ah! is this really you?" he exclaimed, in his simple, straightforward manner, holding out his hands and coming toward me. "Can it be possible you have changed so much? How you have grown! Where is my violet gone? Now you are a full-blown rose."

He took my hand in his big hand, pressed it so firmly, so heartily, that it almost hurt me. I supposed that he was going to kiss it, and I bent toward him; but he merely pressed it again, and looked straight into my eyes with his frank, merry glance.

I had not seen him for six years. He had changed much, had grown older and darker, and now wore side-whiskers, that were very unbecoming to him; but he had the same unaffected manners, a frank, honorable face, with large features, intelligent, brilliant eyes, and an affectionate, almost childlike smile.

In five minutes he had ceased to be a stranger, and seemed to all of us like a member of the family — even to the servants, who were delighted at his coming, as was evident by their alacrity in serving him.

His behavior was entirely different from that of the neighbors who came after mamasha's death, and who felt constrained to speak in whispers and to shed tears while they were in the house; he, on the contrary, was talkative and jolly, and did not say a word about mother, so that, at first, this apparent indifference struck me as strange and even unbecoming in a man who had been so intimate with our family. But afterward I discovered that it was not indifference, but sincerity; and I was grateful to him for it.

In the evening, Katya sat down, in mamasha's old place in the drawing-room, to pour the tea. Sonya and I took our seats near her; old Grigori brought him one of papasha's pipes that had been put away, and, just as in days gone by, he began to walk up and down the room.

"How many terrible changes in this home, when you come to think of it!" he exclaimed, and stopped short.

"Yes," said Katya, with a sigh, and, putting the cover on the samovar, she looked at him, and almost burst into tears.

"And I suppose you remember your father?" he asked, addressing me.

"A little," I replied.

"And how much you would be to each other now!" he continued, looking gently and thoughtfully at my forehead and hair. "Your father was a very dear friend of mine!" he added, in a still gentler voice, and it seemed to me that his eyes became more luminous than ever.

"Well, it seemed good to God to take *her* also!" rejoined Katya, and immediately she laid her napkin on the teapot, took out her handkerchief, and burst into tears.

"Yes, terrible changes in this home!" he repeated, turning away. "Sonya, show me your toys," he added, in a moment or two, and went into the "hall." With my eyes brimming with tears, I looked at Katya as he went out.

"He's such a splendid friend!" was her answer.

And, in truth, I felt a sensation of warmth and comfort around my heart, at the thought of this good man, though he was such a stranger.

As we sat in the parlor, we heard Sonya's piping voice, and his merry romping with her. I poured out his tea, and heard him sit down at the piano, and begin to touch the keys with Sonya's little fingers.

"Marya Aleksandrovna!" I heard him say, "come here and play me something."

I liked the simple and friendly way in which he laid his commands upon me; I got up and went to him.

"Here, play this," said he, opening the copy of Beethoven to the adagio of the *Sonata quasi una Fantasia*.[1] "Let us see how you play," he added, and went with his glass of tea into a corner of the room.

For some reason I felt that with him it was useless to refuse or to make excuses for playing badly; I sat

[1] Op. 27, No. 2, known familiarly as the "Moonlight" Sonata. — ED.

down obediently at the piano, and tried to play to the best of my ability, though I was afraid of his criticism, for I knew that he understood and loved music.

The adagio corresponded with the sentiment of the reminiscences awakened at the tea-table, and I imagine that I played tolerably well. But he did not ask me to play the scherzo.

"No, you wouldn't play that well," said he, coming up to the piano, "no matter about it; but you didn't play the first badly. You must have some comprehension of music."

This praise, which was certainly not extravagant, so delighted me that I even blushed. It was such a novel and pleasant experience for me that he, a friend and equal of my father, should talk seriously with me as if I were worthy of his notice, and no longer as with a child, as used to be the case.

Katya went up-stairs to put Sonya to bed, and we two remained in the "hall."

He told me about my father, and what a bond of sympathy united them, and what a happy life they led in those days when I was a mere child, amusing myself with picture-books and dolls. And his stories made me see my father for the first time in the light of a simple-hearted and lovable man, such as I had never thought of him before.

He also asked me about my tastes, my reading, and my ambitions, and gave me advice. He was now no longer merely a merry, jesting playmate, teasing me and making toys for me, but a grave, earnest, and lovable man, to whom I felt involuntarily drawn by affection and sympathy. While I talked with him, I felt perfectly at my ease, and enjoyed it; but, at the same time, I could not help feeling a certain strain on me. I was afraid for every word that I spoke; I had a strong desire to be worthy of his affection, which hitherto had been given to me simply because I was my father's daughter.

After putting Sonya to bed, Katya rejoined us, and complained to him of my apathy, of which I had said nothing.

"It seems, then, she has failed to tell me the principal thing," he said, with a smile, and shaking his head reproachfully at me.

"Why speak of it?" said I; "it is very stupid, and besides, it will pass away."

It actually seemed to me at that moment that my sense of lassitude not only would pass away, but that it had already passed away, and that it never had been.

"It's unfortunate not to be able to endure solitude," said he. "Aren't you a grown-up young lady?"

"Of course I am," said I, with a laugh.

"Well, she's a poor kind of young lady who is lively only while she is admired, and as soon as she is alone loses her spirits and takes no interest in anything; all for mere show and nothing for reality."

"You have a fine opinion of me," said I, for the sake of saying something.

"No!" said he, after a little silence. "It is not all in vain that you look like your father; there *is* something in you," and again his kind, penetrating eyes gave me a flattering look, and filled me with a strangely agreeable confusion.

Now for the first time I noticed that his face, which had impressed me as being so jovial, had a look peculiar to himself; serene at first, but afterward becoming more and more thoughtful, and even rather gloomy.

"There is no reason and no propriety in your being down-hearted," said he. "You have your music, which you understand, your books, your studies; and your whole life lies before you, and now is the only time in which you can prepare yourself for it, so that you will have nothing to regret. In a year it may be too late."

He talked to me like a father or an uncle, and I was conscious that he had constantly to exercise self-control not to look down on me.

I felt offended that he considered me beneath him, and at the same time it pleased me that he found it worth while for my sake, and my sake alone, to make an effort to show his friendship in this way.

The rest of the evening he talked business with Katya.

"Well, good-by, my dear friends," said he, getting up and coming over to me, and taking me by the hand.

"When shall we see you again?" inquired Katya.

"This spring," was his reply, as he still held my hand. "Now I am going to Danilovka," — that was another estate of ours, — "I shall look into your affairs there and make what arrangements I can; then I am going to Moscow on some business of my own, and then in the summer we shall see each other again."

"Now, why must you be gone so long?" I asked, feeling terribly depressed; in fact, I had hoped that we should see him every day, and suddenly I felt so melancholy and sad that all my former unhappiness seemed to return. This must have been expressed in my eyes and voice.

"Try to busy yourself as much as you can, and don't get down-hearted," said he, in a tone which seemed to me altogether too cool and natural. "When spring comes, I shall make you pass your examination," he added, dropping my hand, and not looking at me.

In the anteroom, where we were standing while he put on his shuba, again his eyes seemed to search me.

"It's no use for him to take so much trouble," said I to myself; "I wonder if he thinks I like to have him stare at me in that way. He is an excellent man, very excellent .... but if only .... "

For a wonder, it was very late when Katya and I went to bed, and we talked all the evening, not about him, but about how we should spend the coming summer, and where and how we should live next winter.

My bugbear of a question, *why*, did not recur to me. It seemed to me very simple and clear that one ought to live to be happy, and I imagined that the future would bring much happiness. Suddenly, as it were, our Pokrovsky house, so old and gloomy, presented itself to my imagination overflowing with life and light.

CHAPTER II

SPRING had now come.

My former depression was gone, and its place was occupied by the dreamy melancholy of springtime, and by vague hopes and desires.

Though I lived in a healthier way than at the beginning of the winter, and occupied myself with my sister Sonya, and music and reading, still I used often to go into the garden, and wander long, long, up and down the paths, or sit on the bench, my mind filled with all sorts of thoughts, hopes, and desires.

Sometimes, especially when there was a moon, I would sit at the window of my room all night long, and when morning came I would throw on a single garment, and often go, without waking Katya, down into the park and across the dewy grass to the pond; once, I even went out into the field, and, alone and in the night, made the entire circuit of the park.

Now it is hard for me to recall and understand the illusions which at that time filled my imagination. Even when I succeed, I can scarcely believe that my dreams were made of such stuff, they were so strange and remote from the reality.

Toward the end of May, Sergyeĭ Mikhaĭluitch returned from his journey, as he had promised.

His first call was toward evening, and he took us entirely by surprise. We were sitting on the terrace and preparing to drink tea. The park was already clothed in green, and the nightingales made their haunt in every thicket over all Petrovka. The tufted branches of the lilac bushes were everywhere covered with white and purple, with a hint of flowers on the point of bursting into bloom. The foliage of the linden alley was translucent in the setting sun. A fresh, cool shadow lay across the terrace. The grass was already wet with the heavy fall of evening dew. In the yard back of the park were heard the last sounds of day, the bustle of the cattle driven in from pasture. The simple-minded

Nikon crossed in front of the terrace, along the little path, with his watering-pot, and the cooling stream from the nozzle soon began to make the broken soil dark around the stems of the dahlias and their supports.

Near us, on the terrace, on a white cloth, stood the brightly polished samovar, bubbling and boiling, together with cream, biscuits, and cold meat. Katya, with her plump hands, was dipping the teacups like a careful housewife. I could not wait for my tea, for I was hungry after my bath, and was eating a piece of bread spread with thick, fresh cream. I had on a gingham blouse with flowing sleeves, and my wet hair was covered with a handkerchief. Katya was the first to see him through the window.

"Ah! Sergyeï Mikhaïluitch!" she exclaimed, "we were only just talking about you!"

I jumped up, and was going to run up-stairs to change my dress, but he met me just as I was at the door.

"Now, what is the use of ceremony in the country?" said he, glancing, with a smile, at my head and the handkerchief. "You see, you are not ashamed to wear it before Grigori, and I am no more than Grigori."

But at that very instant it seemed to me that he looked at me in a way Grigori would never have thought of doing, and I felt ill at ease.

"I will be back immediately," said I, starting away from him.

"What's the harm as you are?" he cried after me. "You are quite like a young peasant girl."

"How strangely he looked at me," said I to myself, as I hurriedly dressed myself up-stairs. "Well, thank God, he's come; now, it will be more lively."

After a hasty glance at the mirror, I gayly ran downstairs, and, without disguising the fact that I had hurried, I went on the terrace all out of breath. He was sitting at the table, and telling Katya about our affairs. When he saw me, he smiled, and went on talking. According to him, our affairs were in a satisfactory condition. It was necessary for us merely to spend the

summer in the country, and then we could go for Sonya's
education either to Petersburg or abroad.

"Well, now, if you could only be with us while we
were abroad," said Katya. "But if we must be by ourselves it would be worse than being in the woods."

"Ah, how glad I should be to go round the world
with you!" he said, half serious, half in jest.

"All right!" said I, "let us go round the world."
He smiled and shook his head.

"But my mother, and my business?" he asked.
"Well, as that is out of the question, now tell me, please,
how you have been spending your time. Have you
been melancholy any more?"

When I told him that during his absence I had been
busy, and had not been troubled with depression, and
when Katya corroborated my words, he praised me;
and both his words and his looks were flattering, as if I
were a child, and he had the right to patronize me. It
seemed to me necessary to give him a faithful and cir-
cumstantial account of all that I had done in the right
direction, and to confess, as before a priest, all that he
might not approve.

The evening was so warm and pleasant that, after the
tea things had been carried away, we still sat on the terrace; and the conversation was so full of meaning for
me that I did not notice how, little by little, the sounds
of the people about us had died away. From all sides
arose more fragrantly the perfumes of the flowers; the
abundant dew was falling on the sward; the nightingale,
trilling in the privet bushes near us, hushed his song
when he heard our voices; the starry sky seemed to
bend down nearer to us.

Only when a bat suddenly flew under the awning over
the terrace, and fluttered noiselessly about my white
shawl, did I notice that it was already dark. I huddled
close to the wall, and was opening my mouth to scream;
but the bat, with the same swift, noiseless flight, darted
out from under the awning, and disappeared in the darkness of the park.

"How I like your Pokrovskoye!" said he, making a

sudden change in the conversation. "I should like to spend my whole life sitting here on this terrace!"

"Well, then, why not sit here?" suggested Katya.

"That is very well," he went on, "but life does not sit still."

"Why don't you get married?" asked Katya. "You would make any one a splendid husband."

"Why, because I like a quiet life, think you?" and he laughed. "No, Katerina [1] Karlovna, there's no hope for you and me. Long ago all my friends ceased to regard me as a marrying man; and all the more for this very reason I have come to the conclusion that it is best this way; that's a fact!"

It seemed to me that he said that with a sort of affected gayety in his manner.

"Indeed, that's good! You have lived all of thirty-six years and are tired of life!" said Katya.

"Ah, but how much I have gone through!" he continued. "My only wish is to live a quiet life. But, to get married, something else is necessary..... Ask her," he went on to say, nodding his head toward me. "It is for such girls as she to get married. And you and I will look on and rejoice in their happiness!"

There was an undertone of sadness in his voice, and an intensity which did not escape my attention. He was silent for a little, and neither Katya nor I said a word.

"Now, just conceive of such a thing," he went on, turning around on his chair; "supposing I should suddenly, by some unfortunate chance, marry some maiden of seventeen, such a girl as Mash .... as Marya Aleksandrovna. That's an admirable illustration, I am very glad that I found such a one, it is the very best one possible!"

I laughed, and could not see any reason for his gladness at such an illustration, or where its application lay. ....

"Now," said he, addressing me in a bantering tone, "tell me honestly, your hand on your heart, would it not

[1] Katya is the diminutive of Katerina; Sonya of Sofia, Masha of Marya.

be a trial for you to marry an old man who has lived out all his days, whose only desire is a quiet life, while God knows where you'll go or what you want?"

I felt awkward, and made no answer, not knowing what to say.

"Now, see here, this must not be taken as an offer," said he, smiling, "but truly tell me, do you dream of such a husband when evenings you wander down the linden alley, or would you be unhappy with such a one?"

"No, not unhappy ...." I began.

"Nor yet contented," said he, taking the words out of my mouth.

"Yes, but you see, I may be mis...."

But again he interrupted me.

"Well, now you see she is perfectly right, and I am so grateful to her for her frankness, and glad that we could have had this talk. Nevertheless, as far as I am concerned, such a marriage would be the greatest unhappiness," he added.

"What a queer man you are; you haven't changed in the least," said Katya, and she went in from the terrace to order the supper put on.

After she left us we sat in silence; around us not a sound was heard, except that the nightingale, not now in fitful snatches, as his habit is earlier in the afternoon, but with deliberate calmness, since now it was already night, poured out his plaint over all the garden, and another, down in the ravine below, for the first time this spring, replied to him from afar. The one nearest to us seemed to be listening for a moment, and still clearer and more intensely rang out the liquid harmonious trill. And with sovereign calmness their songs resounded in this world of night, so peculiarly their own, so strange to us.

The gardener went to the orangery to sleep, the sound of his heavy boots growing fainter and fainter along the path. Some one gave a shrill whistle twice, at the foot of the hill, and then there was silence again. The foliage rustled almost inaudibly, the canvas awning over the terrace stirred a little, and a delicious fragrance was wafted across the terrace.

It seemed to me awkward to sit in silence, after what had been said; but I now was at a loss for something to say.

I looked at him. His eyes, gleaming in the twilight, were fixed on me.

"It is good to be alive in the world," said he.

For some reason I sighed.

"What is it?"

"Yes, indeed, it is good to be alive in the world," said I, echoing his words.

And again we relapsed into silence, and again I felt a sense of constraint. It occurred to me that I had offended him by agreeing with him that he was an old man; and I was anxious to soothe him, but I did not know how to do so.

"Well, good-by," said he, getting up. "Matushka is expecting me home to supper. I have scarcely seen her to-day."

"But I wanted to play my new sonata to you," said I.

"Some other time," said he, coolly, as it seemed to me.

"Good-by." [1]

It now more than ever seemed to me that I had offended him, and I felt sorry. Katya and I escorted him to the porch; and we stood in the courtyard, looking down the road, where he was soon lost to sight.

As soon as the sound of his horse's feet died away, I went around on the terrace and began once more to gaze down into the garden; and, in the dewy darkness, which muffled the sounds of night, long I saw and heard all that fancy made me see and hear.

He came a second and a third time, and the constraint arising from the strange conversation which had arisen between us entirely wore away, and did not return.

As the summer went on, he rode over to see us two or three times a week, and I became so accustomed to his visits that when any unusual length of time elapsed without our seeing him I became lonely, and was vexed

[1] *Prashchaïte*, adieu.

with him and thought that he was not nice to neglect me so.

He treated me as a dear young comrade, asked me questions, encouraged the most cordial frankness, gave me advice, stimulated me, sometimes scolded me and checked me.

But in spite of all his endeavor to keep himself down on a level with me, I was conscious that, back of what was manifest to me in him, there lay a whole world into which he felt it unnecessary to admit me; and this it was which had the greatest influence on my imagination, and most attracted me to him.

I knew from Katya and our neighbors that, over and above his care for his aged mother, with whom he lived, over and above his responsibilities as a landed proprietor and as our guardian, he had to exercise certain functions connected with the nobility, which were most distasteful to him.

But how he looked on all this, and what his convictions, plans, and hopes were, I never could get the slightest intimation from him. As soon as I led the conversation round to his own affairs, he frowned in his characteristic manner, as much as to say, " Please, I beg of you; this does not concern you," and brought up some other topic of conversation.

At first this offended me, but afterward I became so accustomed to talking about matters concerning myself alone that it seemed quite natural.

Another thing which used at first to displease me, but afterward came to be even pleasant, was his perfect indifference and apparent contempt for my personal appearance. Never by a look or a word did he hint that I was pretty; but, on the contrary, he frowned or smiled when I was called pretty in his presence. He even took pains to pick out my defects and banter me on the subject of them. The fashionable gowns and the way in which Katya liked to do up my hair for festive occasions aroused merely his sarcastic comments, which hurt the good Katya's feelings, and at first quite disconcerted me.

Katya, who was convinced in her own mind that I pleased him, could not understand at all why he did not like the woman who pleased him to appear in the most attractive light.

But I quickly came to see what he wanted. He was anxious to feel assured that I was free from coquetry. And when I understood that, then I made it evident that there was not a shadow of coquetry about me, in my dress or my hair or my actions. But this very thing showed like an embroidery in white worsted, that I had the coquetry of artless simplicity at a time when as yet artlessness was not natural to me.

I was aware that he loved me, but whether as a child or as a woman I did not ask myself; I prized his love, and, being conscious that he considered me the very best girl in the world, I could not help hoping that he might still persist in this illusion.

And I involuntarily helped to deceive him. But the very act of deceiving him in this way made me better. I felt how much wiser and nobler it was for me to show the better side of my soul than of my body.

My hair, my hands, my face, my manners, whatever they were, good or bad, it seemed to me, he understood and appreciated at a glance, so that I could not add anything to my exterior, except the desire to deceive.

But my soul he did not know, because he loved it, and because it was all the time expanding and developing; and thus it was that I could and did deceive him. And how easy it was to manage him when I clearly understood this. My unreasonable agitation, my awkwardness of movement, entirely disappeared.

I had the consciousness that, no matter how he saw me, whether from front face or in profile, whether sitting or standing, whether my hair was up or down, he knew me thoroughly, and, as it seemed to me, was satisfied with me as I was.

I am certain that if, contrary to his habit, he had followed the example of others, and told me that I was pretty, I should not have been in the least delighted. But, on the other hand, how happy and light-hearted I was when, after some insignificant remark of mine, he looked steadily at me, and said, in a voice which trembled a little, in spite of his attempt to impart a bantering tone : —

"Yes, yes, there is *something* in you. You are a splendid girl ; I must tell you so."

And why was it that at that time I received a reward such as filled my heart with pride and joy? Because I said that I sympathized with the love of old Grigori for his little granddaughter, or because I was moved to tears by reading some poetry or novel, or because I preferred Mozart to Schulhof !

And the preternatural keenness of intuition, by which, at that time, I selected what was good, and worthy of admiration, struck me as marvelous ; and yet, assuredly, I was perfectly ignorant of what was good and what ought to be liked.

The most of my former habits and tastes had not pleased him, and a movement of his brow, a glance, was all that was needed to show that he did not like what it was on my tongue to say, and my peculiar disgusted and almost scornful expression, as it seemed to me, made him see that I detested what I had loved before.

It often happened that, when he was going to give me advice about anything, it seemed to me that I knew beforehand what he was going to say. He would ask me a question and look into my eyes, and that look of his sufficed to draw from me the thought which he was after. All my thoughts and feelings at that time were his, not mine ; but by becoming mine they went to make up my life, and fill it with light. Absolutely, without being myself conscious of it, I began to look at all things with different eyes — at Katya and at our domestics and at Sonya and at myself and my occupations.

The books which I had formerly read, simply for the sake of killing time, suddenly became for me one of the greatest pleasures of my life, and the reason of it was simply this : that he and I talked about them, or read them together. He kept me well supplied with books.

Formerly, the time that I spent in superintending

Sonya's lessons was burdensome, and I undertook it only perfunctorily, as a duty. He interested himself in her lessons, and it became a pleasure to me to see what progress and success the child made.

Hitherto it had seemed an impossibility for me to learn a whole piece of music by heart, but now, knowing that he would listen to it, and perhaps commend me for it, I would practise over a single passage forty times in succession, so that poor Katya stopped up her ears with cotton, but I found it not in the least tedious. The old sonatas, somehow or other, seemed to phrase themselves in an entirely different manner, and produced a different and vastly better effect.

Even Katya, whom I knew and loved as myself, underwent a change in my eyes. For the first time I understood that she was under no obligation to be our mother, our friend, our slave, such as she had been. I appreciated all the dear soul's self-renunciation and devotion, appreciated all that I owed to her, and loved her more than ever before.

He taught me to look on all of our dependents — peasants, domestics, maid-servants — in an entirely different way from before.

I am ashamed to confess that I had lived among these people for seventeen years, and knew less about them than about people whom I had never seen; it had never once occurred to me that these men and women had the same affections, desires, and sorrows as my own.

Our park, our groves, our fields, which I had known so long, suddenly acquired a new beauty in my eyes. Nor vainly spoken was his remark that there is only one enduring happiness in life — to live for others. It seemed to me strange at the time; I did not understand it; but this conviction had unconsciously penetrated into my heart. He opened up for me a whole life of joy in the present, not making any apparent change in my life, adding nothing except himself to every impression. Everything which, since childhood, had been inert around me suddenly became endowed with life. He had only to make his appearance for everything to break into speech, and, at the same time, for all the powers of my soul to spring into life, filling it with joy.

Often I would go up-stairs to my room, fling myself on my bed, and give myself up to the sway, not of the melancholy longings, hopes, and desires with which spring endowed the future, but of present happiness. I could not go to sleep, but would get up, go over to Katya's bed, and confide to her sympathetic ears the story of my perfect happiness; now, as I look back upon it, I can see no reason for telling her; she could see it with her own eyes. But she told me that she needed nothing, and that she, also, was very happy, and gave me a kiss. I believed her, for it seemed to me right and proper for every one to be happy.

But Katya was not superior to thoughts of sleep, and she would pretend to grow stern, and drive me off from her bed, and go to sleep; but I would still remain awake, reviewing all my reasons for happiness.

Sometimes I got up and said my prayers for a second time, thanking God in my own words for the happiness which He had vouchsafed me.

And in my room it was still; the only sound was Katya's deep, regular breathing, the clock ticking by her side, and my restless turning, and murmuring broken words, or crossing myself and kissing the crucifix which hung around my neck. The doors were closed, the shutters in the windows were drawn, a fly or mosquito was buzzing in some spot. And I felt as if I should like always to stay in my little room, to have the morning forever delay her coming, to retain forever about me my present spiritual atmosphere. It seemed to me that my dreams, my thoughts, and my prayers were living creatures, abiding there with me in the darkness, flying about my bed, hovering over me.

And every thought was his thought, every feeling his feeling. And at that time I did not as yet know that this was love. I thought that this state of feeling might exist forever, that this feeling was unreciprocated.

CHAPTER III

ONE day, at the time of the grain-harvesting, I went out with Katya and Sonya, into the garden, after dinner, to our favorite seat, in the shade of the linden overlooking the ravine, beyond which stretched a view of forests and fields.

Sergyeï Mikhaïluitch had not been to see us for two days past, and we were expecting him this day, the more confidently because our overseer had said that he promised to go out into the field with him. About two o'clock we saw him riding across the field of rye. Katya told the maid to bring some peaches and cherries, of which he was very fond, and then, glancing at me with a smile, stretched herself out on the bench, and was soon dozing.

I broke off a crooked branch of the linden that hung down with succulent leaves and juicy bark, which moistened my hand, and, while I fanned Katya, I continued to read, though I kept stopping to look down the field road along which he would come to us.

Sonya, sitting on the root of an old linden tree, was busy making an arbor for her dolls. The day was hot, calm, and sultry; clouds had been gathering and growing black, and ever since morning a thunder-shower had been threatening. I was agitated, as always before a thunder-shower. But since noon the clouds had begun to dissipate, the sun came out bright, and only in one quarter of the sky was there low-muttered thunder, and one heavy cloud, piling up above the horizon and blending with the dust over the fields, was occasionally cut by the vivid zigzag flashes of the lightning darting to earth. It was clear that we at least should escape for that day.

All along the road back of the park, as we could see, here and there, moved the uninterrupted lines of creaking teams, heaped high with sheaves, slowly lumbering toward the barns, while the empty carts were hastening out for fresh loads, accompanied by peasants dressed in variegated shirts.

The thick dust neither moved off nor settled, but hung in the air, behind the hedges, among the translucent leaves of the trees in the park.

Farther away, at the threshing-floor, were heard voices, the creaking of wheels, and the rustle of the yellow sheaves slowly moving by the fence, then they seemed to fly through the air, before my eyes grew into oval houses, and I could see the outlines of the sharp, pointed roofs, and the figures of the peasants swarming about them.

Out on the dusty field also the carts were moving about, and there also the yellow sheaves could be seen, and the sounds of wheels, of voices, and of songs were borne in to my ears.

On one side, the stubble-field became more and more open, with patches of wormwood growing here and there.

Farther down toward the right, scattered over the unsightly, still encumbered field that had just been reaped, could be seen the bright-colored dresses of the women binding the sheaves, bending over and waving their arms, while the encumbered field grew clear, and the beautiful sheaves were disposed at intervals upon its level surface.

Suddenly, as it were, before my very eyes, summer was transformed into autumn. Dust and heat were all about, except in our beloved nook in the park. On all sides, in this dust and heat, and exposed to the rays of the sun, were the laboring folk, talking, and moving about with noise and bustle.

But Katya was snoring so peacefully under her white cambric kerchief, and was so comfortably curled up on the cool bench, the cherries looked so black, juicy, and tempting on the plate, our gowns were so fresh and clean, the water in the pitcher gleamed so refreshingly cool in the sun, and I felt so happy!

"What can I do about it?" I asked myself. "How am I to blame that I am happy? But how to share my happiness? And how and to whom shall I give all that I am and all my happiness?"....

The sun had already gone behind the crown of the

birch alley, the dust was settling down over the field, the atmosphere became clearer and brighter under the slanting rays of the sun; the clouds had passed entirely off; at the threshing-floor, beyond the trees, the tops of three new sheaf-ricks could be seen, and the peasants were going away from them; the carts, loudly creaking, were hastening down into the field for the last time; the peasant women, with rakes over their shoulders, and sheaf-withes in their belts, hurried home with ringing songs, but still Sergyeï Mikhaïluitch did not come, although it had been long since I saw him riding down the road.

Suddenly, his tall form appeared, coming along the alley, a direction from which I had not been expecting him; he had ridden round the ravine. With his face shining with pleasure, and taking off his hat, he came up to me with hasty steps. When he saw that Katya was asleep, he bit his lip, shut his eyes, and came up on tiptoe. I instantly perceived that he was in that peculiar state of inexplicable good spirits which I was so awfully fond of in him, and which we called "wild enthusiasm." He was just like a schoolboy released from his lessons; his whole being, from head to foot, was instinct with satisfaction, happiness, and childlike merriment.

"Well, how are you, my young violet? how is your health? Are you well?" he whispered, coming to me, and pressing my hand. .... "Yes, I'm feeling first rate," said he, in reply to my inquiry. "I am thirteen years old to-day; I want to play horse and climb trees!"

"In wild enthusiasm?" I asked, looking into his laughing eyes, and feeling that this *wild enthusiasm* was taking possession of myself also.

"Yes," said he, in reply, winking one eye, and trying to look sober. "But why do you keep hitting Katerina Karlovna in the nose?"

I had not noticed, while I was looking at him and continued to wave the branch, that I had knocked Katya's handkerchief off, and was tickling her face with the leaves.

I laughed.

"But she will insist that she wasn't asleep," said I, in a whisper, as if I were trying not to awake Katya; but that was not the real reason: it was simply because it was pleasant for me to talk in a whisper with him.

He moved his lips, imitating me, mimicking me because I spoke so low that it was impossible to hear what I said.

Seeing the plate of cherries, he pretended to steal it, went over to Sonya, under the linden, and sat down on her dolls. Sonya was angry at first, but he soon made peace with her by devising a game in which he and she were to see which could eat the most cherries.

"If you like, I will have some more brought," said I. "Or get them yourself."

He took the plate, set the dolls on it, and he and I went together to the inclosure. Sonya, laughing, ran after him, tugging at his coat, to make him give her back the dolls. He gave them back to her, and turned to me in all seriousness.

"Now, why aren't you a violet?" said he to me, softly, as if he were still afraid of waking some one. "As soon as I came to you, after all the dust and heat and work, I seemed to smell a violet, and not the fragrant violet, ... but you know that first variety, which is rather dark, and smells of melting snows and the spring vegetation!"

"Well, but how is everything getting along on the estate?" I asked, in order to hide the delicious confusion caused by his words.

"Splendid! These peasants are splendid wherever you find them. The more one knows them, the fonder of them one becomes."

"Yes," said I. "This very day, before you came, I was looking from the garden at their work, and suddenly I felt so ashamed because they were working and I was sitting there comfortably doing nothing that .... "

"Don't take this subject lightly, my dear," said he, interrupting me. He suddenly grew grave, but looked into my eyes affectionately. "It is sacred; God keep you from making a show of such a thing."

"Yes, it is only to *you* I say this."

"Well, yes, I know; but how shall we get the cherries?"

The inclosure was locked up, and no gardener was about (he himself had sent them all off to work). Sonya ran off to find the key, but he, without waiting for it, climbed up by one corner, lifted the netting, and sprang down upon the other side. "Will you have some?" I heard him say from within. "Give me the plate."

"No, I want to pick them myself. I will go after the key myself," said I. "Sonya won't find it."....

But at that very time I had the strongest desire to see what he was doing there, how he looked, how he moved, when he supposed that no one was observing him. Yes, the truth of the matter was that at that time I did not want to lose him from sight for a single moment. I crept round on my tiptoes, on the nettles, to the other side of the inclosure, where it was lower, and, standing on an empty tub, so that the wall came just below my breast, I looked over into the inclosure.

My eyes searched the whole interior of the inclosure, with its ancient, gnarled trees and their wide, dentated leaves, under which hung down, heavy and straight, the luscious black cherries; bending my head under the net, I saw Sergyeï Mikhaïluitch standing under the bough of an old cherry tree.

He evidently supposed that I had gone, and that no one saw him. With his hat off, and his eyes shut, he was sitting on the crotch of the old tree, and was busy rolling a morsel of cherry gum into a little ball. Suddenly he shrugged his shoulders, opened his eyes, and, muttering something, smiled. The word he said and his smile were so peculiar that I repented of having played the spy. It seemed to me that he had muttered the word "Masha."

"It cannot be," said I to myself.

"Milaya Masha — dearest Masha," he repeated, still more gently and affectionately. But I heard those words distinctly. My heart beat so violently, and such extreme, and as it were forbidden, joy seized me, that I clung fast with both hands to the fence, so as not to fall and betray myself. He heard my motion, looked up in alarm, and suddenly, dropping his eyes, reddened, and grew as flushed as a child.

He tried to say something to me, but was unable, and his face grew hotter and hotter. He smiled, however, as he looked at me. I smiled in return.

His whole face was radiant with pleasure.

It was no longer the old uncle flattering and lecturing me: it was a man, neither superior nor inferior to myself, a man who loved and feared me, and whom I also feared and loved.

Neither of us spoke, but we looked at each other. But suddenly he frowned; the smile and gleam vanished from his eyes, and his attitude toward me grew cold and paternal again, as if we had been doing something improper, and he had come to his senses and advised me to come to mine.

"You would better get down; you will fall and hurt you," said he. "And smooth your hair; you have no idea how you look!"

"Why does he play the hypocrite? Why does he want to hurt my feelings?" I asked myself, indignantly. And at that minute I was seized by an irresistible desire once more to confuse him and try my power over him.

"No, I want to pick them myself," said I, and, grasping a branch that hung conveniently near, I stood up on the wall, and got my feet over. He made no attempt to assist me as I leaped down to the ground inside the inclosure.

"What foolish things you do!" he exclaimed, reddening again, and trying to hide his confusion under the guise of annoyance. "You see, you might have hurt yourself. And how will you get out of here?"

He was still more confused than before, but this time his confusion frightened rather than pleased me. It was contagious; I blushed, and, going a little distance from him, and not knowing what to say, I began to pick cherries, though I had nothing with me to put them into. I reproached myself, I repented, I was afraid, and it seemed to me that I had forever forfeited his good opinion by my rash behavior. Both of us were silent, and the silence was awkward.

Sonya came running with the key, and rescued us from this constraint. But it was some time before either of us said a word, and we both addressed our remarks to Sonya.

When we returned to Katya, who insisted that she had not been asleep, but had heard everything, I felt more at my ease, and he tried to assume his ordinary patronizing, fatherly tone. But it was not quite in his power to do so, and he did not deceive me in the least. I had at that moment the liveliest remembrance of a conversation which had taken place, a few days before this, between us.

Katya had been saying how much easier it was for a man to love and express his love than it was for a woman.

"A man can say that he loves, but a woman cannot," said she.

"But I have an idea that a man should not and cannot say that he loves," said he.

"Why so?" I asked.

"Because it would always be a lie. What sort of a discovery is it that a man loves? As soon as one says this, a sort of bolt, as it were, is drawn, he becomes a slave — he is in love. As soon as he utters that word, it seems as if some miracle must necessarily take place, some extraordinary phenomenon, as if a broadside of cannon were fired off all at once. It seems to me," he went on to say, "that men who solemnly pronounce the words, 'I love you,' either deceive themselves, or, what is worse, deceive others."

"Then, how is a woman to know that she is loved, if she is not to be told?" asked Katya.

"I don't know," he replied. "Every man has his own form of speech. But it is a feeling, and should be expressed as one. When I read novels I always imagine what an embarrassed face Lieutenant Stryelsky or Alfred must put on at the moment of saying, ' I love thee, Eleonora!' He thinks that there is to be some extraordinary result; but nothing happens to either him or her; they have still the same eyes and the same nose; everything is the same."

Underneath his jesting remark, I felt at the time that there was a serious meaning which had reference to me; but Katya was not satisfied to be put down with the heroes of romance.

"Always paradoxes," said she. "But now tell me truly, have you never told a woman that you loved her?"

"I never have, and I have never yet got down on my knees," said he, with a laugh. "And I never shall."

"Certainly there is no need, now, for him to tell me that he loves me," I said to myself, vividly recalling that conversation. "He loves me, and I know it. And all his efforts to appear indifferent do not succeed in throwing dust in my eyes."

All that evening he had little to say to me, but in every word he spoke to Katya or Sonya, in his every motion and glance, I detected love, and I was not mistaken. I merely felt annoyed and sorry for him, that he should think it necessary to dissimulate and to pretend to be indifferent, when all the time it was so evident, and when it would have been so simple and easy to be happy beyond telling. But how tormented I was by my criminal act of springing down on him in the cherry inclosure! I had an idea that I had lost his esteem in consequence, and that he was angry with me.

After tea I went to the piano, and he joined me.

"Play something for me; I have not heard you for a long time," said he, overtaking me in the drawing-room.

"I was going to. .... Sergyeĭ Mikhaĭluitch!" I exclaimed, suddenly looking him straight in the eye, "you are not vexed with me, are you?"

"Why should I be?" he asked.

"Because I didn't do as you wanted me to, this afternoon," I explained, blushing.

He understood me, shook his head, and laughed. His look told me he would have scolded, but that he did not feel strong enough for it.

"I didn't mean anything by it; we are friends again, aren't we?" said I, taking my seat at the piano.

"Why, certainly," said he.

The large, high-studded drawing-room was lighted only by two candles, set on the piano; the rest of the room was in a semi-darkness. The clear summer night gleamed in through the open window. All was still; occasionally Katya's steps were heard, as she moved about in the dark reception-room, and Sergyeï Mikhaïluitch's horse, fastened under the window, whinnied and stamped his hoofs on the turf.

He sat behind me, so that I could not see him; but everywhere — in the half-light that filled the room, in the music, in my own soul — I felt his presence.

Every glance, every motion of his, though I could not see them, was manifest to my heart.

I played Mozart's sonata fantasia, which he had brought to me, and which I had learned under his direction and for his sake. I was not thinking at all of what I was playing, but I must have played it well, and I felt certain that he was satisfied. I was conscious of the delight which he was experiencing, and, though I was not looking at him, and he was behind me, I felt the look which he fastened on me.

Quite in spite of myself, while I still continued mechanically touching the keys, I turned around and glanced at him. His head was outlined against the clear background of the night. He was sitting, with his head resting on his hand, and looking steadily at me with gleaming eyes.

I smiled when I saw his look, and stopped playing. He smiled back at me, and reproachfully nodded his head at the music, signifying that I should go on.

When I finished, the moon, which had already risen high, was shining in through the other window, and,

blending with the feeble light of the candles, was flood-
ing the floor with its silvery beams.

Katya declared that it was shameful for me to stop at
the best part of all, and insisted that I was not playing
very well, but he maintained that I had never played so
well as that evening; and he began to walk up and down
through the rooms, from the drawing-room into the dark
reception-room, and back again, each time looking at me
and smiling. And I also smiled; I even felt like laughing, though there was no reason for it, — so happy was
I at anything that might happen on that day.

As soon as he was behind the door and out of sight,
I seized Katya, who was near me by the piano, and
began to kiss her in the place that I liked best of all,
on her plump neck, under her chin; as soon as he came
back again, I put on a serious face and did my utmost
to refrain from smiling.

"What has happened to her to-day?" asked Katya.

But he made no reply, and merely laughed at me.
He knew what had happened to me.

"Just see what a beautiful night it is!" said he,
from the reception-room, where he was standing in
front of the balcony door which opened into the
park.

We went to him, and indeed it was such a night as
I have never seen since. The full moon hung over
the house, back of us, so that it was out of sight, and
half of the shadow of the roof, of the pillars, and the
awning of the terrace lay foreshortened obliquely, *en
raccourci*, on the sanded foot-path and the oval grass-
plot. All the rest was bright, and flooded with moonlight gleaming on the silvery dew. The wide path
between the flower-beds, across which, on one side, lay
the slanting shadows of the dahlias and their supports,
stretched away, fresh and cool, and shining with glittering pebbles, into the misty distance.

Under the trees could be seen the bright glass roof
of the orangery, and out of the ravine rose a shadowy
vapor. The still clumps of lilacs, where the flowers
were not as yet in bloom, were bathed in moonlight.

All the flowers, wet with dew, could be distinguished from one another. Light and shade were so mingled in the alleys that it seemed as if they were not composed of trees and paths, but were transparent houses, rocking and swaying.

At the right, in the shadow of the house, all was dark, dim, and weird. But, with all the greater distinctness from contrast with this darkness, the fantastic crest of the poplar seemed to hang strangely suspended, near the house, the top all bathed in bright light, and ready to soar away, far away, into the calm blue sky.

"Let us go out and take a walk," said I.

Katya agreed, but told me to get my overshoes.

"It is not necessary, Katya," said I. "Here, Sergyeï Mikhaïluitch will give me his arm."

Just as if that would prevent me from dampening my feet!

But at that time all three of us understood my meaning, and it did not seem strange at all. He had never offered me his arm, but now I took it of my own accord, and he did not find it strange. He and I went together down from the terrace. All this world, this sky, this park, this atmosphere, were no longer the same as I had known them.

When I looked along the alley through which we were walking, it seemed to me that we should in a moment be brought to a stop, that yonder the world of the possible would end, that all this spectacle must continue forever changeless in its beauty.

But still we moved on, and the magic shadow-wall of beauty gave way before us, and let us pass beyond, where also, so it seemed, were our well-known park, the trees, the paths, the dry leaves. And we were actually walking along the paths, treading on the circlets of light and shadow, and it was actually the dry leaves rustling under our feet, and the cool breeze which fanned my face! And this was really he, who, as he walked quietly beside me, with slow steps, discreetly allowed my hand to rest on his arm; and this was actually

Katya, who, shuffling along, followed just behind us.
And that could be nothing else than the moon itself in
the sky, shining down on us through the motionless
branches!....

But at each step the magic shadow wall seemed to
close behind us and before us, and I ceased to believe
that we might go farther, ceased to believe in the reality
of all that surrounded us.

"Ah! a frog!" exclaimed Katya.

"Who said that, and why?" I asked myself. And I
instantly realized that it was Katya, and that she was
afraid of frogs, and I looked to the ground. A little
frog hopped up before me, and came to a standstill, and
his tiny shadow lay along the bright clay walk.

"And aren't you afraid of them?" he asked.

I glanced at him. One of the lindens of the alley had
been cut down, and at that particular place where we
were passing his face was brightly illuminated by the
moonlight. It was so beautiful and full of happiness.....

He said, "Aren't you afraid?" but there was a deeper
meaning to his words. I heard him say, "I love thee,
dear little maiden! I love thee, love thee!"

His glance and his arm said them; and the light, and
the shadow, and the air, and everything repeated the
same.

We made the circuit of the whole park. Katya went
with us, taking short steps and getting out of breath from
her exertion. She said that it was time to go back, and
I felt sorry, sorry for her, poor old soul!

"Why doesn't she feel the same as we do?" I wondered. "Why are not all young, all happy, as this night
is and as he and I are?"

We returned to the house, but it was long before he
took his leave, although the cocks were crowing, although
all in the house were asleep, and his horse kept stamping more and more impatiently and whinnying under the
window. Katya did not remind us that it was late, and,
as we sat there talking about various trifles, we had no
idea that it was already three o'clock in the morning!

The cocks were beginning to crow for the third time,

and there was a faint tinge of dawn in the sky, when he went away. He took his departure, as usual, without saying anything out of the ordinary course of things; but I well knew that from henceforth he was mine, and that I should not lose him. As soon as I confessed to myself that I loved him, I told Katya the whole story. She was very glad and very much touched because I told her, but the poor soul was able to get some sleep that night, while I, on the contrary, walked long, long, up and down the terrace, and went into the park, and, while recalling every word, every gesture, I walked along the very same alleys where he and I had been together.

I could not sleep that night, and for the first time in my life I sat up till sunrise, and saw the early morning. And never since have I seen such a night and such a morning!

"But why," I asked myself, "why does he not tell me simply that he loves me? Why does he imagine such difficulties, why does he call himself an old man, when everything is so simple and beautiful? Why does he waste golden time, which perhaps can never return again? Let him say, '*I love*,' let him say the words, let him take my hand in his, let him press it to his lips, and say, '*I love*.' All that is necessary is for his face to flush and his eyes to be cast down before me, and then I should tell him all. Or no, not tell him, but rather throw my arms around him and press him to my heart and weep!.... But suppose I am mistaken and he does not love me!"

That thought suddenly came into my mind.

I was alarmed at the feeling that came over me; God knows where it might lead me, — and his confusion and mine also in the cherry inclosure, when I sprang down where he was, came back to my memory, and I became heavy-hearted, very heavy-hearted. Tears sprang to my eyes. I tried to pray. And a strange feeling of peace and hope came to me. I resolved to prepare for the Sacrament from this day forth, to partake of the Holy Communion on my birthday, and on that very day to become his betrothed.

Why? Wherefore? How could it be brought about? I had not the slightest idea, but from that moment my faith was firm, and I knew that this would be so. It was already perfectly light, and the people were beginning to get up, when I went to my room.

CHAPTER IV

IT was the Fast of the Assumption, and therefore no one in the house was surprised at my resolution to prepare for the Sacrament during these days.

During that entire week he did not once come to see us, and I was not only not surprised or alarmed or hurt, but, on the contrary, I was glad that he did not come, and I only expected that he would come on my birthday.

During that entire week, I got up every morning early, and while they were harnessing the horses I would wander alone through the park and meditate on the sins I had committed the day before, and consider what I ought to do on the present day in order to be satisfied with my time and not fall deeper into sin.

At that time it seemed to me so easy to be absolutely without sin. It seemed to me that all that was necessary was to try. As soon as the horses were put in, I would take Katya or one of the maids and drive, in our linerka, three versts, to church. As I entered the church, I always remembered that prayers were offered for all "who came in the fear of God," and I strove to mount the two grass-grown steps of the porch under the influence of this feeling.

At that time of day there were never more than a dozen peasants or household serfs in the church, preparing for the Communion, and I tried with strenuous humility to respond to their salutations, and I myself went to the candle cupboard to get tapers of the old soldier who served as sacristan, and I placed them before the ikons, and this seemed to me to be a meritorious action.

Through the "Holy Gates"[1] I could see the altar-cover which mamasha had embroidered; on the ikonostas were the two angels spangled with stars, which when I was a little girl had seemed to me so huge, and the dove with a yellow nimbus which used to engross my childish attention.

Behind the chancel rail could be seen the modeled font, at which I had stood so many times as godmother for the children of our house-serfs, and where I myself had been christened.

The old priest came in his chasuble, made of cloth that had been my father's pall, and read the church service in the very same tone in which he had so many times read it, since my earliest remembrance, at our own house, at Sonya's christening, at my father's requiem mass, and at my mother's funeral.

And the precentor's trembling voice, as it echoed through the choir, was the same; and there was the same old woman whom I always remembered to have seen at church, at every service, as she stood all bent over, next the wall, looking with tearful eyes at the ikon in the chancel, and pressing her clasped hands to her faded shawl, and mumbling prayers with her toothless mouth.

And there was nothing in all this to arouse my curiosity, nor was it dear to me from associations alone; but it was all grand and holy now in my eyes, and seemed to me full of deep significance.

I listened to every word of the stated prayers, and endeavored to respond to them with my feeling; and where I failed to understand the full depth of them, then I mentally implored God to enlighten me, or, in place of the prayer that I could not understand, I inaudibly murmured one of my own.

When the prayers of repentance were read, I recalled my past, and that childish, innocent past seemed to me

---

[1] The *ikonostas*, or screen, which shuts off the Holy Place from the rest of the church, has three doors or gates, the middle one the "*Tsarskaya dveri*," the Tsar's or the Holy Gates, and the "Northern" and "Southern," on either side. — ED.

so black in comparison with the present enlightened state of my soul that I wept and was terrified; but, at the same time, I felt that all was forgiven me, and that, if my sins had been even more heinous, my repentance would have been correspondingly sweeter.

At the end of the service when the priest said, "The blessing of God be upon you," it seemed to me that I felt a physical sense of well-being instantly take possession of me. A peculiar feeling of light and warmth, as it were, suddenly flowed into my heart.

When the service was over, the good father would come to me and inquire if it would not be a good plan to have an all-night service at our house, and when he should come; but I thanked him warmly for his offer, because I felt that it was for my sake that he suggested it, and I told him that I would come to him or would let him know.

"Do you wish to give yourself the trouble?" he asked.

I did not know what answer to make for fear of laying myself open to the sin of pride.

After mass, I always sent the carriage home, unless Katya were with me, and returned alone on foot, humbly bowing low to all whom I met, and trying to find some opportunity of doing good, giving advice, sacrificing myself for some one, helping lift a load, rocking a child, or stepping out into the mud to make room for some one to pass.

One evening I heard the overseer telling Katya that Semyon, one of the peasants, had come to beg for some boards to make a coffin for his daughter, and a little money for a mass, and that he had given it.

"Why, are they so poor?" I asked.

"Very poor; they can't even get enough to eat,"[1] replied the overseer.

Something seemed to clutch at my heart, and at the same time I felt a sort of joy at hearing this. Giving Katya the mistaken impression that I was going out for a stroll, I ran up-stairs, collected all my money (it was

[1] Literally, "they sit without salt."

very little, but all that I had), and, crossing myself, I went alone over the terrace and through the park, into the village, to Semyon's izba.

This was at the very end of the village, and I, without being seen by any one, went up to the window, laid the money on the sill, and tapped on the glass.

Some one came out of the cottage, making the door creak on its hinges, and called to me; but I, trembling and chilled with fright, ran home like a transgressor.

Katya asked me where I had been, and what was the matter with me; but I did not even comprehend what she asked me, and I made no reply. It all suddenly seemed to me so mean and petty. I shut myself up in my room, and for a long time walked to and fro, unable to act or to think or to account for my feeling.

I thought of the pleasure which the whole family would feel, of the blessings which they would shower down on the one that had bestowed the money, and I began to feel sorry that I had not myself given it to them.

I thought also what Sergyeĭ Mikhaĭluitch would say if he knew about this foolish freak of mine, and I was glad enough that no one would ever know anything about it. And I had such a sense of joy, and all, including myself, seemed so contemptible, and yet I looked with such kindly feelings upon myself and upon all that the thought of death came to me like a vision of happiness. I smiled and I prayed and I wept, and what a passionately ardent love for myself and every one else in the world I felt at that moment!

I read the Gospel as it is found in the prayer-book; and more and more comprehensible seemed to me this book, and more attractive and simple the story of that divine life, and more terrible and impenetrable the deep feelings and thoughts which I found in its doctrines. But for that very reason how clear and simple seemed everything to me when, after laying down this book, I again directed my thoughts and observations to the life about me.

It seemed to me so hard not to live aright, and so simple to love every one and to be loved by all. All were so kind and sweet to me; even Sonya, to whom I continued to give lessons, was entirely different, and tried to understand me, and to satisfy me, and not to give me annoyance.

All behaved toward me as I myself behaved. In trying to think over all my enemies, those whose forgiveness I ought to ask before confession, I recalled only one, a young lady, a neighbor. I had laughed at her, a year before, in presence of guests, and she had ceased to visit me. I wrote her a letter, confessing my fault and asking her forgiveness. She replied in a note, granting it, and, in her turn, asking me to forgive her. I wept with delight as I read those simple lines, in which, at that time, I could see a deep and touching significance. My old nurse wept when I asked her to forgive me.

"Why are they all so kind to me? What have I done to deserve such love?" I asked myself. And I involuntarily recalled Sergyeí Mikhaíluitch, and for a long time thought about him. I could not do otherwise, and I did not look on it as an impropriety. I thought of him now, however, in an entirely different way from what I did that night when, for the first time, I realized that I loved him; I thought about him just as I did about myself, and naturally he entered into every plan concerning my future.

The crushing ascendancy which his presence had over me entirely disappeared from my imagination. I now felt myself on an equality with him, and, from the height of the spiritual mood to which I had reached, I thoroughly understood him. What had hitherto been strange in him now became clear to me. For the first time I understood why he declared that happiness consisted only in living for others, and now I was in perfect accord with him. It seemed to me that we should be so endlessly and serenely happy together. And no thought entered my mind of journeys abroad, or of gay society, of brilliant life, but something entirely different — a quiet, domestic life in the country, with constant self-sacrifice, with constant love for each other, and with constant acknowledgment of a kind and helpful Providence in all things.

I partook of the Holy Communion, as I had proposed to do, on my birthday. My heart was so full of happiness when I returned that day from church that I dreaded life, dreaded every impression, everything that might in the least disturb such happiness. But as soon as we had dismounted from the lineĭka, and were mounting the steps, a well-known cabriolet rattled across the bridge, and I saw Sergyeĭ Mikhaĭluitch. He congratulated me, and we went together into the drawing-room. Never, since our acquaintance began, had I been so calm and self-possessed as I was that morning. I felt that there was within me a whole new world, high above him, and of which he was ignorant. I did not feel in his presence the slightest restraint. He must have understood something of this; for he was affectionately gentle toward me, and treated me with a peculiarly religious deference. I was going to the piano; but he shut it, and put the key into his pocket.

"Don't destroy your present mood," said he. "Your soul is now full of harmony better than any earthly music."

I was grateful to him for his thoughtfulness; but, at the same time, I felt a little disappointment that he should so easily and clearly read all that ought to be kept a secret from every one, in my soul.

At dinner he said that he had come to congratulate me, and at the same time to say good-by, as he was going to Moscow the next day. In saying this he looked at Katya; and then he gave me a fleeting glance, and I saw how he feared to witness the emotion in my face.

But I was neither surprised nor annoyed, and I did not even ask him whether he should be gone long. I knew that he would say these words, and I knew also that he would not go.

How did I know this? I can never, even to the pres-

ent day, explain it to myself; but on that memorable
day it seemed to me that I knew everything, whatever
had been, and whatever would be. I seemed to be in a
blissful dream, when things that have not yet taken place
seem to be already in existence, and long ago a part of
my knowledge, and yet all is still to come, and I know
that it is to come.

He intended to go away immediately after dinner,
but Katya, who was tired in consequence of the service,
went to lie down for a little while, and he was obliged to
wait till she had finished her nap, so as to say good-by
to her.

The sun shone brightly in the "hall"; we went out
on the terrace. As soon as we had sat down, I began
with perfect serenity the conversation that was destined
to decide the fortune of my love. And I began to speak
at the very moment that we sat down, neither sooner nor
later, so that nothing had as yet been said, when there
was nothing as yet to give a different tone or character
to our talk, or to affect unfavorably what I wanted to
say. I myself cannot understand whence came the
calmness, decision, and accuracy that marked my expressions. It seemed as if it were not myself, but something quite independent of my will, that spoke in me.
He took a seat in front of me, leaning his arm on the
balustrade, and, drawing down toward him a branch of
lilac, kept pulling off the leaves. When I began to
speak, he let the branch fly back, and rested his head
on his hand. This might have been the attitude of a
man perfectly calm or very much agitated.

"Why are you going away?" I asked, in a significant
tone, deliberately, and looking him full in the face.

He did not answer at once.

"Business," he exclaimed, dropping his eyes.

I saw how hard it was for him to tell me a falsehood,
in answer to a question put with such frankness.

"Listen," said I. "You know what this day is for
me. In many ways this day is very important. If I
ask you the question, it is not out of mere compliment
(you know that I am so used to seeing you, and that I

am fond of you), but I ask you because I must know. Why are you going?"

"It is very hard for me to tell you the truth why I am going," said he. "This past week I have thought much about you and about myself, and I have come to the conclusion that it is my duty to go. You know why, and, if you are fond of me, you will not ask me."

He rubbed his forehead with his hand, and shut his eyes. "This is hard for me!.... But you understand."

My heart began to throb violently.

"I cannot understand," said I. "*I cannot; you* will tell me. For Heaven's sake, for the sake of this day, tell me; I can hear the whole calmly," said I.

He changed his position, glanced at me, and again pulled down the branch.

"Besides," said he, after a pause, and in a voice that vainly tried to be firm, "though it is stupid and impossible to put into words, though it is hard for me, I will try to explain to you," he went on, contracting his brows as if with physical pain.

"Well?" said I.

"Imagine that there was a certain gentleman. Let us call him A," said he; "old, and weary of life; and a lady, B, young and happy, who has never as yet seen society or life. In various family relations, he had learned to love her as a daughter, and never had any fear that he should learn to love her otherwise."

He paused, but I did not interrupt him.

"But he forgot that B was so young that life for her was still a plaything," he went on, suddenly beginning to speak rapidly and resolutely, and not looking at me, "and that he might easily learn to love her in a different way, and that this would be sport for her. And he himself was deceived and suddenly woke to the consciousness that another feeling, heavy as regret, had taken possession of his soul, and he was frightened. He was frightened lest their former friendly relations might be interrupted, and he resolved to depart before they should be interrupted."

In saying this, he again, as it were, carelessly rubbed his eyes with his hand, and closed them.

"Why, pray, should he be afraid of loving her in a different way?" I asked, in a scarcely audible tone. I controlled my agitation, and my voice was calm; but he really seemed to think that I was jesting.

He replied in a tone that showed he was evidently offended.

"You are young," said he, "and I am no longer young. You enjoy trifling; but I must have something else. Trifle as much as you like, only not with me; otherwise, I verily believe, I should do something rash, and you would feel sorry. This is what A said," he added. "Well, it may be all nonsense, but you understand why I am going. And now let us not say anything more about it. Please!"

"No, no! we will speak more about it!" I cried, and the tears made my voice tremble. "Did he love her or not?"

He made no reply.

"But if he did not love her, why has he trifled with her as with a child?" I demanded.

"Yes, yes; A was to blame," he answered hastily, interrupting me. "But all that came to an end, they parted .... friends."

"But that is horrible! And was there no other possible ending?"

The words were barely out of my mouth when I was appalled at my temerity.

"Yes, there is," said he, uncovering an agitated face, and looking straight at me. "There are two different ways of ending it. But for God's sake do not interrupt me, and hear me calmly. Some say," he began, standing up, and looking at me with a painfully sad smile, "some say that A became crazy, fell madly in love with B, and told her so. .... But she only laughed at him. For her this was merely amusing, but for him it was a matter of life and death."

I shivered, and tried to interrupt him, to tell him that he had no right to speak for me; but he restrained me, laying his hand on mine.

"Stop!" said he, in a trembling voice. "Others say that she had pity on him, that she imagined — poor little girl, who has never seen much of the world — that she might really love him, and so consented to be his wife. And he was mad enough to believe it, to believe that his life might begin anew; but she herself saw that she was deceiving him, and he was deceiving her. ..... Let us not say anything more about this," he concluded, evidently not having the force to speak further, and he began silently to walk up and down in front of me.

He said, "Let us not say any more about this," but I saw that, with all the powers of his soul, he was waiting for my reply. I wanted to speak, but I could not; something seemed to oppress my breast. I looked at him; he was pale, and his lower lip quivered. I felt sorry for him. I put forth all my strength, and, suddenly breaking the chain of silence which bound me, I said, in a weak, choking voice, which I feared each second would fail me : —

"But there is a third ending," said I, and paused, but he kept silence. "But there is a third ending, that he did not love, but gave her deep, deep pain, and thought that he was doing right, and went away, and prided himself on doing so. On your side, and not on mine, is the trifling; from the first day I have loved you — yes, loved you," I repeated, and at the word *loved* my voice, in spite of myself, changed from a gentle tone to a wild shriek, which frightened me.

He stood all pale before me; his lips quivered more and more, and two tears rolled down his cheeks.

"It is cruel!" I almost screamed, and I feared that I should suffocate with angry, unwept tears. "What is the reason?" I cried, and got up to leave him.

But he would not let me go. His head bent forward on my knees; his lips were kissing my trembling hands, and his tears wet them.

"My God, if I had only known!" he cried.

"What is the reason? what is the reason?" I kept repeating; but my soul was already full of joy — a joy never to be taken from me, never to be repeated.

In five minutes Sonya was running up-stairs to Katya, and was shouting all over the house that Masha was going to marry Sergyeï Mikhaïlovitch.

CHAPTER V

THERE was no reason for postponing our wedding, and neither of us desired such a thing. To be sure, Katya was anxious to go to Moscow and make purchases and order a trousseau; and his mother urged him to get a new carriage and furniture, and have the house furnished with new hangings, before he should marry. But we both decided that it would be better to attend to all these things afterward, if indeed they were so necessary; and, accordingly, the wedding was celebrated a fortnight after my birthday, — without a trousseau, without guests, without groomsmen, without a supper and champagne, and all those conventional accessories of a wedding.

He told me how annoyed his mother was to have the marriage ceremony performed without music, without a mountain of trunks, and a complete renovation of the house, so different from her wedding, which cost thirty thousand rubles, and how she was solemnly making a secret search through the trunks in her storeroom, and taking Maryushka, the housekeeper, into consultation in regard to certain rugs, curtains, and salvers indispensable for our felicity.

On my side, Katya did the same with the old nurse Kuzminishna. And it was of no use to speak jestingly with her, in respect to this. She was firmly convinced that when he and I were talking over our future we were merely talking soft sentimentalities, and behaving foolishly, as people in such conditions are usually supposed to do, but that our material happiness in the future would depend on the regular cut and embroidery of my underwear, and the hemming of table-cloths and napkins.

Between Pokrovskoye and Nikolskoye mysterious

messages were exchanged several times each day, respecting various preparations; and, although outwardly Katya and his mother seemed to be on the most affectionate footing, still their intercourse began to be conducted in accordance with a subtle but somewhat hostile diplomacy.

Tatyana Semyonovna, his mother, with whom I now became much more closely acquainted, was a precise, stern housekeeper,[1] and a lady of the old school. He loved her, not only as a son, for duty's sake, but also as a man, through his intellect, regarding her as the very best, most intelligent, kindest, and most lovable woman in the world. Tatyana Semyonovna had always been kind to us, and to me especially, and she was glad that her son was going to marry me; but when I visited her after my betrothal, it seemed to me that she was anxious to make me understand that I was not after all the best match for her son, and that it was well for me never to forget it. But I entirely understood her and agreed with her.

During the last two weeks of my maidenhood, we saw each other every day. He came to dinner and stayed till midnight. But, in spite of his declaration that he could not live without me, and I knew he spoke the truth, he never spent a whole day with me, and tried still to give some attention to his affairs.

Our outward relations continued up to the very day of the wedding the same as before; we still addressed each other formally with *vui*, you; he did not kiss even my hand, and not only did not seek, but even avoided, opportunities of being alone with me. He really seemed to be afraid that the affection which was in his heart would become too overmastering and injurious.

I cannot tell, either he or I had changed, and, now I felt that I stood on the same footing with him, I no longer found in him that affectation of simplicity which had formerly displeased me, and oftentimes I saw before me instead of a man inspiring respect and awe, a sweet child spoiled with happiness.

[1] *Khozyaïka doma.*

"There is nothing so surprisingly great in him," I often said to myself. "He is simply a human being, just as I am, nothing more."

It now seemed to me that there was nothing hidden from me, that I knew him thoroughly. And all that I saw of him was so simple and so congenial to me! even his plans for our future mode of life coincided with mine, only they were expressed more clearly and admirably in his words.

The weather these days was wretched, and we spent most of the time in the house. Our best and most intimate talks were held between the piano and the window. The candle-light was reflected in the black window-panes, against which, now and again, fell the raindrops and trickled down. The rain beat on the roof, and poured from the spout into the pool; the dampness spread over the window. And how much brighter, warmer, and more cheerful, from very contrast, it seemed in our corner.

"Do you know, I have for a long time wanted to tell you one thing," said he, as we were sitting late one evening in this place. "I have been thinking about it all the time that you were playing."

"Do not tell me anything; I know it all," said I.

"Yes, you are right; we will say nothing about it."

"Oh! but tell me; what were you going to say?" I asked.

"Well, this was it: Do you remember when I told you the story about A and B?"

"The idea of not remembering that stupid story! It's well that it ended as it did." ....

"Yes, a little more and I should have ruined my own happiness. You saved me. But the main thing was that I was telling a falsehood all the time, and my conscience pricks me, and I wish to finish telling it."

"Oh, please! it is not necessary!"

"Don't be alarmed," said he, with a smile. "All I wish is to set myself right in your eyes. When I began to speak, I wanted to reason."

"Reason? What for?" I exclaimed. "It is never necessary."

"Yes, I reasoned badly. After all my disillusions, my mistakes in life, when I came to live in the country, I resolutely told myself that love, for me, was at an end, that all that was left for me was the duty of living out my remnant of life, and it was long before I realized what my feelings were toward you, and where they were leading me. I hoped and despaired. Sometimes it seemed to me that you were playing the coquette; then again my faith returned, and actually I did not know what I should do. But after that evening, — you remember, don't you, when we walked in the park that moonlight night? — I was filled with alarm; my happiness then seemed to me too great, and impossible. Well, what would have happened to me if I had allowed myself to hope and found that it was in vain. But, of course, I was thinking only of myself, because I am a miserable egotist."

He stopped talking and looked at me.

"However, it was not absolute nonsense that I spoke at that time. For you see there was good reason for me to fear. I receive so much from you, and can give so little in return. You are still only a child, you are a bud, which is yet to unfold; you love for the first time, while I .... "

"Yes, tell me all the truth about it," said I, but suddenly I felt overmastered by a sudden terror at what his answer might be. "No, no, it is not necessary," I added.

"Whether I have ever loved before, you mean?" he exclaimed, instantly divining my thought. "I can tell you about it. No, I have never loved before. Never have I experienced such a feeling as this." ....

But suddenly some painful memory seemed to flash through his mind. "No, and just here is where I need a heart like yours in order to have the right to love you," said he, gloomily. "Was it not necessary, therefore, for me to think it all over before telling you that I loved you? What is there for me to give you? Love, that is true."

"Is that little?" I asked, looking him in the eyes.

"Little, my dear, little for you," he continued. "You have youth and beauty! Often now I cannot sleep at night, I am so happy, and because I keep thinking how we are going to live together. I have had many experiences in life, and it seems to me that I have now found all that is essential for happiness. The quiet lonely life in our country solitude, with the possibility of being benefactors to people to whom it is easy to do good, and who are so unaccustomed to it, then work, work which brings its own reward, then rest, nature, books, music, love for some congenial spirit, — such is my ideal of happiness, and I cannot conceive of a higher. And then, above all, such a friend as you are; a family perhaps, and all that any man could desire in this world."

"Yes," said I.

"For me, since I have lived out my youth, yes; but not for you," he went on to say. "You have not as yet seen anything of life; you very likely have still some desire to seek happiness in another, and perhaps you would find it in another. It seems to you now that this is happiness because you love me."

"No, this quiet home happiness has always been my aim and ambition," said I. "And you have simply expressed what I have always thought."

He smiled.

"It only seems so to you, my dear. This is little to you. You have youth and beauty," he repeated thoughtfully.

But I was annoyed, because he did not believe me, and because he, as it were, made my youth and beauty a reproach.

"Then, why do you love me?" I asked angrily. "For my youth or for myself?"

"I don't know, but I love you," he replied, looking at me with his keen, fascinating glance.

I made no answer, and could not help looking into his eyes. Suddenly, something strange took place in me; first I ceased to see all surrounding objects; then his face disappeared from before me; his eyes alone seemed to be gleaming in front of my eyes; then it seemed to me that those eyes took possession of me; then everything grew dim, everything faded from my sight, and I had to shut my eyes in order to get rid of the sense of passionate bliss and terror which that glance of his gave me.....

On the eve of the day set for the wedding, late in the afternoon, the weather cleared. And after the rains, which had begun while it was still summer, we had our first clear, cool autumn evening. Everything was wet, cool, and bright, and now, for the first time, the park began to open out its vistas through the autumnal coloring of the leaves which already had begun to fall.[1] The sky was clear, cold, and wan. I went to bed happy in the thought that the morrow — the day of our wedding — would be fair.

On that day I woke with the sun, and the thought that it was *to-day*, as it were frightened me and filled me with fear and wonder.

I went down into the park. The sun had only just risen, and was shining through the thin yellow foliage of the linden trees along the driveway. The path was strewn with rustling leaves. The wrinkled, bright clusters of berries on the mountain ash gleamed red on the branches, where still hung a few crumpled leaves killed by the frost; the dahlias stood shriveled and black. Frost, for the first time, lay like silver across the pale green grass, and on the broken burdocks near the house. On the clear, cold sky not a single cloud was or could be seen.

"Can it be to-day?" I asked myself, not daring to believe in my happiness. "Can it be that I shall wake up to-morrow not here, but in that strange house at Nikolskoye, with its columns? Is it possible that I shall no longer have to wait for his coming, no more be going out to meet him, talk no longer about him with Katya? Shall I no more sit with him at the piano in our

---

[1] Literally, could be seen the autumnal spaciousness, variegation, and bareness.

Pokrovskoye drawing-room? Shall I no more see him to the door and worry about him, when the nights are dark?"

But then I remembered he had told me, the evening before, that he had come for the last time, and Katya had called me to try on my wedding-dress, and said, "It is for to-morrow," and, for a moment, I really believed it and again doubted.

"Can it be that after to-day I am going to live there with my husband's mother, without Nadyozha, without old Grigori, without Katya? Shall I no longer kiss my nurse good-night, and have her, according to old custom, make the sign of the cross over me, and say, 'Good-night, my young lady'?[1] I shall no longer teach Sonya, and play with her, and knock on the wall for her in the morning, and hear her ringing laughter! Must I to-day be changed into another person, a stranger to myself, and is a new life, the realization of my hopes and desires, opening out before me? Will this new life last forever?"

I waited impatiently for him to come; it was hard for me to be alone with these thoughts.

He came early, and only when I saw him did I really believe that this day I was to be his wife, and cease to tremble at the thought.

Before dinner we went to our church, to hear a mass in memory of my father.

"If he were only alive now!" I thought, as we were returning home, and I silently leaned on the arm of the man who had been the warmest friend of him of whom I was thinking. During the prayer, while I knelt, with my forehead pressed to the cold stones of the chapel floor, I recalled my father so vividly, I had such a firm belief that his spirit was cognizant of me and approved of my choice, that it seemed to me that even now it was hovering over us, and was conscious of him giving us his blessing. And recollections and hopes and happiness and grief mingled within me in one triumphant and delicious feeling, which was still further intensified by the calm, fresh air; the calmness, the wide

[1] *Pakoïnoï nochi, baruishnya.*

bare fields, the pale sky, from which fell over all things bright but gentle rays, striving to kindle the color in my cheeks.

It seemed to me that the man who was by my side understood and shared my feeling. He walked quietly and silently, and his face, into which I looked from time to time, expressed the same serious emotion in which blended both grief and joy, and which was both in nature and in my heart.

Suddenly he turned to me, and I saw that he wished to say something. It occurred to me, "Suppose he should not speak of what I am thinking?"

But he spoke of my father, though he did not even mention him.

"Once he said to me in jest, 'You must marry my Masha!'"

These were his words.

"How happy he would be now," said I, warmly pressing the arm on which I leaned.

"Yes; you were then only a child," he went on to say, looking into my eyes. "I used to kiss those eyes, and loved them only because they were like his, and I had no thought then that they would be for their own sake so dear to me. I called you Masha then."

"Say *thou* to me," said I.

"That is what I have wished," he went on. "But only now does it seem possible to me that *thou art* wholly mine."

And his calm, happy, fascinating glance rested on me, and we walked still without hurrying along the field path, scarcely traceable amid the trampled piles of stubble; our footsteps and our voices alone broke the silence. On one side, beyond the ravine, stretched away toward the distant forest, now stripped of leaves, the brown stubble-field, where, not far from us, a peasant, with his rude plow, was noiselessly marking a black strip, which grew constantly wider and wider. The drove of horses, scattered at the foot of the hill, seemed close at hand.

On the other side, and straight ahead of us, the dark

field of winter wheat, touched by the frost, and marked here and there with greenish patches, stretched away clear up to the park and the house which could be seen rising directly behind it. Everything was bathed in the autumnal rays of the sun. Long filaments of cobwebs stretched in every direction. They floated through the air around us, and hung over the field dried by the frost; they got into our eyes and clung to our hair and our garments. When we spoke, our voices were resonant, and seemed to hover over us in the motionless atmosphere, as if we were alone in the midst of the great world, and alone under the blue arch, over which played an unscorching sun, flashing and trembling.

I also wanted to use the familiar *tui*, thou, to him; but I felt abashed.

"Why *dost thou* walk so fast?" I asked, hurrying over the words, and almost whispering them, and feeling the blood rush to my face.

He slackened his pace, and looked still more affectionately, still more gayly and joyfully, at me.

When we reached the house, his mother and the guests whom we could not avoid asking were already assembled, and, up to the moment when, on leaving the church, we took our seats in the carriage to ride to Nikolskoye, I was no longer alone with him.

The church was almost empty; I saw, out of the corner of my eye, only his mother, standing prim and precise on the carpeting in the choir; Katya, in her cap with lilac ribbons, and with tears on her cheeks; and two or three house-serfs, who stared at me with curiosity.

I did not look at him, but I was conscious of his presence near me. I listened to the words of the prayers, and repeated them with my lips, but there seemed to be no echo of them in my soul. I could not pray; I looked stupidly at the ikons, the tapers, the embroidered cross on the back of the priest's chasuble; at the ikonostas, the church windows, — and everything was like a dream.

I only had a confused consciousness that something

unusual was happening to me. When the priest, with
the cross, turned to us and congratulated us, and said
that he had christened me, and now God had granted
him the privilege of marrying me; when Katya and his
mother kissed us, and Grigori's voice was heard as he
drove up the carriage, I was amazed and frightened,
because it was all over and nothing extraordinary had
taken place in my soul; nothing that corresponded to
the mysterious sacrament which had been performed
over me.

He and I exchanged kisses; and this kiss was so
strange, so alien to our feelings.

"Is that all?" I asked myself.

We went to the church porch; the wheels echoed
with a hollow sound under the vaulted roof; my face
was fanned by the cool breeze; he put on his hat and
handed me into the carriage. From the carriage
window I saw the crescent of the frosty moon.

He took his seat next me, and shut the door.
Something throbbed in my heart. The self-assurance
with which he did this seemed to me insulting.

Katya's voice screamed something about protecting
my head; the wheels struck against a stone, and then
we turned into the smooth road and were off. Throwing myself back in one corner, I looked out of the
window on the distant fields and the road, seeming to
reflect a pale light from the chill rays of the moon.
And, though I did not look at him, I felt the consciousness that he was next to me.

"And is this all that the moment for which I have
waited so anxiously has to give me?" I asked myself,
and it began to appear mean and humiliating to sit
alone so near to him. I turned to him with the intention of saying something, but no word found utterance;
it was as if there were in me none of that former feeling
of affection, and as if humiliation and dismay had taken
its place.

"Till this moment I have not been able to persuade
myself that this was to be," he softly murmured, in reply
to my look.

"Yes; but somehow or other it is terrible to me," I replied.

"Am I terrible to you, my love?" he asked, taking my hand and bending his head down to it.

My hand lay lifeless in his, and in my heart there was a sense of painful coldness.

"Yes," I whispered.

But then, suddenly, my heart began to beat more violently, my hand trembled and suddenly pressed his hand; a feeling of warmth came o'er me, my eyes tried to look into his, in the twilight, and I suddenly felt that I was not afraid of him; that this dismay was — *love;* new and vastly more tender and strong than before. I felt that I was wholly his, and that I was happy in his power over me.

PART SECOND

CHAPTER I

DAYS, weeks, two months of lonely country life went by, imperceptibly as it seemed at that time; but, at the same time, the emotions, sensations, and delights of those two months would have sufficed for a whole lifetime.

Neither my dreams nor his of how our life in the country should be organized were realized at all as we had anticipated. But our life was in no respect a disappointment of our dreams. There was none of that strenuous labor, the fulfilment of duty, self-renunciation, and life for others, which I had imagined when I became his betrothed; it was, on the contrary, one absorbing, selfish affection for each other; a desire to be loved, a constant, causeless delight, and oblivion of all in the world.

To be sure, he sometimes went into his library, and shut himself up to attend to his affairs; sometimes he went to town, and, again, he was absent on business about the estate; but I saw how hard it was for him to tear himself away from me. And he himself acknowledged that everything in the world seemed to him such perfect triviality, unless I were there, that he could not conceive the possibility of taking any interest in them.

It was exactly the same with me. I read, occupied myself with my music, with his mother, with the school; but I did this only because each one of these occupations was connected with him and met with his approbation; but, as soon as ever the thought of him failed to be connected with any particular task, my hands would fall at my side, and it would seem so queer to think that there was any one besides him in the world.

Possibly this was an unworthy, selfish feeling; but it gave me pleasure and elevated me high above all the world.

In my eyes he was the only being on earth, and I considered him the handsomest and most perfect man in the world; consequently, I could not live for any one besides him, or help trying to be in his eyes what he thought me to be. And he considered me the first and the most beautiful woman in the world, endowed with every possible perfection, and I strove to be this woman in the eyes of the first and best man in all the world.

Once he came into my chamber while I was engaged in prayer. I glanced at him and continued with my devotions. He sat down at the table, so as not to disturb me, and opened a book. But it seemed to me that he was looking at me, and I looked round. He smiled; I began to laugh, and could not go on with my devotions.

"And have you already said your prayers?" I asked.

"Yes, but go on; I will leave you."

"You say your prayers, I hope; don't you?"

He made no reply, and was about to go; but I detained him.

"My sweetheart,[1] please, for my sake, read a prayer with me."

He stood by my side, awkwardly dropping his hands, and began with a serious countenance, but falteringly, to read. Now and then he turned to me, as if to find approbation and encouragement in my face.

When he had read it through, I laughed and gave him a hug.

"That's the way with thee; it's just as if I were ten years old again!" he exclaimed, reddening, and kissing my hand.

Our house was one of those old country mansions in which had lived, in mutual love and reverence, several generations of one family. It was all redolent of sweet, pure family recollections, and these, when I came to live in it, seemed suddenly to have become part and parcel with my own traditions.

[1] *Dusha moya*, "my soul."

The furnishing and adornment of the house were in the old-fashioned style such as Tatyana Semyonovna preferred; it could not be said that they were elegant and magnificent; but there was an abundance of everything, from servants to furniture and food; everything was tidy, solid, stiff, and awe-inspiring. In the drawing-room, the furniture was arranged with symmetrical precision; the wall was hung with portraits; homemade rugs and striped linen were spread on the floor.

In the divan-room stood an old grand piano, chiffonniers of two distinct styles, divans, and brass and mother-of-pearl tables. My boudoir, by the care of Tatyana Semyonovna, was furnished with the most beautiful furniture of different centuries and styles, and, among other things, an old pier-glass, into which I could never glance without a sense of bashfulness, but which finally became as dear to me as an old friend.

Tatyana Semyonovna did not let her voice be heard in the house; but everything went like clockwork, though there were a great many superfluous servants. All of these servants, who wore soft shoes, without heels, — Tatyana Semyonovna considered squeaking shoes and the noise of heels as the most unpleasant things in the world, — all the servants seemed proud of their station, trembled before the old lady, looked on my husband and me with patronizing affection, and evidently did their work with extraordinary contentment.

Regularly every Saturday, all the floors in the house were washed, and the rugs beaten; on the first day of the month a *Te Deum* was performed, and holy water sprinkled; every time that a name-day occurred — Tatyana Semyonovna's, her son's, or mine (mine the first time it occurred, that autumn) — a banquet was given to all the neighborhood. And all this sort of thing had been done, without ever a break in the custom, since Tatyana Semyonovna's earliest remembrance.

My husband did not interfere in the domestic economy, and merely took charge of the management of

the farm [1] and the serfs; and that occupied him a good
deal. Even in winter he got up very early, and was
usually gone when I woke. He returned generally to
morning tea, which we drank by ourselves, and almost
always at this time, after the troubles and annoyances
of his work, he would appear in that extraordinarily
jolly frame of mind which we used to call "wild
enthusiasm."

Oftentimes I tried to induce him to tell me what he
did in the morning, and he would relate such absurdities
that we almost died laughing; sometimes I urged him
to give me a serious account, and he would restrain himself and tell me. I looked into his eyes, at the motion
of his lips, and remembered nothing, but I was merely
delighted to see him and to hear his voice.

"Well, what have I been telling you? Let us hear
it," he would say, and I could not tell him the first
word. It was so absurd that *he* should tell *me* about
anything else than our own selves. It scarcely made
any difference what it was that he had been doing.
It was not until long afterward that I began to understand or feel any interest in his labors.

Tatyana Semyonovna did not make her appearance
till dinner-time; she drank her tea alone, and only sent
a messenger to inquire how we had slept. In our especial, insanely happy little world, it sounded so strange
to hear the voice from her solemn, orderly quarters, so
different from ours, that oftentimes I could not refrain
from laughing heartily in reply to the maid who, with
folded arms, gravely announced that "Tatyana Semyonovna has sent to inquire how you slept after your yesterday's ride, and she begs to inform you, in regard
to herself, that she suffered all night long from the
neuralgia, and that a stupid dog in the village barked
and prevented her from getting any rest. And she
also would be pleased to know how you liked to-day's
baking; and begs to remark that Taras did not make
the bread to-day, but that Nikolashka was allowed to
try his hand for the first time, as an experiment, and

[1] *Polyevoye khoyaïstvo.*

has done not at all badly, says she, especially in the rolls, but he cooked the biscuits too much."

Till dinner-time we were very little together. I played, read to myself; he wrote or went out again; but at four o'clock, when we had dinner, we went to the drawing-room; "mamasha" sailed out of her room, and several visitors, indigent ladies of noble birth, several of whom we always had at the house, made their appearance. Regularly, each day, my husband, in accordance with immemorial custom, offered his mother his arm, to take her out to dinner; but she insisted that he should give me his other, and regularly, each day, we got into a tangle at the door, which was too narrow for all of us.

"Matushka" presided at dinner, and the conversation proceeded with dignified sobriety and not a little solemnity. The few simple words that my husband and I exchanged made an agreeable contrast to the stiffness of these dinner-table conferences. Occasionally, disputes arose between mother and son, and they said sarcastic things to one another; I especially enjoyed these disputes and sarcasms, because they served to bring out in all the stronger light the firm and tender love that united them.

After dinner, *maman* went into the drawing-room and sat down in her great arm-chair, rubbed tobacco or cut open the leaves of newly purchased books; while my husband and I would read aloud, or go into the divan-room to the clavichord. We read a great deal during these weeks, but music was our favorite and supreme enjoyment; for each time it touched new chords in our hearts, and, as it were, revealed each of us to the other again. When I played his favorite pieces, he would sit on the divan at the other end of the room, where I could hardly see him, and from very shyness would try to conceal the impression which the music made on him; but often, when he did not expect it, I would jump up from the piano, run over to him, and try to detect on his face the traces of the emotion, an unnatural light and moisture in his eyes, which he tried in vain to hide from me.

Mamasha often wanted to visit us in the drawing-room, but she was afraid of interrupting us, and sometimes, apparently not looking at us, she would pass through the room with a pretended grave and indifferent face; but I knew that she had no reason to go to her room, and so would quickly return.

In the evening I poured tea in the great drawing-room, and once more all the people of the house gathered at the table. This solemn seat of ceremony before the polished samovar, and the distribution of the glasses and cups, for a long time filled me with trepidation. It seemed to me that I was not yet fitted for this responsibility, that I was too young and frivolous to turn the tap of the big samovar, to put the glass on the butler's salver, and say, "For Piotr Ivanovitch," "For Marya Minitchna, and ask her if it is weak enough," and to put in the lumps of sugar for the nurse and the servants.

"Splendid, splendid," my husband used often to say, "just like a grown-up lady!" and this confused me more than ever.

After tea, *maman* played patience, or heard Marya Minitchna tell fortunes; then she would kiss us and make the sign of the cross over us, and we would retire to our own rooms. Generally, however, we would sit up till midnight, and this was the best and pleasantest part of the day. He would tell me about his past; we would make plans. Sometimes we would discuss philosophy, and do our best to talk low so as not to be heard up-stairs, and that no suspicion of it might reach Tatyana Semyonovna, who believed in early retiring. Sometimes we would be hungry, and go softly down to the sideboard, find some cold supper, provided by Nikita's thoughtfulness, and eat it in my boudoir, by the light of a single candle. He and I lived quite like visitors in this big old mansion, over which brooded the stern spirit of old personified in Tatyana Semyonovna. Not only she, but the servants, the old serving-maids, the furniture, and the paintings, inspired in me a certain respect, a certain awe, and a consciousness that we were not exactly fitted for such associations, and that it was our duty to live a circumspect and careful sort of existence here.

As I look back on it now, it seems that much must have been really stiff and uncomfortable — that stern, unchangeable order, and that throng of lazy, inquisitive people in the house; but then, at that time, that very restraint gave an additional strength to our love.

Neither he nor I gave the slightest sign that anything displeased us. On the contrary, he would have resolutely shut his eyes to what was disagreeable. Mamenka's valet, Dmitri Sidorof, a great lover of smoking, regularly, each day, while we were in the divan-room, after dinner, went to my husband's library and took tobacco from his drawer; and it was worth while to see with what merry dismay Sergyeï Mikhaïluitch came to me on his tiptoes, and, making a warning gesture with his finger, and winking, pointed to Dmitri Sidorof, who never suspected that he was seen. And, when Dmitri Sidorof went out without noticing us, my husband, in his joy that all had ended so satisfactorily, as in everything else, said that I was charming, and kissed me.

Sometimes, this easy-going way, this forgiving disposition and apparent indifference, were not pleasing to me; I did not realize that I was open to the same fault, and I called it weakness. "Just like a child who does not dare to show his will," I said to myself.

"Ah, my dear," he replied, one time, when I told him how much surprised I was at his weakness, "would it be possible for me to be angry with any one when I am so happy? It is easier for me to let things go than to oppress others; I became convinced of that long ago — and there is no position where it would be impossible to be happy. And we are having such a good time! I cannot be angry; for me now there is no such thing as *bad*; it is only pitiful, and rather amusing. But the main thing is — *le mieux est l'ennemi du bien.* Would you believe me, when I hear the door-bell, or read a letter, or simply when I wake up, I have a feeling of terror. Terror because I must live, lest some change may take place; for nothing could be better than what is now."

I believed him, but I did not understand him; it was delightful to me, but it seemed to me that it was just as it ought to be; that it could not be otherwise, that it was always so, with all people, and that if elsewhere there were other forms of happiness, they were different, perhaps, but not greater.

Thus passed the two months; winter came, with its cold weather and snowstorms; and, though he was still with me, I began to feel the loneliness, began to feel that life was monotonous, and that it offered neither of us anything new; and that we seemed to be returning forever in our old tracks. He began to busy himself more than before with his own affairs, and to leave me out; and again my former idea came back to me — that he had in his soul an especial world, into which I was not admitted.

His perpetual self-complacency irritated me. I loved him no less than before; I was no less happy in his love. But my love had come to a standstill, and ceased to grow; and now, besides love, a new feeling, of restlessness, began to take possession of my soul.

The continuance of love was very insignificant after the first happiness of finding that I loved him. What I longed for was activity, and not the calmness of a settled life; I wanted emotions, perils, and self-renunciations, instead of thought. I had within me an exuberance of strength, which found no field of activity in our quiet life. I was attacked by storms of melancholy, which I tried to hide from his knowledge, as something naughty, and fits of unnatural tenderness and gayety that frightened him.

He noticed my state of mind even before I did, and proposed that we should go to town; but I begged him not to go, and not to change our way of living, not to destroy our happiness. And, indeed, I was happy; but it tormented me that this happiness caused me no exertion, no sacrifice, when I was tormented by all the potentiality of labor and self-sacrifice. I loved him, and I saw that I was everything to him; but I wanted all to see our love, I wanted something to come as a stumbling-block in the way of my loving, and still I should have loved him.

My mind and even my feelings were occupied, but there was still above and beyond all that another feeling, that of youth, the necessity for exertion; and these found no scope in our quiet life.

Why did he tell me that we might go to town, when that was the only thing that I wanted? If he had not told me so, perhaps I should have understood that the feeling that tormented me was unwholesome nonsense, and my fault, that the very sacrifice which I was searching for was there before me — in the stifling of this feeling.

The thought that I had the power of saving myself from melancholy by merely going to town constantly recurred to me, in spite of myself, and at the same time it seemed mean and detestable, simply for my own pleasure, to tear him away from all that he loved.

But time passed on, the snow piled up higher and higher above the walls of the house, and we were always and forever alone, alone, and still we were always the same in each other's eyes; but yonder, somewhere, in the brilliancy, in the whirl of life, were throngs of men and women suffering and rejoicing, without a thought of us or our petty existence.

Worse than all was my consciousness that each day the habits of our life were forging it into one definite form, that our sensations were growing dull, and corresponded to the smooth, passionless course of time. In the morning we were cheerful, at dinner deferential, in the evening affectionate.

"To do good!" said I to myself; "it is excellent to do good and to live honorable lives, as he says; we have still time for that, but there is something for which now and now only I have the requisite power."

This was not what I needed; I needed a struggle; what I needed was that feeling should guide life, and not that life should guide feeling. I wanted to go with him to the edge of an abyss, and say, "Here a step, and I will throw myself over; here a motion, and I have gone to destruction;" and for him, turning pale, to seize me in his strong arms, hold me over it till my heart grew cold within me, and then carry me away wherever he pleased.

This state of affairs had a bad effect on my health, and my nerves began to suffer. One morning it was worse than usual; he came back from the office out of spirits; this was a rare event for him. I immediately noticed it, and asked him what the matter was; but he was not inclined to tell me, saying that it was not worth while. I afterward learned that the police ispravnik had called upon our peasantry, and, out of an unfriendly disposition to my husband, had made illegal claims on them, and threatened them. My husband could not as yet look with any degree of coolness on all this, a merely wretched and impertinent piece of business; he was angry, and therefore he did not wish to talk with me about it. But it seemed to me that he did not want to tell me about it because he considered me still a child, who could not understand what interested him.

I turned from him, said nothing, and sent to invite Marya Minitchna, a visitor of ours, to tea. After tea, which I brought to a most remarkably hasty conclusion, I took Marya Minitchna into the divan-room, and began to talk in a very loud tone about some trifle or other, of absolutely no interest to me. He walked about the room, and from time to time looked at us. These glances of his had such a peculiar effect on me that I had all the time a stronger and stronger inclination to talk and even to be merry; everything that I said, as well as everything that Marya Minitchna said, seemed to me ludicrous. Without saying anything to me, he went off to his library and closed the door behind him.

As soon as he was out of hearing, all my gayety suddenly vanished, so that Marya Minitchna was struck by it, and asked me what was the matter.

Without answering her, I sat down on a divan, and felt a strong inclination to cry.

"And what does he think of this performance?" I asked myself. "Some trifle which seems important to him; but just let him try to tell me, I will show him that it's all nonsense. No, he must think that I have no sense; he must needs humiliate me with his majestic calmness, and always be so superior to me. But I am as right as he is, though it is so stupid and dull here, though I have such a desire to live and stir about," I said to myself, "and not to stay always in one place, and feel how time is passing. I want to advance, and every day, every hour, I want something new; but he wants to stand stock-still, and hold me back too. And how easy it would be for him. For this it is not necessary to take me to town; it needs only for him to be like me, not to make a display, not to put checks on one's self, but simply to live. This is the very advice he gave me, but he himself does not follow it. That's what the trouble is!"

I felt that my heart was filling with tears, and that I was angry with him. This exhibition of temper alarmed me, and I went to him. He was sitting in his library writing. When he heard my steps, he glanced up for a moment calmly and indifferently, and went on with his writing. This look of his displeased me; instead of going to him, I stood by the table at which he was writing, and, opening a book, I began to turn the leaves of it. Once more he stopped and looked at me.

"Masha!" said he, "are you out of sorts?"

I answered with a chilling glance, which said, "What makes you ask?— mere curiosity?"

He shook his head, with a sweet, affectionate smile; but for the first time I did not give him an answering smile.

"What has been the trouble with you to-day?" I asked. "Why wouldn't you tell me?"

"A mere trifle, a slight unpleasantness," he replied. "However, I can tell you now. Two peasants have been summoned to town." ....

But I did not give him a chance to finish his story.

"Why didn't you tell me this when I asked you at tea?"

"I should have made some foolish remark, for I was angry then."

"But then was the time that I wanted to know."

"Why?"

"Because you think that I can never be of any help to you."

"What is that?" he exclaimed, throwing down his pen. "I think that I cannot live without you. You not only help me in everything, but you do everything. How did you get such an idea!" he cried, laughing. "I live only for you. Everything seems good to me. I am happy simply because you are here, because you need...."

"Yes, I know that I am a dear child, who needs to be calmed," said I, in such a tone that he was amazed, and, apparently for the first time noticing what a state of mind I was in, gazed at me. "I don't want calmness; you have enough, quite enough for us both," I added.

"Well, now you see what the trouble was," he began hurriedly, interrupting me, apparently fearing to let me say all that I had in mind. "How should you decide the question?"

"I don't want to now," I replied. Though I had a strong desire to hear him, still I took a keen delight in disturbing his equanimity. "I don't want to play at life, I want to live," said I, "just as you do."

Over his face, which always answered so readily and quickly to every emotion, passed an expression of pain and earnest attention.

"I want to live in the same way as you do, on an equality with you."....

But words failed me, such grief, such deep grief, was expressed in his face. He was silent for a little.

"Yes; but you do live on an equality with me, don't you?" he asked; "except that I and not you have to deal with police ispravniks and drunken peasants."....

"No, not in this thing alone," I said.

"For God's sake, understand me, my love," he went on to say. "I know that it is always painful for us to have anxieties; I have had experience of life, and I know this. I love you, and really I cannot help wishing to save you from anxiety. My life consists in this — in love for you; and so don't disturb my life."

"You are always right!" I cried, not looking at him.

I felt annoyed that his soul had again become clear and calm, when mine was still filled with vexation and a feeling like repentance.

"Masha! what is the matter with you?" he exclaimed. "The question is not whether I am right or you are right, but something quite different; what have you to complain of against me? Don't speak rashly, think it all over, and tell me all that you have in your mind. You are angry with me, and of course you must have good reason, but do let me understand wherein I am to blame."

But how could I tell him what was in my soul? The very fact that he understood me so immediately, that I was again like a child before him, that I could not do anything without his understanding all about it and even foreseeing it, — all this made me still more indignant.

"I have nothing at all to complain of against you," said I. "Simply everything seems tedious to me, and I do not wish it to be so. But you say it must be so, and there again you are right."

I said this and did not look at him. I attained my purpose: his calmness disappeared; pain and apprehension were in his face.

"Masha!" he exclaimed in a low, agitated voice, "this is no trifling matter, what you are doing now to me. Now our fate is being decided. I beg of you not to reply to me, but to listen. Why do you want to torture me?" ....

But I interrupted him.

"I know that you are right. You had better not speak; you are right," said I, coldly, as if it were not myself, but an evil spirit which spoke in me.

"If you knew what you were doing!" said he, in a trembling voice.

I burst into tears, and it gave me relief. He sat near me, and said nothing. I was sorry for him, and ashamed of myself, and vexed at what I had done. I did not look at him. I had an impression that he must be looking at me, either sternly or in perplexity, at that moment. I looked up; his sweet, affectionate glance was fixed on me as if asking my forgiveness. I seized his hand, and said: —

"Forgive me! I myself did not know what I was saying."

"Yes; but I know what you said, and that what you said was the truth."

"What?" I asked.

"We must go to Petersburg," said he. "There is nothing for us to do here now."

"Just as you please," I replied.

He took me in his arms and kissed me.

"Forgive me!" he murmured; "I was to blame toward you."

That evening I played a long time to him, and as he walked up and down the room, he kept repeating something. He had the habit of whispering, and I often asked him what he was saying; and he always, after a little thought, told me pretty nearly what he was repeating; generally poetry, and sometimes awful rubbish, but I was enabled by it to tell how he felt in his mind.

"What are you repeating to yourself?" I asked.

He stopped walking, and after a little thought, he smiled, and repeated two lines by Learmontof: —

> *But he, insensate, begged for tempests, ...*
> *As if in tempests peace were found.*" ....

"No! he is more than a man; he knows everything," said I to myself. "How is it possible not to love him?"

I jumped up, took his arm, and began to walk with him, trying to keep step.

"Well?" he asked, with a smile, looking at me.

"Well," I replied, in a whisper; and a strangely

merry frame of mind took possession of both of us; and, taking longer and longer steps, and standing higher and higher on our tiptoes, and with the same step, to the great indignation of Grigori, and to the amazement of mamasha, who was playing patience in the reception-room, we rushed through all the rooms, into the dining-room, and there we stopped, looking at each other, and burst into hearty laughter.

At the end of a fortnight, just before Christmas, we were in Petersburg.

CHAPTER II

Our journey to Petersburg, our week in Moscow, his relatives and mine, our settling down in new quarters, the road, strange cities, faces,—all this went by like a dream. It was all so varied, so new, and so gay, it was all so warm and brightly lighted by his forethought, his love, that the quiet country existence seemed long past and insignificant.

To my great amazement, instead of worldly pride and coolness, which I had expected to find in society people, I was met by all with such sincere affection and hearti-ness—not only my relatives but also strangers—that it seemed as if I were their principal preoccupation, as if they had been only waiting for me to have their happi-ness complete. Unexpectedly, also, my husband dis-covered many acquaintances in the circle of society which seemed to be the best of all; he had never spoken to me of them, and I had often thought it strange, and not altogether pleasant, to hear him pass such harsh judgments on some of these people, who seemed to me so nice. I could not understand why he was so curt in his treatment of them, and why he tried to avoid many acquaintances whom I liked. It seemed to me the more intimately acquainted you become with good people the better, and they were all good.

"Well, you see how we are situated," said he, before we left the country. "Here we are little Crœsuses, but there we shall be very far from rich; and so we can stay in town only till Easter, and not go into society, otherwise we shall get into trouble; yes, and for your sake, I should n't wish...."

"Why society?" I asked. "Only let us go to the theater, see our relatives, hear the opera and good music, and we will return to the country even before Easter."

But as soon as we reached Petersburg these plans were forgotten. I found myself suddenly in such a new, delightful world, I was occupied with so many pleasures, such new interests rose up before me, that I forthwith, though quite unconsciously, recanted all the past, and all the plans that I had made.

"All that was such nonsense! I had not even begun to live; this is the real life! yes, what more is there in store for us?" I asked myself.

The restlessness and moods of melancholy which had disquieted me in the country suddenly and entirely disappeared like magic. My love for my husband became calmer; and here the thought that my husband's love might be growing less never occurred to me. Yes, and I could not doubt his love; my every thought was immediately understood, my every feeling divined, my every desire fulfilled by him. His excessive calmness here disappeared, or, at least, no longer annoyed me.

Moreover, I was conscious that he was even more in love with me than before. Often, after making a call on a new acquaintance, or after having had company at our own apartments, when I, inwardly trembling for fear lest I should commit some blunder, fulfilled the duties of a hostess, he would say:—

"*Ai da!* little girl, famous! don't be worried! truly it was capital!"

And I was very happy. Soon after our arrival, he wrote to his mother, and, when he called me to add a line, he was not willing for me to read what he had written; but afterward, of course, I had my way and read it.

"You would not know Masha," he wrote. "And I

myself hardly know her. Where did she get this gentle, gracious self-confidence, her *affableness*, her clever wit, and her sweetness? And it is all so simple, so gentle, so kindly. Every one is enthusiastic about her, and I myself cannot love her enough, even if it were possible to love her more."

"Ah! so that is what I am, is it?" I said to myself; and I felt so happy and good, and it even seemed to me that I loved him more than ever.

My success with all our acquaintances was entirely unexpected to me. On every side I heard that I had immensely pleased this uncle, that there a certain aunt was quite crazy over me; one person told me that there were no such women as I was in all Petersburg; another assured me that it was within my power to be the most exquisite woman in society. More than all, my husband's cousin, the Princess D., an elderly society lady, who had taken a sudden fondness for me above all, told me the most flattering things, which quite turned my head. When, for the first time, this cousin invited me to go to a ball, and asked my husband's consent, he turned to me, with a slightly crafty smile, and asked if I wanted to go. I nodded my head in sign of assent, and was conscious that I blushed.

"The culprit confesses what she wants," said he, with a good-natured laugh.

"Yes, but you said that it would be impossible for us to go into society, and that you did not like it," I replied, smiling, and looking at him with a supplicating glance.

"If you would like very much to go, then we will," said he.

"Truly, nothing could be better."

"So you would like to go? Very much?" he asked again.

I made no reply.

"Society is not a great misfortune in itself," he went on to say, "but the unattainable ambitions of the world are bad and unworthy. Certainly we must go, and we will!" said he, firmly, in conclusion.

"To tell you the truth," said I, "there is nothing in the world that I was so anxious for as to go to this ball."

We went, and the enjoyment that I experienced exceeded all my expectations. At the ball, it seemed to me, more than ever, that I was the center around which everything revolved; that it was for my sake alone that the great drawing-room was lighted up, the music played, and all this throng of people, admiring me, was gathered together. All, from the hair-dresser and chambermaid to the young men who danced and the old men who promenaded through the ball-room, it seemed to me, spoke to me and made me feel that they liked me. The general consensus of opinion in regard to me at that ball, and reported to me by the Princess D., agreed in this: that I was quite unlike any other woman; that there were a peculiar rustic simplicity and charm about me.

This triumph so elated me that I coolly told my husband how much I should like to go to two or three more balls this year, " so as to be satisfied for once," I added, acting against my conscience.

My husband consented, and the first time went with me with apparent willingness, being pleased with my success, and, as it seemed, entirely forgetting or disavowing what he had said before.

At last he evidently began to grow tired of it, and to be weary of the life that we led. But such was not the case with me; even if I noticed occasionally his significantly serious look fixed questioningly on me, I affected to ignore its meaning. I was so carried away by this suddenly kindled liking that all these strangers seemed to show me, by this atmosphere of elegance, these pleasures and novelties, which I now for the first time in my life experienced, — his moral influence, restraining me, seemed so suddenly to disappear; it was so agreeable to me to feel that in this new world I was not only on an equality with him, but even stood on a higher footing, and therefore could love him more and deeper than before, — that I could not understand how he could find anything unpleasant for me in worldly life. I experienced a new feeling of pride and self-respect when, on entering the ball-room, all eyes were turned upon me; but he, apparently feeling ashamed to lay claim to me before all that throng, made haste to leave me, and disappeared in the black mass of dress-coats.

"Just wait," I often thought. "Wait till we go home, and then you will find out, and know for whose sake I have striven to be handsome and brilliant, and whom I love out of all those that have surrounded me this evening."

It really seemed to me that I rejoiced at my successes, merely for the sake of being in the condition of sacrificing them to him.

One way, I thought, in which this society life might be injurious to me was the possibility that I might fascinate some of the men who met me in society, and arouse my husband's jealousy; but he had such a firm confidence in me, he seemed so calm and equable, and all these young men seemed to me so insignificant in comparison with him, that the only danger in society, as far as my observation went, was not alarming to me. But still, the attentions of many of these young men in society added to my conceit, fanned my selfishness, caused me to reflect that there was considerable merit in my love toward my husband, and made my behavior toward him more independent and perhaps careless.

"Ah! I saw how you had a very lively conversation with N. N.," said I, one time, as we were returning from a ball; and threatened him with my finger, mentioning by name one of the best-known ladies of Petersburg, with whom he had really been talking that evening. I said this in order to stir him up, because he was extraordinarily silent and depressed.

"Ah! why say such a thing? And for you to say it, Masha!" he muttered, through his teeth, and frowning as if from physical pain. "How little this concerns you and me! Leave that to others; these false relations have the power of destroying our peace of mind, and I still hope that the reality will return."

I was ashamed, and said nothing.

"Will it return, Masha? What do you think?" he asked.

"It never has been destroyed, and never will be destroyed," said I ; and at that time it really seemed to me that such was the case.

"God grant that it may not!" he exclaimed. "For then it would be time for us to return to the country."

But this was the only time that he spoke so to me ; the rest of the time it seemed to me that he was enjoying himself as much as I was, and I was so happy and gay. If sometimes he felt the sense of tedium, I consoled myself by thinking how bored I had been for his sake in the country.

"If our relations are somewhat altered, then all will be the same as before as soon as summer comes and we are again alone with Tatyana Semyonovna, in our home at Nikolskoye."

Thus for me the winter passed imperceptibly away, and, contrary to our plans, we spent Easter-tide also in Petersburg. The following week, just as we were all ready to start, — everything was packed up, and my husband, having purchased various gifts, and flowers and articles for home use in the country, was in a remarkably gay and affectionate mood, — his cousin, the Princess D., came to see us, and began to urge us to stay until Saturday, so as to go to the Countess R.'s reception. She declared that the Countess R. was very anxious to have me be present, and that Prince [1] M., who was at that time in Petersburg, and, ever since the last ball, had wished to make my acquaintance, was going to the rout simply for this, and insisted that I was the most beautiful woman in Russia. The whole city was going to be there, and, in one word, it would n't be anything if I did not go.

My husband was at the other end of the drawing-room, engaged in conversation with some one.

---

[1] *Prins*, of a royal family; not *kniaz*, which, though ordinarily translated prince, is a Russian title so common through inheritance as to lose significance. — ED.

"Well, you will come, will you not, Marie?" asked our cousin.

"We were going to the country, day after to-morrow," I replied doubtfully, and looked at my husband. Our eyes met; he turned hastily away.

"I will tell him to stay," said our cousin. "And we will go Saturday and turn all heads. What?"

"But this would upset all our plans, and besides, we are all packed," I replied, beginning to yield a little.

"Yes, it would be better for her to go and pay her respects to the prince this evening," said my husband, from the end of the room, in a repressed tone of indignation, which I had never before heard from him.

"Ah! he is jealous; now I see it for the first time," remarked our cousin. "But you see, I am not trying to persuade her for the sake of the prince, Sergyeï Mikhaïlovitch, but for all of us. How anxious the Countess R. is to have her come!"

"This depends wholly upon her," rejoined my husband, coldly, and went out.

I saw that he was more than usually excited; this troubled me, and so I gave our cousin no definite answer.

Only, as soon as she had gone, I went to my husband. He was walking thoughtfully back and forth, and did not see or hear me when I stole on tiptoe into the room.

"He is recalling his dear Nikolskoye home," I said to myself, as I looked at him. "And the morning coffee, in the bright reception-room, and his fields, and his peasants, and the evenings in the divan-room, and our mysterious midnight suppers. No!" I said to myself, decidedly, "I will sacrifice all the balls in the world, and the flattery of all its princes, for his joyous mood, for his gentle caresses."

I was going to tell him that I was not going to the rout, that I did not care to go, when he suddenly looked up, and, on seeing me, frowned, and the sweetly thoughtful expression of his face changed. Once more, keen sagacity, wisdom, and patronizing calmness appeared in his expression. He was unwilling for me to look on him simply as a man: it was essential for him always to stand before me like a demi-god on a pedestal.

"What is it you want, my dear?" he asked, turning toward me with calm indifference.

I made no reply. It vexed my very soul to have him wear a mask before me, to have him unwilling to be as I liked him best.

"So you would like to stay till Saturday and go to the rout?" he asked.

"I did want to, but I see that it does not suit you. Besides, we are all packed," I added.

Never before had he looked at me so coldly, never before had he spoken to me so coldly.

"I am not going till Tuesday, and I will have the things unpacked," he said; "so you can go if you would like. You will please do me the favor of going. I shall not leave town."

As always when he was agitated, he began to stride up and down the room, and he did not look at me.

"I really do not understand you," said I, without moving from where I stood, and following him with my eyes. "You say that you are always so calm." (He had never said such a thing.) "Why do you speak to me so strangely? For your sake I was ready to deprive myself of this pleasure, and you speak to me in such a sarcastic tone, in such a way as you have never spoken with me before, and compel me to go."

"Well, now! You make a *sacrifice* of yourself" (he laid a special stress on that word), "and I make a sacrifice of myself; which is better? A contest of magnanimity! Such is the basis of *family happiness*, is it not?"

This was the first time I had heard him make use of such bitterly sarcastic words. And his sarcasm did not touch me, but rather offended me; and the bitterness did not frighten me, but hardened me. Could it be that *he* said such things, he who always feared formality in our relations, he who was always so simple and true?

And for what reason?

Simply because I wanted to sacrifice for him a pleasure in which I could see no harm, and because a moment before this I had understood and loved him so! Our *rôles* were exchanged; he avoided my simple and straightforward words, and I was in search of them.

"You have changed very much," I said, with a sigh. "What crime have I been guilty of, in your eyes? It is not this reception, but some old grudge that you have in your heart against me! Why this lack of frankness? Once you did not avoid it. Speak honestly, and tell me what fault you have to find with me." "What will he say to this?" I asked myself, remembering, with self-congratulation, that not once during the winter had he had cause to find fault with me.

I went into the middle of the room, so that he would have to pass close by me, and I looked at him. "He will come to me, he will take me into his arms, and that will be the end of it," I thought, and I even began to feel sorry that I should not have the chance to show him how much in the wrong he was. But he paused at the end of the room, and looked at me.

"So you still don't understand me?" he asked.

"No."

"Well, then, I will explain to you. The feeling that I have, and cannot help having, is nasty; and 't is the first time I ever felt so."....

He paused, evidently startled by the harsh sound of his voice.

"Well, what is it?" I asked, with tears of indignation in my eyes.

"It is nasty that this prince thinks you are beautiful, and because you are, therefore, eager to make his acquaintance; forgetting your husband, and your own self, and your dignity as a woman, and because you are unwilling to understand what your husband must feel for you, if you have no sense of your dignity as a woman; on the contrary, you come and tell your husband that you are *sacrificing* yourself; in other words: 'To be presented to his highness is a great honor for me, but I am willing to *sacrifice* it.'"

The longer he spoke, the more excited he became

through the sound of his own voice, for this voice sounded harsh, cutting, and brutal. I had never seen him so, and never expected to see him so. The blood rushed to my heart; I was frightened, but at the same time I was supported by a sense of undeserved injury, and of insulted pride, and I was bound to have my revenge.

"I have been expecting this for a long time," I said. "Go on, go on!"

"I know not what *you* have been expecting," he continued, "but I had good reason to look for the worst, seeing you every day growing more and more absorbed in the vileness, the idleness, the luxury, of this senseless society; and I have expected .... I have expected this very thing which to-day fills me with shame and pain such as I never felt before; pain for myself, when this friend of yours, with her vulgar hands, pried into my heart, and began to talk about jealousy, *my* jealousy!.... and toward whom? a man with whom neither of us is acquainted! And you, as if purposely, have no desire to understand me, and you speak of making a sacrifice for me! Of what?.... And shame on you, shame on your degradation!.... Sacrifice indeed!" he cried.

"Ah! now we see a husband's power," I said to myself, "to insult and humiliate a woman who has not done the slightest thing wrong. This is what it means by a husband's rights, but I won't give in to them."

"No, I will not make any sacrifice for you," I said, feeling how unnaturally my nostrils were dilated, and how the blood was rushing to my face. "I shall most certainly go to the rout Saturday; nothing shall hinder me!"

"Well, God give you much pleasure; but all is at an end between us!" he cried, carried away by uncontrollable rage. "Henceforth you shall not torment me. I was a fool when I ...." he began again, but his lips twitched, and he restrained himself by an evident effort from finishing the sentence he had begun.

I was afraid of him and loathed him at that instant. I had many things I wanted to tell him, so as to retaliate for his insulting remarks; but if I had opened my lips I should have burst into tears, and lost my dignity before him. I left the room without saying a word. But, as soon as I ceased to hear the sound of his steps, I was overwhelmed by the horror of what we had done. I felt terribly at the thought that the bond on which my happiness depended was torn asunder forever, and I felt strongly drawn to return.

" But is he sufficiently calm," I asked myself, " to understand me, if I should silently stretch out my hand and look at him? Would he understand my magnanimity? What if he should call my grief pretense? Or would he accept my repentance and forgive me, with the consciousness of being in the right, and with proud calmness? And why? Why should he whom I have loved insult me so cruelly?"

I went, not to him, but to my chamber, where I sat long alone, weeping, remembering with horror each word of the conversation that had passed between us, substituting for these words other friendly words, and then again, with dismay and a sense of insult, recalling the whole scene.

When I went to tea in the evening, and met my husband in the presence of S., who was staying with us, I had the consciousness that this day a wide abyss had opened between us. S. asked me when we were going.

Before I had time to reply, my husband said: —

" Next Tuesday. We are going to the rout at the Countess R.'s. You intend to go, do you not?" he asked, turning to me.

I was terrified at the sound of this simple question, and looked timidly at my husband. His eyes were fixed directly upon me; their expression was angry and sarcastic; his voice was steady and cold.

" Yes," I replied.

In the evening, when we were alone, he came to me, and, holding out his hand, " Please forget what I said to you," said he.

I took his hand, a smile trembled over my lips, and

the tears were ready to well up in my eyes; but he withdrew his hand, and, as if he feared a sentimental scene, he sat down in an arm-chair, at some distance from me.

"I wonder if he can consider himself wholly in the right?" I thought, and I was ready for a reconciliation; a request not to go to the rout was on my tongue's end.

"I must write to matushka that we have postponed our return," said he; "otherwise she will be anxious."

"And when do you expect to go?" I asked.

"On Tuesday, after the rout," he replied.

"I hope that you are not doing it on my account," said I, looking into his eyes, but his eyes merely looked, and gave me no reply, as if a veil had been drawn over them between him and me. His face suddenly seemed to me old and disagreeable.

We went to the rout, and, to all appearances, our relations were again most friendly. But really these relations were absolutely unlike what they had been.

At the rout, I was sitting with other ladies, when the prince came to me, and I was obliged to stand up in order to talk with him. As I stood up I involuntarily looked for my husband, and caught sight of him at the other end of the drawing-room. He looked at me and turned away. I suddenly felt such a sense of mortification and pain that I grew painfully confused, and blushed to the roots of my hair under the prince's gaze. But I was compelled to stand and listen to what he said, while he looked down on me.

Our conversation was not of long duration; there was no place for him to sit near me, and he evidently saw that I felt very much constrained. We talked about the last ball, about where I lived in the summer, and other things. As he left me he expressed his desire to make my husband's acquaintance, and I saw them meet and talk with each other at the end of the room. The prince was evidently talking about me, because, in the midst of a sentence, he looked around to where I was and smiled.

My husband's face suddenly flushed; he made a low bow, and turned away from the prince. I also blushed, for I was mortified on account of the remark which the prince had evidently made about me, and especially at my husband. It seemed to me that all must have observed my awkward bashfulness at the time the prince was talking with me, and must have noticed my husband's strange behavior; God knows how they may have interpreted that. Was it possible they knew of my quarrel with my husband?

My cousin brought me home, and on the way we talked about my husband. I could not refrain from telling her everything that had occurred between us because of this unhappy rout. She calmed me, saying that this was a perfectly insignificant misunderstanding, such as were very frequent in married life, and led to no consequences; she explained to me what from her point of view my husband's character was; she declared that he was reticent and proud; I agreed with her, and it seemed to me that I myself began now to have a calmer and better appreciation of him.

But afterward, when my husband and I were alone together again, this judgment of him lay like a crime on my conscience, and I was conscious that the abyss that separated us had grown wider than ever.

CHAPTER III

HENCEFORTH, our life and relations underwent a complete change. It was no longer so pleasant as before to be alone together. There were questions which we avoided, and it was easier for us to talk in the presence of a third person than when by ourselves.

Whenever the talk turned on country life or a ball, we felt that we were treading on dangerous ground,[1] and we avoided each other's eyes.

We both seemed to feel where lay the abyss which separated us, and tried to avoid falling into it.

[1] Russ: "As it were, little boys ran in our eyes."

I was persuaded that he was proud and passionate, and that it was necessary to be on my guard not to irritate him. He was persuaded that I could not live without society, that the country was not to my mind, and that it was necessary to give in to this unhappy taste. And we both avoided direct reference to these subjects, and each judged the other falsely.

We had both ceased long ago to be in each other's eyes the most perfect people in the world, but made comparisons with others, and secretly criticized each other.

I became ill before we left Petersburg, and, instead of going to the country, we took a *datcha* or summer place near the city, and my husband went alone to see his mother. When he went, I was sufficiently recovered to go with him, but he insisted that I should stay behind, alleging, as an excuse, that he was afraid for my health. I felt that, in reality, he had no fear about my health, but was afraid that we should not be happy in the country.

I was not very urgent, and I stayed behind. Without him it was dull and lonely, but when he came back I discovered that he did not bring into my life what he had once brought. Our former relations, when every thought unshared with him caused the impression of being guilty of a crime, when every act, every word of his, seemed to me the model of perfection, when from very joy, in looking at each other, we felt like laughing at every little thing, — these relations passed so insensibly into others that we could not tell what had become of them.

Each of us had separate interests and occupations, which we no longer thought of sharing. It even began to seem no longer mortifying that we each had our own special world, from which the other was excluded. We became used to this idea, and at the end of a year "the boys ceased to run in our eyes" when we looked at each other.

His boyish fits of gayety, in which we shared, entirely ceased; his lenience, and his indifference to everything, which formerly troubled me, disappeared; that significant glance, which once confused and delighted me, was seen no more; no longer did we share in our prayers and our enthusiasms; and indeed it now happened that we saw little of each other; he was constantly away on journeys, and he had no fear or regret at leaving me alone; I went constantly into society where I had no need of him.

We had no more scenes or open quarrels, and I endeavored to satisfy his requirements; he fulfilled all my desires, and, to all outward appearance, we still loved each other.

When we were together, which happened rarely, I had no sensation of pleasure, or emotion, or confusion, any more than as if I were alone. I knew very well that he was my husband and not a stranger, but a worthy man, — my husband, whom I knew as well as myself.

I was persuaded that I could foretell all that he would do or say, and how he would look at any matter; and if his actions or views disappointed my expectations, then it seemed to me that he was mistaken.

I had nothing to expect from him; in a word, he was my husband, and that was all. It seemed to me that this was so, and inevitably so; that there never could be, and never had been, other relations between us.

When he went away, especially at first, I felt terribly lonely; when deprived of his support, I realized, as never before, the meaning of it; when he returned, I would throw myself into his arms with joy, and yet within two hours I had entirely forgotten this joy; it quite passed out of my memory, and I had nothing to say to him.

Only in these quiet, sober moments of affection, which we sometimes had, it seemed to me that there was something wrong, that there was a pain in my heart, and it seemed to me that I read the same in his eyes. I felt that this affection had a limit, beyond which, it seemed to me, he had no desire and I no power to go. Sometimes I felt some regret, but I never allowed myself time to meditate on the reason for it; and I tried to forget this vague melancholy, by plunging into all the diversions which were always within my reach.

Society life, which from the very first had dazzled me with its brilliancy and its power of flattering my conceit, quickly attained complete ascendancy over my inclinations, and became a second habit with me, and imposed its fetters on me, and usurped in my mind all the place to which feeling was rightfully entitled.

I never stayed by myself alone, and I was afraid to look my position fairly in the face. All my time, from my waking hour, late in the morning, till I went to bed, late at night, was full, and, even when I did not go out, there was something to occupy me. I was neither happy nor unhappy; but it seemed to me that it must always be this way, and never change.

Thus passed three years, and our relations remained the same; it seemed as if everything remained stationary, congealed, and unable to change, either for the better or the worse.

During these three years of our married life, two important events occurred; but neither of them brought about any change in my life.

They were the birth of my first baby, and the death of Tatyana Semyonovna. At first, the feeling of motherhood took possession of me with such force, and such unexpected exultation welled up in my heart, that I thought a new life was going to begin for me; but after two months, when I was able once more to go out, this feeling, growing weaker and weaker, changed into the habitual and cold fulfilment of duty.

My husband, on the contrary, from the time of the birth of our oldest son, became his old self again, gentle, unruffled, contented with staying at home, and he poured out all his affection and gayety on the child.

Often, when, dressed for some ball, I went into the nursery, to make the sign of the cross over my child, I would find my husband there; I noticed his reproachful and sternly observant glance fixed on me, and my conscience would upbraid me. I would suddenly repent of my indifference to my child, and ask myself : " Can it be that I am worse than other women ?.... But what can I do ?" I asked myself. "I love my son, but I cannot spend all my time with him; it would be tiresome, and not for anything in the world would I make a pretense."

His mother's death was a great grief for him; it was hard, as he said, to live without her at Nikolskoye; but, though I also missed her, and sympathized with my husband's sorrow, I found now much more pleasure and comfort in the country.

During all these three years, we lived, for the most part, in the city, spending only two months one summer in the country, and the third year we went abroad.

We spent the summer at the baths.

I was then twenty-one years old; our circumstances were, I supposed, in a flourishing condition; I did not expect from domestic life anything more than it already gave; everybody whom I knew, it seemed to me, was fond of me; my health was excellent; my toilets were the handsomest at the baths; I knew that I was pretty; the weather was lovely, a peculiar atmosphere of beauty and elegance surrounded me, and I felt very light-hearted.

I was not so light-hearted as I used to be at Nikolskoye, when I had the consciousness that I was happy in myself, that I was happy because I deserved to be, that my happiness was great but was capable of being greater, that I longed for still greater joy.

Then it was another thing; but this summer, also, everything was delightful, I had nothing to desire; I had nothing to hope for, I had nothing to fear, and it seemed to me that my life was full and my conscience was untroubled.

Out of all the young men that season there was not one whom I should have singled out for special distinction, or should have preferred, even to old Prince K., our envoy, who paid me great attention.

One was young, another old; there was a fair-haired Englishman, a Frenchman with an imperial — to all of them I felt perfectly indifferent, yet all of them were indispensable to me.   All these faces had the same monotonous lack of distinction, and yet they formed a part of the joyous atmosphere of life which shed its light on me.

Only one of them, an Italian, the Marchese D., attracted my attention more than the others, by his absurd way of showing his admiration of me.   He never missed an opportunity of being with me, of selecting me as his partner at the hops, of riding with me, of being at the casino, etc., and of telling me that I was beautiful!

Several times I saw him from our windows, loitering near the house, and often the disagreeable boldness of his brilliant eyes made me blush and turn away.

He was young and handsome and elegant, and, strangely enough, his smile and the expression of his forehead were like my husband's, though vastly more attractive.   I was amazed by this resemblance, though on the whole, in his lips, in his eyes, in his long chin, instead of the charming expression of goodness and ideal serenity peculiar to my husband, there was in him something coarse and animal.   I surmised then that he was passionately in love with me.   I sometimes thought of him with proud pity, I sometimes tried to soothe him, to bring him to a state of quiet, trustful friendship ; but he bitterly resented these attempts, and continued unpleasantly to disturb me with his passion, unexpressed, it is true, but ready at any moment to break forth.

Although I did not acknowledge it to myself, I was afraid of this man, and against my will I often thought of him.   My husband had made his acquaintance, and treated him with even more coolness and hauteur than the rest of our acquaintances, to whom he was only the husband of his wife.

At the end of the season I was taken ill, and did not leave my room for a fortnight.   When, for the first time after my illness, I came out one evening to hear the music, I learned that, while I was housed, the long-expected Lady S., a renowned beauty, had arrived.   A group gathered around me, and I was greeted warmly ; but a much more interesting circle was attracted around the newly arrived lioness.   Every one around me was talking only about this lady and her beauty. She was pointed out to me, and truly she was charming; but I was disagreably impressed by the conceited expression on her face, and I said so.

This day everything that had before seemed bright and gay was wearisome to me. On the next day, Lady S. arranged an excursion to the castle, but I declined to go. I was almost the only one left behind, and everything had undergone a complete transformation in my eyes. Everybody and everything seemed to me stupid and tiresome; I felt like crying, and I wanted to finish the baths as soon as possible and return to Russia.

At the bottom of my heart there was a strange wicked feeling, but still I would not acknowledge it to myself. I pretended that I was ill, and ceased to go into large gatherings; only, in the morning, occasionally, I went out to drink the waters, or, with L. M., a Russian lady of our acquaintance, rode into the suburbs. My husband was absent at this time, having gone to Heidelberg for a few days, until I should have finished the course of treatment, when he would return and take me back to Russia.

Once Lady S. had invited all the people of our circle to go on some pleasure excursion, but L. M. and I, after dinner, drove to the castle. While we slowly drove along in our carriage, over the winding highway, between the century-old chestnut trees, through which could be seen far away those exquisitely beautiful suburbs of Baden, bathed in the rays of the setting sun, we conversed seriously, as we had never done before. L. M., though I had known her long, now for the first time appeared to me as a beautiful, intelligent woman, with whom one might safely indulge in confidences, and with whom it was delightful to be on friendly terms.

We talked about our families, our children, and the emptiness of Baden life; we both longed to get back to Russia, to our country homes, and we fell into a mood at once pleasurable and melancholy.

Under the influence of these serious thoughts and feelings, we went into the castle. Within the walls it

was shady and cool; above our heads the sunlight
played on the ruins.

We heard steps and voices.

Through the gate, as in a frame, we could see that
charming view of Baden, which, nevertheless, to us
Russians, seems so cold. We sat down to get breath,
and in silence looked at the sunset.

The voices grew louder, and I thought that I heard
my name mentioned. My attention was attracted, and
I could not help hearing every word that they said. I
knew the voices; they were the Marchese D. and a
French friend of his whom I also knew. They were
talking about *me* and Lady S.

The Frenchman was making comparisons between
us, and descanting on our respective charms. He said
nothing derogatory, and yet the blood rushed to my
heart when I heard what he said. He entered into an
elaborate eulogy of what was beautiful in me and in
Lady S. I was the mother of a child already, but Lady
S. was only nineteen; my hair was prettier, but, on the
other hand, Lady S. had a more graceful figure; Lady
S. was of high birth, while your friend, said he, "is
nothing but one of those petty Russian princesses who
are beginning to flock here in such numbers."

He concluded with the observation that I had done
excellently well not to enter the lists as Lady S.'s rival,
and that my day was practically over, as far as Baden
was concerned.

"I am sorry for her. .... Unless, indeed, she should
take it into her head to console herself with you," he
added, with a gay and cruel laugh.

"If she should go, I should follow her," rudely exclaimed the voice with the Italian accent.

"Happy mortal! he can still love," sneered the
Frenchman.

"Love!" exclaimed the Italian, and then paused. ....
"I cannot help loving! Without love there is no life.
To turn life into a romance, this is the one thing that is
beautiful. And my romance never breaks off in the
middle, and this one I shall carry out to the very end."

"*Bonne chance, mon ami !* " said the Frenchman.

We did not hear any more, because they passed around
the corner, and soon their steps sounded on the other
side. They came down-stairs, and in a moment or two
they entered through a side door, and stopped in amazement to see us. I blushed when the marchese joined
me, and felt terribly when, as we came out of the castle,
he offered me his arm. I could not refuse it, and he
and I followed L. M., who started for the carriage under
the escort of his friend.

I was mortified at what the Frenchman had said
about me, though in my heart of hearts I recognized
that he had only expressed my own convictions; but the
marchese's words had surprised and disturbed me by
their audacity. I was tormented by the thought that I
had overheard what he said; and yet it did not in the
least make him abashed to see me. I felt annoyed to
have him so close to me; and, without looking at him,
without answering him, and trying to take his arm in
such a way as not to hear his words, I hurried after L. M.
and the Frenchman.

The marchese said something about the exquisite view,
about the unexpected pleasure of meeting me, and many
other things still; but I did not heed what he said. I
was thinking at this moment of my husband, of my son,
of Russia; somehow I felt a strange sense of shame and
pity and longing; I was anxious to get home as quickly
as possible, and go to my lonely room in the Hôtel de
Bade in order to think at leisure over all that had so suddenly arisen in my soul. But L. M. went slowly; it was
still quite a distance to the carriage; my cavalier, it
seemed to me, stubbornly slackened his steps, with the
express purpose of keeping me back.

"This must not be!" I said to myself, and tried hard
to walk faster. But he actually detained me, and even
pressed my arm. L. M. disappeared around a turn, and
we were left absolutely alone. I was overwhelmed with
terror.

"Excuse me," said I, coldly, and tried to disengage
my arm, but the lace on my sleeve caught on one of

his buttons. Bending over, he tried to detach it, and his ungloved fingers touched my hand. A strange, new feeling, of horror and of pleasure blended, made a cold shiver run down my back. I looked at him with the intention of expressing, by a cutting glance, all the contempt I felt for him; but my eyes failed to express that; they expressed only apprehension and agitation.

His moist, burning eyes, in close proximity to my face, looked passionately at me, at my neck, at my bosom, his two hands clasped my arm above the wrist, his parted lips said something — were uttering a declaration of love, were vowing that I was all the world to him, and his lips drew closer to mine, and his hands pressed mine more firmly, and seemed to burn me!

Fire flashed through my veins, a cloud came into my eyes, I trembled, and the words with which I intended to restrain him stuck in my throat. Suddenly I felt a kiss on my cheek, and, all of a tremble, and cold, I paused and looked at him. Without the power of speech or motion, terrified, I waited and longed, for — what?

All this lasted but a second. But this second was terrible. I seemed to have such a complete view of the man in that time. His face was so plain to me; his low, curved brow, showing under his straw hat, and looking like my husband's; his handsome, straight nose, with dilated nostrils; his long mustaches, twisted to a point, and his imperial, his smooth-shaven cheeks, and his sunburned neck. I detested him, I feared him, so foreign he appeared to me! But at that moment how powerfully I was under the influence of the emotion and passion of that hateful stranger!

I had such an irresistible desire to return the kiss of his bold and handsome mouth, the pressure of those white hands with their delicate veins and with the rings on the fingers! So strongly tempted was I to throw myself headlong into the abyss of forbidden delights suddenly yawning before me. .....

"I am so unhappy," I said to myself. "So why not let an unhappiness still greater and more hopeless accumulate on my head!"

He threw one arm around me, and bent his face down to mine.

"Why not let still greater shame and sin accumulate on my head!"

"*Je vous aime,*" he whispered, in a voice which was so like my husband's!

My husband and child recurred to my memory as dear objects loved in other days, long ago, and now forever disconnected with my life.

But suddenly, at this instant, we heard L. M.'s voice at the turn of the path, calling me. I came to my senses, tore myself away from his arms, and, without looking at him, almost ran after L. M. We took our seats in the carriage, and I scarcely deigned to give him a parting glance. He took off his hat and asked some question with a smile. He could not understand the inexpressible loathing which I felt for him at that moment.

My life seemed to me so unhappy, my future so hopeless, my past so dark! L. M. spoke to me, but I did not heed her words. It seemed to me that she was talking only out of pity, in order to hide the contempt which she felt for me. In each word, in each glance, I detected her scorn and insulting pity. That shameful kiss burned on my cheek; the thoughts of my husband and my boy were unendurable.

Alone in my room, I hoped to be able to comprehend my situation, but it was terrible to me to be alone. I could not drink the tea which was brought to me, and, without knowing why, with feverish haste I immediately began to pack up so as to take the evening train to Heidelberg, where my husband was.

When I was safely seated with my maid in the empty carriage, and the engine had started, and the cool breeze blew in on me through the window, I began to come to myself, and more clearly to realize my past and my future.

All my married life, from the day of our arrival at Petersburg, suddenly appeared before me in a new light, and lay like a burden on my conscience. For the first time I had a lively recollection of our early married life in the country, and our plans. For the first time the question came into my mind: "How has he been enjoying himself during all these months?"

And I felt that I was guilty toward him.

"But why did he not stop me? Why has he played the hypocrite before me? Why has he avoided any reconciliation? Why has he insulted me?" I asked myself. "Why, why did he not exercise the power of his love over me? Or has he not really loved me?"

But, however much he had been to blame, another man's kiss had been imprinted on my cheek, and I still felt it.

The nearer and nearer I came to Heidelberg, the more distinctly I saw my husband in my imagination, and the more I dreaded the approaching meeting.

"I will tell him all, all, I will weep tears of repentance," I thought, "and he will forgive me."

But I myself did not know what this "all" was that I should tell him, and I myself did not believe that he would forgive me.

As soon as I entered my husband's room, and saw his calm though astonished face, I felt that I had nothing to tell him, no acknowledgment to make, and nothing for which to ask his forgiveness. My inexpressible grief and rue were still to be kept in my own secret heart.

"What made you think of doing this?" he asked. "I was intending to join you to-morrow."

But, looking more closely into my face, he seemed to be alarmed.

"What is the matter? What is there wrong?" he exclaimed.

"Nothing," I insisted, with difficulty repressing my tears. "I have come away for good. Let us go home to Russia to-morrow."

He looked at me attentively for some time, without speaking.

"Come, now, tell me what has happened to you," he said.

I could not help blushing, and cast down my eyes. His eyes flashed angrily, as from a sense of injury. I was alarmed at the suspicion that he might have, and, with a power of dissimulation which was quite unexpected even to myself, I said : —

"Nothing has happened; I simply became bored and melancholy at being alone, and I got to thinking much about our life and about you. How long I have been to blame toward you! What made you come with me where you had no desire to come? I have been to blame toward you," I repeated, and again the tears welled up in my eyes. "Let us go to the country and stay there."

"O dear! spare us sentimental scenes," said he, coldly. "It is well that you are willing to go to the country, because we are short of money; but, as for staying there, that is a delusion. I know that would not suit you. But now have a little tea, you will feel better," said he, in conclusion, getting up to call his man.

I imagined all that passed through his mind, and I felt humiliated by the terrible ideas which his incredulous and evidently censuring glance made me know that he had conceived in regard to me. No, he could not and would not understand me!

I said that I would go and see my child, and left him. All I wanted was to be alone and to weep, weep, weep. ....

CHAPTER IV

THE long-uninhabited, empty house at Nikolskoye came to life again, but what had once been alive in it could not come to life again. Mamasha was no more, and my husband and I were alone there, face to face. But now being alone was not only not desirable, but it was irksome to us. The winter passed all the more gloomily for me because I was ill, and my health was not restored until after the birth of my second son.

The relations between my husband and me continued to be the same, coldly amicable, just as when we lived in the city; but in the country every floor, every wall, the divan, reminded me of what he had once been for me, and of what I had lost. It seemed as if an unforgiven offense separated us, as if he were punishing me for something and pretending not to notice that he was doing so. To ask forgiveness was useless, what was there to ask mercy for? he punished me only by not giving me all of himself, all of his soul as before; but he never gave it to any one or to anything. So that it might have been thought it was lacking in him.

Sometimes it occurred to me that he only pretended to be what he was for the sake of torturing me, but that in reality his old feeling still existed, and I tried to bring it out. But every time it seemed as if he avoided all frankness, as if he suspected me of duplicity and feared any sentimentality as something ridiculous. His look and voice seemed to say: "I know all, I know all; there is nothing to say; I know what you mean. And I know too that you talk one way and act another."

At first I was offended at this fear of frankness, but afterward I became wonted to the idea that it was not frankness, but lack of any necessity for frankness. My tongue would not have been tempted now to tell him impulsively that I loved him, or to ask him to read the prayers with me, or to invite him to hear me play.

We felt ourselves subject to the rules of conventional propriety. We each lived separate existences. He with his own occupations, in which I had now no need or wish to share; I with my idle amusements, which did not humiliate and pain him as once they did. Our children were still too young to be able to reconcile us.

But the spring came. Katya and Sonya returned to the country for the summer; our house at Nikolskoye was undergoing repairs, and we moved over to Pokrovskoye. It was the same old mansion with the terrace, with the folding table, and the piano in the bright drawing-room, and my old room with its white curtains and my maidenhood dreams, which seemed to have been forgotten there. In this room stood two little beds; one had once been mine, and here every evening I made the sign of the cross over my fat, frolicsome little Kokosha;[1] the other was still smaller, and here Vanya's cunning little face peered out of his swaddling-clothes.

After making the sign of the cross over them, I often lingered in the quiet chamber, and suddenly from all the corners, from the walls, from the curtains, would arise the old forgotten dreams of my youth. Old voices began to sing my maidenhood songs. And where were these visions? Where were these dear, sweet songs?

All that I had hardly dared hope for had been realized; vague, confused dreams had taken form; but the reality was a dull, hard, and unhappy life.

Yet all was the same — the same park into which I looked from the window, the same lawn, the same paths, the same bench yonder above the ravine, the same song of the nightingales ringing over from the pond, and the same moon rising over the house; and yet all was so terribly, so hopelessly changed! So cold and cheerless was everything that ought to have been near and dear!

Just as of old, Katya and I sat together in the drawing-room and talked about him. But Katya had grown wrinkled and wan, her eyes no longer gleamed with pleasure and hope, but expressed sympathetic melancholy and grief. We did not go into raptures about him, as we used to do; we criticized him; we did not wonder why it was that we were so happy, and we had no desire, as in old times, to tell the whole world what we thought; like conspirators, we whispered together, and a hundred times we asked each other why such a melancholy change had taken place.

And he too was just the same as always, only the line between his eyes was heavier, there were more gray hairs around his temples, but his deep, thoughtful gaze was constantly veiled from me as by a cloud. And I too was still the same, but there was no longer any love or desire for love in my heart. No necessity for work, no self-content. And how distant and impossible seemed to me my early religious enthusiasms and my former love to him, and my former fullness of life! I could not

[1] Kokosha, diminutive of Konstantin; Vanya, of Ivan.

now comprehend what formerly seemed to me so clear and true, the happiness of living for others. Why live for others when I did not even care to live for myself?

I had entirely given up my music from the day we went to Petersburg; but now the old piano, the old music-books, inspired me with a longing for it.

One day I was not feeling well, and had stayed alone at home. Katya and Sonya had gone with my husband to Nikolskoye to see the improvements. The tea-table was set; I went down-stairs, and, while waiting for their return, I took my seat at the piano. I turned to the *Sonata quasi una Fantasia*, and began to play it. No one was in sight or hearing; the windows into the garden were opened, and the familiar notes, plaintive and solemn, echoed through the room. I finished playing the first movement, and, quite unconsciously, through old habit looked round to the corner in which he used to sit when he listened to me. But he was not there; the chair stood in its place, from which it had never been removed; and from the window I could see the lilac bush against the bright western sky, and the afternoon sunlight pouring in through the open window.

I leaned my elbow on the piano, hid my face in both hands, and was lost in thought. I had been sitting so a long time, recalling, with anguish, the old days which would never return, and thinking with apprehension of the unknown future. But it seemed as if there were only a blank ahead of me, as if I had no expectations and no hope!

"Can it be that my life has been wasted?" I asked myself with horror, lifting my head; and, in order that I might forget and not think, I began once more to play, and the same andante as before.

"God forgive me," I thought, "if I have been at fault; restore to me all that was so beautiful to my soul or teach me what to do! how to live now!"

The noise of wheels was heard on the grass. The carriage stopped in front of the steps; then across the terrace came the familiar, cautious footsteps, and then they ceased. But the old feeling was no longer stirred in me by the sound of those well-known footsteps. When I had finished, I heard footsteps behind me, and a hand was laid on my shoulder.

"How clever you are to play that sonata," said he.

I made no reply.

"Haven't you had tea?"

I shook my head and did not look at him, lest I should show the traces of emotion remaining in my face.

"They will be in directly; one of the horses was restive, and they are coming on foot from the main road," said he.

"Let us wait for them," said I, and went out on the terrace, hoping that he would follow me; but he asked after the children and went to them.

Once more his presence, his unaffected kindly voice, made me feel that not all was lost.

"What is it that I lack? He is good and kind, a good husband, a good father; I myself do not know what is for my own good."

I went to the balcony and sat down under the awning of the terrace, on the very same bench where I had sat on the day of our engagement. The sun had already set; it was beginning to grow dark, and a black cloud, heavy with a spring shower, was coming up over the house and park; low in the west, through the trees, could be seen a clear space of sky touched with the fading twilight, and the faint golden radiance of the evening star. Over everything lay the shadow of the cloud, and everything was waiting for the gentle vernal shower.

The breeze had died down. Not a leaf, not a grass-blade stirred, the odor of the lilac and wild cherry trees was strong as if all the air were in bloom; it hung over the park and the terrace, and seemed to come in waves, now stronger, now fainter, making you feel like closing your eyes so as to shut out sight and hearing, and revel in this sweet perfume.

The dahlias and rose bushes, not as yet in bloom, stood motionless in the dark, newly turned soil of the flower-beds, and seemed to be slowly growing on their white supports; the frogs, as if making the most of their opportunity before the rain should drive them into the water, were whistling with loud, cheerful notes down in the ravine. The mellifluous sound of falling waters rose perpetually above their clamor. In the meantime the nightingales were singing, and could be heard flying in alarm from spot to spot. Again this spring one nightingale had tried to build his nest in the bush near the window, and when I went out I listened as he flew beyond the alley, and from there gave one burst of melody and then ceased, also full of longing. In vain I tried to calm myself; I also seemed to be waiting and longing for something.

He came down-stairs and took a seat near me.

"I am afraid they will get wet," said he.

"Yes," said I, and we both were silent for a long time.

The cloud hung lower and lower, though there was no wind; everything had grown more silent, more fragrant, and more motionless; then suddenly a drop fell, and seemed to dance along the canvas awning of the terrace; another fell on the rubble walk, it began to splash on the burdock, and the cool round drops, increasing, began to fall in a smart shower. The nightingale and the frogs entirely ceased; only the mellifluous sound of the falling waters, although it seemed far off beyond the rain, filled the spaces of the air, and some bird, which must have sought shelter under the dry leaves not far from the terrace, at regular intervals repeated its monotonous notes. He got up and started to go away.

"Where are you going?" I asked, detaining him. "It is so pleasant here."

"I ought to send an umbrella and some overshoes," he replied.

"It is n't necessary, it will be over in a moment."

He agreed with me, and we stood together by the parapet of the terrace. I rubbed my hand along the wet, slippery railing, and put my head out over. The cool raindrops irregularly sprinkled my head and neck. The cloud, growing lighter and thinner, was passing over us; the even sound of the rain changed into the pattering of a few drops, falling from the awning and from the foliage. Again the frogs set up their piping, again the songs of the nightingales gushed forth, answering one another from the wet bushes, now in this direction, now in that. Everything grew light before us.

"How lovely!" he exclaimed, sitting down on the balustrade and smoothing my wet hair with his hand.

This simple caress had the effect on me of a reproof, and I felt like bursting into tears.

"And what more does a human being want?" he went on to say. "I am so content now! there is nothing that I lack, I am perfectly happy."

"That was not the way that you used to speak to me of your happiness," I said to myself. "However great it was, you used to say that still there was something that was lacking. But now you are calm and satisfied, while in my soul there seem to be inexpressible remorse and unwept tears."

"I like it too," said I, "but at the same time it makes me feel melancholy, for the very reason that everything is so beautiful around me. Everything in me is so incoherent, so shallow, so full of longing, and here it is so calm and beautiful. Can it be that for you no pain is mingled with the beauty of nature, as if there were a longing for something that was past?"

He drew away his hand from my head, and was silent for a little.

"Yes, I used to feel that way, especially in spring," said he, apparently collecting his thoughts. "And I sometimes used to sit up whole nights, wishing and hoping! such lovely nights they were! .... But then everything was in prospect, but now it is in retrospect; now I am satisfied with all that is, and that is excellent," he added, with such perfect nonchalance that, however painful it was to me to hear him say so, I was convinced that he was speaking the truth.

"And have you no longings?" I asked.

"Not for anything impossible," he replied, divining my thought.

"Here you are wetting your head," he added, caressing me as if I were a child, and again laying his hand on my hair. "You think because you see the shower wetting the leaves and the grass that you ought to be the grass and the leaves, and the shower too. But I take pleasure in them only as in everything else in the world that is beautiful, young, and happy."

"And have you no regrets for what has passed?" I went on to ask him, feeling that my heart was growing heavier and heavier.

He pondered a moment, and sat in silence. I saw that he was anxious to answer me with perfect sincerity.

"No," he replied laconically.

"'T is false! 't is false!" I exclaimed, drawing nearer to him, and looking him full in the face. "Have you no longing for what is past?"

"No," he maintained; "I am thankful for it, but I have no desire for it to return."

"But why would you not want it to return?" I asked.

He turned away, and began to look down into the park.

"I do not wish for it any more than for wings," said he. "It is an impossibility."

"And you would not like to live your life over, so as to live it better? You do not reproach yourself or me?"

"Certainly not! All has been for the best."

"Listen," said I, touching his arm so as to attract his attention. "Listen to me! Why have you never told me what you wished, so that I might have lived in exact accordance with your wishes? Why have you given me such perfect freedom, when I was unfit to make good use of it? Why did you cease to teach me? If you had only been willing, if you had only led me in any other way, then nothing, nothing of this sort would have been," said I, in a tone which expressed more and more energetically cold vexation and reproach, but not a trace of the old love.

"What would not have been?" he asked, in surprise, turning round to me. "Why, there is nothing wrong. It is all well, perfectly well," he added, with a smile.

"Can it be that he does not understand, or is it worse

still, that he does not care to understand?" I asked myself, and the tears stood in my eyes.

"Can it be that, if I had not been guilty in your eyes, you would have punished me so, by your indifference, by your scorn even?" I exclaimed suddenly. "Can it be that for no fault of mine you have suddenly taken from me all that I held dear?"

"What is the matter, my love?" he asked, evidently not understanding what I had said.

"No, let me speak. ..... You have taken from me your trust, love, respect even; because I do not believe that you love me now, after what has passed. No, I must have a chance to speak to the end all that has been tormenting me this long time!" I exclaimed, without allowing him to interrupt me. "Was I to blame that I did not know life, and that you left me to acquire a knowledge of it alone?.... Am I to blame because, having learned all that was necessary, I have been struggling for a year to return to you? and yet you repulse me, as if you did not comprehend what I wanted, and all the time in such a way that it has been impossible to blame you and yet you have made me feel guilty and wretched. Yes, you would cast me back into a life which could make only your unhappiness and mine!"

"But when did I do such a thing?" he asked, with genuine dismay and amazement.

"Did you not say, last evening, and have you not constantly said, that I would not be content to live here, and that we must go back for the winter to Petersburg, which I detest so?" I continued. "Instead of helping me, you have avoided every frank explanation, every true affectionate talk with me. And then, if I should fall altogether, you would reproach me, and rejoice in my fall."

"Stop, stop!" he cried sternly and coldly; "what you have just said is not true. It only shows that you occupy a false position in regard to me, that you do not ...."

"That I do not love. Speak it! speak it!" I said, taking the words out of his mouth, and bursting into

tears. I sat down on the bench and buried my face in
my handkerchief.

"That is the way that he has misunderstood me!" I
thought, trying to restrain the sobs that choked me.
"It is all over, all over with our old love," said some
voice in my heart.

He did not come to me or try to comfort me. He
was offended at what I had said. His voice was calm
and dry.

"I do not know what you have to reproach me for,"
he began; "if you mean that I do not love you as
much as formerly, then...."

"Love!" said I, with my face buried in my handkerchief, which was more copiously wet with scalding
tears.

"For this, time and we ourselves are to blame. Each
period in life has its own love."....

He was silent.

"And shall I tell you all the truth, if, as you say, you
desire frankness? When I first knew you, I spent
sleepless nights thinking about you, and fashioned my
own ideal of love; and this love grew and grew in my
heart. Then, at Petersburg, and when we were abroad,
I no longer spent terrible nights, and I tore this love to
tatters, and demolished it, since it tormented me. I did
not destroy it, but I only destroyed that part of it that
tormented me; I calmed myself, and still I love you,
but with a different kind of love."

"Yes, you call it love, but it is torture!" I exclaimed.
"Why did you let me go into society if it seemed to
you so harmful that on account of it you ceased to love
me?"

"It was not society, my love."

"Why did you not exert your power?" I continued.
"Why did you not bind me, kill me? It would have
been better for me now than to be deprived of all that
constitutes my happiness; it would have been well for
me, and not shameful!"

And again I sobbed and hid my face.

At this moment Katya and Sonya came on the terrace, merry and dripping, and with loud voices and laughter; but when they saw us they became quiet, and immediately went into the house.

For a long time we did not speak, even after they had gone. I had had my cry, and felt relieved. I looked at him. He sat there with his head resting on his hand, and tried to make some reply to my glance; but he only sighed deeply, and still leaned on his elbow.

I went to him and took his hand. His glance rested thoughtfully on me.

"Yes," he continued, as if carrying out his thought, "to all of us, and especially you women, it is necessary to have personal experience of all the triviality of life in order to return to life itself; and it is impossible to believe any one else's report. You had at that time as yet had no experience of this brilliant and charming triviality which I admired in you. And I left you to have your own taste of it, and I felt that I had not the right to prevent you, although for me the time of this had gone by long before."

"Why, then, did you experience with me and let me experience this triviality, if you love me?" said I.

"Because, even if you had had the desire, still you would not have had the power of believing me; you yourself had to learn for yourself, and you have learned."

"You have reasoned much, very much," said I, "but your love was small."

Again we relapsed into silence.

"What you have just said is cruel, but it is true," he broke out suddenly, rising and beginning to walk up and down the terrace. "Yes, it is true. I have been to blame," he added, halting in front of me; "I should either not have permitted myself to love you at all, or to have loved more simply, yes."

"Let us forget it all," said I, timidly.

"No, what has passed will never return, thou wilt never return," and his voice grew tender as he said this.

"It has already returned," said I, laying my hand on his shoulder. He took my hand and pressed it.

"No, I did not tell you the truth when I said that I did not regret the past; yes, I regret it, I mourn over your vanished love, which is gone never to come back. Who is to blame for that? I know not. Love remains, but not the same; its place is occupied, but by a feeble love, lacking strength and vigor; recollections and thankfulness remain, but .... "

"Don't speak so," said I, interrupting. "Let all be again as it used to be. It can be, can it not?" I asked, looking into his eyes. But his eyes were bright and calm, and gazed at me without showing their depths.

Even while I said this, I felt that what I desired and asked him for was an impossibility. He smiled a serene, sweet, but, as it seemed to me, an old man's smile.

I stood silently near him, and my mind became calmer.

"Let us not try to repeat the experiment of life," said he. "Let us not deceive each other. There will be none of the old anxieties and agitations, and thank God for it! There is nothing for us to seek for, and nothing to trouble us. We have already made our experiments, and sufficient happiness has fallen to our lot. .... Now it is necessary for us to step aside and give room for some one to pass," said he, pointing to the nurse, who, with Vanya, came and stood at the terrace door. "And so it is, dear friend," he said in conclusion, drawing my head to his breast, and kissing me on my hair. It was not a lover, but an old friend, who kissed me.

And from the park arose stronger and sweeter the fragrant coolness of the night, the sounds and the silence grew more solemn, and the stars burned more brilliantly in the sky.

I looked at him and my soul grew suddenly calm; as it were, that moral, painful nerve which had been torturing me was relieved. And suddenly I understood clearly and serenely that the feeling of that time had passed irrevocably, like time itself, and now it would be not only impossible, but even be hard and grievous, for it to return. Yes, and, after all, was that time, which had seemed to me so happy, was it really good? And it was already so long, long ago!....

"Now let us have tea," said he, and we went together into the drawing-room. At the door we were again met by the nurse, with Vanya. I took the child in my arms, covered up his bare, red legs, pressed him to my heart, and, scarcely touching him with my lips, kissed him. He, as in a troubled dream, waved his little hand, with its spreading, dimpled fingers, and opened his troubled eyes as if he were searching or trying to remember something. Suddenly those little eyes rested on me, the spark of intelligence shone out in them, his chubby pouting lips began to pucker and parted in a smile.

"Mine, mine, mine," I repeated to myself, with a happy sensation in all my being, and I pressed him to my heart, finding it hard to keep myself from hurting him. And I began to kiss his cold feet, his little belly, his hands, and his head where the hair was just beginning to grow. My husband came to me; I quickly covered the child's face, and then uncovered it again.

"Ivan Sergyeïvitch!" exclaimed my husband, tickling him under his little chin with his finger. But I again quickly covered Ivan Sergyeitch's face. No one but me had a right to look long at him! I glanced at my husband, his eyes rested on me with a bantering expression, and for the first time for many days it was easy and pleasant to look into them.

From that day forth my romance with my husband was ended; the old feeling became a precious, irrevocable memory; but the new feeling of love to my children and to the father of my children formed the beginning of another life, happy indeed, but in an entirely different way, and this I have continued to live up to the present moment. ....

A PRISONER IN THE CAUCASUS

CHAPTER I

A RUSSIAN gentleman was serving as an officer in the army of the Caucasus. His name was Zhilin.

One day a letter from his home came to him. His old mother wrote him : —

I am now getting along in years, and I should like to see my beloved son before I die. Come and bid me farewell, lay me in the ground, and then with my blessing return again to your service. And I have been finding a bride for you, and she is intelligent and handsome and has property. If she pleases you, why then you can marry and settle down together.

Zhilin thought the matter over.

"It is very true : the old lady has been growing feeble ; maybe I shall not have a chance to see her again. I 'll go, and if the girl is pretty — then I might marry."

He went to his colonel, got his leave of absence, bade his comrades farewell, gave the soldiers of his command nine gallons [1] of vodka as a parting treat, and made his arrangements to leave.

There was war at that time in the Caucasus. The roads were not open for travel either by day or night. If any Russian rode or walked outside of the fortress, the Tartars were likely either to kill him or carry him off to the mountains. And it was arranged that twice a week an escort of soldiers should go from fortress to

[1] Four *vedros*, equivalent exactly to 8.80 gallons.

331

fortress. In front and behind marched the soldiers, and the travelers rode in the middle.

It was now summer-time. At sunrise the baggage train was made up behind the fortification; the guard of soldiery marched ahead, and the procession moved along the road.

Zhilin was on horseback, and his effects were on a cart which formed part of the train.

They had twenty-five versts[1] to travel. The train proceeded slowly; sometimes the soldiers halted; sometimes a wagon-wheel came off, or a horse balked, and all had to stop and wait.

The sun was already past the zenith, but the train had only gone halfway. It was dusty and hot, the sun was fierce, and there was no shelter. A bald steppe; not a tree or a shrub along the road.

Zhilin rode on ahead, occasionally stopping and waiting till the train caught up with him. He would listen, and hear the signal on the horn to halt again. And Zhilin thought, "Had I now better go on alone without the soldiers? I have a good horse under me; if I fall in with the Tartars, I can escape. Or shall I wait?"

He kept stopping and pondering. And just then another officer, also on horseback, rode up to him; his name was Kostuilin, and he had a musket.

He said:—

"Zhilin, let us ride on ahead together. I am so hungry that I cannot stand it any longer, and the heat too,— you could wring my shirt out!"

Kostuilin was a heavy, stout, ruddy man, and the sweat was dripping from him.

Zhilin reflected, and said:—

"And your musket is loaded?"

"It is."

"All right, let us go. Only one condition: not to separate."

And they started on up the road. They rode along the steppe, talking and looking on each side. There was a wide sweep of view in all directions. As soon as

---

[1] Sixteen and a half miles.

the steppe came to an end, the road went into a pass
between two mountains.

And Zhilin said : —

"I must ride up on that mountain, and reconnoiter;
otherwise you see they might come down from the
mountain and surprise us."

But Kostuilin said : —

"What is there to reconnoiter? Let us go ahead."

Zhilin did not heed him.

"No," says he, "you wait for me here below. I'll
just glance around."

And he spurred his horse up the mountain to the
left.

The horse that Zhilin rode was a hunter; he had
bought her out of a drove of colts, paying a hundred
rubles for her, and he had himself trained her. She
bore him up the steep slope as if on wings. He had
hardly reached the summit when before him, on a place
a little less than three acres, mounted Tartars were standing. There were thirty of them.

He saw them, and started to turn back, but the Tartars had caught sight of him; they set out in pursuit of
him, unstrapping their weapons as they galloped. Zhilin
dashed down the precipice with all the speed of his
horse, and cried to Kostuilin : —

"Fire your gun!" and to his horse he said, though
not aloud : —

"Little mother, carry me safely, don't stumble; if
you trip up, I am lost. If we get back to the gun, we
won't fall into their hands."

But Kostuilin, as soon as he saw the Tartars, instead
of waiting for him, galloped on with all his might toward
the fortress. With his whip he belabored his horse,
first on one side, then on the other; all that could
be seen through the dust was the horse switching her
tail.

Zhilin saw that his case was desperate. The gun
was gone; nothing was to be done with a saber alone.
He turned his horse back toward the train; he thought
he might escape that way.

But in front of him he saw that six were galloping down the steep. His horse was good, but theirs were better; and besides, they had got the start of him. He attempted to wheel about, and was going to dash ahead again, but his horse had got momentum, and could not be held back; he flew straight down toward them.

He saw a red-bearded Tartar approaching him on a gray horse. He was gaining on him; he was gnashing his teeth; he was getting his gun ready.

"Well," thought Zhilin, "I know you devils; if you should take me prisoner, you would put me into a hole, and flog me with a whip. I won't give myself up alive."

Now, Zhilin was not of great size, but he was a uhlan. He drew his saber, spurred his horse straight at the red-bearded Tartar. He said to himself, "Either I will crush him with my horse, or I will hack him down with my saber."

Zhilin, however, did not reach the place on horse-back; suddenly, from behind him, gunshots were fired at the horse. The horse fell headlong, and pinned Zhilin's leg to the ground.

He tried to arise; but already two ill-smelling Tartars were sitting on him, and pinioning his hands behind his back.

He burst from them, knocking the Tartars over; but three others had leaped from their horses, and began to beat him on the head with their gun-stocks.

His sight failed him, and he staggered.

The Tartars seized him, took from their saddles extra saddle-girths, bent his arms behind his back, fastened them with a Tartar knot, and lifted him up.

They took his saber from him, pulled off his boots, made a thorough search of him, relieved him of his money and his watch, and tore his clothes in pieces.

Zhilin glanced at his horse. The poor beast lay as she had fallen, on her side, and was kicking, vainly try-ing to rise. In her head was a hole, and from the hole the black blood was pouring; the dust for an arshin around was wet with it.

A Tartar went to the horse to remove the saddle. She was still kicking, so the man took out his dagger and cut her throat. The throat gave a whistling sound, a trembling ran over the body, and all was over.

The Tartars took off the saddle and the other trappings. The one with the red beard mounted his horse, and the others lifted Zhilin behind him; and, in order to keep him from falling, they fastened him with the reins to the Tartar's belt, and thus they carried him off to the mountains.

Zhilin sat behind, swaying, and bumping his face against the stinking Tartar's back.

All that he could see before him was the healthy Tartar back, and the sinewy neck, and a smooth-shaven nape, showing blue beneath the cap.

Zhilin's head ached; the blood trickled into his eyes. And it was impossible for him to get a more comfortable position on the horse, or wipe away the blood. His arms were so tightly bound that his collar-bones ached.

They rode along from mountain to mountain; they forded a river; then they entered a highway, and rode along a valley.

Zhilin tried to follow the route that they took him; but his eyes were glued together with blood, and it was impossible for him to turn round.

It began to grow dark; they crossed still another river, and began to climb a rocky mountain. There was an odor of smoke. The barking of dogs was heard.

They had reached an *aul*.[1]

The Tartars dismounted. The Tartar children came running up, and surrounded Zhilin, whistling and exulting. Finally they began to hurl stones at him.

The Tartar drove away the children, lifted Zhilin from the horse, and called a menial.

A Nogayets, with prominent cheek-bones, came at the call. He wore only a shirt. The shirt was torn; his whole breast was bare. The Tartar gave him some order. The menial brought a foot-stock. It consisted of two oaken blocks provided with iron rings, and in

[1] *Aul*, Tartar's village. — AUTHOR'S NOTE.

one of the rings was a clamp with a lock. They un-
fastened Zhilin's arms, put on the clog, and took him to
a shed, pushed him in, and shut the door.

Zhilin fell on the manure. As he lay there, he felt
round in the darkness, and when he had found a place
that was less foul, he stretched himself out.

CHAPTER II

ZHILIN scarcely slept that night. The nights were
short. He saw through a crack that it was growing
light. Zhilin got up, widened the crack, and managed
to look out.

Through the crack he could see a road leading down
from the mountain; at the right, a Tartar saklia [1] with
two trees near it. A black dog was lying on the road;
a she-goat with her kids was walking by; they were
shaking their tails.

He saw coming down the mountain a young Tartar
girl in a variegated shirt, ungirdled, in pantalettes and
boots; her head was covered with a kaftan, and on it
she bore a great tin water-jug.

She walked along, swaying and bending her back,
and holding by the hand a little shaven-headed Tartar
urchin, who wore a single shirt.

After the Tartar maiden had gone into the saklia with
her water-jug, the red-bearded Tartar of the evening
before came out, wearing a silk beshmet, a silver dagger
in his belt, and *bashmaks*, or sandals, on his bare feet.
On the back of his head was a high cap of sheepskin,
dyed black. He came out, stretched himself, stroked his
red beard. He paused, gave some order to the menial,
and went off somewhere.

Then two children on horseback came along on their
way to the watering-trough. The snouts of the horses
were wet.

Other shaven-headed youngsters, with nothing but
shirts on, and nothing on their legs, formed a little

---

[1] A mountain hut in the Caucasus.

band, and came to the shed; they got a dry stick, and stuck it through the crack.

Zhilin growled "ukh" at them. The children began to squeal, and scatter in every direction as fast as their legs would carry them; only their bare knees glistened. But Zhilin began to be thirsty; his throat was parched. He said to himself:—

"I wonder if they won't come to look after me?"

While he was listening, the barn doors were thrown open.

The red Tartar came in, and with him another, of slighter stature and of dark complexion. His eyes were bright and black, his cheeks ruddy, his little beard well trimmed, his face jolly and always enlivened with a grin.

The dark man's clothing was still richer,—a beshmet of blue silk, embroidered with gold lace. In his belt, a great silver dagger; red morocco bashmaks, embroidered with silver, and over the fine bashmaks he wore a larger pair of stout ones. His cap was tall, of white lamb's-wool.

The red Tartar came in, muttered something, gave vent to some abusive language, and then stood leaning against the wall, fingering his dagger, and scowling under his brows at Zhilin, like a wolf.

But the dark Tartar, nervous and active, and always on the go, as if he were made of springs, came straight up to Zhilin, squatted down on his heels, showed his teeth, tapped him on the shoulder, began to gabble something in his own language, winked his eyes, and, clucking his tongue, kept saying:—

"A fine Russ, a fine Russ!"[1]

Zhilin did not understand him, and said:—

"Drink; give me some water."

The dark one grinned, and all the time he kept babbling:—

"A fine Russ!"

Zhilin signified by his hands and lips that they should give him water.

---

[1] *Korosho Urus, horosh Urus.*

The dark one understood, grinned, put his head out of the door, and cried : —

"Dina!"

A young girl came running in, — a slender, lean creature of thirteen, with a face like the dark man's. Evidently she was his daughter. She also had black, luminous eyes, and she was very pretty.

She was dressed in a long, blue shirt, with wide sleeves and without a belt. On the bottom, on the breast, and on the cuffs it was relieved with red trimmings. She wore on her legs pantalettes and bashmaks, and over the bashmaks another pair with high heels. On her neck was a necklace wholly composed of Russian half-ruble pieces. Her head was uncovered; she had her hair in a black braid, and on the braid was a ribbon, and to the ribbon were attached various ornaments and a silver ruble.

Her father gave her some command. She ran out, and quickly returned, bringing a little tin pitcher. After she had handed him the water, she also squatted on her heels in such a way that her knees were higher than her shoulders.

She sat that way, and opened her eyes, and stared at Zhilin while he was drinking, as if he were some wild beast.

Zhilin offered to return the pitcher to her. She darted away like a wild goat. Even her father laughed.

He sent her after something else. She took the pitcher, ran out, and brought back some unleavened bread on a small, round board, and again squatted down, and stared without taking her eyes from him.

The Tartars went out, and again bolted the door.

After a while the Nogayets also came to Zhilin, and said : —

"*Aï-da, khozyaïn, aï-da !*"

But he did not know Russian either. Zhilin, however, perceived that he wished him to go somewhere.

Zhilin hobbled out with his clog; it was impossible to walk, so he had to drag one leg. The Nogayets led the way for him.

He saw a Tartar village, a dozen houses, and the native mosque with its minaret.

In front of one house stood three horses saddled. Lads held them by their bridles. From this house came the dark Tartar, and beckoned with his hand, signifying that Zhilin was to come to him. He grinned, and kept saying something in his own tongue, and went into the house.

Zhilin followed him.

The room was decent; the walls were smoothly plastered with clay. Against the front wall were placed feather-beds; on the sides hung costly rugs; on the rugs were guns, pistols, and sabers, all silver-mounted.

On one side a little oven was set in, on a level with the floor.

The floor was of earth, clean as a threshing-floor, and the whole of the front part was covered with felt; rugs were distributed over the felt, and on the rugs were down pillows.

On the rugs were sitting some Tartars with bashmaks only on their feet — the dark Tartar, the red-bearded one, and three guests. Behind their backs, down cushions were placed; and before them on wooden plates were pancakes of millet flour, and melted butter in a cup, and the Tartar beer, called *buza*, in a pitcher. They ate with their fingers, and all dipped into the butter.

The dark man leaped up, bade Zhilin sit on one side, not on a rug but on the bare floor; going back again to his rug, he served his guests with cakes and buza.

The menial showed Zhilin his place; he himself took off his outside bashmaks, placed them by the door in a row with the bashmaks of the other guests, and took his seat on the felt as near as possible to his masters; and while they ate he looked at them, and his mouth watered.

After the Tartars had finished eating the pancakes, a Tartar woman entered, dressed in the same sort of shirt as the girl wore, and in pantalettes; her head was covered with a handkerchief. She carried out the butter and the cakes, and brought a handsome finger-bowl, and a pitcher with a narrow nose.

The Tartars proceeded to wash their hands, then they folded their arms, knelt down, and puffed on all sides, and said their prayers. Then they talked together in their own tongue.

Finally one of the guests, a Tartar, approached Zhilin, and began to speak to him in Russian.

"Kazi Muhamet made you prisoner," said he, pointing to the red-bearded Tartar; "and he has given you to Abdul Murat," indicating the dark one. "Abdul Murat is now your master." [1]

Zhilin said nothing.

Abdul Murat began to talk, all the time pointing toward Zhilin, and grinned as he talked:—

"*Soldat Urus, korosho Urus.*"

The dragoman went on to say:—

"He commands you to write a letter home, and have them send money to ransom you. As soon as money is sent, he will set you free."

Zhilin pondered a little, and then said:—

"Does he wish a large ransom?"

The Tartars took counsel together, and then the dragoman said:—

"Three thousand silver rubles."

"No," replied Zhilin, "I can't pay that."

Abdul leaped up, began to gesticulate and talk to Zhilin; he seemed all the time to think that Zhilin understood him.

The dragoman translated his words.

"He means," says he, "how much will you give?"

Zhilin, after pondering a little, said:—

"Five hundred rubles."

Then the Tartars all began to talk at once. Abdul began to scream at the red-bearded Tartar. He grew so excited as he talked that the spittle flew from his mouth.

But the red-bearded Tartar only frowned, and clucked with his tongue.

[1] *Khozyaïn.*

When all became silent again, the dragoman said:—

"Five hundred rubles is not enough to buy you of your master. He himself has paid two hundred for you. Kazi Muhamet was in debt to him. He took you for the debt. Three thousand rubles; it is no use to send less. But if you don't write, they will put you in a hole, and flog you with a whip."

"Ekh!" said Zhilin to himself, "the more cowardly one is, the worse it is for him."

He leaped to his feet, and said:—

"Now you tell him, dog that he is, that if he thinks he is going to frighten me, then I will not give him a single kopek nor will I write. I am not afraid of you, and you will never make me afraid of you, you dog!" The dragoman interpreted this to them, and again they all began to talk at once.

They gabbled a long time, then the dark one got up and came to Zhilin.

"*Urus*," says he, "*jigit, jigit Urus!*"

The word *jigit* in their language signifies a brave young man. And he grinned, said something to the dragoman, and the dragoman said:—

"Give a thousand rubles."

Zhilin would not give in:—

"I will not pay more than five hundred. But if you kill me, you will get nothing at all."

The Tartars consulted together, sent out the menial, and they themselves looked first at the door, then at Zhilin.

The menial returned, followed by a rather stout man in bare feet and almost stripped. His feet also were fastened to a clog.

Zhilin uttered an exclamation; he saw it was Kostuilin. So they had captured him too.

They placed him next his comrade; the two began to talk together, and the Tartars looked on and listened in silence.

Zhilin told how it had gone with him; Kostuilin told how his horse had stood stock-still, and his gun had missed fire, and that this same Abdul had overtaken him and captured him.

Abdul sprang to his feet, pointed to Kostuilin, and made some remark. The dragoman translated his words to mean that they now both belonged to the same master, and that the one who paid the ransom first would be freed first.

"Now," said he to Zhilin, "you lose your temper so easily, but your comrade is calm; he has written a letter home; they will send five thousand silver rubles. And so he will be well fed, and he won't be hurt."

And Zhilin said:—

"Let my comrade do as he pleases. Maybe he is rich. But I am not rich; I will do as I have already told you. Kill me if you wish, but it would not do you any good, and I will not pay you more than five hundred rubles."

They were silent.

Suddenly Abdul leaped up, brought a little chest, took out a pen, a sheet of paper, and ink, and pushed them into Zhilin's hands, then tapped him on the shoulder and said by signs:—

"Write."

He had agreed to take the five hundred rubles.

"Wait a moment," said Zhilin to the dragoman. "Tell him that he must feed us well, clothe us, and give us good decent foot-wear, and let us stay together so that it may be pleasanter for us. And lastly, that he take off these clogs."

He looked at his Tartar master, and smiled. The master also smiled, and when he learned what was wanted, said:—

"I will give you the very best clothes; a cherkeska[1] and boots, fit for a wedding. And I will feed you like princes. And if you want to live together, why, you can live in the shed. But it won't do to take away the clogs; you would run away. Only at night will I have them taken off." Then he jumped up and tapped him on the shoulder: "You good, me good."

Zhilin wrote his letter, but he put on it the wrong address so that it might never reach its destination. He said to himself:—

[1] A sort of long Circassian cloak.

" I shall run away."

They took Zhilin and Kostuilin to the shed, strewed corn-stalks, gave them water in a pitcher, and bread, two old cherkeski, and some worn-out military boots. It was evident that they had been stolen from some dead soldier. When night came they took off their clogs, and locked them up in the shed.

CHAPTER III

THUS Zhilin and his comrade lived a whole month. Their master was always on the grin.

"You, Ivan, good — me, Abdul, good."

But he gave them wretched food, — unleavened bread made of millet flour, cooked in the form of cakes, but often not heated through.

Kostuilin wrote home again, and was anxiously awaiting the arrival of the money, and lost his spirits. Whole days at a time he sat in the shed, and counted the days till his money should arrive, or else he slept.

But Zhilin knew that his letter would not reach its destination, and he did not write another.

"Where," he asked himself, — "where would my mother get so much money for my ransom? And besides, she lived for the most part on what I used to send her. If she made out to raise five hundred rubles, she would be in want till the end of her days. If God wills it, I may escape."

And all the time he kept his eyes open, and made plans to elude his captors.

He walked about the aul; he amused himself by whistling; or else he sat down and fashioned things, either modeling dolls out of clay or plaiting baskets of osiers, for Zhilin was a master at all sorts of handiwork.

One time he made a doll with nose and hands and feet, and dressed in a Tartar shirt, and he set the doll on the roof. The Tartar women were going for water. Dina, the master's daughter, caught sight of the doll.

She called the Tartar women. They set down their jugs, and looked and laughed.

Zhilin took the doll, and offered it to them. They kept laughing, but did not dare to take it.

He left the doll, went to the barn, and watched what would take place.

Dina ran up to the doll, looked around, seized the doll, and fled.

The next morning at dawn he saw Dina come out on the doorstep with the doll. And she had already dressed it up in pieces of red cloth, and was rocking it like a little child, and singing a lullaby in her own language.

The old woman came out, gave her a scolding, snatched the doll away, broke it in pieces, and sent off Dina to work.

Zhilin made another doll, a still better one, and gave it to Dina.

One time Dina brought a little jug, put it down, took a seat, and looked at him. Then she laughed, and pointed to the jug.

"What is she so gay about?" wondered Zhilin.

He took the jug, and began to drink. He supposed that it was water, but it was milk.

He drank up the milk.

"Good," says he.

How delighted Dina was! "Good, Ivan, good!"

And she jumped up, clapped her hands, snatched the jug, and ran away.

And from that time she began to bring him secretly fresh milk every day.

Now, sometimes the Tartars would make cheese-cakes out of goat's milk, and dry them on their roofs; so she used to carry some of these cakes secretly to him. And another time, when her father had killed a sheep, she brought him a piece of mutton in her sleeve. She threw it down, and ran away.

One time there was a heavy shower, and for a whole hour the rain poured as from buckets; and all the brooks grew roily. Wherever there had been a ford, the depth of the water increased to a fathom, and boulders were rolled along by it. Everywhere torrents were rushing, the mountains were full of the roaring.

Now, when the shower was over, streams were pouring all through the village. Zhilin asked his master for a knife, whittled out a cylinder and some paddles, and made a water-wheel, and fastened manikins at the two ends.

The little girls brought him some rags, and he dressed up the manikins, one like a man, the other like a woman. He fastened them on, and put the wheel in a brook. The wheel revolved, and the dolls danced.

The whole village collected; the little boys and the little girls, the women, and even the Tartars, came and clucked with their tongues: —

"*Aï, Urus! aï, Ivan!*"

Abdul had a Russian watch, which had been broken. He took it, and showed it to Zhilin, and clucked with his tongue. Zhilin said: —

"Let me have it, I will mend it."

He took it, opened the penknife, took it apart. Then he put it together again, and gave it back. The watch ran.

The Tartar was delighted, brought him his old beshmet, which was all in rags, and gave it to him. Nothing else was to be done, — he took it, and used it as a covering at night.

From that time, Zhilin's fame went abroad, that he was a "master." Even from distant villages, they came to him. One brought him a gun-lock or a pistol to repair, another a watch.

His master furnished him with tools, — a pair of pincers and gimlets and a little file.

One time a Tartar fell ill; they came to Zhilin: "Come, cure him!"

Zhilin knew nothing of medicine. He went, looked at the sick man, said to himself, "Perhaps he will get well, anyway." He went into the shed, took water and sand, and shook them up together. He whispered a few words to the water in presence of the Tartars, and gave it to the sick man to drink.

Fortunately for him, the Tartar got well.

Zhilin had by this time learned something of their language. And some of the Tartars became accustomed to him; when they wanted him, they called him by name, "Ivan, Ivan;" but others always looked at him as if he was a wild beast.

The red-bearded Tartar did not like Zhilin; when he saw him, he scowled and turned away, or else insulted him.

There was another old man among them; he did not live in the aul, but came from down the mountain. Zhilin never saw him except when he came to the mosque to prayer. He was of small stature; on his cap he wore a white towel as an ornament. His beard and mustaches were trimmed; they were white as wool, and his face was wrinkled and brick-red. His nose was hooked like a hawk's, and his eyes were gray and cruel, and he had no teeth except two tusks.

He used to come in his turban, leaning on his staff, and glare like a wolf; whenever he saw Zhilin, he would snort, and turn his back.

One time Zhilin went down the mountain to see where the old man lived. He descended a narrow path, and saw a little stone-walled garden. On the other side of the wall were cherry trees, peach trees, and a little hut with a flat roof.

He went nearer; he saw beehives made of straw, and bees flying and humming around them. And the old man was on his knees busy doing something to one of the hives.

Zhilin raised himself up, so as to get a better view, and his clog made a noise.

The old man looked up, — squealed; he whipped his pistol from his belt, and fired at Zhilin, who had barely time to hide behind the wall.

The old man came to make his complaint to Zhilin's master. Abdul called him in, grinned, and asked him:

"Why did you go to the old man's?"

"I didn't do him any harm. I wanted to see how he lived."

Abdul explained it to the old man; but he was angry, hissed, mumbled something, showed his tusks, and threatened Zhilin with his hands.

Zhilin did not understand it all; but he made out that the old man wished Abdul to kill the two Russians, and not keep them in the aul.

The old man went off.

Zhilin began to ask his master: —

"Who is that old man?"

And the master replied: —

"He is a great man. He used to be our first jigit; he has killed many Russians. He used to be rich. He had three wives and eight sons. All lived in one village. The Russians came, destroyed his village, and killed seven of his sons. One son was left, and surrendered to the Russians. The old man went and gave himself up to the Russians also. He lived among them three months, found his son, killed him with his own hand, and escaped. Since that time he has stopped fighting. He went to Mecca to pray to God, and that's why he wears a turban. Whoever has been to Mecca is called a hadji, and wears a chalma. But he does not love you Russians. He has bade me kill you, but I don't intend to kill you. I have paid out money for you, and besides, Ivan, I have come to like you. And so far from wishing to kill you, I would rather not let you go from me at all, if I had not given my word."

He laughed, and began to repeat in broken Russian: —

"*Tvoya Ivan, khorosh, moya, Abdul, khorosh* — Ivan, you good; Abdul, me good."

CHAPTER IV

THUS Zhilin lived a month. In the daytime he walked about the aul or did some handiwork, but when night came, and it grew quiet in the aul, he burrowed in his shed. It was hard work digging because of the stones, and he sometimes had to use his file on them: and thus he dug a hole under the wall big enough to crawl through.

"Only," he thought, "I must know the region a little first, so as to escape in the right direction. And the Tartars would n't tell me anything."

He chose a time when his master was absent, then he went after dinner behind the aul to a mountain. His idea was to reconnoiter the country.

Now when Abdul went away he commanded his little son to follow Zhilin, and not take his eyes from him. The little fellow tagged after Zhilin, and kept crying:—

"Don't go there. Father won't allow it. I will call the men if you go!"

Zhilin began to reason with him.

"I am not going far," says he, "only to that hill; I want to find some herbs so as to cure your people. Come with me; I can't run away with this clog. If you will I will make you a bow and arrows to-morrow."

He persuaded the lad, they went together. To look at, the mountain was not far, but it was hard work with the clog; he went a little distance at a time, pulling himself up by main strength.

Zhilin sat down on the summit, and began to survey the ground.

To the south behind the shed lay a valley through which a herd was grazing, and another aul was in sight at the foot of it. Back of the village was another mountain still steeper, and back of that still another. Between the mountains lay a further stretch of forest, and then still other mountains rising ever higher and higher. And higher than all, stood snow-capped peaks white as sugar, and one snowy peak rose like a dome above them all.

To the east and west also were mountains. In every direction the smoke of auls was to be seen in the ravines.

"Well," he said to himself, "this is all their country."

He began to look in the direction of the Russian possessions. At his very feet was a little river, his aul surrounded by gardens. By the river some women, no larger in appearance than little dolls, were standing and washing. Behind the aul was a lower mountain, and beyond it two other mountains covered with forests. And between the two mountains a plain stretched far, far away in the blue distance; and on the plain lay what seemed like smoke.

Zhilin tried to remember in what direction, when he lived at home in the fortress, the sun used to rise, and where it set. He looked.

"Just about there," says he, "in that valley, our fortress ought to be. There, between those two mountains, I must make my escape."

The little sun began to slope toward the west. The snowy mountains changed from white to purple; the wooded mountains grew dark; a mist arose from the valley; and the valley itself, where the Russian fortress must be, glowed in the sunset as if it were on fire. Zhilin strained his gaze. Something seemed to hang waving in the air, like smoke arising from chimneys.

And so it seemed to him that it must be from the fortress itself, — the Russian fortress.

It was already growing late. The voice of the mulla calling to prayer was heard. The herds began to return; the kine were lowing. The little lad kept repeating, "Let us go!" but Zhilin could not tear himself away.

They returned home.

"Well," thinks Zhilin, "now I know the place; I must make my escape."

He proposed to make his escape that very night. The nights were dark; it was the wane of the moon. Unfortunately the Tartars returned in the evening. Usually they came in driving the cattle with them, and came in hilarious. But this time they had no cattle; but they brought a Tartar, dead, on his saddle. It was the red-headed Tartar's brother who had been killed. They rode in solemnly, and all collected for the burial.

Zhilin also went out to look.

They did not put the dead body in a coffin, but

wrapped it in linen, and placed it under a plane tree behind the village, where it lay on the sward.

The mulla came; the old men gathered together, their caps bound around with towels. They took off their shoes, and sat in rows on their heels before the dead.

In front was the mulla, behind him three old men in turbans, and behind them the rest of the Tartars. They sat there, with their heads bent low and kept silence. Long they kept silence. The mulla lifted his head and said: "Allah!" (That means God.) He said this one word, and again they hung their heads, and were silent a long time; they sat motionless.

Again the mulla lifted his head, saying, "Allah!" and all repeated it after him:—

"Allah!"

Then silence again.

The dead man lay on the sward; he was motionless, and they sat as if they were dead. Not one made a motion. The only sound was the rustling of the foliage of the plane tree, stirred by the breeze.

Then the mulla offered a prayer. All got to their feet; they took the dead body in their arms, and carried it away.

They brought it to a pit. The pit was not a mere hole, but was hollowed out under the earth like a cellar.

They took the body under the armpits and by the legs, doubled it up, and let it down gently, shoved it forcibly under the ground, and laid the arms along the belly. The Nogayets brought a green osier. They laid it in the pit; then they quickly filled it up with earth, and over the dead man's head they placed a gravestone. They smoothed the earth over, and again sat around the grave in rows. There was a long silence.

"Allah! Allah! Allah!"

They sighed and got up.

The red-bearded Tartar gave money to the old men, then he got up, struck his forehead three times with a whip, and went home.

The next morning Zhilin saw the red-haired Tartar leading a mare through the village, and three Tartars following him. They went behind the village. Kazi Muhamet took off his beshmet, rolled up his sleeves, — his hands were powerful, — took out his dagger, and sharpened it on a whetstone. The Tartars held back the mare's head. Kazi Muhamet approached, and cut the throat; then, he turned the animal over, and began to flay it, pulling away the hide with his mighty fists.

The women and maidens came, and began to wash the intestines and the viscera. Then they cut up the mare, and carried the meat to the hut. And the whole village collected at the Kazi Muhamet's to celebrate the dead.

For three days they feasted on the mare and drank buza, and they celebrated the dead. All the Tartars were at home.

On the fourth day about noon, Zhilin saw that they were collecting for some expedition. Their horses were brought out. They put on their gear, and started off, ten men of them, under the command of the red-headed Tartar; only Abdul stayed at home. There was a new moon, but the nights were still dark.

"Now," said Zhilin to himself, "we must escape to-day." And he told Kostuilin.

But Kostuilin was afraid. "How can we escape? We don't know the way."

"I know the way."

"But we should not get there during the night."

"Well, if we don't get there we will spend the night in the woods. I have some cakes. What are you going to do? It will be all right if they send you the money, but you see, your friends may not collect so much. And the Tartars are angry now because the Russians have killed one of their men. They say they are thinking of killing us."

Kostuilin thought and thought. "All right, let us go!"

CHAPTER V

ZHILIN crept down into his hole, and widened it so that Kostuilin also could get through, and then they sat and waited till all should be quiet in the aul.

As soon as the people were quiet in the aul, Zhilin crept under the wall, and came out on the other side. He whispered to Kostuilin : —

"Crawl under."

Kostuilin also crept under, but in doing so he hit a stone with his leg, and it made a noise.

Now, the master had a brindled dog as a watch, — a most ferocious animal; they called him Ulyashin.

Zhilin had been in the habit of feeding him. Ulyashin heard the noise, and began to bark and jump about, and the other dogs joined in.

Zhilin gave a little whistle, threw him a piece of cake. Ulyashin recognized him, began to wag his tail, and ceased barking.

Abdul had heard the disturbance, and cried from within the saklia : —

"Haït! haït! Ulyashin."

But Zhilin scratched the dog behind the ears. The dog made no more sound, rubbed against his legs, and wagged his tail.

They waited behind the corner.

All became silent again; the only sound was the bleating of a sheep in the fold, and far below them the water roaring over the boulders.

It was dark, but the sky was studded with stars. Over the mountain the young moon hung red, with its horns turned upward.

In the valleys a mist was rising, white as milk. Zhilin started up, and said to his comrade, "Well, brother, *aï-da !* "

They set out again.

But as they got under way, they heard the call of the mulla on the minaret : —

"*Allah ! Bis'm Allah ! el Rakhman !* "

"That means, the people will be going to the mosque."

Again they sat down and hid under the wall.

They sat there long, waiting until the people should pass. Again it grew still.

"Now God be with us!" [1]

They crossed themselves, and started.

They went across the dvor, and down the steep bank to the stream, crossed the stream, and proceeded along the valley. The mist was thick, and closed in all around them, but above their heads the stars could still be seen.

Zhilin used the stars to guide him which way to go. It was cool in the mist, it was easy walking, only their boots were troublesome, — they were worn at the heels. Zhilin took his off, threw them away, and walked barefoot. He sprang from stone to stone, and kept glancing at the stars.

Kostuilin began to grow weary.

"Go slower," said he; "my boots chafe me, my whole foot is raw."

"Then take them off, it will be easier."

Kostuilin began to go barefoot, but that was still worse; he kept scraping his feet on the stones and having to stop.

Zhilin said to him : —

"You may cut your feet, but you will save your life; but if you are caught they will kill you, which would be worse."

Kostuilin said nothing, but crept along, groaning. For a long time they went down the valley. Suddenly they heard dogs barking at the right. Zhilin halted, looked around, climbed up the bank, and felt about with his hands.

"Ekh!" said he, "we have made a mistake; we have gone too far to the right. Here is a strange aul. I could see it from the hill. We must go back to the left, up the mountain. There must be a forest there."

But Kostuilin objected : —

[1] *Nu, S Bogom !* — literally, "with God."

"Just wait a little while, let us get breath. My feet are all blood."

"Eh, brother! they will get well. You should walk more lightly. This way."

And Zhilin turned back toward the left, and uphill toward the forest.

Kostuilin kept halting and groaning. Zhilin tried to hush him up, and still hastened on.

They climbed the mountain. And there they found the forest. They entered it; their clothes were all torn to pieces on the thorns. They found a little path through the woods. They walked along it.

"Halt!"

There was the sound of hoofs on the path. They stopped to listen. It sounded like the tramping of a horse: then it also stopped. They set out once more; again the tramping hoofs. When they stopped, it stopped.

Zhilin crept ahead, and investigated a light spot on the path.

Something was standing there. Whether it was a horse or not, on it there was something strange, not at all like a man.

It snorted — plainly!

"What a strange thing!"

Zhilin gave a slight whistle. There was a dash of feet from the path into the forest, a crackling in the underbrush, and something rushed along like a hurricane, with a crashing of dry boughs.

Kostuilin almost fell to the ground in fright. But Zhilin laughed, and said: —

"That was a stag. Do you hear how it crashes through the woods with its horns? We were afraid of him, and he is afraid of us."

They went on their way. Already the Great Bear was beginning to set; the dawn was not distant. And they were in doubt whether they should come out right or not. Zhilin was inclined to think that they were on the right track, and that it would be about ten versts farther before they reached the Russian fortress, but there was no certain guide; you could not tell in the night.

They came to a little clearing. Kostuilin sat down and said:—

"Do as you please, but I will not go any farther; my legs won't carry me."

Zhilin tried to persuade him.

"No," said he, "I won't go, I can't go."

Zhilin grew angry; he threatened him, he scolded him.

"Then I will go on without you. Good-by!"

Kostuilin jumped up and followed. They went four versts farther. The fog began to grow thicker in the forest. Nothing could be seen before them; the stars were barely visible.

Suddenly they heard the tramping of a horse just in front of them; they could hear his shoes striking on the stones.

Zhilin threw himself down on his belly, and tried to listen by laying his ear to the ground.

"Yes, it is,—it is some one on horseback coming in our direction."

They slipped off to one side of the road, crouched down in the bushes, and waited. Zhilin crept close to the path, and looked.

He saw a mounted Tartar riding along, driving a cow, and muttering to himself. When the Tartar had ridden by, Zhilin returned to Kostuilin.

"Well, God has saved us. Up with you! Come along!"

Kostuilin tried to rise, and fell back.

"I can't; by God, I can't. My strength is all gone."

The man was staggered, and was bloated, and the sweat poured from him; and as they were caught in the forest in the midst of the cold fog, and his feet were torn, he lost all courage. Zhilin tried to lift him by main force. Then Kostuilin cried:—

"Aï! it hurts."

Zhilin was frightened to death.

"What are you screaming for? Don't you know that

Tartar is near? He will hear you." But he said to himself, "Now, if he is really played out, what can I do with him? I can't abandon a comrade. Now," says he, "get up; climb on my back. I will carry you if you can't walk any longer." He took Kostuilin on his shoulders, holding him by the thighs, and went along the path with his burden. "Only," says he, "don't put your hands on my throat, for Christ's sake! Hold on by my shoulders."

It was hard for Zhilin. His feet were also bloody, and he was weary. He stopped, and made it a little easier for himself by setting Kostuilin down, and getting him higher up on his shoulders. Then he went on again.

Evidently the Tartar had heard Kostuilin scream. Zhilin caught the sound of some one following them, and shouting in his language. Zhilin hid among the bushes. The Tartar aimed his gun; he fired it off but missed; began to whine in his native tongue, and galloped up the path.

"Well," said Zhilin, "we are lost, brother. The dog .... he will be right back with a band of Tartars on our track. .... If we don't succeed in putting three versts between us, we are lost." And he thinks to himself, "The devil take it, that I had to bring this clod along with me! Alone, I should have got there long ago."

Kostuilin said : —

"Go alone. Why should you be lost on my account?"

"No, I will not go; it would not do to abandon a comrade."

He lifted him again on his shoulders, and started on. Thus he made a verst. It was forest all the way, and no sign of outlet. But the fog was now beginning to lift, and seemed to be floating away in little clouds; not a star was any longer to be seen. Zhilin was tired out.

A little spring gushed out by the road; it was walled in with stones. There he stopped, and dropped Kostuilin.

"Let me rest a little," said he, "and get a drink. We will eat our cakes. It can't be very far now."

He had just stretched himself out to drink, when the sound of hoofs was heard behind them. Again they hid in the bushes at the right under the crest, and crouched down.

They heard Tartar voices. The Tartars stopped at the very spot where they had turned in from the road. After discussing awhile, they seemed to be setting dogs on the scent.

The refugees heard the sound of a crashing through the bushes; a strange dog came directly to them. He stopped and barked.

The Tartars followed on their track. They also were strangers.

They seized them, bound them, lifted them on horses, and carried them off.

After they had ridden three versts, Abdul, their master, with two Tartars, met them. He said something to their new captors. They were transferred to Abdul's horses, and were brought back to the aul.

Abdul was no longer grinning, and he said not a word to them.

They reached the village at daybreak; the prisoners were left in the street. The children gathered around them, tormenting them with stones and whips, and howling.

The Tartars gathered around them in a circle, and the old man from the mountain was among them. They began to discuss. Zhilin made out that they were deciding on what should be done with them. Some said that they ought to be sent farther into the mountains, but the old man declared that they must be killed. Abdul argued against it.

"I have paid out money for them," said he. "I shall get a ransom for them."

But the old man said:—

"They won't pay anything; they will only be an injury to us. And it is a sin to feed Russians. Kill them, and that is the end of it."

They separated. Abdul came to Zhilin, and reported the decision.

"If," says he, "the ransom is not sent in two weeks, I will flog you. And if you try to run away again, I will kill you like a dog. Write your letter, and write it good!"

Paper was brought them; they wrote their letters. Clogs were put on their feet again; they were taken behind the mosque. There was a pit twelve feet [1] deep, and they were thrust down into this pit.

CHAPTER VI

LIFE was made utterly wretched for them. Their clogs were not taken off even at night, and they were not let out at all.

Unbaked dough was thrown down to them as if they were dogs, and water was let down in a jug. In the pit it was damp and suffocating.

Kostuilin became ill, and swelled up, and had rheumatism all over his body, and he groaned or slept all the time.

Even Zhilin lost his spirits; he saw that they were in desperate straits. And he did not know how to get out of it.

He had begun to make an excavation, but there was nowhere to hide the earth; Abdul discovered it, and threatened to kill him.

He was squatting down one time in the pit, and thinking about liberty, and he grew sad.

Suddenly a cake [2] fell directly into his lap, then another, and some cherries followed.

He looked up, and there was Dina. She peered down at him, laughed, and then ran away. And Zhilin began to conjecture, "Could n't Dina help me?"

He cleared out a little place in the pit, picked up some clay, and made some dolls. He made men and women, horses and dogs; he said to himself: —

"When Dina comes, I will toss them up to her."

But Dina did not make her appearance on the next

[1] Five *arshins*, 11.65 feet. [2] *Lepyoshka.*

day. And Zhilin heard the trampling of horses' hoofs; men came riding up; the Tartars collected at the mosque, arguing, shouting, and talking about the Russians.

And he also heard the voice of the old man. Zhilin could not understand very well, but he gathered that the Russians were somewhere near, and the Tartars were afraid that they would attack the aul, and they did not know what to do with the prisoners.

They talked awhile, and went away.

Suddenly Zhilin heard a rustling at the edge of the pit.

He saw Dina squatting on her heels, with her knees higher than her head; she leaned over, her necklace hung down, and swung over the pit. And her little eyes twinkled like stars. She took from her sleeve two cheese-cakes, and threw them down to him. Zhilin accepted them, and said: —

"Why did you stay away so long? I have been making you some dolls. Here they are."

He began to toss them up to her, one at a time.

But she shook her head, and would not look at them. "I can't take them," said she. She was silent for a while, but sat there; then she said, "Ivan, they want to kill you."

She made a significant motion across her throat.

"Who wants to kill me?"

"Father. The old men have ordered him to. But I am sorry for you."

And Zhilin said: —

"Well, then, if you are sorry for me, bring me a long pole."

She shook her head, meaning that it was impossible.

He clasped his hands in supplication to her.

"Dina, please! Bring one to me, Dinushka!"

"I can't," said she. "They would see me; they are all at home."

And she ran away.

Afterward, Zhilin was sitting there in the evening, and wondering what was going to happen. He kept looking up. He could see the stars, but the moon had not yet risen. The mulla uttered his call, then all became silent.

Zhilin began already to doze, thinking to himself, "The little maid is afraid."

Suddenly a piece of clay fell on his head; he glanced up; a long pole was sliding over the edge of the pit, it slid out, began to descend toward him, it reached the bottom of the pit. Zhilin was delighted. He seized it, pulled it along, — it was a strong pole. He had noticed it before on his master's roof.

He gazed up; the stars were shining high in the heavens, and Dina's eyes, at the edge of the pit, gleamed in the darkness like a cat's.

She craned her head over, and whispered, "Ivan, Ivan." And she waved her hands before her face, meaning, "Softly, please."

"What is it?" said Zhilin.

"All have gone, there are only two at home."

And Zhilin said: —

"Well, Kostuilin, let us go, let us make our last attempt. I will help you."

Kostuilin, however, would not hear to it.

"No," says he, "it is not meant for me to get away from here. How could I go when I haven't even strength to turn over?"

"All right, then. Good-by.[1] Don't think me unkind."

He kissed Kostuilin.

He clasped the pole, told Dina to hold it firmly, and tried to climb up. Twice he fell back, — his clog so impeded him. Kostuilin pushed him from below; he managed to get to the top; Dina pulled on the sleeves of his shirt with all her might, laughing heartily.

Zhilin pulled up the pole, and said: —

"Carry it back to its place, Dina, for if they found it they would flog you."

She dragged off the pole, and Zhilin began to go down the mountain. When he had reached the bottom of the cliff he took a sharp stone and tried to break the

[1] *Prashchaï.*

padlock of his clog. But the lock was strong; he could not strike it fairly.

He heard some one hurrying down the hill, with light, skipping steps. He said to himself: —

"That is probably Dina again."

Dina ran to him, took a stone, and said: —

"*Daï ya.* — Let me try it."

She knelt down, and began to work with all her might. But her hands were as delicate as osiers. She had no strength. She threw down the stone, and burst into tears.

Zhilin again tried to break the lock, and Dina squatted by his side, and leaned against his shoulder. Zhilin glanced up, and saw at the left behind the mountain a red glow like a fire; it was the moon just rising.

"Well," he said to himself, "I must cross the valley and get into the woods before the moon rises." He stood up and threw away the stone. He would have to go as he was, even with the clog.

"Good-by," says he. "Dinushka, I shall always remember you."

Dina clung to him; searched with her hands for a place to stow away some cakes. He took the cakes.

"Thank you," said he; "you are a thoughtful darling. Who will make you dolls after I am gone?" and he stroked her hair.

Dina burst into tears, hid her face in her hands, and scrambled up the hillside like a kid. He could hear, in the darkness, the jingling of the coins on her braids.

Zhilin crossed himself, picked up the lock of his clog so that it might not make a noise, and started on his way, dragging his leg all the time, and keeping his eyes all the time on the glow where the moon was rising.

He knew the way. He had eight versts to go in a direct course, but he would have to strike into the forest before the moon became entirely visible. He crossed the stream, and now the light was increasing behind the mountain.

He proceeded down the valley; and as he walked along, he kept glancing around; still the moon was not visible.   The glow was now changing to white light, and one side of the valley grew brighter and brighter.   The shadow kept creeping nearer and nearer to the mountain, till it reached its very foot.

Zhilin still hurried along, all the time keeping in the shadow.

He hurried as fast as he could, but the moon rose still faster; and now, at the right, the mountain tops began to be illuminated.

He struck into the forest just as the moon rose above the mountains.   It became as light and white as day. On the trees all the leaves were visible.   It was warm and bright on the mountain side; everything seemed as if it were dead.   The only sound was the roaring of a torrent far below.   He walked along in the forest and met no one.   Zhilin found a little spot in the forest where it was still darker, and sat down to rest.

While he rested he ate one of his cakes.   He procured a stone and once more tried to break the padlock, but he only bruised his hands, and failed to break the lock.

He arose and went on his way.   When he had gone a verst his strength gave out, his sore feet tortured him. He had to walk ten steps at a time and then stop.

"There's nothing to be done for it," says he to himself.   "I will push on as long as my strength holds out; for if I sit down, then I shall not get up again.   If I do not reach the fortress before it is daylight, then I will lie down in the woods and spend the day, and start on to-morrow night again."

He walked all night.   Once he passed two Tartars on horseback, but he heard them at some distance, and hid behind a tree.

Already the moon was beginning to pale, the dew had fallen, it was near dawn, and Zhilin had not reached the end of the forest.

"Well," said he to himself, "I will go thirty steps farther, strike into the forest, and sit down."

He went thirty steps, and saw the end of the forest. He went to the edge; it was broad daylight.   Before him, as on the palm of his hand, were the steppe and the fortress; and on the left, not far away on the mountain side, fires were burning, or dying out; the smoke rose, and men were moving around the watch-fires.

He looked, and saw the gleaming of firearms; Cossacks, soldiers!

Zhilin was overjoyed.

He gathered his remaining strength, and walked down the mountain. And he said to himself:—

"God help me, if a mounted Tartar should get sight of me on this bare field! I should not escape him, even though I am so near."

Even while these thoughts were passing through his mind, he saw at the left, on a hillock not fourteen hundred feet away, three Tartars on the watch. They caught sight of him — bore down upon him. Then his heart failed within him. Waving his arms, he shouted at the top of his voice:—

"Brothers! help, brothers!"

Our men heard him — mounted Cossacks dashed out toward him. They spurred their horses so as to outstrip the Tartars.

The Cossacks were far off, the Tartars near. And now Zhilin collected his last remaining energies, seized his clog in his hand, ran toward the Cossacks, and, without any consciousness of feeling, crossed himself and cried, "Brothers, brothers, brothers!"[1]

The Cossacks were fifteen in number.

The Tartars were dismayed. Before they reached him, they stopped short. And Zhilin was running toward the Cossacks.

The Cossacks surrounded him, and questioned him: "Who are you?" "What is your name?" "Where did you come from?"

But Zhilin was almost beside himself; he wept, and kept shouting, "Brothers, brothers!"

The soldiers hastened up, and gathered around him; one brought him bread, another kasha-gruel, another vodka, another threw a cloak around him, still another broke off his clog.

[1] *Bratsui, bratsui, bratsui!*

The officers recognized him, they brought him into the fortress. The soldiers were delighted, his comrades pressed into Zhilin's room.

Zhilin told them what had happened to him, and he ended his tale with the words:—

"That's the way I went home and got married! No, I see such is not to be my fate."

And he remained in the service in the Caucasus.

At the end of a month Kostuilin was ransomed for five thousand rubles.

He was brought home scarcely alive.